PRAISE FOR

BITCH FACTOR

"BITCH FACTOR is going to rank as one of the year's most stellar debuts. The story is exciting, gripping the reader immediately and never letting go. Sexual tension and out-and-out suspense abound in this outstanding first novel. Keep the name Chris Rogers in mind, for she is definitely going to be a force to reckon with in women's fiction. Move over Stephanie Plum and make way for Dixie Flannigan, the new kid on the bounty hunter block!"

—*Romantic Times*

"Incendiary . . . Chris Rogers has certainly kicked off her writing career with a bang."

—*New York Post*

"Dixie is funny, clever and entertaining and Miss Rogers is a skilled storyteller. They are indeed a promising twosome."

—*The Washington Times*

"A nontraditional romance full of sass and surprises."

—*Woman's Own*

"An original voice, a strong female character, and an interesting plot . . . combine in a winner."

—*Booknews* from The Poisoned Pen

BITCH FACTOR

FACTOR

CHRIS ROGERS

BANTAM BOOKS

New York London Toronto

Sydney Auckland

This edition contains the complete text
of the original hardcover edition.
NOT ONE WORD HAS BEEN OMITTED.

BITCH FACTOR
A Bantam Book

PUBLISHING HISTORY
Bantam hardcover edition published February 1998
Bantam paperback edition / October 1998

ISBN 0-553-58001-9

Published simultaneously in the United States and Canada

Bantam Books are published by Bantam Books, a division of Bantam
Doubleday Dell Publishing Group, Inc. Its trademark, consisting of the
words "Bantam Books" and the portrayal of a rooster, is Registered in U.S.
Patent and Trademark Office and in other countries. Marca Registrada.
Bantam Books, 1540 Broadway, New York, New York 10036.

PRINTED IN THE UNITED STATES OF AMERICA

OPM 10 9 8 7 6 5 4 3 2 1

This book is dedicated:

To Krystal, Connie, Cullen, and Kelly, my greatest creations, and to Nathan, Matthew, Brandon, Dean, Charlie, Jolly, Steven, Jennifer, and Tyler, for the joy they bring into my life and for loving me no matter how weird I get;
To Dean K, my inspiration, and to Day, for listening to all my stories;
To Lois, Rex, Dorothy, Alice, and Judy for always caring;
To Amelia, Amy, Ann, Kay, Laurel, Linda, Mary, Margaret, Ron, Shirl, and Stan for needling me with gentle criticism until I got it right;
To the entire audit staff, for their tolerance, friendship, and encouragement;
To the masters I shamelessly modeled;
To the taxi driver who unknowingly begot Dixie's character;
And to Barry, because he insisted.

Acknowledgments

For helping me keep the facts straight, I wish to thank Jeff Beicker, former bounty hunter; Glenn Gotschall, former Assistant District Attorney for Harris County, Texas; and the entire Houston Police Department—some of the finest people and one of the best-trained crime-fighting teams in this country.

It is also my pleasure to acknowledge: Peter Miller, Jennifer Robinson, all the staff at PMA Literary & Film Management, Inc.; Kate Miciak, Amanda Powers, and everyone at Bantam Books. Without their belief in me, and in Dixie, the publication of this book would not have been possible.

BITCH FACTOR

Prologue

Friday, May 1, Houston, Texas

If Betsy Keyes had known about the car waiting at the curb that morning, waiting for the moment she stepped into the intersection, she would have worn the purple shirt. Purple was for special days, days she marked with stars in her diary. The *most* important days got the purple shirt and three stars.

Hopping over a jagged hump in the sidewalk, she shoved a hand in her pocket and pressed a thumb-size metallic noise-maker: *Click!* Released it. *Click!*

Sometimes the dark secret Betsy held inside made her feel exactly like a teakettle about to boil over. Squeezing her toy clicker allowed tiny bits of worry to escape, like steam from a teakettle's whistle. The shiny black cricket painted on top had worn thin from rubbing against her finger. Crickets were supposed to be lucky, weren't they?

Click, click.

But today's worry wasn't the bad kind. Today she would read her story to her sixth-grade classmates, which was worth two stars in her diary, at least. The story was exceptional. The class would love it. . . . Betsy hoped they would love it. They would laugh, certainly, and clap.

A honeybee zipped from a smelly wisteria vine trailing a chain-link fence and buzzed past her hair. She dodged it, skirting a puddle from last night's rain. Maybe she'd write a story about an angry honeybee that could only buzz-buzz-buzz, while its secrets stayed locked inside forever.

From the time Betsy was five years old, reading picture books out loud to her younger sisters, she'd known she would someday be a fabulous writer. She often skipped the real words and made up her own, inventing new adventures, new characters. Her sisters liked the made-up stories best.

She wished Courtney and Ellie hadn't played sick today. If they'd walked to school with her, she could have practiced her story. She'd whispered to them, before Mama went out to jog, that she didn't think they were really sick. After all, they were both fine at Daddy Jon's party last night.

An empty school bus rumbled past, snorting like an old bear. Betsy wrinkled her nose at the smell. Maybe she'd write a story about a girl bear with two lazy sisters.

She liked going to school early, before engine roar and car horns and the crossing guard's whistle cluttered the morning with noise. It gave her time to think about . . . things . . . like what she might have done to make her real daddy go away. She remembered his dark eyes and the way his hair flopped over his forehead like Courtney's, but she could no longer remember his smile.

Click, click.

Sidestepping a pink and yellow buttercup that had poked up through a crack in the concrete, dewdrops glistening on its petals, Betsy pushed the empty feeling away. Today was for happy thoughts. As she neared the intersection, she recited the first line of her story over and over, because teacher said the opening was so important. It had to grab a reader and pull, like reeling in a fish.

Betsy was so caught up in her words, she didn't notice the car waiting for the moment she crossed the street. She didn't hear the engine ripping toward her until it was too late. As the shiny black cricket bounced from her hand, Betsy knew she should have worn the purple. Today was the last important day of her life.

HOUSTON POLICE DEPARTMENT
ACCIDENT DIVISION

RECORDED INTERVIEW: January 4, 19—

I felt the bump and looked in my rearview mirror at the body lying beside the road. . . . I honestly thought the killing would end there.

Chapter One

Wednesday, December 23, Houston, Texas

From the forty-seventh floor of the grandiose Transco Tower, the law offices of Richards, Blackmon & Drake command a panoramic view of the city. Dixie Flannigan scarcely noticed the view as she pushed through the mahogany doors. Pine needles clung to her denim jacket from shouldering a Christmas tree into the back of her pickup, and her hands smelled of pine sap. A janitor, lazily mopping an inch of water off the women's rest-room floor, had refused to let her enter—even the men's—and Belle Richards' message had said *hurry*.

Pausing at the receptionist's desk, Dixie tossed a green and red handful of Hershey's Hugs on a document the woman was proofing. The military-strict assistant glanced up.

"Cheers, Sergeant!" Dixie grinned.

The woman's scowl lifted almost a centimeter. "What's cheery about adding another damned inch to my hips?"

The law firm had hired receptionist Sally Grimm, former martial-arts instructor, after a client stormed through the offices hell-bent on shooting the firm's senior partner. Such mayhem would never happen on Sergeant Grimm's watch. Today Dixie couldn't resist trying to break through the woman's armor—after all, 'twas the season to be jolly. Didn't

that include stone-faced door wardens? Leaning across the
desk, Dixie lowered her voice.

"A copulation consultant once told me a woman's chances
of getting laid increase proportionately with the size of her
derriere."

Grimm's thin lips twitched at the corners, then rippled
into a tight, reluctant smile. Dixie beamed back at her, dropping a few more candies on the desk. As she continued down
the hall, she heard a low chuckle, followed by the sound of a
foil wrapper ripping open.

Turning the brass handle to Belle's office, Dixie found the
defense attorney on the phone, pacing behind her desk. High
heels *thupped* into plush gray carpet, marking cadence with a
Muzak version of "Little Drummer Boy." Attractive, fortyish,
and tough as boot leather, Belle Richards had once been described by *Fortune* magazine as Texas' hottest female lawyer.
Today Belle looked rattled. Her hair sprigged out where she'd
been running fingers through it, her lipstick was bitten off,
and her white silk blouse had a coffee stain on the left tit.

Dixie shed her jacket and settled into a red leather guest
chair. She hoped the attorney hadn't put her heart and soul
into another case that was going sour. She and Belle had been
friends since law school, and normally, Dixie didn't mind
rallying forces to help slay a few legal dragons, but at Christ-
mastime, family outranked even the best of friends. On the
long elevator ride to the forty-seventh floor, Dixie had practiced seventeen ways of saying "no."

Ending her conversation with a "Thanks, anyway," Belle
cradled the phone and pushed an open file across the desk.

"You're going to think I'm crazy, Flannigan. Dann and I
left the courthouse together only three hours ago, but I think
he's skipped."

Dixie glanced at the file: *Parker Dann, Intoxication Manslaughter*, which was Texas Penal Code language for driving
while drunk and accidentally killing someone. Evidently,
he'd also left the crime scene—a hit-and-run case.

"Three hours is a short call." She thumbed the file open to

flip through the pages. "Tough spot in the trial for a holiday recess?"

Belle bit the last flake of color from her bottom lip.

"A very tough spot. The jury has my client ninety-nine percent convicted already. And you know how strong public opinion gets in the death of a child—"

"Foolish sentimentality."

Belle ignored the sarcasm. "Dann can't leave his house without being harassed, sometimes physically attacked. People throw eggs, beer bottles—"

"Baby killers make terrific targets."

"Something in his eyes told me to call and check on him this afternoon." Belle tapped the desk with the eraser end of a well-chewed wooden pencil. "He was too cheerful, just too damn cheerful."

"So you think he'll run during the holiday break."

Belle nodded. "Expecting no one to miss him until court reconvenes after New Year's."

"By then, he'll be as gone as a spit in the Gulf." Before Dixie resigned as a Harris County Assistant District Attorney, she and Belle had often found themselves opponents: Texas' Hottest Defense Lawyer vs. the State's Courtroom Bitch, as one yellow-press headline had put it.

Dixie didn't mind a good fight; justice demanded it. But after ten years as ADA, with one too many bad guys beating the system, her bitch quotient had maxed out. Being a continual badass hardened a person, first on the outside, like a beetle's armor, then on the inside. When Dixie felt her very core turning stone-cold mean, she hadn't liked herself much. Now she was content working the legal fringes, rounding up bail jumpers and runaways. Someday she'd figure out what to do with the rest of her life.

She studied Parker Dann's mug shot: thick brows, an insolent stare, a hard mouth. He looked guilty as hell.

"From Dann's point of view, Flannigan, and considering the way the trial has gone so far, running could make sense. Sometimes justice is a damn poor gamble."

In Belle's eyes, her clients were never guilty. But Dixie

remembered this case from local news reports. Driving while intoxicated, Parker Dann had allegedly struck and killed eleven-year-old Elizabeth Keyes. The cops found Dann's car parked in his driveway, three blocks from the crime scene, front headlight smashed, the girl's blood and tissue on the bumper. Dixie was afraid her friend's loyalty might, this time, be misplaced.

A snapshot clipped inside the folder showed three brown-eyed, smiling girls seated on a brick hearth hung with Christmas stockings. *The Keyes children*, the photo was labeled, *Courtney, Betsy, Ellie*. Betsy, the oldest, sat in the middle, arms spread wide to embrace her sisters' shoulders.

Beneath the snapshot was a news photo from Dann's arraignment—Betsy's family in the courtroom, the mother wan and teary-eyed, the father flushed, angry. Courtney, about nine, perched at the edge of her seat, studying Parker Dann with serious eyes and a determined mouth. Wisps of dark hair had wriggled free from a tightly drawn ponytail to flop across her forehead and feather around her ears. One hand clutched the bench in front of her; the other arm rested protectively around her smaller sister, who sat solemnly turning pages in a worn picture book.

Dixie looked back at the Christmas photo, dated five months before Betsy's death. Big grins spread across all three young faces. If Dann was guilty, he had ripped this family's life apart and deserved whatever the jury handed down.

"I know what you're thinking, Flannigan. It looks bad. Hell, I know it looks bad, but trust me, every piece of evidence against him is circumstantial."

"The kid should've waited for an eyewitness before crossing that street."

Belle tossed her a fierce glare, crossed her arms over the coffee stain, and *thup-thupped* behind the desk to stare out the window.

"The DA is still trying to come up with someone who saw Dann driving the car on the morning of the accident. And I'm still looking for a witness who saw *somebody else* driving Dann's car."

Belle had good instincts. Dann might actually be innocent—not likely, but possible. Dixie decided to ease up on
the needling. "The DA's staff could be digging as dry a hole
as you are."

"Could be." Belle turned and slapped her pencil down
hard on the desktop. "But that *idiot* will *clinch* a conviction by
running."

"Maybe he hasn't skipped. Maybe he's doing some last-
minute shopping." Which was exactly what Dixie should be
doing. "Or tying one on. You've tried his favorite watering
holes, I take it?"

"He swears he hasn't touched a drop since the accident."

"And you believe him?"

"Don't be such a skeptic. People *can* change, you know."

"Right. And the government can reduce spending."

"It's possible he's out shopping or visiting someone . . .
but he doesn't have any family here—"

"And you have a hunch." Dixie grinned. In law school, she
and Belle had both been chastised for listening to some inner
voice that goaded them to inexplicable decisions. Ordinarily,
she'd have been glad to help her friend follow a hunch.
"Look, Ric." Dixie hoped the college nickname would soften
her refusal. "I have to pass—"

"Flannigan, I know this is the worst possible time, with the
holidays and all—"

"—on this one. I'm already in Dutch with Amy for being
gone at Thanksgiving."

Belle sighed. "How *is* your sister?"

"Stubborn as ever. Still wants me to lead the kind of storybook life she does."

"You're all she has left. She doesn't want to lose you."

"Bullshit. Amy has a money-magnet husband and the
world's greatest son—who, by the way, will be disappointed as
hell if I don't show up on time for tree-trimming in two
hours." Dixie hesitated. "Besides, the bail bondsman won't
issue a contract until Dann's officially missing."

"I don't want the bondsman involved." When Dixie
frowned, Belle hurried on. "If we can get Dann back here

before court convenes on January fourth, no one else will
have to know—"

"Including the jury."

"*Especially* the jury. Dixie, trust me, he won't have a
chance, otherwise."

"Ouch! You sure know how to pass around the guilt."
Though she didn't share Belle's conviction of Dann's innocence, she had to admit the jury would crucify him if they
learned he'd jumped bail. "Despite my bleeding heart, I must
remind you of one other minor consideration—"

"Your fee. Of course. I'll pay it myself."

Dixie raised an eyebrow. "You?" Belle Richards could
squeeze a buck hard enough to make George Washington
weep green ink.

"Well . . . not me, *personally*, but Richards, Blackmon
and Drake."

"Which means it ultimately comes out of Dann's substantial retainer." Dixie's grin widened. "Now that's a bit of irony
I can appreciate." She skimmed Dann's background sheet. It
listed seven residences in five different states in the past three
years. "A drifter."

"A salesman. And a damn good one, according to his tax
returns."

"Forty-two years old. This doesn't mention any exes." One
of the most frequent places to find a skip was with an ex-
spouse.

"Never married."

Dixie looked up. "Is he gay?"

Belle shrugged. "He tried to hit on me."

"No priors?"

"Picked up twice for DWI—"

"And you want to put this hairball back on the road to kill
another kid?"

"He's *innocent*, Flannigan, until *proven* guilty. Remember?"

Dixie shook her head. "You'll always be a soft touch, Ric."

Dann's file listed next of kin in Bozeman, Montana, and a
second contact in Canada—a long haul if he decided to head

for home ground. Most Houston skips beat feet for the Mexican border, scarcely a day's drive, but since Dann wasn't a local, he'd probably opt for familiar territory. If so, it'd take some heavy traveling to round him up and get back in time for dinner on Christmas night.

"Look at it this way," Belle persisted. "If he's skipped, then he's already on the street where he can 'kill another kid,' as you put it. The only way justice can be served is if we bring him back to stand trial."

"Yeah, well, you know what I think of Texas justice." Dixie slid the Christmas snapshot of the Keyes girls from under its paper clip and compared it to the news photo taken the previous May in the courtroom, the two girls looking bewildered and older than their years. Her mouth filled with bitterness. It galled her to know the man who killed Betsy was running free while the family sat with an empty chair at the Christmas table this year.

She turned the snapshot over. On the back, in big, loopy, girlish script was written, *The Keyes 3–2gether Forever.*

"You know I wouldn't ask you to do this," Belle coaxed, "if it wasn't important. I hope you can find him quickly—"

"Ric, he's probably draped over a bar stool within a few blocks of his house. Which means that *if* I decide to look for him, this will be the quickest ten thousand bucks I ever made."

"Ten thousand?"

"He's out on a hundred thousand dollars bail, right? At ten percent, you're getting my preferred customer discount."

"On second thought, I hope he gives you a merry damn chase."

Dixie got to her feet. "Tell you what. If I find this guy tonight, I'll keep him tucked away nice and tight until midnight on January third. That way you can worry all through the holidays and feel grateful as hell when he walks in before the judge drops his gavel."

Glancing at the darkening sky beyond Belle's window, Dixie headed for the door. If she wasn't home when Amy arrived, the evening would start with Dixie's feeble apology, and she hated that. She hoped to enjoy a pleasant evening with no arguments.

"You'd really do it, wouldn't you?" Belle said. "Keep Dann hidden away and let me sweat."

"Just want you to feel you're getting your money's worth." She closed Dann's file and slipped the Christmas photo into her pocket.

"Flanni?"

Dixie raised an eyebrow at the familiar nickname.

"If I'm wrong, if Dann really is guilty, he won't be easy to bring in. He's already facing a manslaughter charge. Adding one more felony to his record won't seem too high a risk to a desperate man. He could be dangerous."

"Don't let Amy hear that. She already worries too much." Dixie snapped a rubber band around the folder.

"Dixie, this case—"

"I'll let you know later tonight whether you'll need to find another skip tracer." Dixie grinned and rained a few Hershey's Hugs in the middle of Belle's desk. "Meanwhile, sweeten up, Ric. It's almost Christmas."

But as she pushed through the mahogany doors, thinking of those two dark-eyed girls with a dead sister, Dixie's own holiday spirit fell like loose gravestones.

Chapter Two

Eight months earlier, Sunday, May 3

Courtney Keyes looked at the room full of reeking flowers and darkly clad grown-ups standing around in hushed groups and thought a cuss word. She didn't want to go into that room.

Courtney had never said a cuss word out loud, not even the D-word, because Mama had about the best ears in the world. (*"If I ever hear you girls talking filth, I'll wash your mouths out with Tide."*) But Courtney *thought* cuss words plenty of times, especially the F-word, because she liked the sound of it.

This time, though, she wasn't even specific. She tightened her lips and thought: *Cuss word! Cuss word! Cuss word!*

Ellie tugged at Courtney's hand to get attention. "I want to see Betsy."

"Okay, shhh. You can see Betsy in a minute."

There were no other kids in the room, which meant she and Ellie would STAND OUT. Everyone would know who they were and either whisper to each other as they walked by or cluck like their neighbor Mrs. Witherspoon. (*"I swear, those girls were so close, it must be awful for them, like cutting off an arm. Thank the good Lord the little ones still have each other."*)

"I want to see Betsy NOW."

"Okay, Ellie. Just be quiet for another minute."

One way Courtney was like Betsy was that neither liked to STAND OUT. Being the oldest, though, Betsy naturally took the lead, and sometimes she got too damn bossy, especially when Mama left her IN CHARGE. Courtney ignored her, which made Betsy really mad. But mostly Betsy had a magical way of making things happen without causing a fuss. Now Courtney was the oldest and wished she had paid more attention to her sister's magic.

She slid her gaze toward the object she'd been avoiding, the long box on the table crowded with flowers at the back of the room. The COFFIN.

Having never seen a coffin before, except on TV, she expected it to be black. Instead, it was a pearly grayish-white, a puke color, but not as bad as black.

Betsy would hate being here today, being the center of attention, with everybody standing around whispering and walking by to look at her inside the box. Courtney wanted to yell, "Go away! She's our sister. We want to be alone with her." Of course, she'd never do that.

"COURTNEY, I WANT TO SEE BETSY!"

Oh, fuck, Ellie, now you've done it.

But it wasn't as bad as she expected. Only *half* the people in the room turned to look at them. Mama, surrounded by a knot of ladies, hadn't even heard, and Daddy Travis was outside smoking with some men.

Courtney straightened her shoulders, clasped Ellie's hand tighter, and started toward the coffin. Actually, Ellie had been pulling her toward the coffin all along; now Courtney stopped resisting. Too bad Ellie wasn't the oldest. Ellie *loved* to STAND OUT.

Courtney avoided looking inside the box until she stood right beside it. She had never seen a dead person before, except on TV, of course, which didn't count because everybody knew the actors weren't really dead. She'd had a cat once that died. The cat didn't look any different, except it got stiff. But one time Mama ran over a dog—Mama didn't mean to, it darted right in front of her car—and the dog looked really gross, its head all mashed and bloody.

Mama said *Betsy* was run over by a car.

"Courtney, I can't SEE!"

"Okay, Ellie, I'll pick you up, but be quiet."

First, she had to make sure it wasn't too gross. She didn't want Ellie having nightmares about her own sister. She peeked real quick—

and it wasn't gross at all.

But it wasn't really Betsy, either. More like a doll made to look like Betsy.

"COURTNEY . . ."

She picked Ellie up, and they stood looking at the Betsy doll in the coffin.

"Can Betsy come home now?"

"No, she can't come home," Courtney whispered. Now that she had finally made herself look, she couldn't seem to stop looking. Was Betsy really in there? Or was this a big dumb doll someone had made to fake them out? And why the fuck had Mama made Betsy wear that pink dress?

Betsy *hated* that dress. She'd have wanted the purple shirt.

Hot tears crowded behind Courtney's eyes, threatening to spill over. She blinked hard, willing them to BACK OFF. Betsy would hate knowing her sister was standing here blubbering over her.

"Betsy's sleeping, Courtney. Wake her up."

"I can't wake her up, Ellie."

"I can wake her!" Ellie lunged toward the doll in the box.

Courtney pulled away in time to keep Ellie from smacking the doll's face, but Ellie grabbed the side of the coffin and held on.

"BETSY, WAKE UP. LET'S GO HOME."

A man appeared instantly beside them.

"Now, now, child. Elizabeth doesn't want to wake up just now. Let's let her rest awhile longer." His voice was low and friendly, but firm. The man loosened Ellie's fingers and turned the girls toward a larger room with fewer people and more chairs.

Courtney had never seen the man before. He wore a black suit and looked like part of the furniture. She was glad he came along when he did. A few minutes later, she and Ellie were seated, each with a cinnamon sugar cookie and a plastic cup half filled with syrupy red punch.

"Will Betsy *ever* come home?" Ellie's voice sounded smaller.

"No." The doll in the box was not Betsy. Courtney didn't know whether she believed in heaven, but she knew Betsy was someplace good, because even when she was too damn bossy she was a good sister.

Courtney scooted her chair closer to Ellie's. Ever since Betsy's . . . accident . . . she hadn't let Ellie get too far away. "Bad things always come in threes," Mrs. Witherspoon had once said. Betsy getting killed was the first *really* bad thing that ever happened to them. A part of Courtney felt sure that what Mrs. Witherspoon said was only superstition, like "seven years bad luck" when you broke a mirror, but another part of her had squeezed down around a terrible feeling that Mrs. Witherspoon might be right.

Daddy Jon, who was Ellie's real daddy but not Courtney's or Betsy's, had said all three of his girls had special gifts. Betsy was a storyteller—a "philosopher," Daddy Jon called her. Ellie was a performer. She loved to dress up in Mama's high heels and put on a show when friends came over.

Daddy Jon called Courtney his "clairvoyant," because she sometimes got these feelings that something would happen. Maybe if she had gone to school with Betsy that day, one of her feelings would have tapped her on the shoulder to warn, "Don't let Betsy cross the street."

"No," she said again, smoothing Ellie's dress. "Betsy won't be coming home. Ever." She felt a squeeze inside as she rubbed at a tiny wrinkle. "But eat your cookie now and drink your punch. When we get home, if you put on your pajamas without a fuss, I'll read you a story."

"A Betsy story?"

"Yeah." Courtney blinked hard. "A Betsy story."

Courtney had gotten one of her feelings when she looked at Betsy in the coffin—an awful feeling—that if she didn't take special care of Ellie, another bad thing might happen.

Chapter Three

Wednesday, December 23

"Aunt Dixie! We might get snow!" Ryan bounded through the back door, enthusiasm bubbling ahead of him.

Hearing her nephew's bullfrog voice, which had started to change the past few weeks, Dixie's own enthusiasm welled up. Ryan was the best part of every holiday. Maybe trimming the tree with him would rekindle her Christmas spirit.

"Snow? It's seventy-five degrees." She pitched the Parker Dann file on the buffet, out of sight, out of her indecisive mind, at least for the moment, and found Ryan halfway down the hall, cradling two Tupperware containers. "This is Houston," she told him. "We get rain, or maybe sleet. Once in a coon's age we get hail. We *never* get snow."

"Dad says every eleven years. Last time I was a baby. We have pictures!"

"I know we have pictures. Who do you think bought you that baby snowsuit, special overnight delivery from Denver—and you only wore it three days?" She ruffled his hair, an affection Ryan hated. But with his hands full, he was at her mercy. "What smells so great?"

"Chocolate chip cookies and pecan pie. I made the cookies!" He grinned, standing hunched over from the weight of his backpack. Dixie could see the bulge of his laptop computer stuffed inside, and a favorite game, Gorn & Tribbles, threatening to tumble out. "Where's Mud?" he asked.

"At the vet, getting poked and clipped." When Ryan's grin faded in disappointment, she punched him playfully. "Hey, kid, who'd you come to see, anyway, that mongrel pup or me?" Aiming him toward the dining room, she copped a swift kiss. "Put the food on the buffet."

Then Dixie turned to help her sister carry a pair of enormous shopping bags. Amy looked all cushiony and warm, in a rose-pink nubby sweater and wool pants. Pearl earrings dangled beneath her blond bob. In high school, she'd been a knockout cheerleader, the girl everyone wanted to chum with. To Dixie—short, plain, brainy, a total nerd—Amy had been a goddess. You didn't compete with a goddess, you worshiped her, even when she asked your help with homework two grades harder than your own, or when she cried in your room over a different boy every week, but especially when she knuckled your head and said you were the world's greatest sister. Now Amy's glamorous curves had softened and spread. "Happy fat," Dixie often teased. "The downside of a contented lifestyle."

"Here, Amy, give me one of those!" Dixie said now. Red and gold Christmas balls peeked from the top of the bag. "What is all this?"

"Christmas decorations. You didn't buy anything new for the tree, did you?" Freed from carrying the shopping bag, Amy patted Dixie's shoulder and tucked her hair back. She could win first prize in a patting-and-tucking contest.

Dixie waited until Amy looked away, then untucked her hair.

"I thought we could use the stuff from the attic." Actually, Dixie had stopped at a Trim-a-Tree store, but the vast selection there had overwhelmed her. She hated shopping for anything that came in more than one color. Besides, her adoptive parents, during their fifty-odd years of marriage, had collected boxes and boxes of trimmings.

"Dixie, you'll have enough Christmas ghosts in this old house without drenching it in memories."

"I'm not afraid of ghosts—certainly not Barney and Kathleen. And Christmas would be damned empty without memories." Dixie bit down on a grain of annoyance. Kathleen had been dead only eighteen months, Barney less than a year. She *wanted* to remember them, and she couldn't understand why Amy, their own blood daughter, wanted to bury the memories like old bones. She stopped short of saying it, though, having promised herself no arguments tonight. But dammit, it was Dixie's house, Dixie's tree, and if she wanted to deck the place with cobwebs of Christmas Past, why shouldn't she?

"That porch has a loose rail," Carl called from the doorway. The smell of smoked meat drifted down the hallway with him. Carson Royal had his faults, but no one could barbecue a yummier brisket. "What I'm saying, someone's going to fall, and you'll have a lawsuit. Mailman takes a tumble, sue you for everything you own and then some."

"Thanks for pointing that out, Carl. Cheers to you, too." As they entered the living room under one of Kathleen's needlepoint maxims—*Visitors Always Give Pleasure: If Not The Coming, Then The Going*—Dixie congratulated herself on keeping the edge out of her voice. Her brother-in-law could get under her skin quicker than anybody, but tonight Carl's tiny barbs were going to bounce like water off a glass dome.

She mentally encased herself in a bubble . . . filled it with tranquillity . . . and lifted the corners of her mouth. Yes, that would work. That would definitely work. She would enjoy this evening if it killed her.

"I see you haven't stained the fence lately." Carl shook his head. "Got to keep that wood treated, keep the damp out, or it'll rot. I told Barney you'd never be able to keep this place up."

Bounce . . . bounce . . . bounce . . .

"Too much work for a woman, running a pecan farm. Best thing is to sell the place now, while you can still get top dollar. What I'm saying, once you let it run down—"

"Carl, the same people are handling the orchard who handled it for three years before Barney died. You and Amy received the financial reports and your profits from this year's

crop." Dixie dropped the bulging shopping bag near the
Christmas tree, where Amy was already unloading ornaments.
The room smelled pleasantly of wood smoke. By turning the
air conditioner down to freeze, Dixie had felt justified in
building a fire in the fireplace.

"Now, Carl, stop nagging," Amy said, patting a huge red
velvet bow into place on a tree limb. "Mom and Dad left the
orchard to Dixie because they knew she'd take care of it." She
twirled a faceted gold ball. Light fragments darted around the
room.

"All I'm saying is she'll never get top dollar—"

. . . *bounce* . . . *bounce* . . . *bounce* . . .

What Carl was *not* saying was that he'd rather have thirty
percent of a two-million-dollar sale to invest in the stock mar-
ket than twenty-thousand-a-year income.

Actually, it had been Amy's idea that Dixie inherit the
family home and pecan orchard. From the day twenty-seven
years ago when the Flannigans adopted Dixie as a troubled
adolescent, they'd treated her as their own. Amy, an only
child nearly three years older, had been eager to have a little
sister. And Dixie had clung to all their love and attention like
a flagging swimmer to a life raft—but she'd never hoped to
inherit more than a few family mementoes. Then the day
Kathleen learned she had cancer, Barney called a family
meeting to discuss the property. "I don't want to run a pecan
farm," Amy had told her parents. "And Carl wouldn't know
how. I'll never understand why Dixie loves this moldy old
house, but she does, so she should have it. We'll take the
summer house in Maine." After Barney's death, the will specified that proceeds from the pecan farm would be split sev-
enty-thirty in Dixie's favor, with a provision that she could sell
at any time. So far, she hadn't wanted to.

A thunder of drums blasted from the stereo.

"Ryan!" Amy shouted. "Turn off that racket."

"It's Christmas music, Mom."

"Find a station playing *traditional* carols. And turn it
down." Amy handed Carl a string of colored lights. "Plug

these in, would you, honey? I think they're supposed to wink."

Dixie opened one of the boxes she'd brought down from the attic. Some of the decorations were still in their original boxes, but older ones were wrapped in recycled gift paper. Dixie found the beaded balls she and Amy had made in a craft class, then the salt-and-cornstarch gingerbread men Kathleen had baked and the girls had painted. She carried them to the tree. Amy had already tied several gold balls to the limbs with red velvet bows.

"Now, Dixie! We can't use those things. They'll upset the color balance. These are designer decorations. The latest fashion."

"Gold balls and red bows. That's new?"

"Look at the impressions in the gold. Computer chips!"

Dixie tucked the gingerbread men back in their box. "These beaded balls won't clash. They're mostly red and gold." Ignoring Amy's exaggerated sigh, she hung the two ornaments in prominent positions, then stepped aside to let Carl work another string of lights among the branches.

"I said *traditional*!" Amy shouted at the paneled wall—on the other side, "Jingle Bells" was being rendered in something between rap and reggae.

Carl anchored the light string, then stood back to scowl at the electrical outlet.

"Must be fifty years old. This whole house likely needs rewiring. Cost you a bundle, changing all that wire."

. . . *bounce* . . . *bounce* . . . *bounce* . . .

As Dixie resumed her exploration of the boxes from the attic, Ryan charged into the middle of them. He found a snow family Kathleen had bought one Christmas—snowman, snowwoman, two snowbabies, the Flannigans' names embroidered on their hats.

"Cool!" Ryan carried them to the tree. "I remember these. Gramma used them every year."

Amy heaved another martyred sigh. "Put them somewhere inconspicuous, please, Ryan. Carl, what's wrong with those lights? They're not winking."

"It's the wiring. Old wiring's not going to work with these new-style lights."

"I think you have to replace one of the bulbs with that special bulb in the plastic bag," Amy pointed out. "Dixie, maybe you *should* consider selling this house—or rent it out—and move closer to town. There's a nice place for sale right down the street from us." She paused, then, offhanded, like it was nothing special, she added, "The nicest man has joined our choir."

Dixie felt bad news coming like a blast of cold air.

"You mean Mr. Snelling, Mom?" Ryan rummaged through the attic boxes for more treasures. "Snelling's *old*, and he stares at everybody over the top of his glasses."

"Old? Delbert Snelling is younger than me!" Amy pinched her son playfully on the ear. "And your Aunt Dixie's not getting any younger."

Dixie had turned thirty-nine in November.

"Anyway, I invited him to dinner Christmas night—"

"Amy! I asked you not to fix me up—"

"Now, Dixie, this isn't a *date*. I just thought . . . well, the poor man doesn't have any family here, not a *soul*. I know how you hate to see anybody spend Christmas alone."

True. But what a coincidence that this solitary soul happened to be near Dixie's age and unmarried. Amy would never understand that some women preferred solitude. She believed people should be paired off like socks.

"My empty stomach tells me it's time to set the table," Dixie announced, making a beeline for the dining room. Dating had never been her strong suit. Men she met were always too tall, too short, too macho, too sensitive, too rude, or too quick with a lasso. In college, she'd dated sporadically, and in the years that followed had enjoyed several long-term "situations." But she always bailed out when they looked like becoming permanent.

Kathleen's good china gleamed behind the glass doors of the oak hutch. Dixie lifted down four plates, inspected them for dust, then set them around the oak table. The room rarely was used anymore, but until the final stages of Kathleen's illness, every Sunday had found it filled with noisy good humor and the mouthwatering aroma of peaches and cinnamon. Kathleen had made the best peach cobbler in Texas, attested to by a State Fair blue ribbon that hung framed on the dining-room wall, under another of Kathleen's needlepoint maxims—*When You Make Your Mark in the World, Watch Out For the Guys With Erasers.*

Dixie moved Carl's brisket to a carving plate, then peeled plastic covers from a bowl of coleslaw and the pecan pie. Flannigan holiday meals always included dishes made with the rich meat of paper-shell pecans—from pecan rolls at breakfast to tuna-pecan sandwiches at lunch to pecan stuffing and buttered-pecan ice cream at dinner. Each Christmas Eve, the family would gather in the kitchen, Kathleen rubbing oil on a turkey in a blue granite roaster, Barney chopping pecans from the family stash. Heat from the stove turned their faces rosy. Kathleen, her knot of white hair springing loose to halo around her face, always looked happiest in her kitchen, and Barney sang the goofiest Christmas songs. While Amy mixed cookie dough, Dixie, who'd never been much of a cook even under Kathleen's watchful eye, had kept the dishes washed. Flannigan holidays were a buzz of mundane activities made festive with wacky moments, colorful trappings, and marvelous food.

Holidays now were the times Dixie missed her adoptive parents most. She knew that's why Amy had insisted on coming over this evening to trim the tree. Shortly after Kathleen's death, when Barney started moping around looking like he wanted to join her, Dixie had moved back home. Six months later, despite Dixie's best efforts, Barney was dead, too. This would be her first Christmas alone in the house.

She sliced a fresh loaf of bakery bread, her solitary contribution to the night's meal, and arranged it in a basket under one of Kathleen's embroidered dish towels. A boyish hand slipped under the towel and snatched a slice. Ryan had come up quietly behind her.

"Snelling isn't really so bad, I guess." He picked up a carving knife and began drawing designs in the butter.

Dixie took the knife away and gave him a handful of utensils to arrange beside the plates. "You think I should meet him? Think he's prime uncle material?"

Ryan shrugged. "Mom thinks you should get a life."

"I have a life. Only it's not the kind your mother wants me to have."

"Mom thinks I need an uncle to round out my extended family."

"What do you think?"

He picked at a stray bit of meat that had clung to the foil cover. "I think if I had to live all alone I'd be lonely."

Dixie winced. Sometimes Ryan's perception at twelve was sharper than her own at thirty-nine. "Sometimes I do get lonely, but not because I'm alone. I get lonely for . . . people I miss."

"Like Gramma and Grampa Flannigan?"

"Sometimes. And like *you*, and your mother. That's when your beeper goes off with a message to call your Aunt Dixie." She goosed him lightly in the ribs. "What do *you* think? Think I need a life?"

He rolled his shoulders again in that lazy shrug, then turned to peel the plastic lid off the plate of cookies on the buffet. After a moment, he said, "I think, if I was you, living here in Gramma and Grampa's house, with all their things here, but not them, I'd be sad."

Dixie studied the framed family pictures on the bottom shelf of the hutch and searched for sadness in those familiar treasures. She didn't find it.

"Mom says there's lots of guys around who wouldn't mind being an uncle." He opened the Parker Dann file, where she had tossed it on the buffet, and stood flipping the cover lazily back and forth. "She says, pick up any newspaper and read the personals."

"Did you tell her some of those guys are creeps you wouldn't want for an uncle?"

The shoulder roll again. "She says the men you meet doing the work you do are creeps." He hurried on, tugging a crumpled page of newsprint from his pocket. "Look at this. Some of the ads are guys with motorcycles and speedboats."

"Hey, whose side are you on, kid?" Dixie could hear Amy's influence in Ryan's words. She was used to Amy trying to pat and tuck Dixie's life into her own idea of perfection, but Ryan had always thought his aunt's work was "cool." And what he thought mattered. Dixie couldn't help wanting to be a hero in her nephew's eyes.

"I'm on your side," he said. "I asked Mom if I could stay here and keep you company during school break." He dipped his head. "She said you wouldn't be home enough to notice."

Unfolding the paper, he showed her an ad he'd circled in red marker.

" 'DWM, forty-five,' " she read. "Divorced white male? *'Six-foot-five, two hundred pounds'*?" At five-four, 120 pounds, Dixie would feel like a dwarf by such a man. "The age is okay, I guess."

"Look at the best part. He likes to hang glide and bungee jump. That's dangerous stuff, like you chasing criminals."

"Dangerous?" She grinned at him. "Bungee jumping is *insane.*"

Then her gaze fell on the file Ryan was fingering, and she remembered she needed to call Belle Richards. Frankly, she didn't want to risk missing Christmas with her family just to chase down some drunk driver. She should call now, give the attorney enough time to hire another skip tracer.

"Hey, I know her!" Ryan was looking down at the file. The Richards, Blackmon & Drake label was plastered on the front.

"Ms. Richards? Sure, you met her in the summer." In August Ryan had spent a week with Dixie, and she'd taken him by the lawyer's office.

"I mean Elizabeth Keyes, the girl who was run over."

"Are you sure?" Their schools were miles apart.

"Yeah. We met last year, during the Kids in the Arts project. Remember, my drawing won a District Honorable Mention. So did Betsy's story. And after the accident, a safety cop came to talk to us about it." Ryan turned to the newspaper photo taken in the courtroom. "They're going to *fry* this guy that killed Betsy, aren't they?"

Watching the taillights on Carl's Buick fade into the night, Dixie mentally ticked off the places Parker Dann was most likely to be found at nine o'clock two nights before Christmas. According to the depositions in his file, the man's closest friend was a bartender at the Green Hornet Saloon. A neighbor woman, obviously an admirer, had called Dann "a charming, thoughtful gentleman who always ran the lawn mower over her front yard when he finished cutting his own." Perhaps the neighbor invited the "charming gentleman" over for some Christmas cheer.

In addition to the Green Hornet, Dann frequented neighborhood coffeehouses, restaurants, movies—places where people were likely to congregate. He didn't travel, except for work-related trips, which had ceased with his arrest and subsequent release on bail. Most of Dann's bumming-around time appeared to be spent within a few city blocks.

All through dinner, Ryan's words had kept nagging at her: *They're going to fry this guy . . . aren't they?* Sure. If he didn't skip the country while the judge and jury were opening their Christmas gifts. When Amy offered to serve the pecan pie, warmed in the microwave and topped with buttered-pecan ice cream, Dixie had slipped into the bedroom, phoned Belle, and agreed to keep an eye on Dann over the holidays. What could it take, an hour maybe, to check out his favorite haunts? Once she found him, she'd slap a tracking transmitter on his car—an expensive little toy that would let her know if he exceeded a fifty-mile radius from Houston. Then she'd go back to celebrating Christmas.

When Carl's taillights finally turned the corner, Dixie shut the front door and began to seal up the Christmas boxes she'd brought down from the attic. A brass horn clattered to the rug. She picked it up. Amy's designer tree had turned out fine, but a few pieces from the family collection might help the red and gold spectacle fit in better with Dixie's traditional living room. The brass horn had adorned the Flannigan tree every Christmas Dixie could remember. She clipped it near a red bulb that immediately warmed the brass with a rosy glow.

About to close the box again, she noticed a string of crystal snowflakes. She had always loved those snowflakes—and the tree needed a spot of white.

During dinner, she'd also figured out how to handle Amy's holiday matchmaking: *simply play along*. Later, while she and Amy were loading the dishwasher, Dixie "confessed" that she looked forward to meeting Delbert Snelling. She could pretend to be smitten when the day actually arrived—"Delbert's really the *nicest* man, Sis, just as you said"—which would keep Amy from dragging up any other strays. At the same time, Dixie could come off so obnoxious Snelling would never call her for a date. By the time Amy figured it out, the holidays would be long past.

Hanging the last ornament, a pudgy Santa's face fashioned from cotton and yarn, Dixie pronounced the tree finished. She tossed the empty box in a corner, unplugged the lights, and heaved a resigned sigh: might as well start looking for Parker Dann. By now, he should be mildly sotted and easy to find. She grabbed his file from the buffet and her jacket from the closet.

As she strode through the kitchen, a piece of paper fluttered on the refrigerator door, anchored with a magnet Ryan had made in art class—a ceramic heart framing his school picture. Dixie stopped to look. On the notepaper, a neatly printed block read:

SWF, 39, BROWN HAIR, BROWN EYES, AND STILL PRETTY FOXY. LIKES AWESOMELY DANGEROUS SPORTS LIKE DOWNHILL DIRT BIKING. SOMETIMES BRINGS HER 12-YEAR-OLD NEPHEW.

Below that, Ryan had scrawled: *Dear Aunt Dixie: I'll put this on the Internet tonight and scan in a snapshot of you from when we went swimming last summer. You'll have loads of replies by New Year's. So don't worry about Old Snelling.*

Chapter Four

Feed a cop and you've got a friend for life, an attorney had told Dixie when she joined the DA's staff. At the time, the remark had rubbed her naive sense of ethics the wrong way.

In fact, the value of networking—building a grid of people who knew other people who knew other, possibly very important, people—eluded her until the day a patrolman in Denver witnessed a situation that helped Dixie nail a husband-wife burglary team in Houston. Working off-duty at a Rockies game, the patrolman saw the couple talking to a local fence they claimed never to have met. Bingo! Dixie closed the case quick as a hiccup. Now she had law enforcement contacts in forty-two of the fifty states—and the night truly had a thousand eyes.

She'd need all of them if Parker Dann had fled to Canada.

Slim Jim McGrue of the Texas Highway Patrol had come through more than once over the years. McGrue could be a big help tonight, too, if Dixie could only talk him into it. Unfortunately, the fact that Dann had not yet officially jumped bail prevented her from being totally honest.

After checking around Dann's neighborhood without luck, Dixie had jimmied the lock on his back door. She found the small house neat and clean. A few hangers swung empty in the closet, but that didn't mean much. A couple of empty suitcases were stacked behind the suits. His shaving gear remained in the bathroom cabinet, but not his toothbrush or toothpaste. The most permanent personal item in the house was a well-stocked bookcase. Dixie thumbed through a volume of Shakespeare's sonnets. Either Dann bought it used or he had spent many hours reading it. Nothing told her specifically Dann had skipped, yet she knew he had. The house *felt* like its owner wouldn't be returning.

Calling in a few favors, Dixie had set up watch posts at the nearest border towns, Brownsville and Laredo, and at the Louisiana state line. Then she'd phoned McGrue. When he agreed to meet, she'd had to fight off her usual case of the shivers. Watching him now through the diner window as he unfolded from his patrol car, Dixie was reminded of a praying mantis. How many lawbreakers had watched that sight in their rearview mirrors and soiled their car seats?

Six-foot-eight and thin as a shadow, the Highway Patrolman moved through the diner with a loose-jointed, sticklike grace. People stared. He didn't seem to notice. Once, in apprehending a criminal, Dixie had seen McGrue stretch his long legs to cover the length of a football field in an eye blink, as if time itself had folded a stitch. Scary. With his deepset eyes, the iridescent green of pond algae, finely chiseled nose, and sensuous mouth, McGrue was admittedly handsome, but as spooky as a walking cadaver.

He nodded a greeting and slid into the booth. Dixie recalled Amy's comment that the men Dixie worked around were all creeps—meaning the criminal element, of course. What would she think of McGrue?

When the waitress arrived, Dixie ordered an unwanted cup of coffee for herself. The patrolman ordered grapefruit juice.

"Tell me this, Counselor," he said, after swallowing half the juice in one gulp. "With six major highways leaving Houston, not counting the Gulf Freeway to the coast, why would your friend choose to go through Oklahoma?" McGrue's voice reminded Dixie of dead leaves scudding along a sidewalk.

"Habit, mostly. Dann travels all over the state on sales calls, but his favorite route is I-45 north. He'll know the speed traps and the stretches where he can make the best time. He'll know I-59 is currently rerouted for construction. Forty-five is flat, multilane, easy traveling."

"Could head south."

"Could." While she told him about Dann's former residences in Montana and Calgary, and her lookouts along the Mexico border, McGrue took some time over the menu, finally settling on steak, four eggs, hash-brown potatoes, biscuits with gravy, a side of ham, and double apple pie à la mode for dessert. Dixie regarded the skin stretched tight over his rangy frame. Maybe it was true that grapefruit juice burned fat.

"Dann was here in town as late as seven o'clock," she said. "A neighbor saw him come home, stay a few minutes, then leave, carrying a couple of plastic grocery bags. I cruised his favorite hangouts. No sign of him or his car." Dann's Cadillac had been impounded after Betsy's death. Now he drove a four-year-old Chevy sedan with a patched fender.

"Might ditch the car," McGrue drawled in his raspy voice.

"Probably would, if he knew we were looking for him."

"Now it's *we*, is it?" McGrue took a handful of Jolly Rancher candies out of his pocket and laid them on the table, lemon, sour apple, and one peach. He slid the peach across to Dixie with a bony finger, the nail glossy and perfectly trimmed. Then he thumbed the cellophane off a lemon candy and crunched rather than sucked it. The sound made Dixie's teeth hurt.

"I was hoping you'd put out a 'suspicious vehicle' watch," she said, "along with a 'do not attempt to apprehend,' of course." Asking the Highway Patrol to watch for Dann's car was her best bet for picking the skip up fast, without an official contract. But it was also like issuing McGrue a Gold Card for paybacks.

"Hot plates, sugar!" The waitress covered their table with steaming dishes. "If the steak's not done just right, now, I'll take it back. Y'all hear?" She lingered, eyeing McGrue, her smile turned up to maximum wattage.

He held the woman's gaze impassively a moment, then sliced into the steak, which promptly bled into the eggs. Turning back to the waitress, his gaze slid downward to an inch of cleavage above an open button.

"Looks good."

She smiled even brighter. "Let me know if y'all want *anything* else."

Dixie studied McGrue as he watched the waitress swivel down the aisle. Even in December, his skin was leathery and nut brown from the sun. His hair, almost the same shade, was expensively styled to fall magically into place after the weight of his uniform cowboy hat was lifted. McGrue was a man women noticed, no denying that. Dixie had seen others come on to him as blatantly as their waitress had just now. Maybe they didn't notice the danger.

Or maybe that's what attracted them.

"Tell me, Counselor," he said, after he'd put away a dozen bites. "Just why *are* you looking for this guy?"

Dixie mulled that over. McGrue could be trusted not to get in her way, even if he ran Dann's plates and recognized the name. But the people McGrue would be spreading the word to might not be as cooperative.

"A friend of his is worried about him. Thinks he's . . . unstable."

The patrolman looked up sharply. "Psycho?" Coming unexpectedly upon a raging lunatic was every officer's nightmare.

"Let's just say he needs careful handling." This story was getting complicated. Dixie didn't like fibbing, but she'd promised Belle to keep Dann's whereabouts quiet, if he'd indeed fled the state. An overexuberant patrolman might throw Dann in jail. The paperwork would certainly find its way back to the DA's office. The DA would leak the information to the press. The jury, despite the judge's reminder not to read or listen to news about the case, would discover Dann had tried to escape justice, and the fact would undoubtedly sway the verdict. Dixie was bitterly regretting she'd ever agreed to look for Dann.

But how could she disappoint Ryan? The kid trusted his Aunt Dixie to make things right in the world. *They're going to fry this guy . . .*

McGrue's narrow gaze inched over Dixie's face with the glacial precision of an insect testing the air with its feelers. He knew she wasn't being completely candid. She resisted the urge to look away.

"All you need is a sighting, then. That right?"

She nodded, reluctantly. "I'll pick him up myself."

In normal bail jumps, it worked the other way around. She located the skip, then alerted the local law enforcement agency to bring him in. Safe. Smart. Uncomplicated.

McGrue sliced a ribbon of steak, cut it in half, and speared it with his fork.

"Last time I noticed, Counselor, I didn't owe you any recompense." He chewed the steak, slow and thorough.

"I'll owe *you* a payback if we find Dann before he crosses a state line."

"One?"

Dixie shrugged. "Whatever's fair." She was in no position to haggle.

A radio crackled on the seat beside him. He flipped the control switch. "McGrue."

"Chevy sedan, Texas plates, 266 ZPM," the radio crackled. *"Sighted seventy-two miles south of Dallas."*

"Got it." McGrue switched off and speared another bloody chunk of meat. "I put out the BOLO right after you called me," he said, without looking up from his meal.

Just like McGrue to act quickly, yet keep her flapping like a butterfly on a collector's pin until he decided how much the favor was worth. Dixie looked at her watch.

"A two-hour lead. I'd better start making time." Dann would stick close to the speed limit, knowing the highway would likely be thick with cops during the holidays. Her own 5.0-liter Mustang could tap out 110 miles an hour without breathing heavy. Even at that, and even with the state police looking the other way, it would take five hours to catch up with Dann, another five to bring him back to Houston. She picked up the dinner tab.

"Counselor?" McGrue stacked a thick slice of ham atop his biscuit and gravy. "If your friend crosses the Canadian border, best let him go about his business. Our northern neighbors don't take bounty hunters to their bosoms like we do."

Dixie nodded. A pair of skip tracers had been convicted of kidnapping recently when they tried to bring a bail jumper back from Canada. Technically, she might very well run into the same trouble here in the States, since Belle had insisted on leaving the bondsman out of the loop. But if all went as planned, Parker Dann would stop soon after midnight to bed down. That'd put him still in Texas or, at the outside, Oklahoma. One of McGrue's lookouts would radio Dixie with his motel location, and Dann would get a surprise wake-up call. Easy.

"If he gets as far as Kansas, give me a buzz," McGrue said. "I know a few people up there." He speared the last triangle of ham. "Got plans for Christmas?"

The change of subject caught her by surprise.

"Usual family stuff. Lots of eggnog and fruitcake." After the briefest pause, she added, "You?"

"My son . . . *maybe.* Lately, we haven't been too close."

Dixie hesitated. Even spooky Slim Jim McGrue shouldn't spend Christmas alone. Divorced, he had hinted around more than once about catching a beer together. Dixie wondered how he'd stack up against Delbert Snelling.

Chapter Five

Dixie zipped her denim jacket against a frigid wind and hustled across the motel parking lot. Even best-laid plans occasionally went awry. Dann had managed to dodge all her bird dogs and stay ahead of her on the all-night drive. Twice she'd wasted time checking out likely motels while the skip pressed on. Now here she was, twelve hundred miles north of Houston, in a state where she didn't know a soul to call on for backup.

She hunkered behind a four-year-old Chevy sedan parked outside room 114. Her knees popped. Her back and leg muscles shrieked from too many hours on the road with too few stops. Scraping snow and grime off the Chevy's license plate, she compared the numbers to those on her notepad. No match—yet the car looked right.

Another blast of icy wind ruffled her short hair. Shivering, she unzipped her jacket far enough to reach her shirt pocket and pull out a grainy photo. She flipped it over, tilted it toward the morning sun, almost hidden behind a bank of ugly clouds, and studied the dealer's description jotted on the back: *cream, 1993 four-door Caprice, patched dent in right rear fender.* Dann had probably snatched the plates off a parked car somewhere. Still, Dixie needed to be certain she had the right man.

She studied the faded blue drapes at room 114.

You in there, Dann?

Spying a maid's cart stationed by the open door of room 120, Dixie ambled past and scooped up an armload of cheap white towels that smelled of soap. Snowflakes dampened her face. Catching a few flakes on her tongue, she filed the sensation in her memory for a hot Texas night. The frivolous part of her mind hoped the snowfall would continue. If she had to be in North Dakota on Christmas Eve, it should at least be a white one. Back home, snow was as scarce as snake feathers.

Approaching 114, Dixie considered retracing her steps to get the semiautomatic stored in the Mustang's trunk. She didn't like using deadly force when she didn't need it, and Dann's file hadn't mentioned his owning any weapons. He was a salesman, for Pete's sake, not a street punk. Walk in with a gun, he might panic, make a stupid move. Get one of them killed. No, she'd leave the .45 in the Mustang.

Cradling the towels, she unlocked a small stun gun from her belt and held it hidden in her right hand. Her palm felt damp. She juggled the stunner and wiped her hand on the top towel, then rapped on the dingy blue door.

"Maid service!" She flavored the words with a Mexican accent. Sometimes she found the smidgen of Apache blood that darkened her skin and hair to be remarkably handy. Pretending not to understand English might buy her enough time to study the man's face, get a quick take on the room, hazard a guess at whether he was alone; and she spoke a damn sight more Tex-Mex than Apache.

When the door remained shut, she rapped louder.

"Fresh linen, señor?"

The door swung open. A hairy chunk of a man with bushy dark brows, a bold mustache, an angry jaw—and a hell of a lot more muscle than she'd expected—glared at her from the doorway. Dixie resisted a sudden urge to back away and try a different tack. He looked bigger, rougher than his mug shot. No shirt. Jeans zipped but unsnapped. Purple bags under fierce blue eyes. He needed a shave, and his hair was hiked up as if slept on crooked.

It was Dann, all right, drunk, child killer, bail jumper.

"The hell you want?" he thundered.

"I clean your room now, señor?" Dixie's gaze swept past him to take in the rumpled bed and the clothes spilling out of two plastic grocery bags.

"Hell no! Go clean somewhere else."

"*Que hora*, señor? What hour?" No roommate in sight. No weapons, either.

"The sign says I don't have to check out till noon—hellfire, it's only ten-thirty." Dann started to shut the door.

"*Por favor*, señor, you take fresh linen."

Dixie thrust the towels at his chest. At the same instant, she shoved the stun gun to his solar plexus, a fist-size mass of nerves nestled beneath the heart. Eighty thousand volts traveled from that sensitive mass to scramble his brain patterns.

Surprise, Dann.

Despite its limitations, Dixie preferred the stunner to more serious weapons. It was useless at farther than arm's reach, dangerous on wet ground, and if you were actually touching your opponent, you'd get the full voltage yourself. But a stun gun was quiet and, in the right situation, remarkably effective.

When Dann jerked and started to fall, Dixie steered him awkwardly toward the bed. He landed half on, half off, eyes unfocused, mouth opening and closing soundlessly, like a fish. She rolled him on his stomach, with only his bare feet hanging off the mattress—a quick glance outside to make sure no one had witnessed the scuffle—then kicked the door shut. Locked and bolted it. Then she studied Dann for a moment: he looked dead to the world.

Unhitching the cuffs from her belt, Dixie scanned the sparsely furnished motel room. A heavy down jacket was draped over a ratty chair, a shirt tossed on the closet floor; still no weapons visible. She snapped the cuff on Dann's thick left wrist, then had to reach across the bed for the other hand.

Incredibly, he rolled over.

The unexpected movement shoved Dixie off balance. As

Dann rolled, the arc of his right forearm collided with the side of her head. Not much strength behind the blow, but *damn!* He should've been out for at least five minutes. The stunner's battery must be low.

As Dixie stumbled back, Dann hit the floor. He landed seated on his rump, legs out straight, hands splayed behind him on the worn beige carpet, bracing him from falling backward. His eyes were already flashing with comprehension. Dixie swept a quick appraisal over the powerful chest muscles and knew instantly she didn't want to tackle this guy one-on-one. Her only hope was to restrain the bastard while he was still dazed. Or to get the hell out of there. For a shaky instant, she wished Slim Jim McGrue were here to scare Dann into submission.

Stomping hard on his left hand from behind, she fished her key ring from her jeans pocket, wrapping her fingers around the Kubaton she carried there. Thick as a thumb, long as a ballpoint pen, and hard as steel, the Kubaton, like the stunner, was an up-close-and-personal weapon. Simple but persuasive. When applied with force to sensitive spots, a Kubaton could make grown men as docile as doves.

Thankfully, it didn't require batteries.

Reaching around him, Dixie pressed it to the nerves in Dann's right ear, forcing his head against her hip. Too much pressure and he'd black out. She wanted to avoid that, wanted him mobile to walk to her car. But without *enough* pressure, he could snatch the Kubaton and slap her against the wall like a bothersome horsefly. She wanted to avoid that, too.

"Put your right hand behind you," she ordered, grateful to hear her voice sound strong and fearless. "Slowly."

Dann didn't move. She applied another ounce of pressure.

"You know the drill, Dann. We can do this hard or we can do it easy. So far I've been mercifully easy."

When he tried to pull away, she pressed harder. She heard a satisfying grunt, but also felt his powerful back muscles tense against her leg. He still wasn't convinced.

"The cosh in my back pocket," she explained reasonably, "was invented by the Nazi SS. It can break a kneecap with one blow, quick as breaking eggs." Absolutely true. She didn't add that she'd never used it. "I'll ask once more, Dann, nice. Put your left hand behind you."

She gave him time, holding the pressure steady, letting him think about it. After a moment she felt his shoulder move as he tried to comply, dazed neurons sending sluggish impulses to the arm. Then his left hand slid behind him, the spare cuff dangling.

"I'm going to move my foot," she told him. "I want you to put the other hand back here, both wrists together so I can fasten the cuffs."

Maintaining the pressure on his ear, she eased back on her boot heel and released his hand. He didn't move. She knew what he was thinking—once the cuffs were locked, he'd lose any advantage.

Another ounce of pressure on the Kubaton.

He didn't move. The pain in his ear had to be nearly unbearable. Dixie waited, mentally counting to ten.

At five, she felt his back muscles flex . . . *six* . . .

She wished she could see what he was doing. She leaned forward . . . *seven* . . .

He was stretching his fingers. Plotting a sudden grab? *Eight* . . .

Her hand around the Kubaton began to cramp. She wondered if the stun gun had any zap left. *Nine* . . .

Wincing at the pain in her hand, she applied more pressure . . . and his arm brushed her leg as he finally, with a gravelly curse, complied.

Dixie reached down to snap the lock one-handed, then stuffed the Kubaton back in her pocket and wiped the sweat off her upper lip. After a moment, her heart stopped hammering.

The easy part was over. Now she had to ferry this scumbag all the way to Houston, a twenty-six-hour trip after already being up all night. Taking this job had been as dumb as spitting upwind.

Chapter Six

The way Parker Dann figured it, he'd gotten careless, let his guard down, and deserved to be caught. But it still felt lousy being outsmarted after all his careful plotting, playing the "model citizen," waiting for the holiday court break so no one would miss him for a week or two. That bounty hunter must be part bloodhound to guess he'd head for Canada.

How many years since he'd lived there? Twenty? Twenty-five? Next time he got loose he'd throw a dart at the map, shoot for someplace he'd never lived before. The beach, maybe. Yeah, he'd always wanted a waterfront home, surf pounding right outside his door.

He yanked the heavy chain that shackled him to the rear floorboard. The chain slid out of his numbed hand and rattled around his feet.

Flannigan, she'd said her name was. Wasn't that the name he'd heard muttered around the jailhouse, waiting for bail to be set? Inmates talked about her like she was some kind of mind-reading magician, showing up at places she couldn't possibly know about. One guy'd been successfully dodging the law for nine years. Joined the Mexican army, and nobody even came close to finding him. Then he crossed back into

Texas to see his daughter get married. When he left the church, there was Flannigan waiting at his car.

Parker rubbed his chest where she'd hit him with the friggin stun gun. Felt like a mule kicked him in the gut, then trampled his head.

Nudging the chain aside with his stocking foot, he studied the U-bolt attaching the chain to the car floor. She hadn't even let him put on his shoes or shirt before hustling him out to the Mustang. Now there she was in the motel room, poking around, packing up his stuff, he hoped. Maybe she'd bring him a shirt before he froze solid.

He yanked the chain again, hands flexing quicker this time. No way he'd ever work that U-bolt loose. The shackle locked around his ankle looked simple enough, if you knew how to pick locks, which he didn't. If he could find a nail or a piece of wire, might as well give it a try. Might get lucky.

Otherwise, he'd bide his time till he got a chance to snatch her keys. Twelve hundred miles back to Houston . . . she'd have to let him out sometime . . . and he must outweigh her by eighty pounds. Pure mass had to account for something, magician or not. He'd shove her down and sit on her.

Mighty Mouse, that's what the inmates had called her. Big Joe Bonner swore she'd brought him down in ten seconds flat.

"Shee-ut. Reached out to knock the little runt out of my way, maybe cop a feel of those fine tits while I'm at it. She grabbed my wrist in some kind of devil's grip, had me on my knees before I could spit." Exaggerating, of course. Bonner must weigh three hundred pounds. Only way to save face after being brought in by a woman was to make her out to be Superbroad.

But Pico, a quiet, hard-eyed Hispanic, his acne-scarred face devoid of expression, had taken up the story from where he squatted on his heels in a corner to avoid sitting on the floor.

"Same bitch brought my brother in. Rudy makes it halfway to Monterrey, stops at a cousin's house maybe ten minutes. Gets back in his car, drives twenty feet down the road—the engine quits. While Rudy's head's under the hood, Flannigan cuffs him, man, throws him in her trunk. Hauls him back across the border." Pico gave everybody a look that said the punch line's still coming. "Cousin finds the car. Later he tells Rudy the bitch stuck a potato up his tailpipe. A goddamn *potato*, man."

After that, half the guys in hearing distance had bounty hunter stories, each one trying to top the last. But the ones featuring Flannigan were the most colorful.

Dann watched the motel-room door open and close, Flannigan striding toward the car, carrying his plastic bags, stun gun clipped to her belt. Have to stay clear of that thing.

The inmates all agreed on a couple of points. Said if Flannigan got on your trail there was no shaking her. Someone said she used to be a hotshot ADA, had a good chance at the top job. Then one day she up and quit, no explanation.

Dann heard her pop the trunk, toss his bags in, close it. When she strode around to the passenger side, he caught a brief full-length profile, and an unexpected stir of appreciation gave him a start. The woman was a looker, no denying that. The cut of her curves awakened carnal appetites that had gone woefully dormant these past few months.

She opened the front passenger door, leaned in, and slid a panel open in the steel mesh separating the front and back seats. Parker got his first unobstructed view of her face: full mouth, well-shaped lips, sunny complexion over fine bones, no-nonsense chin. But it was the lusty brown eyes that gave her away. This bitch might walk, talk, and kick butt like a man, but inside she was all woman. And women had soft hearts.

"Here's a shirt and coat, Dann." She shoved them through the opening. "And some dry socks."

The rolled-up socks bounced off his chest, hitting the chain with a thud and a rattle.

"Guess you think I'm Houdini." He jiggled his cuffed wrists with just the right amount of impotence. Wasn't a woman alive could resist male helplessness. "How am I supposed to put them on?"

She motioned him to turn around. Parker suppressed a smile as he heard a click and felt the cuffs separate.

"What about my shoes?"

"Packed."

"Guess you didn't notice the snow. Guy could get frostbite." He grinned his most puppyish grin.

"You won't be walking anywhere until we get to Houston." So much for charm.

"Well, what about my car?" It was a wreck, sure. He'd bought it to get by until the city released his impounded Cadillac. Paid hard-earned money for it. "Can't just leave it here in the parking lot."

"You won't need any wheels where you're going."

Shit! "Tell me, lady, were you born a bitch, or did it come with your training bra and pubic hair?"

She cocked an amused eyebrow, then snapped the mesh panel shut and slammed the passenger door.

What a lousy friggin mess. Bracing one foot against the door, as high as he could lift it, Parker studied the shackle lock.

"The mass of men lead lives of quiet desperation," Thoreau had written. Parker had never felt desperate until the day he was arrested and charged. Mostly, he took life as it came, hard or easy. Never accomplished much, but then he hadn't aimed at making any great marks in the world. He had lusty appetites, and he was unashamed of those. "In the long run men hit only what they aim at." Henry David Thoreau hadn't minded jail, but then *he* wasn't facing twenty years. Parker aimed to stay out of jail. No way he was going back to court. He'd watched the jurors' faces that last day. If the trial had ended there, he'd be in Huntsville now, staring at up to twenty years behind bars. He'd rather they shot him.

Chapter Seven

Thursday, December 24, Grandin, South Dakota

Dixie swallowed another caffeine tablet and pulled off the highway to look for a coffee shop. The noonday sky had muddied up with storm clouds. The snow fell harder now, a blinding white curtain that stretched miles into forever. She barely felt safe going sixty. If she could drive far enough south, she'd leave the storm behind, but that meant staying awake a few more hours. No matter how it kicked and sputtered in her stomach, coffee was a must.

Spying a red neon DINER sign, its message softened by a snowy scrim, Dixie coasted to a stop and pulled on her gloves. The Mustang's feisty heater kept the car toasty, but from the buildup of fresh snow outside, she figured the temperature had dropped considerably.

"Hey!" Dann called from behind the steel mesh. "Where you going? Don't leave me in here. I'll friggin freeze."

"How do you want your coffee?"

"*Coffee?* What the hell happened to breakfast?" He rattled the chain that shackled him to the Mustang's floorboard.

"You won't starve and you won't freeze, so don't get your panties in a wad."

"Come on, lady, I'm not going to run. How far would I get in this weather?"

"You think I intend to find out?" She zipped her jacket and turned up the collar. "That backseat is your home all the way to the Harris County lockup, so you may as well get comfortable."

"Yeah? Suppose I have to take a leak?"

"See that plastic bottle back there? Label says 'Fresh Mountain Water'? Consider that your personal urinal." Dixie tucked her thermos under one arm and flipped the door latch.

"Aw, come on, lady—"

A blast of icy wind wrenched the door from her hands, flung it wide, and peppered her skin with snow and sleet like gravel. Turning her face from the wind's force, she wrestled the door shut, then fought her way down the sidewalk to the front of the diner. She had parked away from the windows to avoid curious eyes. Glancing back now through the swirling snow, she could barely see the car. Surely no one would notice Parker Dann in the backseat. In this squealing wind, if he yelled, no one would hear him, either.

A wave of heat and the smell of hamburgers greeted her when she stepped inside the diner. Her taste buds snapped to attention. Around midnight, she'd stopped at a drive-through burger stand. She hadn't eaten since.

Raking snow from her hair, she scanned the diner. The ambient noises dropped a notch. Dishes slowed their clatter; voices leveled to a hum. Local citizens sized up the wayfaring stranger.

A somewhat crooked Christmas tree decked with tinsel and candy canes twinkled in one corner, while Elvis crooned "I'll Be Home For Christmas" on a vintage jukebox. To be home for Christmas, Dixie would have to cross three states and half of Texas in less than thirty hours.

She sighed and slid onto a stool at the counter as she checked out her fellow customers. Two young couples sat at a square table across the room, thick down-filled ski jackets padding their chair backs. At the counter, a pair of middle-aged men in plaid flannel shirts drank coffee, and in a booth on the back wall, an elderly couple had just finished lunch. They shoved their plates aside and stared openly at Dixie.

The waitress, twenty-odd, with bouncy chestnut hair, pushed through a swinging door from the kitchen. Her gingham uniform had a loose button dangling from the top buttonhole, a long run marred her stockings, and an artistically penned card Scotch-taped to her name tag said "Smile, it's almost Christmas." She set plates of food in front of the plaid-shirted men, then turned a ready smile at Dixie.

"Yes'm. What can I get for you?"

Dixie eyed the wall-hung menu. "Four burgers, two orders of fries, a large milk, and a thermos of black coffee to go." She didn't plan to stop again anytime soon. "I'd also like a coffee to drink while I wait."

The waitress wrote it all down, then flashed the smile. "We have some fresh cherry pie. You guys want to take some of that along, too?"

Dixie checked the stool beside her to make sure she was alone. So much for anonymity. Everybody in town had probably watched the Mustang pull in, spotted the Texas tags even through the snow, and, with their keen country eyes, noticed Dann in the backseat. Smalltown folks didn't miss much.

"Cherry pie sounds real good," Dixie said.

The waitress jotted that on her pad, too, and scurried off to the kitchen. Minutes later she was back with Dixie's coffee.

"We got a room vacant if you guys want to bed down for the storm. Weatherman says the roads north of Hillsboro are closed. Expect they'll be closed farther south inside an hour."

"Hillsboro? I just came through there. The roads aren't closed."

"Yes'm, they are now. Storm's coming in fast." She slid two generous slabs of pie into a foam carrier.

One of the men at the counter said, "Your first time up this way, is it?" His flannel shirt was red and green plaid.

"First time and a quick trip at that," Dixie told him. "I was hoping to make Omaha before stopping for the night." Driving up early that morning, even with light snowfall, and the muddy remnants of earlier snowfalls along the shoulders, the roads had been clear. She couldn't believe the highway would shut down completely.

"Blue Norther's pushing a ton of snow and ice down from Canada," the man said. "Wet front's moving up from the southwest. Be the devil of a mess when they get together—"

"—and tougher'n the devil to outrun," said the man beside him in blue flannel. "You got chains for that Mustang, have you?"

"Chains?" Dixie had left sixty-degree weather in Houston the night before. Even if there'd been time, she wouldn't have thought to bring chains.

Blue plaid shook his head doubtfully. "Those roads will turn to ice before you get five miles."

In Texas, a favorite small-town pastime was teasing the tourists. She couldn't help wondering if these South Dakotans were pulling her leg.

"I don't suppose you have a spare set of chains I could purchase, do you?"

The two men looked at each other and shook their heads.

"Harold would have some up at the Texaco," said red shirt. "Only he shut down at noon."

"Good set of snow tires might do," said blue shirt. "You guys have snow tires on that Mustang, do you?"

Dixie was beginning to regret she'd even stopped. Ten minutes wasted here would've taken her ten miles farther south. But the snow snaking across the road in hypnotic waves had started her nodding off.

"No snow tires," Dixie admitted. Her tires were the best for driving through mud and sand. This time, she'd have to trust them on ice.

The waitress reappeared from the kitchen, to-go bags already turning dark where grease from the fries seeped through. At home, Dixie dosed up on salad greens every day to compensate for the junk food she couldn't avoid on trips. She dropped some bills on the counter when the waitress presented the check, then eyed the loose button and ruined stockings, dropped another bill, and told the girl to keep the change.

"Watertown's about a hundred and fifty miles," red shirt said. "You might make that before dark, if the storm doesn't close the road south."

The clock above the counter said twelve thirty-five. Even poking along at fifty, Dixie could make Watertown in three hours. "What time does the sun go to bed around here?"

Red shirt scratched his unshaven jaw. "Four, four-thirty, this time of year. Earlier, maybe, with this storm."

"Sisseton's only a hundred miles," the waitress said. "In case the road gets really bad, you might want to stop there. It's only three miles off the interstate, and they'll have a room. Emma Sparks will be sure to stay open for late travelers." She smiled encouragingly. "Merry Christmas."

"Thanks," Dixie said. "I hope you don't have to work through yours."

"No, but thanks for asking. We close at one."

"I was lucky, then, to get here when I did." Dixie waved at the two men. "Cheers!"

"You guys take care," blue shirt said.

The elderly couple were still staring, as if Dixie'd walked in naked. Pulling the door shut behind her, she shivered at the shock of frigid wind and started back toward the Mustang.

Her leather boot soles hit a slick of ice. Without warning the sidewalk zipped out from under her. She whumped down on concrete, jarring her spine, tailbone to teeth. Bags and thermos scooted away as tears of pain welled in her eyes.

"Damn! How did it get so fucking cold so damn fast?"

During the few minutes she'd spent in the diner, the sidewalk had iced over. The cold pierced her light jacket as if it were cheesecloth.

Groaning under her breath, Dixie struggled to her knees and clamped a gloved hand around the thermos, thwarting the gust that threatened to roll it into the street. She clutched it to her chest, scooped up the bags, then stretched a hand to a windowsill to pull herself to her feet. The Mustang was only twenty paces away, but looked like a mile.

Head down, she moved off the sidewalk onto the snow-covered dirt and, testing her footing with every step, fought the wind back toward the car. She couldn't recall ever being so cold. Why the hell did people live with such weather? She wanted to holler back into the diner, tell all those folks to come on down to Texas where a body can breathe without freezing her pipes.

When she finally ducked into the car and shut the fierce wind outside, Dixie fought down a shock of trembling that was only partially due to the cold. She couldn't help wondering if she was courting disaster to try to drive in the coming storm. Stalling out anywhere along the highway would likely mean freezing to death.

She considered taking the room the waitress had said was available here at the diner. But in the backseat of the Mustang, Dann hadn't a prayer of escaping; in a motel room, with space to maneuver and Dixie asleep, he might get free. People could get hurt—the men in their plaid shirts, the helpful waitress with her dangling button. Dann was big enough to do some serious damage if he took a mind to hurt someone.

She could always call the Houston judge trying Dann's case and let him know Dann had violated the terms of his bail agreement. But if the judge managed to get him back to Houston, Dann stood a good chance of being convicted—precisely the situation Belle had hired Dixie to avoid. Sure, she'd be able to look at that Christmas photo of the Keyes girls, knowing she'd done her part in avenging Betsy, and Ryan would still think of his Aunt Dixie as a hero, tracking down bad guys, but she'd forever hear Belle's yammering scold: *Innocent until* proven *guilty, Flannigan.*

Dixie could argue that she hadn't bargained for hauling the bail jumper across four state lines in a raging snowstorm. It was dangerous. Crazy as bungee jumping.

So when the job gets tough, Flannigan, you quit? What kind of hero is that? Dann wasn't a murderer, after all. He was a useless, thoughtless drunk driver, possibly guilty of vehicular manslaughter, but not murder. She could handle him. And she had no choice but to brazen the storm.

As she eyed the lowering clouds, Dixie started the Mustang. Once she put the weather behind her, she could park at a roadside camp and grab a few winks. She didn't feel a bit sleepy at the moment, with a roaring fire of caffeine in her belly, but she wasn't fooled. Out on the highway, swirling snow and droning tires would work on her like a snake charmer's flute.

Chapter Eight

Thursday, December 24, Interstate 29

The Mustang's tires felt solid enough on the snow-covered gravel stretching back to the highway, but the icy blacktop was less forgiving. When Dixie stepped on the gas, the big engine surged and the car's rear end fishtailed all over the road, swerving inches from an oncoming pickup truck.

She fought for control, panic snapping at her. Suddenly the tires grabbed the pavement and the car settled into the lane, steady and straight.

Dixie filled her lungs, waited a beat, then let the air seep out between her teeth, countering the surge of adrenaline that tensed her muscles.

"Let me guess," Dann said. "Got your driver's license by mail order."

It'd happened so fast, everything fine one minute, out of control the next. Usually, she was a good driver, facing tricky situations with a cool head, but she was tired, wired, and sleepy—the worst driving conditions she could imagine. Loosening her grasp on the steering wheel, she flexed her fingers, mentally counting to ten.

Losing control was a special fear of hers, a deep-rooted fear. As a youngster, she'd played football with the tough kids on the block, but roller skating left her hugging the rail. Where was the logic?

Just now, though, she'd done all right. Both truck and Mustang sped unmarred toward their destinations. By midnight or bust, she'd make Omaha, even without chains or snow tires.

Easing up on the gas, she relaxed into a comfortable cruising speed a hair over forty-five. Driving would be a damn sight easier if she could give her eyes a rest from the blinding whiteness. Squinting made her head ache, yet her sunglasses were too dark. Their comforting shade would coddle her right to sleep.

A silent barrage of snowflakes flying straight at the windshield was sleep-inducing enough, every bit as mesmerizing as the glistening ribbons snaking along the highway in front of her. Dixie cast her gaze into the distance and tapped her foot to an imaginary rock band, refusing to be lulled.

"No ketchup for these fries," Dann groused.

"Look in the other bag."

Dixie heard a rustle of paper followed by the crinkle of plastic packets. She'd tossed everything to the back except the thermos of coffee.

"Damn good burgers. Don't you want one?"

"Later, maybe. Not now."

Her stomach felt as empty as a winter ballpark, but tanking up on food would only encourage sleep. With the lane stripes buried under the snow, she had to keep sharp to stay on the road. Luckily, the highway was straight and flat.

"Saw you thump your bumper back there at the cafe. Nasty fall. Surprised you didn't break something."

Dixie ignored him. Conversing with skips made as much sense as laundering bullshit. Skips bitched about how the cops handled their investigation, bitched about their own attorneys, and bitched about the system in general. They could spin heartrending stories asserting their innocence, but anyone guppy enough to listen would be broadsided later by the truth.

If she made a list of people to scrape off the face of the

earth, drunk drivers would crowd right up near the top. Dumb, self-centered, and lethal. She could understand anyone getting snockered—hell, she'd been snockered a few times herself, had even curled up in the backseat to sleep it off. But a drunk behind a steering wheel turned a car into a weapon. Parker Dann might as well have held a gun to Betsy Keyes' head and pulled the trigger.

"Probably stepped on a patch of black ice back there," Dann mumbled around his hamburger.

Sure was a talkative bastard.

A shock of wind slapped the side of the car, sending it scudding across the road. Startled, Dixie clenched the wheel and took her foot off the gas until the car righted itself. It had swerved only a few inches into the other lane, but the incident left her shaken. Crosswinds could be devastating. She had battled them on Texas flatlands, usually during spring or fall, not dead of winter; never on icy pavement. She slowed to forty.

"Black ice," Dann was saying, "dangerous stuff. Slick as oiled glass . . ."

At forty miles an hour, Dixie calculated, *we'll make Watertown in three hours, Sioux Falls in five.*

". . . builds up in thin sheets. So clear you see the pavement through it and don't notice you're on ice until it's spinning you nine ways to Sunday."

The entire sky now roiled with clouds, forward horizon as murky as the one behind. Folks at the diner hadn't been joking when they called it a devil of a storm. Dixie nudged her speed back up to forty-five. She wanted to be clear of this mess before dark.

The buzz-saw sound of Dann's snoring drifted from the backseat. Much better than listening to his prattle. The next twenty hours would be nerve-racking enough without his voice to grind on her. A dismal damn way to spend Christmas Eve.

At home, she could be finishing her Christmas shopping, buying batteries for Ryan's new remote control model airplane. Recalling her nephew's beaming face the day they'd come upon the Cessna in the hobby store, Dixie smiled.

"If I had this, Aunt Dix, we could go flying together!"

One day while exploring the attic, he'd seen Dixie's identical model, a gift from Barney her first Christmas after the adoption. With visions of dueling Cessnas, and showing off her model-flying skills, Dixie had waited until Ryan's interest was captured by a rack of CDs, then skulked back to have the Cessna wrapped and shipped to Amy's. What were kids for, after all, if not a chance to relive the best parts of our own lives?

Dixie glanced at the sun visor, where she had clipped the Christmas snapshot of the Keyes girls. Dixie had been just a year older than Betsy the day her blood mother, Carla Jean, dropped her on the doorstep of Founders Home and disappeared—the best thing that could have happened. Within a month, Barney and Kathleen rescued Dixie, and a few months later, their lawyer tracked down Carla Jean to sign the adoption papers. Withdrawn at first, Dixie had soon warmed to the love that permeated her new home. Amy was fifteen, and the two girls became inseparable.

Dixie's gaze flicked once more to the big grins in the Keyes snapshot. Living with the Flannigans had erased the horrors of her first twelve years. But Betsy's young life had been snuffed before it had a chance.

The buzz saw in the backseat grew quiet, made a few rustling, clanking noises, and resumed snoring.

According to the dash clock, Dixie'd been driving half an hour, but had travled barely twenty miles. Maybe Omaha-by-midnight was a trifle ambitious.

A crust of ice covered the windshield outside the fan-shaped area scraped clear by the wipers. That same icy crust would be building up on the pavement. Her arms ached from fighting the crosswind. Her eyes felt grainy and raw from the tiresome whiteness.

She closed them briefly for relief. . . .

Snapped them open again.

Damn, she needed sleep!

Jabbing the radio's ON button, she set the scanner to search
for a local station. It swept the band, found nothing but static.
Dixie turned up the volume, rotated the tuning dial, and
picked up a few words. They faded. Her next sweep got only
dead air.

Turning it off, she listened instead to the hum of the
heater fan . . . the scrape, scrape, scrape of the wipers . . .

A grunt from the backseat signaled her prisoner's awakening. Snow fell so furiously now that Dixie could scarcely see
past the hood. The Mustang's speed had dropped to thirty,
and they'd traveled fewer than fifty miles since leaving the
diner.

"Look at those taillights," Dann said suddenly. "See them
up ahead there?"

Dixie could barely make out the twin red specks. Where
had they come from?

"That's a truck. A big one. Lights are too high off the
ground for anything else. Probably turned in from one of the
state roads."

You mean there's another fool on this highway? Dixie had
begun to think the world ended at the Grandin Diner.

"If you catch those taillights," Dann said, "we can travel in
the truck's wake . . ."

Like riding behind the windshield wipers.

". . . plow right along behind him all the way to Watertown. Yep, catch those taillights, we might make it."

The distance between the Mustang and those red lights
was tantamount to leaping the Grand Canyon. The truck
driver must have been going fifty, at least. Dixie nudged the
Mustang to forty and instantly felt the tires lose their traction,
the same way she'd lost her footing on the icy sidewalk. The
brutal crosswind threatened to blow them into Iowa.

Yet those taillights were the only sign of life Dixie had seen
in nearly an hour. Tightening her grip on the steering wheel,
she pushed her speed past forty, past forty-five.

She'd driven through stretches of Texas as desolate as
this, miles of highway without passing a car, no sign of a town,
nothing to break the monotony but fence posts, road signs,

and, from time to time, a cow lumbering along the road. Here, even the fence posts were buried.

A bleak white emptiness stretched all around, the delineation between highway and prairie no longer discernible. Dixie felt like an ant skating on whipped cream. Only her intuition and the occasional reflector kept the Mustang from running off the road.

A flash of movement streaked across the highway.

Dixie stomped the brake—

The steering wheel whipped through her hands.

The car spun out of control—whirling in sickening, gut-wrenching circles—skidded sideways, tires skimming the ice like new skates, gliding, sailing, sliding—and whammed bumper-deep into a snowbank.

"Dammit to hell, woman. You sure know how to make a bad day worse."

Chapter Nine

In the rearview mirror, which had jolted sideways, Dixie's eyes were dark pinpoints of strain, her complexion ash-gray. A tiny muscle twitched beside her mouth. Her hands were shaking. She tightened her grip on the wheel.

What a damn dumbass predicament. She knew better than to stomp the brake.

"Must've been a deer," Dann commented. "Lot of white-tail around these parts."

The engine had died, and the sudden quiet stretched like a vast cotton blanket, broken only by the relentless wind whistling at the window. With the fog lights off, Dixie realized how much the sky had darkened in only an hour.

"Natural reaction, you know. Stomping the brake like that. Been a real mess if you'd hit that deer."

Dann's words triggered a rerun in Dixie's mind of the sudden streak of movement across the highway. This time she felt the impact, heard the crunch of glass, saw the Mustang smashed, herself unconscious . . . snow, blowing through the broken window, burying her still form, while her prisoner froze to death in the backseat . . . the Mustang slowly disappearing into an endless white terrain.

She wiped a hand across her face to dispel the image.

"You ever hit a deer?" she asked quietly, suddenly needing to hear a voice. Dann's voice, she'd noticed, was resonant and oddly pleasing. Most of all, it was warm and human. The only thing she could think of worse than being stuck in the middle of God knows where in a blizzard was being stuck and alone.

"Nope, not a deer. Knew a guy hit a horse, though. Bashed up the front of his rig, put himself in the hospital."

"What about the horse?"

"Dead."

Dixie grimaced. True, they could be in worse trouble. But the thought offered little comfort.

She turned the key to start the engine. When it cranked right up, she heaved a sigh of relief, shifted into reverse, and stepped lightly on the gas. The Mustang kicked up a spurt of snow, started to pull out—then the tires whirled in place.

"Damn it all!" She killed the engine.

"Lady—"

Dixie opened the car door, had to shove it hard to clear the drift. The wind's fury pushed her back, but her own fury won out. She slammed the door, sank knee-deep in snow, felt it trickle over the tops of her boots.

Sucking in a breath of frigid air, she kicked her way through the snow to the edge of the highway, almost relishing the dull ache in her lungs. Any feeling, even the worst pain, was better than the helpless reeling as the Mustang spun across the ice. Dixie closed her eyes. Instantly she was a child hugging the rail at a roller rink, small, nauseated with fear, yet determined not to let panic get the best of her. A common phobia, a doctor had assured her once, akin to one of only two fears humans are born with—fear of loud noise and fear of falling. Dixie wasn't fond of loud noises, but she got white-knuckled terrified at losing control.

All right. So she had *momentarily* lost control of her car. All she had to do was put it back on the road and start driving. She was in South Dakota, after all, not the frozen tundra.

As if mocking her, the wind gusted fiercely, knocking her off balance. Dixie braced so hard against it—teeth clenched, hands fisted as if to punch the wind back in its corner—that when the gust abruptly let up, she fell forward on one knee.

"Hah! At least I didn't fall on my Texas ass this time!" she yelled at the sky.

The wind lapped up her words and spit them into the distance.

Catching a glimpse of Dann's face at the car window, Dixie flushed. *Well, if he believes he's traveling with a crazy woman, maybe he'll think twice before trying anything stupid.* Nevertheless, it was time to stop railing and find a way out of this mess.

A four-pronged diagonal rut marked the Mustang's path where the tires had skidded treacherously into the drift. Snow had leveled the ditches and turned the fence rows to hills. If she was right, the car had landed on the opposite side of the road, headed in the wrong direction from where they started. The car, buried to its bumper, canted downhill.

Teeth chattering hard enough to bite off her tongue, Dixie scanned the distance for signs of life. A tow truck would sure as hell be welcome. But nothing stirred, except for the wind and snow.

Then out of the wind came a low moaning, like the bleat of a foghorn. Shielding her eyes against the flurry of snow-flakes, she peered toward the sound. At first all she saw was a frenzied blur of twisting, whirling whiteness; then a brown patch shifted into view.

When the moaning sounded again, instinctive dread pulsed at the back of her neck. Behind her, Dann rapped on the window. Dixie ignored him, trying to discern the source of the moaning. When it came again, recognition struck like a wet snowball. *A cow, you ignorant city fool.*

But one cow wouldn't present such a wide mass of brown. A number of cows, then. Hadn't she heard that sheep and cattle would bunch against a fence on the downwind side of a storm—especially a sudden and violent storm? Each animal pushed mindlessly ahead until they sometimes smothered one another in panic.

Dixie's teeth, chattering like castanets, began to ache. The biting cold stung her face. She tugged open the car door and sank onto the seat.

"Two things," Dann said. "Here's what's happening under the car right now . . ." He paused a beat. When she didn't respond, he continued. "Residual exhaust heat is melting the snow. As fast as it melts, the wind freezes it again while the car's weight compresses it. Soon we'll be stuck in ice. I'll give you one guess which is easier to get out of."

Maybe trying to get out wasn't the best idea. She'd played a game once called "Lost in the Arctic." Survival hinged on whether to stay put and wait for rescue or to start walking. Players who elected to walk died.

Watertown was a hundred miles ahead of them, hours ahead, considering driving conditions that worsened by the minute. Even if she succeeded in getting the Mustang back on the road, what made her think she could keep it there?

Parker Dann had grown up with this sort of weather in Montana. He would know a hell of a lot more than she did about surviving it.

"You said *two* things," she reminded him.

"If you're considering waiting out the storm, you may as well shoot us both and save us a lot of misery."

She turned to look at him through the steel mesh.

"You think it's cold now," he said. "Wait till the sun goes down. That Levi jacket you're wearing is better than my shirt, but not by much."

She eyed his brown flannel shirt and the thick down-filled parka that lay beside him on the seat.

"If we sit here," he continued, "we'll have to run the heater to keep from freezing. We'll be out of gas before daylight. Or dead from carbon monoxide poisoning."

"What about rescue trucks?"

"Sure, there'll be a few snowmobiles out. But unless you have a CB radio hidden in the glove box, Flannigan, we've no way to signal for help."

She had a CB, all right, a portable. It'd been useful during the drive up, for maintaining contact with her patrol buddies through Oklahoma, Kansas, and Nebraska. But here in South

Dakota, where she had no friends on a police force, and no contract to legitimize her picking up Dann, a potential kidnapping charge was a very real possibility.

"Stay here," Dann said, "and by morning we'll be just another snowdrift."

The thought of being buried alive turned her bowels to water. Was Dann counting on that? She had noticed his subtle shift from "you" to "we." Was he baiting her, betting on her inexperience for a chance to escape?

"Okay, snowbird, do you have a suggestion for getting out of this ditch?"

"Got anything in the trunk to dig with?"

"Wrenches, screwdrivers. A claw hammer, maybe. No shovel."

"We can cut the top off this plastic water bottle. Use it as a scoop."

Better yet, she had a gallon jug of laundry detergent in the trunk that she forgot to carry in after yesterday's shopping trip. Since they were likely to freeze before needing clean underwear, she supposed the detergent was expendable. "Okay, so we have something to dig with. Now what?"

"Scoop the fresh snow away from the tires, then straighten the front wheels. We'll try to take it out on the same ruts it made going in, but first we'll have to find some gravel—or dirt, whatever—to throw under the tires for traction. Chances are they're sitting on weeks of packed snow and ice from earlier storms."

A light blinked on in Dixie's mind. This was the same drill she'd use to get unstuck from Texas mud, except there she'd look for scraps of wood to wedge under the tires. She'd lived that scene often enough to know *exactly* what to do. If she could get out of a Texas mud hole, she could sure as hell get out of a snowdrift. Turning up her collar, she reached for the door handle.

Dann slammed his palm against the steel mesh. "Hey! Aren't you going to let me out of here?"

And have him knock her in the head first chance he got? She might know zip about blizzards, but she knew plenty

about skips. In Houston, Dann was ninety-nine percent convicted, and his running would clinch the jury's decision. Only
a fool would return willingly; Parker Dann was nobody's fool.
Either he'd leave her here to freeze, or he'd lock her in the
trunk and dump her at the first town on his way to Canada.

"Dann, your part in this project is to continue offering sage
advice. You might also pray a little."

"Aw, lady . . ."

She pushed the door handle and felt the first blast of cold.

"Hey!" Dann held up his parka. "At least take this. If you
freeze, neither one of us gets out of here."

Dixie nodded and lowered the back driver-side window
enough for him to push the coat through. It was too big, only
the elastic cuffs preventing the sleeves from hanging to her
knees, but once she was zipped into it, she felt a damn sight
better about digging in the snow. Turning back, she opened
the door again to flip the trunk latch.

"Find some big rocks," Dann instructed. "Pile them in the
trunk for weight."

"Right." Dixie squinted into the wind, wondering how to
tell a rock from a clump of old cow dung when everything
was buried under a swirling white coat.

Twenty-two minutes later, she yanked the door open and
slid across the seat, pain needling her nose and fingers, feet
numb inside her boots. Dann had been right about ice form-
ing under the car. The top layer of snow had already started to
crust over. She'd dug through it, though, scraping away fresh
powder until she hit the packed snow that formed solid
ground. She still needed some gravel to throw under the tires,
but her hands had stiffened until she could scarcely bend her
fingers. They had to warm up some before she could dig
again.

She skinned off her frozen gloves and jammed her fists
into the pockets of Dann's parka. Better. But she couldn't
afford the luxury of sitting still for long. She glanced in the
mirror; Dann was watching her through the mesh barrier, a
cynical amusement in his eyes.

"Got a pair of dry gloves back there?" She'd noticed a pair

stuffed in a pocket of his coat before pushing it through the mesh opening earlier.

"Wouldn't need the gloves if you'd let me help. Be back on the highway by now."

"Just hand me the gloves, Dann." She fumbled the keys from the ignition switch and opened the mesh panel.

Dann handed the gloves through, then hooked his fingers over the bottom edge of the opening. "It's getting cold back here. How about a cup of that coffee?"

Eyeing the thermos, Dixie decided a few sips would be welcome before braving the cold again, and she supposed she owed Dann something for the use of his coat. She observed a rigid set of rules, however, when transporting skips.

"Move your hand away from the screen," she said.

"What the hell, one cup of coffee—"

She slammed the panel down on his fingers. The sharp steel edge cut into his knuckles.

"Goddamn!" He jerked his hand back. A narrow line of blood oozed across his middle finger. "Are you nuts?"

Dixie snapped the lock shut and pocketed the keys. She opened the thermos, poured a single cup of coffee.

"Hellfire, woman. You're a real piece of work."

The first sip burned her tongue, but the second felt good going down. She finished a third of the coffee before opening the panel and passing the cup to Dann. When he took it, she relocked the pass-through.

"Parker Dann, I don't have to be civil to you," she said. "I'm not a cop—"

"No, you're a goddamn bounty hunter!"

"—and you're no longer a man. You're chattel. The bondsman owned your ass the minute you skipped bail." She opened the glove box and removed a first-aid kit. The single-wrapped alcohol swabs and Band-Aids slipped easily through the mesh.

"I could have waited out this storm in a nice warm bed back in Grandin," Dixie said, pulling on the heavy gloves. They were too big for her hands. "You'd have spent the night in the trunk. Maybe you should be thanking your lucky stars that I'm reasonably humane."

Outside, Dixie swallowed a surge of shame for being such a badass bitch. She hated doing it. But with a burly male prisoner, a 120-pound female couldn't afford to relinquish control, even a little. She was already showing weakness in her ability to handle the storm. If she and Dann were stuck with each other overnight, he could become a threat, not only to her, but to others. Dann had to believe she'd shoot him rather than let him escape.

She kicked at the snowbank, wondering how far she'd have to dig to find gravel. The air felt colder than before. The driving snow felt wetter, clinging to her hair, clotting her lashes. Visibility had closed to a few feet. Using the lug wrench, she chipped through packed snow and ice until she hit a road sign that had been knocked down. Underneath it, she found a gravel shoulder. Hunching against the cold, she laboriously filled the makeshift scoop with dirt and rocks. Although the clumsy gloves impeded her, they kept her hands from stiffening up. Her ears felt cold enough to snap off.

She carried the scoop of gravel to the car and spread it out, barely covering the ice behind one tire. As she watched with sinking spirits, the wind picked up the smaller pieces and scattered them.

Another numbing gust knocked her sideways. Rocking on her heels, she braced her fall with one hand. She'd weathered a hurricane once, and the winds hadn't felt much stronger than the one blowing now. Despair curled in a corner of her mind and nested. How the hell was she supposed to keep the car on the road once—*if*—she got it out of the ditch?

Sheilding her eyes, she scanned the highway in both directions, hoping for a search beacon, or at least a break in the clouds. As she watched the lashing snow, it occurred to her that no vehicle had passed during the half hour they'd been stranded.

She turned back to the patch of gravel at the roadside and refilled her scoop.

Chapter Ten

Sunday, July 12, Houston, Texas

"Why can't we go to the same camp?" Ellie persisted, sorting forks and spoons into separate plastic bins.

Courtney noticed her sister's yellow sundress had puckered in front where she'd spilled lemonade. Ellie was still a baby, too young to pay attention to spills and such.

Smoothing out wrinkles as she worked, Courtney folded a green napkin into a neat triangle, then folded it in thirds. On Sundays, they worked with Mama at the restaurant. The smell of tomatoes and spices drifted from the kitchen, where Mama was cooking spaghetti sauce. The restaurant's air conditioner hummed, pumping cool air on the back of Courtney's neck.

"We can't go together because I'm nine and you're barely six," Courtney explained for the zillionth time—even though she didn't totally understand it herself. She'd volunteered to go to the younger camp. Going alone her first year, Ellie would be frightened.

Actually, Courtney wasn't too keen on trying out a new camp alone, either. She'd never been away from home without Betsy. But Mama had just shrugged when Daddy Travis INSISTED.

"It's time you two girls spent some time apart. Ellie acts more like your shadow than your sister."

That had been on Friday, Courtney's day to work with Daddy Travis at the hardware store. She had watched him choose a blue pencil, from a collection in the breast pocket of his orange overalls, and note something on an order form, his short fingers pressing hard to write through all the carbons.

"Ellie and I *like* doing things together," Courtney explained in her most persuasive voice, the one that usually got them fifteen extra minutes before bedtime.

"I know you do." He tapped the pencil's eraser on her nose. "And you might be lonely at first. But then you'll meet new friends, and before long you'll be having a great time. A *great* time, you'll see."

She waited until he looked back at the order form before rubbing the tickle off her nose.

"What if something happens to Ellie and no one's there to take care of her?" Taking care of Ellie was Courtney's job, now that Betsy was gone.

"There'll be a whole camp full of people to make sure nothing happens to Ellie." His pale blue eyes twinkled in the morning sunlight. "A whole camp full. Now, stop being such a worrywart, and ask Mr. Collins if he wants a basket for those tools he's carrying."

Nobody EVER won an argument with Daddy Travis. A few weeks earlier, the whole family had gone to the courthouse to see the man who ran over Betsy. Mama hadn't wanted her and Ellie to go, but Daddy Travis said it would be good for them.

"They need to see for themselves that the bastard who killed their sister won't get away with it. Won't be out driving drunk to run down some other kid."

Courtney was glad the bastard had been caught—if he were still driving around, she'd worry even more about Ellie—but she was surprised to see that it was Mr. Parker Dann. Mr. Dann seemed like a nice person when he came into the hardware store and cafe, always smiling and usually with a new joke to tell the other customers. He always told Mama how good her cooking was. On Sundays, when Betsy served him coffee at the counter, Mr. Dann sometimes gave her a dollar.

Courtney tried to imagine Mr. Dann running his car over Betsy. She pictured his big smiling face over the windshield like Betsy would have seen it. Couldn't he TELL he was about to hit her?

"No skid marks," Daddy Travis had said. "The bastard didn't even slow down."

Maybe Betsy had run in front of the car, like when Mama hit the dog. Maybe it was an accident.

Courtney remembered seeing the brown and black dog dart across the street, then feeling a *thud* when it hit the wheel. Mama had stopped the car and jumped out to see if the dog was all right.

Mr. Dann hadn't stopped to see if Betsy was all right.

That Friday, at the hardware store, Courtney had seen him walking along the sidewalk.

"They let the bastard out on bail," Daddy Travis explained.

Now, Courtney dropped the hopelessly messed-up napkin and hugged herself. Goose bumps pimpled her arms. She would try one more time to convince Mama that she and Ellie should go to the same camp, but Mama would probably only shrug again and listen to Daddy Travis.

Chapter Eleven

Thursday, December 24, South Dakota

"Take it slow," Dixie muttered to herself, shifting into reverse. "Slow and steady."

"And go light on the gas," Dann warned, over her shoulder. "You don't want to set the wheels spinning again."

But Dixie didn't need his advice to tackle this part. She'd coaxed the Mustang out of plenty of mud banks; a snowbank couldn't be a hell of a lot different. All it took was a firm hand on the car's power and a bushel of patience to tease the wheels forward and back, until they rocked free of the trench.

She couldn't see diddly through the sheet of ice on the windshield, but right now she didn't need to see, only to feel. Bit by bit, the Mustang gained ground. Each time it rocked, the wheels traveled another inch, until, finally, the tires bit into the packed snow and the car lurched backward to the highway.

"Whoa!" Dixie said, relieved. "We're back in the race."

Another hard gust whammed the moving car sideways. She thought for sure it would spin into another snowdrift. Despite the cold, sweat beaded her forehead. The car straddled the center lane, but at least it was back on the road, headed in the right direction. She turned on the wipers, hoping their fric-

tion would clear the windshield. The rubber blades scudded
over ice without budging it.

"Got a scraper?" Dann asked.

"An ice scraper?" Dixie heaved an exasperated sigh. "Ask
me if I have a high-intensity spotlight in case I need to change
a tire at night on a dark highway. Ask me if I have road flares
to alert passing motorists. Spare cans of high-performance oil.
Extra coolant for the heavy-duty cooling system. I have *all*
that! But why the hell would I carry an ice scraper in South
Texas?"

"Woman, you're a long way from Texas."

A *damn long way*. At this rate she wouldn't see Houston
again before the New Year. She couldn't even get moving
again until she found some way to clear the cussed ice off the
windshield.

"Got a credit card?" Dann asked.

A credit card?

"Stiff plastic, not one of those paper-thin jobs. It'll take a
few minutes, but you can scrape a hole big enough to see
through."

It took more than a few minutes. Her American Express
card snapped, she had to finish with Visa, but she managed to
clear most of the windshield and a strip across the back window. She decided not to worry about the side glass. They
weren't likely to encounter any passing traffic.

Stiff with cold, yet reenergized by the prospect of moving
out, Dixie slid back inside the car. She'd left the engine running, and the little heater had bullied the cold until the car
felt downright hospitable. She shrugged out of Dann's parka,
removed the cumbersome gloves, and put the Mustang in
gear.

The wind's constant push assured her she was headed
south. All she had to do was step on the gas and tool on down
to Watertown.

Step on the gas, Flannigan.

But as long as the car remained stationary, the wind could
do its worst and they wouldn't be flung off the road. The

moment she started moving again, the Mustang might skid out of control.

Besides, she felt a certain familiarity with her immediate environment, the cattle smothering one another on her right, the snowbank she had interacted with intimately on the left. Ahead lay the unknown, shrouded by a wailing white tempest.

"Turn on the radio," Dann said. "Maybe there'll be a weather alert."

Startled out of her quandary, Dixie shifted into neutral, punched the ON button, and heard "Rudolph the Red-Nosed Reindeer." At least somebody out there was enjoying Christmas Eve. She turned the dial, sweeping half the band before hearing a faint voice. Tried to tune it in. Lost it. Swept past and started over, almost to the station with "Rudolph," when—

"—*Denver's* DIA *reports all flights canceled until further notice. . . . Greyhound bus routes canceled throughout Montana, Wyoming, North Dakota, South Dakota, eastern Colorado, northern Nebraska. . . . State highways closed throughout the Dakotas, check with your local weather bureau for specific routes. . . . Grand Forks airport reports winds at fifty-two miles an hour, temperature at minus two degrees Fahrenheit with windchill pushing that to forty-six below. . . .*"

Even the wind was going faster than she was.

"No wonder I've been freezing my buns off out there—"

"Lady, you better get your buns down the road if you plan on making it to a town. Once they close this highway, we're stuck."

"Surely they can't refuse to let us pass." She put the Mustang in gear, eased up on the gas—

and felt the back wheels spin ineffectively.

You sat here too long with the engine running, you shit-for-brains Southerner. Didn't Dann warn you what happens under the—

Abruptly the wheels gripped the ice. The Mustang shot forward, sliding as much as rolling until Dixie got the steering under control. With a death grip on the wheel, she barreled forward at fifteen miles an hour.

Parker Dann was silent for the first five minutes.

"How far you reckon we are from the nearest town?" he asked.

"Forty, maybe forty-five miles to Sisseton." She didn't want to talk. She needed to concentrate on keeping the car on the road, which was next to impossible with no markers. No lane stripes. No reflectors. Everything covered with snow.

But hey! Was that a road sign ahead? She strained her eyes to read it . . . CHAINS REQUIRED.

"Terrific! Why don't they tell me something useful?"

Her arms ached from gripping the wheel so hard. Her stomach burned with hunger. Her bladder felt full enough to float her eye teeth. Dann could grouse all he wanted about using a water bottle, but at least had an option that didn't involve freezing his ass off.

"How long you reckon it'll take us to get to Sisseton at fifteen miles an hour?" When she didn't answer, Dann speculated. "Three hours, the way I figure it. Oughta be slap-dab dark in twenty minutes. Storm isn't letting up any."

"What's your point, Dann?"

"My point is we aren't going to make it with you driving."

"You're saying you could do better?"

"About twenty miles an hour better—which just might be enough to get us to town before they shut down this highway."

She wished the radio would quit fading in and out. She could do without the Christmas music reminding her of what she was missing at home, but at least it was a connection to civilization. Without that connection, she felt utterly isolated. They could easily be the only souls in a thousand miles.

"What happens," Dann said, "is the highway department swings a steel gate across the road. Couple officers wait around to let stragglers through, but they don't wait forever. And I got to tell you, most folks up this way have enough common sense to stay off the roads in weather like this—"

"*—all flights closed into Denver . . .*" The radio faded in loud again, no change in the weather spiel, except for one cheery announcement: ". . . *record storm sweeping the upper Midwest . . . worst blizzard in more than a decade.*"

Dixie loosened her death grip on the wheel and tried to relax, but the caffeine keeping her awake had racked her nerves. She felt like a piano wire stretched to the snapping point.

Anyone who can rappel a three-hundred-foot cliff, she told herself, *has no business freaking out at a little ice on the road.*

Once, you rappeled a cliff. Once. And lost your breakfast as soon as it was over.

To be truthful, she didn't even like driving in heavy rain. During a flash flood in Houston, the Mustang had hit a sheet of water on the freeway and Dixie found herself whipped around, heading back the way she'd come, wrong way in one-way traffic. After righting the car, she pulled off the freeway for ten minutes, shaking. That split-second loss of control had turned her backbone to jelly.

Barney Flannigan had schooled her to view such episodes as challenges, never to accept defeat. She could hear his lyrical brogue as if he were sitting beside her. "Never say 'can't,' lass. Tackle the fear head-on. Grab it by the horns, and don't let go till you best it."

She'd mastered roller skating, but never learned to *enjoy* it. After the hydroplane incident, she continued to drive on rain-slick streets, but never without the familiar churning in her stomach. This ice was a hundred times worse, and now was not a good time to test her grit.

Dixie didn't want to consider Dann's suggestion to let him drive, but she hadn't seen another vehicle since the truck's taillights disappeared, which seemed to confirm that the highway was closed behind them. If it was also closed ahead, then they were already stranded and it didn't matter what she decided. But if Dann stood a better chance of getting them to a town before the road closed, maybe she should let him take the wheel.

Hidden behind a false wall separating the trunk from the backseat was a small arsenal. She could retrieve the .45 and cover Dann while he drove. For that matter, a shiv was tucked right here in her boot. She'd never use it unless backed into a corner. She hated knives. She had to admit, though, they were better than guns in close quarters—except for the psychological advantage of a gun, which wasn't to be sneezed at.

Then again, maybe she was merely psyched after that close call with the deer. If Dann could handle the road at thirty-five miles an hour, she could, too. She was better acquainted with the Mustang's idiosyncrasies.

It would help if the cussed wind would let up.

She pushed the needle to twenty. *Okay, so far,* she thought. Which reminded her of the idiot who fell off a skyscraper and halfway down yelled to some people looking out a window, "I'm all right, so far."

Ignoring the dread churning in her gut, she pushed the needle to twenty-five. Dann hadn't said a word since his comment about driving. But his anxiety crackled through the air, fueling her own tension.

The folks at the diner had called it close when they said dark would come by four o'clock. In daylight, the driving snow was worse than a thick fog. Now that the sunlight was fading, visibility ended just past the front bumper.

At twenty-five miles an hour, her teeth were clenched so hard her jaw hurt, her fingers felt welded to the steering wheel, and her stomach felt like getting stuck in her throat. When she thought about going faster, panic rose like bile. But at this speed they wouldn't make Sisseton for another two hours. She pressed the accelerator and watched the needle inch toward thirty. *Okay, so far.*

Then the right front tire hit an ice slick. The car whipped into a sickening spin.

Jerking her foot off the gas, Dixie steered into the turn, counting two revolutions before the car shuddered to a stop.

Sweat drenched her clothes. She sat without moving, her forehead on the steering wheel. When she could no longer stand the churning in her stomach, she opened the door and vomited.

Chapter Twelve

Sunday, July 19, Conroe, Texas

Courtney watched the summer rain making ribbons outside the camp bus window and wondered if Ellie felt as gloomy as she did. Probably not. Ellie would already have met half the kids on the squeaky old bus.

Courtney had never worried about meeting people when Betsy was around. Being two years older, Betsy knew just about everyone. Now Courtney would be the new kid all by herself.

When everybody teamed up, she would be the odd one out, the one nobody picked. The stupid snobs wouldn't even realize she was an ace player. She'd have to sit on the bench until one of the camp counselors noticed and made the team let her rotate in. THEN she'd spike a volleyball over the net or hit a home run or shoot the winning basket (fat chance), and her team would wish they'd let her play sooner (yeah, right).

Maybe she should fake a two-week stomachache.

"Your first year?" The girl in the next seat was rummaging through a knapsack. She pulled out a Snickers bar and peeled it like a banana.

"First year at Camp Cade," Courtney answered. "Last year I was at Donovan."

"*Baby* camp. I graduated from there two whole years ago."

The girl had hair the color of tomato soup, and a crooked front tooth. Courtney hoped she also had a mouthful of aching cavities.

Turning back to the window, Courtney wondered if fate had purposely seated her beside the Camp Toad. Why couldn't her seat mate be another new girl, someone to team up with and share all the first-day blunders?

"Ooh swmem?"

"What?" Caramel and chocolate had stuck the girl's teeth together, garbling her words.

"*Swim*. Will you go out for the swim meet?"

"No." Actually, Courtney was a good swimmer, better even than Betsy, but she didn't want to encourage the Camp Toad. "I don't much like swimming."

"Just as well. I'm going to win again this year."

"Again?"

"Sure." The girl rolled the last bite of candy to the back of her mouth, then crumpled the wrapper and dropped it on the floor. "In last year's meet, I beat out everybody. Even the third-year girls. Now I'm even faster."

Courtney hadn't been swimming since last summer at Daddy Jon's house. He'd taught them all to swim, her, Betsy, and Ellie, when they were little. Sometimes she wished Mama were still married to Daddy Jon, even though he wasn't her real father. Her real father went away when she was almost two years old. Daddy Jon was Ellie's real father. He had adopted Courtney and Betsy. Now he and Mama were divorced and the girls spent every other weekend with Daddy Jon. Daddy Travis was okay, but older and never any fun.

"Tennis," the Toad said. A glob of chocolate had stuck to her crooked tooth. "If you play tennis, we could double."

"I haven't played much," Courtney admitted. She'd never played tennis in her life, but the girl seemed to be making an effort to be friends, and Courtney wondered if she had misjudged her. "I catch on quick, though."

"Tough. You'll have to find another partner. I'm a star player. A beginner would drag my score down."

QUEEN TOAD, Courtney decided, turning toward the window. The rain had stopped. They should be getting close to Camp Cade. She wondered if Ellie's bus had arrived at Camp Donovan.

One of the second graders had promised to look out for Ellie, but Courtney had a bad feeling about this summer—bad enough that she'd given Ellie her lucky penny. Inside Ellie's camp book she had written Daddy Jon's telephone number. Daddy Jon was a good person to call if you got scared.

Listening to the other girls' chatter, Courtney missed Betsy so much, she felt as empty as a shriveled-up balloon. She wished she could take back all the mean things she'd ever said and somehow let Betsy know she'd done a pretty good job of being a big sister. Courtney wasn't sure she could ever measure up.

She wished, also, that she could take a BASEBALL BAT to the car that killed Betsy. She'd like to BUST all the windows and FLATTEN all the tires.

Even more, she'd like to BASH Mr. Parker Dann.

Chapter Thirteen

Sunday, July 26, Camp Donovan, Texas

Ellie wriggled into her shorts, slipped her arms into the red camp shirt, and squeezed it over her head fast. She *hated* getting caught inside.

She smoothed the wrinkles over her tummy and scraped with her fingernail at a spot of something yellow. Mama would say to wear a clean shirt, the blue one or the white — both had CAMP DONOVAN on the front — but Ellie liked the red one best. She'd worn it every day since camp started.

Rubbing her eyes with a fist, she tiptoed to the door, praying she wouldn't awaken the other girls in her cabin. She'd woke up early so she could beat Anna to the flag. Yesterday, Miss Bower'd said the person who got to raise the flag to the top of the flagpole had to be an early bird.

Easing the door open, Ellie started down the steps. Then she remembered Courtney's lucky penny.

No, *her* lucky penny. Courtney said she could keep it, and today Ellie needed lots of luck.

Creeping back to her bunk, she tripped on her untied shoestrings and made a loud thump. She crossed her fingers that Anna wouldn't wake up. She and Anna had argued last night about who would get to do the flag today. Ellie knew in her heart that she could do a better job. Anna would probably drop the flag halfway up, and then they'd have to *burn* it. Everybody knew it was very bad luck to drop a flag.

She felt around under her pillow until her fingers closed over the penny. Pushing it deep in her shorts pocket, she hurried back to the door and down the steps. When the door banged behind her, she kept going.

Across the yard, Miss Bower, her blond hair scraggly from sleep, was leaving the Chow Barn, where everybody ate meals except when they had a picnic. Miss Bower had a coffee mug in one hand and the flag box tucked under her arm. Ellie raced across the damp ground to the circle where everyone gathered to salute the flag. Miss Bower was settling into her camp chair to drink her coffee.

"My goodness, Ellie. Aren't you an early bird?"

"I came to do the flag."

"Oh . . ." Miss Bower nodded, but Ellie could tell by the way her smile faded that it wasn't a yes nod. It was the sort of nod Mama used when she said, "I see."

"I won't drop it, Miss Bower. I promise."

"No, I'm sure you wouldn't mean to, but it's an awfully big flag for such a little girl."

"I'm not so little anymore. See, my hands are big." Ellie spread her fingers wide to make her hands as big as possible. She heard footsteps pounding behind her.

"Miss Bower! Miss Bower!"

It was Anna.

"Look!" Ellie clenched her fist to bunch up the muscle in her arm, as she pushed up the sleeve of her camp shirt. "I'm strong, Miss Bower."

"That's not a muscle," Anna jeered, offering both arms. "Look at these."

Just then, the bell rang, calling everybody to the circle.

Ellie had to admit that Anna's muscles might be a *teensy* bit bigger than her own. Anna was already six and *a half*, as tall as second-year girls.

"But, Miss Bower," Ellie argued, "you told us only *early birds* get to do the flag. I was the earliest of anybody."

"Yes, that's true, Ellie. I did say that, didn't I?"

Ellie nodded helpfully.

"That's not fair, Miss Bower. Ellie's the youngest kid in camp. Us older girls should get to go first, and *I've never* done the flag."

Miss Bower wrinkled her forehead. "I don't recall your ever asking before, Anna."

"No, ma'am, but I still—"

"Well, Ellie was the early bird this morning. Maybe you can get up earlier tomorrow." When Anna started to object, Miss Bower put up a hand. "Meanwhile, it takes *two* girls to unfold the flag and keep it from touching the ground while I fasten it to the flag hoist."

Behind them, Ellie heard cabin doors banging, feet pounding, as the other girls gathered around the flagpole. Miss Bower opened the box, took out the flag, and handed it to Ellie.

"One girl holds the end while the other girl unfolds."

Anna pushed forward and grabbed the unfolding end. Ellie had to just stand there while Anna flipped the folded part over and back until it was stretched between them.

"Now, open it wide," Miss Bower said, standing and moving to the flagpole. "Ellie, you hand me the top corner."

Ellie knew the blue part sprinkled with stars was the top. Reaching to hand Miss Bower the metal ring in the blue corner, Ellie felt a tug. The flag slipped through her fingers. She grabbed quick, heart thumping furiously, and caught it before it touched the ground. When she looked up, Anna was grinning.

That grin was too much.

"Butthead," Ellie whispered, with her most ferocious glare. She had learned the word from Courtney, but this was the first time she felt like saying it to anybody.

When Miss Bower finished hooking the flag to the rope, she made Anna step back. Then Ellie pulled hard on the rope, and the flag traveled a little way up the pole. It was heavier than she expected. She looked at Miss Bower, hoping she hadn't noticed that Ellie had raised the flag only a few inches.

Bracing herself, Ellie tugged harder, the muscles in her arms straining with the effort. This time the flag moved a little easier. Hand over hand, like she'd seen the older girls do, Ellie pulled the flag to the top of the pole, where it snapped and waved in the wind. Then Miss Bower tied it off and everybody said the Pledge.

Ellie had only learned the Pledge since she came to camp. She wasn't sure what all the words meant, but she said them in her biggest, most important voice.

Afterward, the bell rang again, calling everyone to break-fast. While the other girls ran past, Ellie looked up at the flag flapping back and forth and couldn't stop smiling. She bet Courtney hadn't got to pull up the flag on her first time at camp.

Watching the flag as she walked, Ellie started toward the Chow Barn—and fell flat in the dirt. Her chin hit hard. She bit her tongue, bringing tears to her eyes. Sitting up, she quickly rubbed the tears away. Big girls, who could pull a flag all the way to the top of the pole, didn't cry.

"Nah, na-na-nah-na!" Anna stood jeering at her from the steps of the Chow Barn. "Forget to tie your shoes?" She stuck out her tongue, then disappeared through the door.

Looking at her untied shoestrings, Ellie saw a dirty smudge where someone had stepped on one of them. She had a good idea who that someone was.

But she wasn't going to let it spoil her best day at camp. She tied her shoes, brushed herself off, and ran to join the other girls at breakfast. Reaching the steps, she fished in her pocket for the lucky penny. Courtney had made Ellie promise to keep it with her to ward off any bad luck. Ever since Mr. Dann's car ran over Betsy, Courtney had been worried about bad luck.

Frowning, Ellie felt in her other pocket, pulled it wide, and peered inside it. She saw a rubber band she had found under her bed and a piece of cookie from yesterday's snack.

But the lucky penny was gone.

Chapter Fourteen

Thursday, December 24, Interstate 29, South Dakota

"I don't want to shoot you," Dixie said, aiming the .45 at Parker Dann's chest. He sat next to her now, in the driver's seat, wearing a cocky grin that had spread across his face the moment she unshackled him. "I especially don't want to shoot you in my car, where I'd have to mop up the blood."

His grin drooped at the corners. "So you want me to start this thing or what?"

She handed him the key. When he put it in the ignition, she leaned across the car and snapped a handcuff on his wrist.

"Hey—"

She snapped the other cuff to the steering wheel.

"Dammit, woman, how am I supposed to drive all chained up like a rabid dog?"

"You have eighteen inches of chain between those cuffs, enough to shift gears and drive." But not enough length to reach her with his big fist. In scoping out a control situation, Dixie always imagined herself in the skip's place. Parker Dann could watch for the moment her attention wavered, grab the back of her head, slam her face into the dash until she was senseless, then kick her out of the car and be as free as a southbound goose. Now that they'd spent half a day together, she found herself thinking of him more as a big teddy bear than a crazed killer. But that sort of thinking could get her in trouble. The cautious part of her mind said "cuff him," so she had.

She rested the gun on her lap. "Do your stuff, snowbird. Get us out of here."

Miraculously, the car had not run into another snowbank coming out of its spin, and Dann seemed to know what he was doing. He handled the Mustang with such skill that Dixie felt doubly embarrassed at her own incompetence. Why didn't the damn car slide with him driving it?

Then, as her tension began to ease, the passenger-side wheels hit a bump.

"Watch out! You're going off the road."

"Gee gosh darn. You're downright perceptive." Dann's cocky grin was back in place, along with his irritating air of assurance. "Hanging two wheels on the shoulder gives us traction. That telltale bump warns us if we start to drift left or right."

"So why didn't you share that pearl of wisdom earlier?"

He tossed her a look of amused insolence. "Actually, fresh snow isn't all that bad to drive on. You were overcompensating, is all. Natural, when you're not used to the weather and road conditions. It's ice *under* the snow that's tricky, but this blizzard came so fast there hasn't been much ice buildup since the roads were cleared."

Dixie nodded, and they rode in silence for a while. For the first time all day, she felt her shoulders and neck relax.

"Guess you know what a legend you are around the jailhouse," Dann said.

"Legend?"

"You know, someone prisoners swap stories about."

She knew what he was getting at, having fabricated a good number of the stories herself. Her reputation as a badass bitch made skips think twice about resisting.

"Did you really follow a guy into the men's room, cuff him at the urinal before he could zip his pecker back in his pants?"

More than once. "Catch a man with his pants down, he's

too surprised to fight back." But she'd never transported a skip in the trunk of her car; those nasty rumors were useful but false.

"Another guy said you started a bonfire outside his bedroom window while he and his girl were getting it on. When they smelled smoke and came crashing out, you were waiting for him."

"Wouldn't call it a bonfire. A few sticks, some newspapers."

Dann laughed. "Hell, you've got a cold heart."

"Only kind to have in my business."

His smile faded. "That's a hint, right? Guess it's not smart to listen to a prisoner's story."

When she didn't answer, he turned his attention to the road. After a few minutes, he cleared his throat, and Dixie knew he was about to lay it on her.

"Truth is, I'd give anything to know for sure I didn't kill that little girl. I honestly don't know."

"It's hard to know anything when you're falling-down drunk."

"I was feeling no pain, for sure. Celebrating my first three-million-dollar sale—to a demolition company out of New Orleans."

Three million? "What the hell did you sell, explosives?"

"Heavy equipment. Dozers, tractors, backhoes."

Tuning him out as he droned on about making the sale, Dixie considered how to handle it if they managed to find a motel room. She'd have to leave him hitched to the steering wheel while she booked a room, then cuff him to the bed.

Her eyes felt sandblasted. She closed them against the strain of the swirling landscape, gray now more than white, with the sun setting. When she snapped her eyes open, twenty minutes had passed.

"Good timing," Dann said. "Looks like a roadblock ahead."

The faint glow of yellow lights dotted the road, one of them blinking.

"Keep that cuff out of sight, or I'll have to turn you over to the sheriff." She knew he'd rather take his chances with her than end up in a small-town jail.

As Dann coasted to a stop, she slid the .45 under her seat. A man in a heavy parka jogged up to the driver's side. Dann lowered the window. When the man hunched over to look in, Dixie saw a highway department emblem on his coat and wondered if he might know McGrue. Doubtful, this far north. The parka's hood was drawn close around the man's face. Snow coated his mustache and brows, turning them white.

"You folks took a big chance coming through without chains."

"Didn't realize we were in for such a storm," Dann said cheerfully. "Found out the hard way."

"Not nearly as hard as it could've been. There's sixty miles more of this and it's still coming. Afraid we'll have to stop you here." He pointed. "Turn right and go about four miles to Sisseton. You'll see the Sparks Motel. Emma Sparks has a room waiting for you."

Dann raised one of his bushy eyebrows.

"Waiting for *us*? Like she knew we were coming?"

The officer knocked snow off his lashes with a padded-gloved hand. "Margie, from the Grandin Diner, said to watch for you guys. Otherwise, I'd be home now, with a warm fire and a hot meal."

"Appreciate your waiting," Dann said.

"You can follow me into Sisseton, get a good night's sleep." The trooper slapped a farewell on the car's roof and jogged back to the pickup. Ten minutes later Dann turned in and stopped at a red neon motel sign. The pickup blinked its lights and drove on.

Dixie eyed the office. Across the drive, four cabins angled toward the road, roofs laden with snow.

"Keys," Dixie said, holding out her hand.

"You don't really think I'd try to drive out of here?"

"I don't think you're that big a fool, but why risk it?"

With a shrug and a yawn, Dann slipped the keys from the

ignition, dropped them into her hand. Dixie zipped herself into his parka, shoving the .45 deep in a pocket, then trudged through gusting snow to the rental office. A bell jangled above the door. The rich aroma of roast pork filled her nostrils. A thin elderly woman in a green calico dress and round eyeglasses smiled across a counter sign that identified her as Emma Sparks, Proprietor. She wore a corsage of holly sprigs and gold Christmas balls. No computer-chip designs stamped into the gold finish, Dixie noticed, and felt absurdly uplifted by that fact.

Emma Sparks handed her a steaming mug of a liquid that smelled like hot apple pie.

"Spiced cider," she said. "It'll warm you right up." The woman had an infectious smile.

"It's wonderful." Dixie hadn't realized how ravenous she was. "Thanks."

"Lord, I was worried sick you folks'd got yourselves stuck someplace. Told Arnie, that's my son, if you didn't turn up in another half hour he'd best go fetch you."

Dixie tugged off her gloves and dug out her wallet.

"We appreciate your staying open for us, being Christmas Eve and all."

"Honey, out on that highway you'd be a snowball come morning." Emma plucked a brass key off a wall peg. "The cabin's not a bit fancy, but it's warm and the bed's good."

"Don't suppose you have two beds in there, do you?" Dixie counted out some bills. Glancing up to see the woman's smile had faded, she forced a grin. "That man kicks like a mule, but I'd hate to put him on the floor on such a cold night."

"Ha! I've been *there* before." Emma Sparks laughed and rang up the sale. "Got a dilapidated old cot, won't be too comfortable. I'd let you have an extra room, but the others are all filled." She opened a closet door behind her and lifted out an aluminum camp cot, the army green canvas worn thin in places.

Dixie rounded the counter to take it from her.

"There's extra bedding in your cabin," the woman said. "On the closet shelf."

"Thank you. This will beat getting kicked blue." Dixie hefted the cot, hating the deception but aware that no good could come from telling Emma Sparks that a child killer would be sleeping under her roof. Turning to go, Dixie remembered the acute emptiness of her stomach.

"Suppose there's any place open in town to get a hamburger?"

The old woman's smile brightened like a Christmas candle.

"Cafe's closed, but I knew you folks'd be hungry, so I put a tray in your room. Nothing fancy, mind. Buck, that's my husband, cooked up a big ham this morning, way more than we'll ever eat. I made some sandwiches. Put some fresh fruit on the tray, too, and a thermos of that hot cider. The room has a little refrigerator stocked with juice and sodas, just pay for what you use, and there's instant coffee packets, tea, cocoa — not the Hilton, honey, but we won't let you starve."

Sounded a damn sight better than the Hilton at the moment. Homemade ham sandwiches? Dixie's mouth was already watering. Emma bustled around to open the door for her.

"Last cabin on the right. You can park on the side there, out of the wind."

"Thanks, Mrs. Sparks. Sure was good of you to be open."

"It's Emma, honey, and listen, there's a phone in your room, if you need anything. Just dial eight. We won't have the office open, so no sense in you trudging over here in the storm."

"How long does a storm like this usually last?"

"This'n's worse than most, but I expect it'll blow over by morning. Clearing the roads might take a day or two."

Dixie couldn't keep the misery from showing in her face. Even if the roads were miraculously clear by morning, no way she'd make it home by Christmas night. Seeing her feelings reflected in Emma Sparks' inquisitive eyes, Dixie forced a smile before pushing back out into the blizzard.

The wind tried to wrestle the cot from her hands as she carried it to the Mustang and shoved it onto the backseat.

"Let's go." She cocked a thumb toward their cabin, handed Dann the car keys, and wished like hell she hadn't let Belle Richards talk her into taking this sorry job.

Chapter Fifteen

Hell is a hard cot in a cold motel room, Dixie decided, pulling the scratchy wool blanket around her neck. The heating system moaned and clanked, doing its damnedest to pump warm air through the vents, but the tempest howling past the windows challenged the aging mechanism beyond its limits. Dixie had slept nearly seven hours. She could easily sleep another seven if only she could get warm and comfortable.

Scooting lower on the cot, she heard a rip and felt the canvas give way under her butt. A knife of cold air promptly stabbed her through the tear. *Terrific.*

She shifted her weight gingerly to elbows and heels, pushed herself toward the top of the cot, and held her breath as she settled. With the rip no longer under the heaviest part of her body, the canvas might hold.

Punching her pillow into a fluffier lump, she looked across the room to where Parker Dann was stretched out on the bed, snoring. Comfortable, no doubt, on his innerspring mattress. And warm. The only place to cuff him securely had turned out to be the bed's curved iron headboard, its vertical bars strong and firmly welded in place.

Funny how bright the room was for just past midnight. The raging snow outside the windows reflected red light from the motel's NO VACANCY sign. Dixie wriggled sideways to avoid an aluminum side bar and slowly relaxed her muscles, listening for the sound of fabric tearing . . . heard only the creak of the cot's frame rocking beneath her . . . and drifted off to sleep.

Three hours later she awoke with her midsection wedged through the rip in the canvas, her frozen rump nearly dragging the pine floor. Flailing her arms, she groped for something to grab hold of to pull herself out; the canvas had trapped her just below the arms and above the knees. She must look like a giant bug tipped on its back, she thought, cursing softly and feeling a flash of empathy for the Kafka character who awoke as a giant cockroach.

She glanced at Dann. He was sitting up, leaning against the pillow-padded headboard, and wearing his cocky grin, a twinkle of malice in his blue eyes.

"Merry Christmas! Be happy to lend a hand, only . . ." He rattled the handcuff along the iron bar where it was fastened. "Afraid I'm temporarily inconvenienced."

"Perhaps you'd be less inconvenienced sleeping in the backseat of the Mustang. Or in that clawfoot bathtub." Dixie swallowed her anger. It wasn't Dann's fault he had the more comfortable bed. She had actually considered cuffing him to a bathtub faucet knob, but there was no way he could've wormed his big frame into a sleeping position, and staying awake all night, he might've figured a way to get the knob off. From where she sat now, her decision needed reconsideration.

Pushing at the sides of the cot with her upper arms, she managed to gain enough leverage to pull herself out of the hole. She rose stiffly and stumbled to the bathroom. Splashed a handful of icy water on her face. Wiped it dry on a thin terry towel with faded yellow flowers.

Through the bathroom door, she heard bedsprings creak as Dann shifted positions, and she knew he could hear the rush of water as she emptied her bladder. Never had she been in such intimate circumstances with a prisoner. She didn't like it.

Emerging from the bathroom, she found he had turned on a reading lamp and was playing solitaire with a dog-eared deck of red bicycle cards. The air had warmed up some and the wind had quieted down. In a partially open drawer of the bedside table she saw a scratch pad, pencils, a box of dominoes, and a book of crossword puzzles alongside the empty playing-card box. Apparently, Sisseton wasn't brimming with tourist attractions.

Dann scooped up the cards and shuffled them.

"I suppose, sooner or later, the *prisoner* will get a turn at using the facilities," he said. "Or did you carry in my Mountain Spring Water bottle?"

Dixie massaged a kink in her neck as she considered the wisdom of uncuffing him. He was smart enough to bide his time until he saw the perfect opportunity to escape, but she didn't expect that would happen until they were out of the storm and into a more populated area, where he'd have a chance of melting into a crowd. Glancing out the window, she noticed it had stopped snowing and ambled over to look out.

"Holy hell," she whispered.

Snowdrifts swooped and dipped across the landscape, level with the knotty pine windowsills. One drift completely covered the motel office entrance. Similar drifts barricaded the doors to the other cabins.

Dixie strode to their own door, twisted the lock, and pulled. For a moment it resisted; then she heard a sucking noise and the door swung free to reveal a solid wall of snow.

Packed tight.

Not a chink of sky showing anywhere. They were snowed in.

Frigid air curled into the room from the white barrier.

Why doesn't it cave in? she wondered.

She touched a tentative hand to the center of the mass. A fist-size section tumbled to the floor. She shut the door quickly.

"Looks of that, we'll be here all day, maybe another night," Dann said.

Dixie strode to the window, an old-fashioned casement like the ones at home. A metal storm window was mounted outside it. She opened the toggle locks and pushed upward. Stuck.

"Probably frozen," Dann offered cheerfully. "Be surprised if these old windows were airtight."

Dixie banged on the casement and tried again to raise it, but it held firm. Ice had caked around the ropes and pulleys. What she needed was a crowbar.

"Sort of like being in jail," Dann said, "only more comfortable."

She could pry the window open and . . .

And what? Surely Buck and Emma Sparks had a back door to their house and tools for dealing with this sort of thing. It was three-thirty A.M., too early for the Sparkses to be awake.

"We won't be going anywhere for a while," Dann said. "Might as well get comfortable."

The Mustang made a hump in the snow, its chrome side mirrors all that distinguished it from other humps, probably shrubs. Eventually, she would have to dig the car out, but until snowplows came through there'd be no place to go. Dann was right. She might as well relax until daylight, when the Sparkses would be up and around. It galled her, though, being trapped.

Behind her she could hear Dann shuffling the cards.

"Gin?" He had smoothed the chenille bedspread and had dealt two hands, the deck centered between them, a discard faceup. Catching Dixie's eye, he wiggled his heavy brows so comically she almost smiled.

What the hell. They'd get through the day a lot easier if they were both comfortable. Might as well start by letting Dann wash up.

She picked up her keys from the windowsill where she'd laid them the night before and tossed them to Dann. So far he'd been a model prisoner, but she wasn't about to get close enough for him to hook one of those tree-limb arms around her neck.

While he worked the handcuff lock awkwardly with his left

hand, she retrieved the .45 from the floor beside the cot, took the gun's magazine from her pocket, shoved it in place, and sat down in one of the wooden chairs. When Dann had freed himself, she held out her hand for the keys.

"Five minutes," she said.

"Right. We're on a tight schedule here."

"You need more time than that, maybe we'll get a doctor in to check you over, see if you're getting enough fiber in your diet."

"Flannigan, we got a bathroom here with no window, no sharp objects, no chemicals to build a bomb—on the off chance that I knew how to build a bomb. I'm flattered you think I'm so crafty, but short of stopping up the plumbing, I don't think I can create much chaos in there."

"Four and a half minutes."

He shot her a dark look and slammed the door.

Dixie laid the gun and keys on the table. She emptied a packet of coffee in the automatic dripolator positioned on a pine shelf that served as a sideboard. Having filled it with water the night before, she now plugged it in. She inspected two cups for spiders. The pot gurgled, filling the air with a rich coffee aroma.

Scooping up one of the gin rummy hands—two aces; king, ten, and three of hearts; five of spades; deuce of clubs—she thought about checking out the other hand, wondered if Dann had already seen it, and before she could make up her mind, the bathroom door opened. Drops of water clung to the front of Dann's dark hair. His shirttail was tucked in neatly. Being shut in together would be less frustrating, she realized, if Dann weren't so obviously male.

She tossed him the keys. "You'll have to double-lock the cuffs to keep them from tightening down as you move."

"Ah, yes. 'Trust not the deviant mind, though it be dulled by sloth or drink or age; 'tis nonetheless twisted and therefore . . . *treacherous.*' Better lock me up, Flannigan. No telling how much mayhem I'd cause if allowed to move about freely."

"Fancy yourself an intellectual, do you, Dann?"

He bounced the keys a few inches into the air, watched them clink back into his palm.

"A student, Flannigan. Merely a student of life."

"Especially when you're a few hours in the bottle, right?"

He flushed, which surprised her. Most drunks she'd known were hardened to criticism about their drinking, always certain they had it under control. She must have hit a nerve.

He bounced the keys in his hand again, making no move toward the handcuff.

"Being chained to this bed might make sense if there were somewhere for me to go. How far you think I'd get with four feet of snow on the ground?"

Dixie couldn't argue the four feet of snow.

"I don't cotton to spending another day and night cramped up with one arm anchored to that friggin headboard."

Better than a cot with no canvas. Dixie sympathized, but she couldn't let Dann roam freely about the cabin. He probably had a whole bag of tricks she hadn't seen yet. She aimed the .45 at his kneecap.

Bunching his fist around the keys, he pointed to the phone.

"Say I *did* get free. Call the sheriff. A snowmobile would run me down in no time."

With each word, she could see his anger mounting.

"Dann, you'll be a damn sight less comfortable with a busted leg."

"And you'd have some explaining to do. Listen to how quiet it is out there. Think that gunshot won't ring out all over the countryside?"

Dixie reached behind her. The gun never wavering, she pulled the wool blanket off her cot and wrapped it around her gun hand.

"Now nobody will hear the shot."

Dann stood his ground, blue eyes fierce in the lamplight.

"I don't think you'll do it, Flannigan. You won't shoot me in cold blood."

"Think again." Dixie cocked the .45, the click barely audible through the folds of wool. "Remember those jailhouse stories you heard?" She hoped he'd heard the meanest ones.

He vacillated another thirty seconds, knuckles pale and rigid around the keys. Then he picked up the loose handcuff, snapped it around his wrist, and locked it.

Dixie put the gun down and accepted the keys, glad as hell he hadn't called her bluff. Then she stood and turned her back to him, her hands shaking as she poured two cups of coffee. She set one cup on the bedside table for Dann.

"You really think we'll have to stay another night?" she said, as if the past few minutes had not occurred.

Anger engraved in every line of his face, Dann picked up the coffee cup. She could see him making an effort to calm down. Finally, he glanced up at her. His blue eyes had regained their amused insolence. He had backed off this time. They both knew he'd try again. Meanwhile, the time would pass easier if they put the incident behind them.

"According to the radio reports," he said, "this was a freak storm. Sudden, violent, widespread. They'll clear the main highways and essential routes first, to airports, hospitals, shelters . . . I'd guess the storm hit this area hard, being on the plains. Means some folks will need emergency rescue." Hooking the other wooden chair with his foot, he scooted it over beside the bed and sat down. The lines in his face had relaxed. He picked up his card hand and moved the deck to where they could both reach it. "Considering also that it's Christmas, the cleanup crews will be shorthanded. All in all, lady, there's not a chance in hell we'll be out of here before tomorrow."

Twenty-four hours, maybe thirty. Dixie recalled the snowflakes she had caught on her tongue, and one of Kathleen's needlepoint maxims came to mind—*Be Careful What You Wish.* Dixie had gotten her white Christmas, all right. Unfortunately, she was spending it with a prisoner.

She fanned her cards, paired up the aces, moved the deuce to one side. Drawing a jack of hearts, she discarded the deuce, and for a few minutes they played in silence, the cards giving the antsy part of her mind something to do while another part wrapped around the problem of what to tell Buck and Emma Sparks about Dann.

If she managed to get the window unstuck and helped shovel snow, they'd wonder why Dann wasn't helping, too. If she sat tight and waited until Buck Sparks dug the snow away from the door, he'd surely knock and she'd have to mince around to keep him from spotting Dann's handcuffs. A lot depended on how friendly their hosts turned out to be.

"Strange job for a woman," Dann said. "Bounty hunting." He drew a card from the deck and tossed down the four of clubs.

"Strange job for anybody, but someone has to do it."

He grinned. "Otherwise scum like me would be shirking their comeuppance all over the country."

"Screwing up the judicial system, putting bail bondsmen out of business."

"Cheating juries out of their moment in the limelight."

"Not to mention disappointing the arresting officers." She drew the four of hearts, thought about it for a moment, and dropped it on the discard pile.

Dann drew a keeper, rearranged his hand to accommodate it, then discarded the six of clubs.

"Heard you were favored for stepping into the DA's seat. Must be quite a story, you giving them the bird and taking up bounty hunting."

Dixie looked at him over the top of her cards. The story wasn't any secret. She'd joined the lower ranks of the DA's office right out of law school. Like the Ghostbusters of movie fame, she wanted to rid the world of slime, but it oozed through loopholes, slithered back into society, and expanded.

"Remember the Leigh Ann Turner murder trial?" Dixie's last case had made national news.

"Turner . . . Turner . . ." Dann eyed the discards. "Accused of killing her aunt, wasn't she?"

"Flora Riggs. A scrawny old woman with pink-tinted hair and clothes recycled from the decadent twenties. Good-hearted and stronger than horseradish."

Dixie had met Flora Riggs a year before her death, after

the old woman witnessed a mugging. When Dixie questioned her eyesight, Flora had retorted, *I saw those two boys beat that man as clear I can see those ugly shoes you're wearing.* Dixie's plain brown pumps were comfortable, which is what she required of all her clothes. She asked Flora if she tried to stop the boys. *Oh, fah! It was over before I could get my old bones out the door. But I sicked Pooch on 'em.* Pooch was the German shepherd that lay at Flora's feet and growled at anyone who came near. *He's old like I am, and not a sharp tooth left in his head, but he can still bark a ghost back in its grave.* Flora's hearty cackle had made Dixie smile. *Those boys took one look at Pooch tearing across the yard and they turned tail fast. Then I dialed 911.*

Thanks to Flora's swift reactions, the victim had lived, and for once the Texas judicial system worked as it should: the two young men went to prison. But the murder of Flora Riggs was not so easily resolved.

"Newspapers said a neighbor found her hanging from a ceiling fan," Dann said.

"Engineered to look like suicide. The chair she supposedly climbed on was tipped over, as if she'd kicked it aside after fixing the rope around her neck."

The neighbor had also found Pooch, dead beside his water dish, a nasty lump between his eyes. *Me and old Pooch keep each other alive out of pure cussedness,* Flora had told Dixie. *We're both too ornery to go first.*

"But Ms. ADA Supersleuth suspected it wasn't suicide, I suppose." Dann's voice held a barb, which Dixie ignored.

"Forensics examined the bruising on Flora's neck, the direction the rope fibers were bent, and said, 'No way it was suicide.' "

Like Pooch, Flora had been murdered. *But why would anybody want to kill Aunt Flora?* her niece, Leigh Ann, had protested. *Everybody loved her.*

Why indeed? The back door was unlocked. A number of family heirlooms, mostly jewelry and silver, were missing. Had Flora surprised a burglar? Dixie didn't think so. A burglar wouldn't have taken time for a trumped-up hanging, would've knocked the woman in the head, same as the dog.

"Leigh Ann's thumbprint was found on the ceiling fan," Dixie told Dann. "Of course, she might have touched the fan while cleaning it, but Leigh Ann didn't strike anybody as a conscientious housekeeper. And she had moved out of Flora's house more than a year earlier."

"Cute little blonde, wasn't she? Delicate, soft-spoken?"

"Picture of innocence." To everyone but Dixie. "At first she couldn't produce an alibi. Claimed she'd spent the afternoon shopping with a friend at the Galleria. But her friend wasn't available to comment. Leigh Ann said she'd mentioned taking a trip."

"Let me guess: the aunt was a rich bitch."

"Not rich, but frugal. Inherited her home, and set money aside for years, living on the interest and the sale of her needlework. She took Leigh Ann in after the girl's parents were killed in a car accident." *All the while that child was growing up*, Flora had told Dixie, *I worried something would happen to me and she'd be left all alone in the world.* "Flora Riggs took out a half-million-dollar insurance policy on her own life so her niece wouldn't be left penniless."

"And you figured she murdered her aunt for the insurance money?"

"Yes, but the policy had a double indemnity clause for accidental death, so why make it look like suicide? Suicide doesn't pay. That's the part I couldn't make fit." Dixie shook her head. "Besides, Leigh Ann didn't exactly need the money. She earned a fancy salary as an interpreter for the State Department, and her fiancé was an ambassador from some unheard of country in South America."

"Came out in the trial, didn't it, that the girl's aunt didn't like the boyfriend?"

"Flora didn't like him, but that's a thin cause for murder."

"Not when you add a cool million. Correct me if I'm wrong, but murder qualifies as accidental, for insurance purposes. Swipe a few fancy baubles, looks like the aunt was killed during a burglary."

"That still doesn't explain the business with the rope, though, does it?" Dixie knew Dann was feigning interest, hoping to win her over. But she was getting a kick out of hearing him puzzle it out the same way she had two years ago. He had a sharp mind.

He stood up, the handcuff sliding to the top of the rounded headboard.

"Here's this sweet-faced blonde. Looks like she wouldn't harm a fly. Yet evidence keeps stacking up against her." He paused, rubbing his stubbled chin with his free hand. "Personally, I thought she was guilty. Reminded me of a Norman Rockwell painting—maybe you've seen it—an angel hiding a slingshot under her wings."

"The jury wasn't fooled, either. When all the evidence was heard, they were ready to convict—"

Dann's eyebrows arched suddenly. "That's when the mysterious friend showed up."

"Myra. Claimed she'd left for Europe the day after her shopping spree with Leigh Ann, and went from there to China, in no hurry to return home until she heard about the trial."

Dann's eyes narrowed, and he went silent for a beat.

"So the friggin jury, *twelve persons good and true,* almost convicted an innocent woman." A slow drawl flavored his words with cynical amusement. "Proving circumstantial evidence can look damning as all hell and still be pure dogshit." He yanked at the chain holding him to the bed. "Guess I know exactly how Leigh Ann felt."

"Then you missed the rest of the story," Dixie said. Dropping her cards on the bed, she stood and walked to the window. To the east, the sky had brightened. Wisps of pink limned the dun-colored clouds. Buck and Emma Sparks would wake up soon, and Dixie hadn't yet decided how to handle the snow-shoveling problem. She trusted inspiration to strike at the right moment.

"You're telling me Leigh Ann was guilty? I saw her and the boyfriend on television, boarding a plane for South America."

Dixie folded her arms against the chill air near the window.

"Shortly after the trial, another witness surfaced. A neighbor recognized the ambassador in the news and remembered seeing him at Flora's house on the afternoon of the murder."

"Then you're saying sweet-cheeks and her boyfriend planned the whole thing together."

"Right down to Leigh Ann's thumbprint on the ceiling fan and the missing Myra, who turned up precisely when her testimony would do the most damage to the prosecution's case."

"The prosecutor being you."

"It couldn't have worked any better if they'd had a ring through my nose, leading me from one clue to the next."

Dann leaned against the wall, studying Dixie, his piratical brow furrowed with interest. "In the end, though, you figured it out."

"Sure, I figured it out. When it was too damn late! The ambassador was exempted from prosecution—diplomatic immunity—and a jury had already found Leigh Ann innocent. She couldn't be tried again, even if two dozen witnesses lined up to swear they saw her string her aunt from the ceiling fan. By the time I pieced it together, Leigh Ann was on that airplane to South America with the insurance check in her pocket."

"So, they both walk—and angel collects a million dollars to boot."

When Dixie nodded, Dann slammed the heel of his fist against the wall.

"Now *that* chaps my butt. Here's *my* jury, ready to fry my ass good on circumstantial evidence. Maybe I even did it, hell, I don't know, I don't remember, but if I *did* hit that child, I never intended it, like you're talking about with this Leigh Ann, and I *damn* sure won't do anything like that again because I'll never again touch a drop of liquor and drive a car. How does a jury justify sending *me* up the road and letting *real murderers* get off?" He stopped, let out a heavy, exasperated breath, then kicked the bed frame. "I don't friggin understand that."

Dixie had heard every drunk-driving story in the books, and they all included the promise never again to drive after drinking. But she agreed with Dann about Flora Riggs' killers. It enraged her that they were walking around free.

"The system's not perfect," she said quietly. "It's rife with political pressures, inadequate prison facilities, incompetent attorneys, corrupt officials. Sometimes it just breaks down."

"Well . . . you should know." He fanned his cards out. "So that was the case that ripped your britches."

Leigh Ann Turner and the ambassador weren't the first killers Dixie had watched walk free, nor the most ruthless. But after the Riggs case, Dixie was filled to her gullet with bitter pills, would choke if she had to swallow another one.

Now her job was pig simple. She never concerned herself with a skip's guilt or innocence. When a bondsman posted bail, the client signed a contract guaranteeing his own physical presence in court on a specified date. The bondsman in turn had to post collateral guaranteeing the court that his client would be available, much like backing a loan. If the client skipped, the bondsman owed the court the entire bail amount and had the right to "repossess" his client's "physical presence," through force if necessary, like repossessing a car. Only hauling back skips paid a lot better than hauling cars. And there were times it carried emotional reward, as well. Such as bringing a child killer to trial.

Turning back to the bed, Dixie started to reclaim her cards, when Dann spread his hand on the bed, faceup.

"Gin," he said, his cocky grin and amused blue eyes full of mocking impertinence.

Chapter Sixteen

Saturday, August 1, Camp Cade, Texas

"I heard it again," Courtney whispered.

"Heard what?" Her bunk mate's voice, thick with sleep, rose from the darkness.

"Lisa, someone's creeping around outside." Courtney held her breath in the muggy dawn, listening for skulking noises. At dinnertime around the campfire, and later, walking back to the cabin, she'd gotten a feeling—a scary feeling.

"It's probably someone going to the latrine."

"The latrine's not around here." In fact, it stood in the middle of camp, near the counselors' quarters. Their own cabin lay farthest out, farthest from the lake.

"It's nobody. Go back to sleep."

But Courtney knew she hadn't imagined it. In nearly two weeks at Camp Cade, nothing like this had happened. She wasn't in the habit of imagining things.

"I *heard* someone—or something—creeping around. *There it is again. Listen!*"

Outside the window, something rustled, like dead leaves. The cabin sat in a clearing, away from the jutting pines and dense underbrush of the woods, but dry bark had been spread in the flower beds as mulch. Someone must be standing in the flower bed, trying to look in.

Courtney peered hard at the window nearest her bunk. Had a shadow shifted outside the pale curtain?

"Probably a raccoon." Her bunk mate's voice sounded more alert. "Who would be creeping around this late?"

"A chain-saw killer." Courtney watched the shadow, waiting to see if it moved.

"There's no such thing as a chain-saw killer, except in the movies."

Maybe. But other kinds of killers were real enough. Like Mr. Parker Dann. *Out on bail*, Daddy Travis had said, *not locked up like murderers ought to be*. Courtney's eyes felt gritty. She needed to blink, but she didn't want to miss—

There! The shadow moved. Didn't it?

"I'm going to wake up Miss Bryant." Bryant was the nicest of their three counselors, the one least likely to get mad at being awakened before reveille. Slipping over the side of the bunk, Courtney dropped quietly to the bare wooden floor.

"Courtney, you're not going *out* there? Suppose it really is someone?"

"Shhhh. If you keep quiet, maybe I'll find out."

She sounded bolder than she felt. She didn't want to go out there like some dumb chucklehead in a TV movie. When told NOT TO GO IN THE ATTIC, where did they always go? To the attic, of course, to get beheaded by the Rhinestone Ripper or gutted by the Shadylane Stabber.

Somebody had to go out there, though. Someone had to alert a counselor.

"But, Courtney—"

"I don't want to lay awake till breakfast worrying about someone chopping us up in our sleep." She shuddered at the thought, and glanced back at the curtain swaying gently in the breeze of the ceiling fan. Was the shadow still there? Maybe she *had* imagined it. Or maybe the killer had moved on to chop up someone in *another* cabin. These girls were all her friends.

She pulled on her bathing suit, then her T-shirt and shorts. She'd planned to get in a few early laps anyway.

"You . . . um . . . want me to go with you?"

Courtney sat on the lower bunk to put on her shoes. Lisa's round brown eyes and chubby cheeks reminded her of Ellie.

"No, stay here. If I don't show up for chow," she made her voice spooky, "send someone to look for my mangled, beheaded body."

"Courtney! I don't think you should—"

"*Shhhh!* Like you said, it's probably just a raccoon."

She slipped out the door. The sultry darkness enveloped her as she turned toward the window where she'd seen the shadow. The rustling came again, then footsteps sounded in the dirt.

Rounding the corner, Courtney saw white running shoes flash in the moonlight as someone darted behind the next cabin in the clearing. Something about the person's shape looked familiar. Willing her feet to hit the ground softly, Courtney followed the muted footsteps . . . away from the cabin . . . into the thicket surrounding the lake.

Then she slowed down.

It was dark under the trees, and the footsteps had stopped.

In the overlapping shadows, someone could be hiding, ready to pounce as she walked past.

Courtney waited, holding her breath again, listening.

Behind her something shifted in the grass. She whirled, her throat tight with fear; but it was only a frog.

All right, 'fraidy-cat, why did you come out here if you were just going to freak out when you got to the scary part? Now suck it in and get MOVING . . . moving . . . moving . . .

Slowly, she edged forward toward the lake, peering around each tree as she passed it, casting frequent glances over her shoulder.

Something splashed in the water.

Probably just a fish, she thought. *Just a fish . . . a fish . . . a fish . . .*

When she emerged into the moonlight, Courtney quietly exhaled and looked out over the inky lake, shrouded now in fog. Nothing moved, not a sound, not a fish, not even a breeze.

But there, in the soft dirt beside the pier—*a shoe print.*

She crept closer, squatting for a better look. A heel print, under the sign announcing today's swim meet: SATURDAY, 1:00 P.M., VISITORS WELCOME. All week Courtney had been swimming laps before breakfast, out to the diving platform and back. The counselors would croak if they knew she swam alone, but how else could she get enough practice? In the afternoon race she planned to knock Queen Toad off her pedestal.

The person she chased must have stopped beside the pier. To read the sign? Or was it one of the other girls, trying to spook her?

Courtney stood up and carefully fitted her sneaker into the heel print; it was too big to be one of the girls'.

Yet the shadow had seemed vaguely familiar.

The sky was already turning from black to gray. Soon there'd be fingers of pink jutting above the trees. Courtney walked to the end of the pier and sat down to wait for sunrise.

Chapter Seventeen

Friday, December 25, Sisseton, South Dakota

Dixie wiped condensation from the window glass to watch the sun's first rays turn the pristine landscape from blue-white to ivory. Minutes later, Buck Sparks made his appearance.

A tall, gray-bearded man, he wore square eyeglasses and a navy-blue overcoat with a matching cap. Wisps of pale smoke rose from his curved-stem pipe. A red hunting dog sniffed at his heels.

Dixie watched him shovel a path from the back of the main house to the front door of the first cabin. The task took less than ten minutes, and amazed at the old man's energy, Dixie immediately felt better about not being out there to help. He cleared the entrance of snow, then knocked on the door, the sound carrying clear and loud in the early hours.

A woman in a woolly robe stuck her head out, long hennaed hair a tangled mass, as if she'd just awakened. She seemed surprised at the amount of snowfall. A man in overalls, pulling on a coat, squeezed past her through the door, but Buck Sparks waved him back.

They talked for a minute, Sparks pointing with his pipe toward the main house. Then Sparks moved on, wide shovel clearing a path for his heavy boots. Apparently, the old man didn't want any help, which was fine with Dixie; she had other things to worry about. In thirty minutes or so he'd knock on their own door, the last of the four cabins, and she hadn't yet decided what to do with Dann.

"Be real handy if you took sick all of a sudden," she muttered.

"Sick? I feel fine."

"No, you don't. You don't feel fine at all. Fact is, you've caught a humdinger of a cold, and much as you'd like to join everybody if we're invited for breakfast, you're worried about spreading germs around."

Dann lowered his eyebrows.

"You must think I'm a friggin Eskimo. Why would I try to escape in the middle of nowhere before the roads are even clear?"

"I don't know what you'll try, Dann, but why risk it?"

"So now I'm supposed to make like an invalid while you go up to the main house and chow down, is that it?"

"We haven't been asked, yet, but I expect our hosts will arrange a meal of some sort."

He was sitting on one of the wooden chairs pulled close to the bed. Now he stood abruptly, knocking the chair to the floor. Snatching his pillow, he plumped it hard against the headboard, but made no move to slide under the covers.

"Suppose I don't feel much like an invalid?"

Dixie leafed through packets of cocoa mix and tea bags that Emma Sparks had left in a straw basket beside the coffeepot. If Dann was already getting cabin fever, he was looking at a long, hard time ahead, cooped up in a cell. But telling him so wasn't likely to calm him down. Finding a packet of instant hot lemonade, she fished it out of the basket.

"Here's the ticket. A cup of this and you'll feel as fine as frog's hair."

"I'm not sick!"

"You look peaked to me." She ran fresh water in the coffeemaker.

Dann glowered at her silently for a long moment. Then he crossed his arms, leaned languidly against the wall, and cocked an insolent eyebrow.

"On second thought, maybe I'm not feeling so good. Maybe I'm sick enough you should call the sheriff, have him take me to the hospital." Dann smiled, but there was no humor in the defiance that sparked in his eyes.

Dixie studied him as water dripped into the glass pot. The possibility of being holed up together for another day and night was likely grating on Dann as much as it was on her. After ten hours of sleep and two hours of gin rummy, she was ready to crawl out of her skin. No reason for him to handle the stress any better.

"Is that what you want me to do, call the sheriff?"

"It'd get me off your hands," he said. "I spend a couple days in a warm bed with three squares, TV, and cute nurses, then the sheriff ships me off to Houston. You still collect your fee, but with only half the work."

He had no way of knowing that such a plan wouldn't fit the arrangement she'd made with Belle Richards.

"You want to take your chances with the locals?"

He hesitated, then his lips twisted in a sour smile. "Small-town cops aren't too chummy with bounty hunters, are they? Might look the other way while I slip out the hospital door."

"And they might not." But hospitals were notoriously easy to escape from.

"So what do you think, Flannigan? Do we call a truce until the roads clear? Maybe cut me a little slack while we're stuck here in this room. Or do I have a convulsion when Sparks knocks on the door, get myself some emergency treatment? My convulsions are Academy Award material—have a brother who suffers grand mal seizures, and I've seen all the moves."

Dixie didn't like being backed into corners. If she told him the deal she'd struck with Belle, he might not be so eager to broadcast his whereabouts. On the other hand, it was his own goose he'd be cooking if the sheriff turned out sharper than Dann expected and delivered him straight into the hands of the prosecuting attorney in Houston.

But it was Dixie's ten thousand dollars he'd be pissing away.

"Choose your own poison," she said at last. "You may be right about small-town cops not liking bounty hunters. I hear they're not too keen on child killers, either."

She poured steaming water over the lemon crystals and watched them burst, filling the cup with a tangy aroma. Dann stood very still, studying her. She could almost see the dilemma behind his blue eyes, and she gave him some space to make his decision. Of course, if he made the wrong decision, there wasn't a handier tranquilizer in the world than the butt of a .45.

"All right, I'll drink the friggin lemonade." He took the cup and sniffed it. "Don't suppose you have a shot of brandy to give it some character. My mother's hot toddies included a healthy measure of spirits."

"Which is probably what started you down the road to dipsomania—"

"I'm not a goddamn alcoholic!"

"No? Then you must be an ordinary drunk."

"Well, yeah. . . . I mean, sometimes I get drunk, but I don't *have* to drink. I can leave the stuff alone if I want to."

Dixie had heard that before. She reached into the bathroom for one of the yellow-flowered towels.

"Just look miserable and cover that handcuff when Sparks gets here." That made twice he'd backed down. Next time wouldn't be as easy. She wrapped the towel around his throat like a muffler.

"Hellfire, woman, you're choking me!" Dann yanked the cloth away from his neck. "Next you'll be smearing me with Vicks VapoRub."

"Too bad we don't have any. The fumes alone would convince Sparks." Dixie replaced the towel, leaving it slightly looser.

Minutes later they heard a shovel scrape the walk outside the door. She finger-combed her hair, smoothed her rumpled clothes, and tried to look domestic. When a loud knock sounded, she opened the door.

"Morning, Miz Flannigan. Buck Sparks. Hope you folks

slept well. Emma sends an invite to come eat breakfast with us up at the house. Plenty of food, plenty of room."

"Those ham sandwiches were about the best I've ever had."

Sparks gave a stiff little nod and puffed on his pipe. "There's more ham to go with your eggs, and I think Emma's cooked up some sausage. There'll be plenty."

Dixie opened the door wider so Sparks could see Dann propped up in bed, wool blanket tucked snugly around his makeshift muffler, lemonade steaming in his cup.

"I'm afraid he's coming down with something," Dixie said, adopting Sparks' speech rhythms. "Been sneezing all night, barking something fierce. Wouldn't want other folks catching the misery."

Parker Dann obliged with a halfhearted cough.

"Think we oughta fetch the doctor?" Sparks asked.

"Not yet. But a dose of aspirin and some cough syrup would help, if you think Emma might have some."

"Sure she will. You come when you're ready, get whatever you need." He started down the walk, the shovel slung across one shoulder.

Dixie shut the door and picked up Dann's heavy coat.

"I'm going to make this as fast as possible," she told him. "As you reminded me earlier, there's no point in your trying to get away, since you don't have a dog sled. So relax and play another hand of solitaire."

She removed the magazine from the .45, studied the room, and decided the best place for the gun was on the closet shelf, under the blanket from her cot, far enough away that Dann couldn't reach it wearing the handcuffs. Shoving the magazine in her jeans pocket, she picked up Dann's white running shoes, which she'd unpacked for him to wear from the car to the motel room, tied the laces together, and carried them along to hide in a snowdrift. Even if he did manage to free himself, he wouldn't get far in his stocking feet.

Chapter Eighteen

Stupid mistake, Parker figured, tipping his hand like that. Should've kept his friggin mouth shut till Sparks knocked on the door. Then go into his act. Writhe around, eyes rolled back, legs jerking, head flopping like a chicken with a wrung neck, making a gurgling, choking noise in his throat. All the time rattling that handcuff. Sparks would've been suspicious of Flannigan right off. So would the sheriff, keeping a sick man chained up like that.

Parker flipped up a black nine to play on a red ten.

The cabin, with its morning muffler of snow, was as quiet as a cell in the dead of night. Parker shuddered. Worst combination he could think of, silence and isolation.

Funny he hadn't heard that bathroom faucet dripping before. Must've left the cock open a bit. He slid off the bed and stretched around the door facing to the bathroom. He'd never seen handcuffs like these, with chain between them. Leg irons, sure, but not cuffs. Must be some kind of special issue. Even with a foot of chain, though, he couldn't quite reach the friggin faucet.

Moving the bed might help. It fell shy of the doorway by six or eight inches—could be exactly the inches he needed.

He eyed the curved iron headboard. His handcuff, attached to the outside, would slide down the curve as far as the mattress, where a horizontal bar stopped it, or up around the curve to the first vertical bar. Dann slid the cuff as far down as it would go, then squatted to lift the bed and scoot it over the wood floor.

Damn, it was heavy! Heaving and pulling, he finally moved the bed flush with the doorway. When he stood up again, he was breathing hard. Hadn't realized he was so out of shape.

He slid the handcuff back up the rail and stretched toward the faucet. Still an inch short.

Studying the distance, he could see there was no way to get any closer. At least he could close the bathroom door, muffle the drip some.

Now it was really too friggin quiet. A radio would help. Understandable, a small-town motel not having television. Crap on TV wasn't worth watching anyway, but a radio, what could that cost? Ten, fifteen bucks?

He sat down on the bed. At least he could see out the window from this new position, see where Sparks had cleared a path around the side of the motel office. Probably where Flannigan had gone for breakfast.

Somehow, he had to get her to unbend a little, let down her guard. She wasn't the easy touch he'd expected. Those brown, velvety eyes looked soft and inviting, but the woman was hard as bedrock. "Though she be but little, she is fierce." Shakespeare might've written more plays about women if he'd met the likes of Flannigan.

Parker turned up the ace of spades and played it beside the other two.

As good a salesman as he was, there had to be a way to convince Flannigan to cut him some slack. He'd sold everything from doorknobs to dump trucks, hair products to helicopters. Amount of money he'd made ought to be a sin. He was a charming, reasonable, agreeable fellow, wasn't he? Nonthreatening. Friendly. Likable.

Lovable, even? Maybe he should romance her a little.

She was a good-looking woman. Dressed like a man, but that didn't necessarily mean . . .

Hellfire, the way her jeans fit, the way she filled out a sweatshirt, could make a man crazy if he hadn't more important things to worry about—like staying out of prison. Maybe women had taken a bottom rung on his priority list, but Parker still knew the right moves. And Flannigan might not be the easy touch he'd first guessed, but she was still a woman.

Parker's neighbor said he reminded her of Clark Gable—sometimes she said Burt Reynolds, her memory wasn't the greatest—Gable, Reynolds, Tom Selleck. Couldn't make his big voice go squeaky like Selleck's, but he could wiggle his eyebrows. Wasn't a woman alive could resist his boyish humor for long. He'd charm the pants off her, like *Magnum, P.I.*

Kind of funny, actually. Flannigan was the PI, so to speak, Parker was the bad guy. Never thought of himself as a bad guy. He was the ". . . man more sinned against than sinning." At least that's what he'd hoped the jury would believe.

Wouldn't let them lock him up again. Those few days in jail had convinced him. But staying out of jail meant getting Flannigan to loosen up, drop her guard.

Information, that's what he needed. Where were her soft spots? What made her happy? What excited her?

Learn what got a person excited and you could sell them anything. Problem was, Flannigan didn't talk much.

Two things, then. Step one, find her talk button. Everybody had a button—he'd learned that as a rookie salesman—a passion that opened them up like turning on a faucet. Once folks opened up, they just naturally felt friendlier.

Parker played a red deuce on a black trey, and realized he was out of cards. Game over.

Out on the highway again, he could use what he learned about Flannigan for step two: romance her. Maybe he'd talk her into letting him sit up front. She'd already let him drive, hadn't she? Eleven hundred miles—should be plenty of time to prove what a reasonable, charming, nonthreatening sort of guy he could be.

Chapter Nineteen

Emma Sparks' kitchen smelled of baked apples and cinnamon, awakening a pang of nostalgia in Dixie. Cheeks rosy from the heat and wisps of white hair springing around her head, Emma was rubbing peanut oil on a plump turkey in a blue granite roaster. She looked as happy in her kitchen as Kathleen had always been in her own.

"Can't recall the last time we had guests for breakfast. God sure does work in mysterious ways. Sends a blizzard to make us take time with each other."

Dixie lifted a warming lid. "Smells great."

"Honey, there's not much trick to whipping up a batch of eggs and sausage. Now you grab a plate from the cabinet and fill it from those pans. There's hot coffee and buttermilk biscuits on the sideboard. Remember, I don't want a mess of leftovers to deal with."

The early sunlight streaming through yellow-flowered curtains gave the kitchen a homey glow. In the adjoining dining room, dishes clinked around a table. Conversations hummed. Dixie saw her henna-haired neighbor and a young man wearing a Ski Canada sweatshirt. She was tempted to sit down with them.

But the antsy part of her mind was back in the room with

Dann. Handcuffed to the bed, he couldn't raise much havoc. Yet why risk leaving him alone to try something stupid?

Emma clucked sympathetically about Dann's "cold."

"You just pile both these plates high, and I'll wrap them up good for you to carry back."

As Dixie scooped spoonfuls from each dish, she watched the redhead chat gaily with everyone at the table. Somehow, the woman had tamed her mass of tangles into a curly mane that bounced like copper pennies around her shoulders, and judging by the freckles sprinkled delicately across her nose, the copper hadn't come from a bottle as Dixie first suspected. The woman's skin had a translucent quality, like fine porcelain. She'd artfully tinted her eyelids lavender, which made her green eyes bright and vivid. A peachy blush colored her cheekbones. Not young—probably Amy's age—but youthful and vibrant, she was the sort of woman who totally baffled Dixie.

Why did anyone spend that much time on looking good? For that matter, how did they know where to start? Somewhere there was a secret women's club that passed these little tricks around. Dixie'd never been invited. Oh, sure, she'd played with makeup. Amy had insisted. "You only need a touch, Dixie, with your strong bones and naturally rich coloring, but you *do* need a touch." And she'd had her "colors done" by a professional—also at Amy's insistence. Dixie knew she wasn't homely; she cleaned up pretty damn good at times. But there was something missing, a distinctly feminine quality this redhead possessed.

Amy had it, too, although the hard edge of her glamour had softened as she matured. Carla Jean had it in spades. Dixie's mother was female extraordinaire, not a masculine bone in her perfumed, powdered, ruffle-clad body, and not a practical thought in her head. Carla Jean always presented herself as a princess, a tawdry princess perhaps, too often used and discarded, but always a princess. Maybe Dixie, in her fear of becoming like her mother, had bent too far the other way.

Scooping butter pats onto the plates, Dixie caught a glimpse of herself in a narrow beveled mirror above the buffet. She hoped she didn't smell as scruffy as she looked. Forty-eight hours without a bath or change of clothes was probably pushing bad grooming to its limit. She turned away from the troublesome reflection—out of sight, out of mind—and was glad, after all, that she hadn't sat down to eat with these people. One thing she didn't have to worry about with Parker Dann was her appearance.

Buck held the door as she started back to the cabin between shoulder-high mounds of shoveled snow, the aroma of baked apples still strong in her nostrils. Now that the wind had died down, she hardly felt the cold. The sun had popped out strong and bright in a sky as blue as Texas blue-bonnets. A brush-stroke of creamy clouds mirrored the snowscape.

She wished Ryan were here. He'd want to jump right in the middle of those tall drifts. Make snowballs. Build a space-age snowman. Hell, Dixie herself felt an urge to jump in the middle of a drift. *God sends a blizzard to make us take time with each other*, Emma had said. Those few minutes with the Sparkses had dredged up a slew of concerns. When Dixie didn't show up for Christmas dinner tonight, Amy would be worried and upset. Ryan would be disappointed, opening his Cessna and having no batteries to fly it. And shucks! Dixie would miss meeting Old Delbert Snelling!

She grinned. Things could be worse. She could be shacked up with an ugly, foul-tempered, illiterate jerk. At least Dann was reasonably good company. Maybe she should loosen his rein some. Even in the harshest of prisons, criminals celebrated Christmas; and as Dann had pointed out, there was no way anybody could leave until the snowplows came roaring through.

With that settled, Dixie felt better about herself. Even a badass bitch should take Christmas off. After breakfast, maybe she'd telephone Amy.

"*South Dakota?*" Her sister's mellow voice had picked up a worried barb. "Dixie, whatever possessed you to drive to South Dakota during a blizzard?"

"The blizzard happened *after* I drove up here. And the weather is beautiful again. I'm only waiting for a highway crew to clear the roads, then I'll start home."

"On Christmas Day? You think people are going to run those snowshovel things instead of being home with their families?"

"Lots of people have to work on Christmas." *Including me.* But Dixie didn't want to remind Amy of the reason for her unplanned trip, because then she'd have to admit she was sharing a motel room with a prisoner. Amy would have nightmares.

"I hope you realize how upset Ryan's going to be. I swear, Dix—"

"If you'll put him on, maybe I can explain."

"Well, I'm sorry. He's not here." She didn't sound a bit sorry, she sounded pleased, but Dixie knew Amy was only venting her frustration. Her notion of jobs that constituted "women's work" was not quite Victorian, but certainly pre-Margaret Thatcher. "Carl and Ryan are driving around, looking at the snow."

"It snowed in *Houston*?"

"Enough to turn the ground white. Of course, it'll burn off by noon. They should be back here in a couple of hours. Dixie, you're not doing anything dangerous, are you?"

"A routine job. Nothing to worry about." Someday lightning would strike her for telling these white lies, but the truth would set Amy to walking the floors.

"South Dakota doesn't sound at all routine to me."

"You should see it, Amy, it's so beautiful up here. The couple who own the motel are cooking Christmas dinner for everyone who got snowed in. They're really sweet. . . . Of course, I'd rather be home with you guys."

"I know. We'll miss you, too." Her sister's voice softened. "Dixie, drive carefully. We'd rather have you arrive in one piece, even if it means you'll get here a little later."

"I will, Amy. Cheers."

"Yeah . . . cheers yourself." She paused. "I think there's a nine-volt battery around here someplace that wil fit the remote control for Ryan's model airplane. I'll tell him to save that package and open it when you call."

"Thanks, Sis. I love you, too."

Cradling the phone with a pang of regret, Dixie regarded Dann. He sat at the yellow table finishing his breakfast, one hand cuffed to the table leg, where he could rest it on his knee. She was not missing a traditional Flannigan Christmas for the ten-thousand-dollar fee, she reminded herself. She was not missing Christmas because of her loyalty to Belle Richards or because Belle didn't want the jury to know Dann had skipped. She had taken the case because an eleven-year-old child would never see another Christmas. Accident or not, Betsy Keyes' death was wrong. Dann could not be allowed to carry on with his own life as if drunkenly killing a child meant nothing.

Reminding herself why she was here helped ease the ache Dixie felt, missing the biggest day of the year with her family. But it didn't ease that ache a whole hell of a lot.

"Guess it messed up your holiday, coming after me," Dann said, as if reading her mind.

Innocent until proven *guilty, Flannigan.*

"Actually, the storm messed up my holiday," she relented.

He stacked his plate on hers and set them both on the shelf above the table. Dixie had found a small radio in the closet. It sat beside Mr. Coffee now, tuned to Christmas music.

"Your family have big holiday plans?" Dann took a box of worn wooden dominoes from the nightstand drawer and turned them out on the tabletop.

"Not big, exactly, but mandatory. To miss a Flannigan family dinner requires a death certificate or, at the very least, a hospital admission slip."

"Big family gatherings," Dann said. "That's what I miss most about Montana. Our whole clan used to pile in the hay truck, drive up the mountain to pick out a Christmas tree. Arguing all the while—which tree had the bushiest limbs, straightest trunk. Back home, Mother would break out the apple cider, a bottle of schnapps, a box of tree trimmings. No matter how much we fooled around, rearranging the lights, by midnight Pop always positioned the angel and hit the light switch." Dann sat down and drew a domino hand. "Good times."

He had washed up and changed his shirt before she set out their breakfast. His chin stubble was starting to fill in, Dixie noted. He had the sort of face that looked good in a beard.

She'd taken her own turn with one of the tiny bars of Ivory soap, washing even her teeth with it, in the absence of toothpaste. Her overnight kit, which she kept in the Mustang's trunk for emergencies, had been conspicuously absent when she brought their things in. After her last trip across the Mexican border, she'd removed the kit to replace the sample-size deodorant and mouthwash. She could see the brown, zippered leather kit sitting exactly where she'd left it, on a shelf in the utility room, handy for the next time she went to the car. But the next time she went to the car, her hands had been full and her mind busy with Christmas tasks.

Dixie ran her tongue over her teeth. She could sure use a slug of that mouthwash right now. And some fresh clothes. She resisted sniffing her armpits.

"At our house, it was Southern Comfort and eggnog," she said, squirming her chair around so she'd be sitting downwind. "And pecan shells burning in the fireplace." Dixie counted only the years after she became a Flannigan, never the earlier years. Holidays with Carla Jean were celebrated with turkey sandwiches from the Stop & Go.

"Had you figured as a teetotaler."

"I've got nothing against alcohol. I just believe in moderation."

Dann looked at her from under his heavy eyebrows, and something in his gaze reminded Dixie of a private investigator on a TV series. She couldn't remember which one.

"Moderation in everything?" he said.

Now what the hell was he up to, flashing those blue eyes and dropping his voice into the sexy zone? She stared back at him.

"Even the best things can be overdone, Dann."

He shrugged and shuffled his dominoes. They made surprisingly loud swishing sounds on the wooden table. Annoying sounds. Dixie glanced at her own hand, but didn't see how it would improve with rearranging.

"Like soap," Dann mumbled. "Soap can be overdone."

"What?"

"You have a soap smudge." He touched his jawline near the ear, and Dixie automatically mirrored him. "Other side."

She slid her chair back, stalked into the bathroom, and closed the door. Soap smudge. Yep, there it was. Good thing she didn't wear makeup, she'd probably paint her eyebrows red and her lips blue. She scrubbed the smudge off and splashed her face with cold water. Watching the droplets drip off her nose in the mirror, she wondered what sort of biological clock made a woman her age finally start worrying about appearances. No gray in her hair yet. No unsightly wrinkles. She wouldn't turn any heads at a beauty pageant, but she looked okay.

Drying her face, she noticed Dann's comb lying on the countertop beside his toothbrush and toothpaste. Borrowing the toothpaste had seemed too intimate a request to make of a man you held prisoner. Of course, it was only her imagination, thinking she could still taste the Ivory soap after chasing it with breakfast. She looked at the comb, about four inches long, black, the kind barbershops gave away free. What could be intimate about that?

When she picked it up, a single dark hair fell into the sink. The same brown as her own. Shorter, of course. Her own collar-length hair was heavy enough that it fell more or less in place, but there was no denying it would improve with combing. She pulled the comb through it. No magical rays zapped her. After a few more strokes, she did look better. Felt better, too.

From the bedroom came the *swish, swish, swish* of Dann shuffling his domino hand. Probably shuffling hers, as well.

She eyed the toothpaste. *In For a Penny, In For a Pound—*

as Kathleen's maxim would state. She squirted a dab of tooth-paste on a clean washcloth, rubbed her teeth and gums, and swished with water. Better. Monumentally better. Absolutely, fantastically, peppermint-flavored better. Only now, of course, she'd have to confess to toothpaste theft.

Chapter Twenty

Fessing up never came easy, though she'd had plenty of practice. Barney had told her there were two kinds of people, those who asked permission and those who forged ahead, begging forgiveness later. Dixie'd never learned the knack of asking for anything. But she understood quid pro quo.

Before resuming their domino game, she'd scraped the Mustang's trunk free of snow and had found another pair of handcuffs. The two pairs linked together with some extra chain gave Dann nearly five feet of mobility, enough to take a bathroom break without asking and to sit comfortably in one of the wooden chairs. Watching him move around, she noticed he favored his right leg. An old injury?

She'd also made a fresh pot of coffee. Dann produced an airline-size pony bottle of Baileys Irish Cream to sweeten it.

"You won't believe this, but I'm a moderate drinker, myself. Most of the time." He played a six-five on her five-two.

"Right. That's why you can't remember what happened the night before the accident."

"Hellfire, woman, I'd just hit a big sales quota. Happens maybe once a quarter, if I'm lucky. Sure, I celebrate! Deposit the check, hit the Green Hornet, buy drinks for the whole room."

"Once a quarter?" She didn't really want to argue about his drinking problem. It was the driving *after* drinking that caused trouble. "According to your file, you're a twice-a-week regular at the Green Hornet."

He flipped a domino down, flipped it back up.

"I stop there couple times a week. Play a few hands of backroom poker, down a drink or two. I'm too old to binge every week—not worth the morning after." He stared at the dominoes, focusing on something deep in his mind. "Especially this last time. God, what a nightmare, like walking into a tunnel that gets blacker and blacker. Only the nightmare didn't start until I woke up."

Hearing the misery in his voice—and wondering if it was genuine—Dixie couldn't resist asking: "What *do* you remember?"

He drew a domino from the bone yard.

"I remember it was a busy damn night at the Hornet. Fifteen, twenty guys from a computer software convention, along with the usual crowd." He paused, spinning the domino facedown. "What I can't figure out, though, is where I was between three A.M., when Augie swept me out the door, and seven forty-five, when . . . the little girl was killed. I mean, it's only four friggin blocks to my house. That time of morning, that neighborhood, I rarely meet another car on the road. Not much chance of an accident. Otherwise I'd sleep it off right there in Augie's parking lot."

"Have you done that often?"

"Once or twice." He flipped the domino up, looked at it, turned it down again. "Anyway, after a big night, I'm usually good for ten, twelve hours sleep. So what was I doing back on the road before breakfast?" He looked up at her, then shook his head wearily. "Sorry. I know you don't want to hear this shit. Even if you gave a damn, what could you do about it?"

He's setting me up, Dixie thought. *Selling me swampland.* "Did anyone see you going back out the next morning?"

"Nope." He scraped at a spot on the back of a domino. "Nobody saw me come, nobody saw me leave. Neighbor lady said she saw *the car* pull out about seven-thirty. Didn't see who was driving."

That much was true. Dixie had read it in his file.

"How were you dressed when the cops roused you?"

"Same clothes as the night before. Looked like dogshit, like I'd slept in them, which I probably had."

"Where were your keys?"

"On the dresser, in this tray where I dump everything out of my pockets."

"The door was locked?"

"Dead bolt, both doors."

Also true. Someday she might tell him how easy the back door could be jimmied.

"Anyone else have a key to your car?"

"Nobody."

"Keep a spare key anywhere?"

"A spare? Yeah. Richards, my attorney, asked that, too. I kept a spare key in a magnetic gizmo under the car frame. Wasn't there when the cops looked. They said it could've jarred loose anytime I went over a bump."

"Plastic or metal?"

"Huh?"

"The key gizmo, was it hard plastic or metal?"

"Metal, I think. Does it matter?"

"It might. The plastic ones can melt and fall off if you put them too close to the exhaust. The metal ones stay on."

"I don't know . . . could probably find out. Bought it at the hardware store around the corner, the one the kid's father owns."

"*Whose* father?" Dixie felt the hair rise on her arms. "*The girl who was hit?*" She hadn't realized Dann knew Betsy Keyes.

"Her folks own the hardware store and cafe. I used to eat in the cafe couple times a week, shopped at the hardware store when I needed anything."

Dixie stared at him. "So you knew Betsy *before* she was killed."

"Her and her two sisters." He must have noticed Dixie's curiosity had turned to suspicion; his brows jutted together.

"How *well* did you know her?"

"Betsy waited on me at the cafe sometimes. Said she wanted to be a writer. I kidded her about being the next Danielle Steel."

"Did you ever see Betsy outside the cafe?"

"Outside—?"

"Were you ever alone with her?"

His face turned red, his eyes hot. "If you're thinking what I think you're thinking—goddamn, Flannigan! I wouldn't hurt that kid on purpose. That's *sick.*"

"Did you ever see the girl outside the cafe?"

He slammed his dominoes down and shoved them away from him. "You want to know if I get a hard-on for little girls? Shit!"

"Dann, did you ever see the child outside the cafe?"

Turning sideways in the chair, he looked out the window, his jaw tight. Dixie stared silently at his back until he decided to answer, his voice hard and flat.

"At the hardware store. She sometimes helped her old man. May've seen her playing with the other girls in their yard when I walked by, maybe stopped to talk. But what you're implying . . . *no.*"

He stormed into the bathroom and slammed the door against the chain connecting the handcuffs.

Dann's denial left Dixie cold. Too many times, when prosecuting a case, she had listened to men deny their sick attractions to children. Once, an outraged father agreed to testify against a friend accused of molesting his own daughter. The witness had a girl the same age, and it turned out during the trial that both men had been sexually abusing their daughters for several years. But the outraged father considered his own situation different, claimed he was teaching his little girl how to satisfy a husband, preparing her for wifedom.

Dixie's anger was like a rock—cold, hard, and heavy in her gut. She knew it had more to do with herself than with Dann, and she had to deal with it. She shuffled and reshuffled her hand, snapping the dominoes with unnecessary force on the wooden table.

Picking up one of the worn black rectangles, she ran her thumb across six smooth, dished-out spots. She'd been six years old the first time one of Carla Jean's men approached her, not yet old enough or savvy enough to know what he wanted; powerless against his advances. Carla Jean wasn't intentionally a bad mother, but she was absolutely self-centered, incurably romantic, and too generous with her body. She believed in "happily ever after," believed that someday a prince would carry her away to a golden castle. Meanwhile, she brought home every man she met who had a sexy smile and a pretty line of bullshit.

Dixie had been sitting in bed, reading a picture book about Amelia Earhart, when the man eased the door open.

"My, aren't you a cute little thing?"

She didn't know how to answer, had never considered herself cute. The other girls in her first-grade class were prettier. The man didn't seem to expect an answer, anyway. He sat down on Dixie's bed and lifted her chin toward the lamplight.

"I'll bet you grow up to be as fine as your mother."

Dixie didn't plan to be anything like Carla Jean, whom she loved devotedly but who cried too often "the morning after." Right now, Carla Jean was probably passed out from all the booze she drank when she had a "date."

"I'm going to be an airplane pilot," Dixie explained earnestly. Amelia Earhart was her current heroine.

The man took the book out of her hands.

"How about I put this aside for now and show you a game?"

Dixie liked games, especially card games. She always beat Carla Jean at Go Fish. But those weren't the sort of games the man had in mind. His hand under the covers stroked Dixie's leg.

From that night on, every time Carla Jean had a date, Dixie hid in the closet with a pillow and a reading lamp. Only a few of her mother's "steadies" realized she had a daughter, and only Tom Scully was persistent enough to find Dixie no matter where she hid. Scully was a big man with strong hands and a temper.

"You don't like it when I slap your mama around, do you?" Scully asked.

I don't like it when you show your ugly face at the door, Dixie wanted to say. But she just shook her head.

"If you ever tattle to anybody about you and me, little girl, I'll do more than black your mama's eye."

Telling Carla Jean had never done any good, anyway. She had a knack for not seeing what she didn't want to, for disbelieving anything that threatened her fairy-tale view of life.

When the closet trick stopped working, Dixie learned other evasions. If she saw Scully's car headed their way, she would duck out and sleep at a friend's house. One night, when she heard his voice after she was already in bed, she slipped out the window and spent the night on the roof.

But there were plenty of times during the next six years when she was powerless to avoid him. Carla Jean remained oblivious to the truth, even when Dixie tearfully admitted she'd missed her period.

"Honey, that's natural at your age. Why, you've just barely even got the curse." At twelve, Dixie had been menstruating for two years, but in Carla Jean's eyes her daughter was still a baby, in ruffles and hair ribbons.

A few nights later Dixie was rushed to a hospital, after a quack doctor finished scraping out the unborn fetus. She awoke at Founders Home, surrounded by teenage girls in similar situations. That night Dixie had vowed never again to be powerless.

Now, hearing water running in the bathroom, she dropped the blank-six in place beside the double and knew that her anger at Dann was the same anger she'd known as a child. The same anger she'd felt as a state prosecutor watching hairballs routinely beat the system.

Why hadn't Belle mentioned this aspect of the case? It might've been in the case notes, of course. Dixie hadn't read the entire file, only the details that would help her locate the skip. But if Dann had tried to molest Betsy Keyes and the child threatened to tell, he might have plotted the drunk-driving scheme to cover outright murder. The DA could be going for manslaughter because it was easier to win.

Or was Dann telling the truth?

He emerged from the bathroom, blue eyes as hard as stones, and Dixie felt the fox of wrath gnaw at her heart. She returned his stare. Would a child molester's gaze be so steady? Or would it sidle away like grabby hands under a little girl's dress when someone came near?

He's as angry as I am, Dixie realized. *But that doesn't make him innocent.*

Child molesters were shape-shifters, the dregs of humanity appearing to the world in the guise of decent men. They played the role so well they fooled most people.

Dixie recalled Carla Jean's furious protests that her good old friend Scully would never diddle a little girl, much less her own daughter. Carla Jean's disbelief had pierced twelve-year-old Dixie like a stab through the heart. In that one instant, Dixie had suffered more than in all the years of grabby hands, more than she suffered under the quack doctor's knife.

Was Parker Dann playing a role?

She watched his fingers on the dominoes.

"What makes you so sure you drove home after the bar closed? Maybe you did fall asleep in your car in the parking lot."

Dann looked at her and then away, as if summoning a memory.

"I guess . . . I don't know for sure. Seem to remember driving home, but maybe I'm confusing that night with some other time. Usually, though, when I sleep in the car I get a neck crick."

"Did anyone see you drive away? The bartender, for instance. You said the two of you closed the place down."

"Augie parks out back and leaves in the opposite direction. No one else was there."

Dixie studied him, knowing she shouldn't believe anything the man said, knowing he was probably selling her an empty sack, but interested in hearing him tell it.

"Okay, take me through the evening. From the time you arrived at the Green Hornet."

He set a domino to spinning.

"Like I said, it was celebration time. Three-million-dollar sale, full commission, you know what that comes to? Two hundred thousand. I bought house rounds all night—"

"Remember any names? People who were there?"

"Sure, a few. Wrote them all down for Ms. Richards. First names, mostly. That's all they ever gave. In my business, person's name is important. Make a point of remembering—"

"What happens when Augie closes down? What's the procedure?"

"*Procedure?*" He glanced up before continuing. "Fifteen minutes to closing, Augie makes last call. Some folks take the hint, leave right then. Others buy another round. Two-ten, he picks up any drinks left on the bar and tables. People drift out. Augie starts washing up."

"I thought you said you didn't leave until three o'clock."

"Usually, I stick around till he finishes cleaning. Sit at the bar drinking coffee, flapping my gums."

"He makes coffee for the two of you?"

"Always has a pot for himself and for coffee drinks—"

"And he doesn't mind you staying there while he cleans up?"

"Actually . . . Augie sort of prefers it. Got robbed last year, three times in one month. Beat up pretty bad, lost four teeth, most of the hearing in one ear. I hang around to scare off the muggers, you might say."

"A real Samaritan."

Dann's eyes sparked. "I hang around, that's all."

"Anything different about that night, other than the big sale? Anybody stay later than usual?"

"No one I recall . . . no, wait a minute. There *was* someone who stayed late. Drinking bourbon and Coke. We talked about selling fishing trips in the Caribbean. John, that's his name. Didn't seem ready to leave when Augie wanted to lock up, so I walked outside with him, talking as we walked. When we got to his car, I said I forgot my keys and went back—"

"Did you get his last name? See what he was driving?"

"Never said his last name." Dann closed his eyes for a moment, frowning. "Climbed into a foreign car of some kind, boxy, not sporty. Volvo, maybe."

"Doesn't sound like you were very drunk, if you remember all that."

"I never said *how* drunk I was. Only that I couldn't remember anything after leaving the bar." He slapped the domino down and spun it. His face looked gray in the sunlight reflecting off the snow, his facial muscles slack, the lines more pronounced. "Look, I can give you everything I remember, step by step, minute by minute, and I still can't say for certain whether I got back in that car the next morning, drove toward the school, and . . . killed that child—"

Something shot past Dixie's face and hit the window with a *crack!* Dann had spun the domino so hard it flew off the table.

"Sorry." He got up to retrieve it, the jerry-rigged handcuffs stretched to the limit.

He's torn with worry. The realization hit Dixie like a brick. *He's worried about whether or not he actually killed Betsy Keyes.* What if he didn't? It looked open and shut, and the caseload for Houston cops was notoriously heavy. Maybe they rushed it through, didn't dig deep enough.

Theories tumbled into Dixie's mind. The man who stayed late that night might've followed Dann home and stolen his car for some illegal use—maybe a drug dealer who wanted an anonymous car for a deal going down. On his way to return the car, he hits the child. Such a scenario was more believable, in many ways, than pinning an ordinary citizen with vehicular manslaughter when he might very well have been at home sleeping off a bender.

Dixie realized then that she had bought Dann's story. She forced herself to back up a step.

He stood at the window, where he'd picked up the errant domino.

"Look, Flannigan, I know what you think of me. High-rolling peddler, drifting from town to town, job to job. Got a little property, a few bucks in the bank. No close family in town, no real friends, no ties. You're right, I'm not much, but I'm harmless. I like kids—not in any *sick, twisted* way—simply because they're kids. I used to tease those girls, gave Betsy big tips to serve me coffee, dropped nickels in the little one's pocket when she wasn't looking. I *never* would've hurt them. Come from a big family myself. I know how this family must have suffered, especially with what happened to the other child so soon after losing Betsy—"

"The *other* child?"

"You didn't know? Some kind of accident at summer camp."

Chapter Twenty-one

August 1, Camp Cade, Texas

Courtney stamped her feet on the grassy lake bank, waiting for dawn to brighten the sky a little and watching for the first sign of lightning. Angry clouds churned overhead, turning the early light eerie. She hoped Counselor Frey wouldn't cancel the race because of the storm, then reminded herself to THINK POSITIVE.

She could scarcely believe her good luck yesterday, beating Queen Toad's best time. Of course, no one knew yet. She'd been practicing, sure, swimming her arms off every single day, building her strength and lung capacity like Daddy Jon had taught her.

In today's meet, when it really mattered, when she'd be swimming against Queen Toad FOR REAL, knowing she absolutely, positively HAD to beat her, and knowing deep in her bones she could win hands down, no ties, no retakes, who could blame her for worrying that something freaky like this storm would wipe out her big chance?

She hugged herself against a chill as a brisk breeze brought goose bumps to her bare skin.

"No lightning, no lightning, no lightning," she chanted softly. Counselor Frey was a safety nut. Even without lightning, she might stop the swim meet if it rained hard enough.

Grown-ups were weird like that, worrying about a little rain when you were already soaking wet in the lake.

Mama had promised to arrive early enough to see the swim contest. Daddy Travis had begged off to take care of some business, something to do with his new computer department, and Daddy Jon had to go out of town. Maybe Mama would stop at Camp Donovan to pick up Ellie. That'd be great, because Ellie would cheer louder than anybody. Ellie was Courtney's biggest fan.

A dark thought slithered through Courtney's mind. All during summer camp she'd worried about Ellie, badgering Counselor Bryant every night until she telephoned Camp Donovan to make sure Ellie was all right. Now the two weeks were almost over. Suppose something happened on this very last day, something terrible?

Think positive. Think positive. Think positive.

The camp floodlights winked off on their timer. Just a few more minutes and the sun would creep up behind the clouds. Courtney imagined the final race—all the girls and their moms and dads crowding around. Having won three heats already, Courtney would be the center of attention when Queen Toad stepped up, tall and sleek in her blue racing suit. She'd sneer down her skinny nose, but with everyone listening, she'd pretend to be a good sport.

"You looked pretty good yesterday, Keyes."

"Thanks. So did you." Admitting it would be worse than eating boiled squash, but Toad really was a good swimmer, a blue streak gliding through the water. Courtney's speed and form had improved, yet she knew she looked more like a squiggle than a streak, with her stupid lopsided freestyle. She'd been working hard to smooth it out. When she forgot about form and went full out for speed, she swam better. Faster.

"Keep it up, Keyes, and you might come in second. Not a close second—I'll be kicking water in your face all the way."

Courtney could almost HEAR the sneering voice, and she tried to think of a clever comeback, something to singe Toad's tomato-soup hair. She'd work on it, have one ready by race time.

A few raindrops sprinkled Courtney's shoulders. The sun still sat low behind the trees, but the sky was bright enough for a practice swim. Imagining the "take your marks" announcement crackling over the speaker, she stood in position, heard the starting gun in her head, and dove. The water wrapped her in silence.

Seconds later she burst through the surface.

DAMN! DAMN! DAMN! Was that Toad half a length ahead? Seeing the blue streak in her mind, Courtney grabbed the water in front of her and shoved it behind with all the force she could manage. She kicked and stroked harder than she ever had before, imagining the cheers from the bank, while concentrating on grabbing water and pushing it behind . . . pull, kick, stroke, stroke, stroke . . .

She could do it, she knew she could do it. Her lungs felt strong, her legs powerful. The opposite bank didn't look so far now.

Courtney closed her eyes and willed her legs to kick harder, smoother. *Remember to follow through . . . follow through . . . follow through . . .*

She opened her eyes. The bank was closer. She was gaining on her best speed—she felt sure of it! And she wasn't a bit tired.

She could make it. She could WIN. A few more strokes, and THEN who would be kicking water in whose face?

What was that grabbing her foot? Something under the water had wrapped around her ankle. Slithery plants grew close to the bank, but they usually didn't grow this far out.

She kicked hard, broke free of the plant's rough grasp, and shot forward—

The plant grabbed her foot again, slowing her down. Slipping underwater, she reached back to pull herself free of the clutchy thing. The lake's undergrowth kept the water dark, especially this early in the morning, greenish-brown, never clear enough to see more than a few feet. And something had churned up muddy gunk from the lake bottom. Courtney couldn't see at all. But she didn't *need* to see, did she? All she had to do was reach down and find the plant with her fingers—

Uhh! The vine pulled tighter, almost as if someone were yanking on it, pulling her toward the bottom of the lake—

Worry skittered around her mind. Something wasn't right here, something was wrong, wrong, wrong, wrong, WRONG.

The creepy rustlings earlier—the shape at the window, the footsteps she'd chased through the trees, the flash of white running shoes—suddenly all the images rushed at her.

Oh, no, now the vine was around both feet, wrapping round and round her ankles, like a rope, tying her feet together . . . how could a plant do that? Fear shuddered through her. If only she could SEE WHAT WAS HAPPENING!

Twisting in the water, she bent double to pull at the vine— or was it a rope? It was scratchy like a rope.

Now something moved just beyond her reach. Not the watery plants but something solid. A person.

Oh, no, no, no. It *was* a person—pulling her deeper and deeper.

Her lungs burned, BURNED. She needed air . . . had to get to the surface.

She let her body go slack, let her bottom drop lower, drew her knees in, gathering the power in her legs . . .

Then pushed!

And broke free, the rope still binding her feet, but free of whoever was pulling her. She shot toward the surface—

And was yanked back. Her lungs were on fire . . . she needed oxygen . . . her head swam with tiny fireflies, buzzing.

Buzzing.

It would feel so good to go to sleep . . . to sleep . . . to sleep to stop the burning . . . burning . . . burning . . .

Courtney opened her mouth and allowed cool water to quench the fire.

Chapter Twenty-two

December 25, Sisseton, South Dakota

Dixie stormed out of the cabin. Lifting her face to the sun's brilliance, she filled her lungs with clean winter air. But the awful images clung to her mind like swamp moss.

She knocked a bead of ice off the Mustang's door handle, opened the door, and slid onto the driver's seat. From the snapshot clipped to the visor, the Keyes girls grinned down at her. On the drive from Texas, their trusting brown eyes had egged her on, willing her to find Betsy's killer. Now she looked at the snapshot and an ache filled her chest. Two of those three girls were dead. Not one, but *two*.

She looked away. Her deep feeling of loss made no sense. Dixie had never met Betsy or Courtney, and both had died months ago. Betsy in the spring, Courtney in the summer.

An accident at camp, Dann had said. What were the odds of two fatal accidents occurring in the same family in three months?

Dixie found a napkin in the burger sack and blew her nose. When she looked back at the snapshot, her throat tightened again. She'd made a silent promise that she could no longer fulfill, because Courtney Keyes was dead. Never mind that she died long before Dixie went after Parker Dann. For Dixie, Courtney had been alive, grinning down at her from that visor. Now her smile would never brighten another snap-shot.

Parker Dann's case file lay on the passenger seat, under the thermos. Dixie picked it up. She slipped off the rubber band, looping it around her wrist, and opened the folder. Midway through the papers she found Belle's notation about Court-ney's death. The nine-year-old had drowned on the last day of camp, on the morning of a swim contest. Swimming alone, before breakfast. Belle had talked with the physician who signed the death certificate. The doctor thought Courtney might have suffered a cramp and then got disoriented under the water. An accident. Three months earlier, Courtney's sis-ter Betsy was killed in an accident. A grotesque coincidence? The mother must be a blathering basket case worrying about her third chick.

Dixie thought about Ryan, the way his twelve-year-old face brightened when he saw his Aunt Dixie, and imagined the agony of losing him. She fished the newspaper clipping of Dann's arraignment out of the file. Rebecca Keyes, pale and thin, sat close to her husband, who looked angry enough to kill. The two girls huddled together, Ellie's small hands clutching the picture book, solemn eyes steady on the page, while her sister glared at Parker Dann.

Dann had been out on bail when the camp accident oc-curred. He could have murdered both girls, setting up both as accidents. But what reason would he have? Dixie had en-countered perversions often enough to know they could sur-face in the most unlikely personalities. But men who killed children to satisfy some sick need generally wanted close physical contact. They strangled or stabbed, they didn't run a child down with a car.

Belle had seen no connection between the two deaths. Apparently neither had the DA. It was tragic, certainly, but not unheard of for two family members to die in rapid, unre-lated succession. If foul play had been suspected, the media would've pounced on it, quick to point out that the man accused of hit-and-run manslaughter of Betsy Keyes was free on bail at the time of her sister's "accident."

Okay, so the deaths happened months apart in different counties.

Dixie recalled Dann's face when the domino spun off the table and hit the window. She'd seen torment there. Every good salesman was part actor, but it would take the skill of an Anthony Hopkins to fake the anguish she'd seen in Dann's eyes. Was he that good? If she hadn't caught up with him, he'd be in Canada—hiding out awhile, then reappearing under a new name. The long arm of the law didn't reach that far in such cases. He'd be a free man.

An innocent man?

Guilty or not, Belle hadn't been happy with the way Dann's trial was going. Unless new evidence surfaced in his favor—a witness who saw someone else driving Dann's car, for instance—Parker Dann would likely spend the next two to twenty years in prison.

Dixie pulled the snapshot off the visor. Her silent promise had been to bring Betsy's killer to justice. Suppose that killer wasn't Dann?

Court would reconvene on January 4. If they arrived back in Houston by the twenty-eighth, say, she'd have five or six days to poke around. Granting they *were* accidents, the stolen-car-drug-dealer theory wasn't too far out. On the other hand, if the answer was that easy, Belle's investigator should have turned up something. Or maybe not. Since Dixie had taken up skip tracing, her information network surpassed anything she'd relied on as ADA. It certainly surpassed any network Belle might be using.

Dixie put the news clipping back in Dann's folder, slipped the rubber band around it, and laid the file on the seat. Then she put the snapshot back on the sun visor. When they hit the highway tomorrow—or the next day—she'd have eleven hundred miles to make a decision.

Chapter Twenty-three

December 27, Interstate 45, Texas

Parker watched the Houston skyline tower into view, buildings like sentries waiting to close in on him. He was in a pissy mood, not at all interested in talking about the night of the hit-and-run. Why was Flannigan so friggin keen on the subject, anyway? They'd be quits soon as she dropped him at the county jail.

"Tell me about the guy who stayed late at the Green Hornet," she said.

"Again? Nothing's changed in two hours."

The bounty hunter'd cut the twenty-two-hour trip to seventeen, driving like a Tasmanian devil—with the fortitude of a camel and the bladder of a friggin elephant. Stopped once, for gas, leaving him locked in the backseat without a prayer of breaking free.

As the mile markers whipped by, he'd tried to get her talking about herself—family, work, anything to give him an edge. The bitch ignored him! Kept asking about his case, same questions over and over, more relentless than the friggin cops who arrested him. Maybe she was brushing up her cross-examination techniques, planning to go back into litigation.

"Humor me," she insisted. "What did the man look like?"

Parker crossed his arms, turned sideways, and leaned against the car door.

"Light brown hair, receding hairline. Ears stuck out from his head. Six-one, hundred and eighty pounds, lanky—"

"Lanky, is that the same as wiry?"

"Hell no. A guy that's wiry, he's slender but muscled. Tightly wound, like a spring. This guy was running on idle."

With downtown Houston still painted in lights against the night sky, they reached the bypass leading to the county lockup. Flannigan took the turn, and Dann's chest tightened. He recalled all too vividly his brief stay in this miserable place. Crowded. Smelly. Volatile. A cauldron of bile with no vent. Even now, months later, he heard doors clang shut behind him and apprehension squirmed like worms in his belly.

Been kidding himself thinking he'd get loose from Flannigan. Charm her, he'd thought. For a while, back at the motel, it seemed to work. She'd combed her hair and softened up a little. Then whap! She shut down. He won so many friggin gin games, he knew she wasn't paying attention. Laughed when he tried to sit up front. She had a great laugh. Gave him the Mountain Spring Water bottle and started on the third degree. So much for his fancy escape plan.

"Lanky," she said now. "Not wiry. How old was this guy?"

"Thirty-eight, forty. But baby-faced, like he could look young even when he's older—"

"Tattoos? Scars? Moles?"

Dann was about to say no, when a picture popped in his mind, a butterfly with a human head. Bright. Intricate. On the man's left forearm. Why hadn't he remembered that before?

He told her about it. "Why are you harping on this, anyway?" There was something screwy about the whole deal, Flannigan getting on his trail so fast.

"Belle Richards believes you're innocent. She doesn't want you screwing up your chance of acquittal. You're lucky she sent me to find you."

"You mean the DA doesn't know I cut out?"

"Not yet."

"Officially, then, I'm not a fugitive. . . ."

"Dann, you were a fugitive as soon as you crossed the state line. Right now I'm the only one who knows."

"What about Richards?"

"I haven't talked to her since I agreed to scout around, see if you were bending an arm at one of your favorite haunts."

That put him back where he started when he left the courtroom. Richards must have picked up somehow on what he was planning.

Flannigan pulled off the road and stopped. Parker looked out to see razor-sharp barbed wire curling along the fence that encircled the Criminal Detention Center. Doors clanged shut in his mind. His stomach started to squirm.

"So . . . ," he said, his voice sounding dry as paper in his ears. "What now?"

"Now we have a dilemma." She turned to face him. Light from the Center's sodium flood lamps cast an orange glow along one side of her face. Her brown eyes were as impenetrable as the night. "If I take you inside, it's all over. You stay locked up until the jury reaches a verdict. The fact that you skipped will tip the scales against you."

"You could drop me at home." He wiggled his eyebrows, tried to smile, feeling how pathetic it must look. "I'll stay put till the trial."

She didn't say anything, just stared with those big, soft eyes. Smirking.

"What do you want, Flannigan, a guarantee signed in blood?"

"You have seven days until your trial resumes. The closer it gets, the more you'll sweat the jury's decision. You'll get itchy feet, Dann."

He hated to admit she was right. The weight of truth settled on his shoulders, and hope seeped out through his teeth in a rush of air. Probably bolt before her Mustang was out of sight.

"Hell. Maybe I'll be lucky. Maybe the jury mellowed out over Christmas."

"I wouldn't count on it."

She was chewing on something. He wished she'd spit it out. "Got an alternative?"

"Maybe." She studied him for a minute, her eyes soft and unreadable. "I could turn you over to Belle Richards, collect my fee, and forget about you. Belle is way too trusting, so you'd soon find a way to skip town again. Then I'd haul you back and collect another fee."

"Sounds like bounty hunting pays well."

"With fewer hours than prosecuting, and less stress." She yawned. He could tell she was taking her time, either stalling to make up her mind or enjoying watching him sweat. "There's another alternative," she said, finally. "How handy are you around a house?"

"Handy? You mean fixing things?" She nodded, and he said, "Fair, I guess. Fix up my own house when it needs it." As long as it didn't include plumbing, wiring, or carpentry.

"I can put you up until your trial resumes. In exchange, you do odd jobs. And maybe I'll look around, see if I can turn up any new evidence."

"Why would you do that?"

She hooked a thumb toward the building across the road.

"There're too many criminals on the streets who ought to be locked up over there, and maybe a few inside who don't belong. The system would work a hell of a lot better if cops, lawyers, and judges did what's right instead of just doing their jobs. Barney Flannigan used to say, 'You're either part of the solution, Dixie, or part of the problem.' I believe that. I also realize it's possible you got a raw deal."

Parker started to speak, but his throat went suddenly tight, and he had to turn his face into the shadows. Crazy, the way hope made your eyes water.

After a few moments, he said, "Think you'll find something the cops missed? And Richards' PI missed?"

"If you didn't drive your car the morning Betsy was killed, someone else did. Let's say someone stole it and hit the girl by accident. Why bring the car back to your house? Why not abandon it across town where no one would connect it with the girl's death, at least not immediately?"

"Sounds like one of the DA's arguments against me."

"Face it, the DA has a tight case. But he didn't start from the position that you might be innocent." She paused, looking thoughtful. "The thief may have brought the car back to your door knowing it would focus the investigation on you, at least until you were cleared, and by that time his trail would be cold. Your being drunk might've been an unexpected bonus."

Parker didn't want to get his hopes up, only to have them smashed in the courtroom, but if Flannigan could find some evidence . . . . "While you're out snooping around, how do you know I won't skip?"

She started the car. In the rearview mirror he saw her smile.

"I have a good friend I can trust to keep you in line."

Friend? Another Superbitch? Parker envisioned a dungeon master with whips and chains.

Driving back the way they'd come, she passed downtown and turned on the Southwest Freeway. A mile or two outside the city, she exited the freeway and turned on a two-lane road.

"I take it you don't live in Houston," he said.

"About twenty miles out, in Richmond." She stopped in front of a sprawling country house. "But right now we're picking up my friend."

He watched her stroll to the door, stretching as she walked. Before she even rang the bell, the porch light flicked on. The screen door opened, and Flannigan disappeared inside. Five minutes later, she came out with a dog, part Doberman pinscher, by the look of it. Maybe part mastiff. Its head reached almost to Flannigan's shoulder. Had the coloring of a Doberman, but heavier, more muscular. Muzzle a foot wide, like a bulldog's.

Parker could hear Flannigan murmuring soothing phrases. When she opened the front passenger door the beast lumbered onto the seat. Snarled through the steel mesh.

"Parker Dann, I want you to meet my best friend, Mud. For the next seven days, he'll be your roommate and bodyguard."

Jesus, that thing's teeth are like daggers. Dann could feel them piercing a leg, crunching right through to the bone. The dog growled low in his throat, eyes steady with malice.

"He hates me," Dann said.

"Don't be silly, Mud doesn't hate anybody. But he can pretend he hates you if you get out of line."

"*Mud?* What kind of a name is that?"

"Short for Mean Ugly Dog."

Chapter Twenty-four

December 27, Houston, Texas

Ellie waited until her mother's bedroom door clicked shut, then switched her night-light back on. She didn't like sleeping in the dark anymore.

Shivering even under the extra blanket Mama had brought, she pushed the covers around Raggedy Ann's chin and hugged her closer. She wished she could go back to camp and find the lucky penny. Maybe if she hadn't lost it, the bad thing wouldn't have happened to Courtney.

She missed Courtney.

She missed Betsy, too.

Scrunching a corner of the pillowcase, she wiped her nose and eyes. Mama said the aspirin would make her feel better. Ellie wished it would hurry. Her tummy hurt and her head made pounding noises in her ears.

Betsy would say, "Don't think about feeling bad, think about something nice."

Like *The Nutcracker*. That had been better than nice, the most beautiful thing she ever saw.

In her new red shoes from Daddy Jon, Ellie'd felt really grown-up. Daddy Jon called her his special lady.

She didn't have to call him Daddy Jon. He was her *real* father, not a stepfather like Daddy Travis. But Betsy and

Courtney always called him *Daddy Jon,* 'cause he wasn't *their* real father.

Ellie wished Betsy and Courtney could see *The Nutcracker.* Together, they could act out the parts—with Ellie as princess. She was better at playacting than either . . . of her . . . sisters.

Her rotten . . . stupid . . . sisters.

Rotten . . . stupid . . . mean . . .

Why did they have to go away and leave her?

Ellie wiped her eyes. She wished the bad thing had happened to her first, so she wouldn't feel so alone.

"Achoo!" She wiped her nose, then grabbed a tissue for Raggedy Ann.

Her head wasn't making those loud noises in her ears anymore, and she didn't feel so shivery. But her stomach hurt something awful.

Turning on her side, she tucked an arm around Raggedy Ann and wriggled her feet up under her nightie. She would ask Daddy Jon where to get another lucky penny. Maybe then the next bad thing wouldn't happen.

Chapter Twenty-five

At half past midnight, after depositing Dann and Mud at her home in Richmond, Dixie turned the Mustang into an alley behind a four-story abandoned brick building at the edge of downtown Houston. The night was still, clear, and unnervingly quiet. No sign of the snow that had thrilled Ryan on Christmas Day.

She slipped the car into a niche between two buildings, then trod gingerly among broken bottles and other trash to a back entrance, where a rusted padlock sealed the door. The lock hadn't been opened in years. Fingering a small black button at the bottom edge of the brick, Dixie watched a double bay door slide silently upward. The room inside was as dark as an oil slick on a moonless night.

Visiting the Gypsy Filchers' headquarters was like visiting another planet. They were only available between midnight and dawn. With first light, they'd be as gone as smoke in the wind. And no matter where they set up shop, the place took on an otherworldliness like nothing Dixie had ever experienced. Their short-circuited youth seemed to heighten their imagination and resourcefulness, like the lost boys from Peter Pan.

Stepping into the dark building, Dixie waited for the door

to close completely, then swept the walls and floor with a penlight, instantly setting off a rustle of activity among the ancient newspapers, empty oil drums, and wooden pallets that littered the floor. Her light caught a pair of tiny red eyes before it swept past to what she was looking for: an ancient hydraulic elevator with a hand-lettered sign that said OUT OF ORDER.

Using the penlight, she located a small rusty wall panel, which she pushed aside to disclose a twelve-digit keypad. She tapped in a code. Moments later, a soft hum started the car downward.

Electricity pirated from a building down the block enabled the team to operate the elevator and other equipment. Blacked-out windows, machinery that ran smooth and quiet, and a schedule enforced with military precision had enabled them to work undetected from this location for almost a year.

The elevator doors yawned open, revealing a cubicle even blacker than the surrounding room. Dixie flashed her light across the walls and floor. She didn't want to step into an open shaft. She was scarcely inside when the car started upward. Halfway between floors, it jerked to a halt. Dixie experienced a momentary panic: *Was the mechanism faulty? Was someone playing games?* But the car started upward again and moved smoothly to the top floor. When the doors opened, she found herself squinting into a halogen spotlight.

A gangly young man shared the spotlight with Dixie—stringy blond hair, freckles, and a double-barreled shotgun aimed straight at her chest. Beyond the lighted circle, everything was dark.

"It's okay, Gabe." The voice came from the darkness. "Let her in."

The overhead fluorescent lights flickered on. Across the room, Brew, a sandy-haired kid just past his teens, slouched behind a computer desk, a telephone at his ear and a keyboard in his lap. He held up a finger, which Dixie interpreted to mean "just a moment," then continued tapping out a string of characters. Her gangly escort disappeared.

She glanced around the warehouse. Packages of disposable

diapers lined one wall, rising four feet high in some places, higher in others, as if some packages had been removed. Near the diapers were piles of toys and a rack of clothes. Boxes of food and other neatly stacked merchandise lined another wall. The desk and a few chairs occupied a corner.

"You don't see a thing, Flannigan," said a voice behind her, a woman's voice, slick with loathing. "Keep your eyes to yourself."

"Hello, Ski." Dixie forced a smile as she turned to face the female member of the Gypsy Filchers' management, a willowy platinum blonde with delicate features and deadly hands. She wore tight black jeans, black boots, a black turtleneck shirt. Dixie had never seen her dressed in anything else. Ski wasn't her real name, of course. The team had taken street names so long ago they probably didn't remember their birth names.

Ski sailed a seven-inch stiletto at a regulation dart board, burying the point in the bull's-eye, then planted three more blades beside the first, *thunk, thunk, thunk*. The center of the board had taken so many hits already that the cork was spongy. One of the knives fell out to land on a rubber mat, apparently placed beneath the board for exactly that purpose.

Dixie watched the girl bend double, as only the young-and-supple can, to scoop the knife from the mat. She plucked the other two from the cork. Whirling abruptly, she sailed a blade past Dixie's right ear, so close the air sang. It took all Dixie's nerve not to flinch.

Ski hefted another knife and aimed.

"I could take out your left eye from here—or the right one—I'll let you choose."

"Frankly, I'm partial to both." Dixie allowed a broad grin to spread across her face. "I have a *strong* attachment, you might say."

A mean little smile hovered on Ski's lips. She feigned a throw, and when Dixie remained unblinkingly steady, the smile turned sour. Then Ski let the knife fly, and it sliced the collar of Dixie's jacket.

Sauntering to the desk, the girl stood behind Brew, her

hand on his shoulder as if marking territory. He mumbled something into the telephone and winked at Dixie.

"Whatever you're peddling," Ski said, "we don't want any."

"Peddling? As I recall, I'm usually on the buying end of our negotiations. Where's Hooch?"

Dixie had met Brew and Hooch, the third, and the oldest, member of the Filchers' management team, four years earlier when the local police charged them with stealing a delivery truck full of goods from one of Houston's successful grocery-store chains. The truck driver identified Hooch as a passenger in a car he saw tailing him, but none of the stolen goods were found in Hooch's possession, and seventeen homeless people swore he was helping them erect a lean-to on the afternoon of the hijacking. Dixie had gotten a tip that the groceries were distributed in great haste to the homeless community, where they quickly disappeared into hungry bellies. As a caring human being, she could sympathize, but as an ADA, she had a duty. In the end, by mentioning the line of homeless people outside her office, ready to swear to Hooch's whereabouts at the time of the theft, she convinced the store owner to endorse a lenient sentence of deferred adjudication. The store got some favorable publicity and the Filchers were scared into staying clean—for a while.

Right or wrong, Dixie believed the three kids and their gang of castaway teens caused fewer problems with these Robin Hood heists than if they turned to less discriminating crime. Maybe they were even doing a little good, so she'd left them alone—but included them in her information network.

From the beginning, she'd hit it off with Brew and Hooch, but Ski was a different story. Something dark in Ski's early years had skewed her thinking. With a vengeance bordering on psychotic, the young woman despised all authority figures, and even though Dixie was no longer with the DA, Ski maintained Dixie would turn them in as soon as she no longer needed their services.

Dixie watched her now, knowing that without the Flannigans' rescue she herself might have turned out as bitter.

"Dixie!" Brew hung up the phone, wheeled his chair

around the desk, and pulled her close in a powerful bear hug. His legs had been crushed in a playground accident before he was school age. To compensate, he spent hours each day developing upper-body strength. "Been too long, Dix. Hope you got our invitation."

Ski plucked her throwing knife from the wall and drifted into the dark recesses of the warehouse.

"Invitation?" Dixie had picked up the mail when she arrived home, but hadn't sorted it.

"Our New Year's Eve bash. You have to come. It'll be a gas. Hey!" He spun the wheelchair around the desk. "I'm glad you're here. You can preview my new magic show for the day-care tours. Watch this." Reaching over the desk, he pulled a huge storybook onto his lap and opened it.

"Once upon a time . . ." he read with grave emphasis, "there were lee pittle thrigs." Three fat rubber pigs popped up to peek over the top of the book. "The first pittle thrig built a haw strouse." Brew snapped his fingers and a handful of straw appeared.

"The second pittle thrig built a hig twouse." A bundle of twigs popped out of his shirt pocket, into the air, and rained all around him. "But the third pittle thrig worked lard and hong, building a brouse out of hicks."

As Brew turned a page in the storybook, a brick appeared in his other hand.

"How'd you do that?" Dixie said.

"Great, huh? How about the spoonerisms? Think the kids will understand?"

"With the visual aids, sure they will." And if the kids didn't understand, they'd love the show anyway. When Brew turned on his showmanship, he was a regular Pied Piper. Kids followed him everywhere. "But, Brew, I need—"

"Wait till you see the wig wad bolf, all clangs and faws—"

A furry puppet popped over Brew's shoulder, baring its fangs and claws. Dixie laughed. But after seventeen hours on the road, she was tired and needed some answers. "Brew—"

"I know. You didn't come downtown for kid stuff." Grinning, he laid the storybook down. The fat little pigs disappeared inside it. "What's happening?"

He scooped two sodas from a foam cooler beside the desk and tossed one to Dixie.

"Last May," she said, popping the aluminum pull tab, "there was a hit-and-run killing in Spring Branch, a girl on her way to school."

Brew nodded. "The dude that did it is on trial right now."

"*If* he did it. Something doesn't feel right about the case. I'm wondering if anyone was working the area that night. Maybe picked up the car, hit the girl by accident, then returned the car to throw the investigating officers off track."

Brew shrugged. "Eight months is like forever. Who remembers what went down eight months ago?"

"People who keep good records. People with long memories who hear stories from other people who can't keep their mouths shut."

He shrugged. "Won't hurt to ask."

Picking up the phone, he pecked out a number. When it answered, he turned away from Dixie to speak privately. Taking her cue, she strolled across the room to a pile of toys and rooted around until she found a rubber ball. Bounced it a few times on the concrete floor. *Pop. Pop.*

She heard the elevator hum. The doors opened and Hooch stepped out. It took him all of five seconds to spot her.

"Say, I knew there be a dang good reason to stop here, my main squeeze paying a visit."

He wrapped his enormous arms around Dixie, lifting her off the floor to plant a substantial kiss on her cheek.

Hooch looked like something out of a horror movie. He stood six-four and weighed 240 without an ounce of fat. His face had never been handsome, but before it was nearly sliced in half by an ax blade, it might have been bearable. The jagged scar crossed the inside corner of his right eye, the bridge of his nose, and the left side of his mouth, where the ax had split his jaw, displacing some teeth and severing nerves and muscles necessary for smiling. Now Hooch only smiled on one side; the other remained frozen in a toothy sneer. Most who saw him preferred he didn't smile at all.

"If Lissie hears that 'main squeeze' bullshit, you'll be needing a patch for the other eye."

His grotesque grin spread across half his face.

"Lissie got selective hearing. She don't hear nothing she know I don't want her to hear."

"Hooch, you might convince somebody else you're a mean mother, but I know you too well."

He chuckled. "Danged if you don't. Say, girlfriend, you see the stuff for the Casa?" He waved an arm toward the wall of diapers and toys.

"The hospice for kids with—?"

"Yeah! We took over a whole truckload of toys and clothes. Diapers, too. Save these for later, you know, so they wouldn't be overstocked—"

"Or get suspicious about where they came from." The Casa took care of children under six who were HIV positive. The Gypsy Filchers had a special soft spot for kids. Many of the team's "charities" were homes for abused or sick children, but Hooch didn't like to think about what happened to HIV kids when they disappeared. The only time Dixie had ever seen him violent was when a boy he'd grown attached to was returned to his abusive parents. Brew, Ski, and Hooch—they would never say whether the names parodied the old cop show team, Starsky and Hutch, or were further bastardizations of slang terms for beer and whiskey, brewsky and hooch—had slipped into the house after everyone was asleep, captured the abusive couple in their bed, and threatened to carve them into dog food if any member of the team ever saw so much as a bruise on the boy again. It seemed to work for a while. Then the child was admitted to the emergency room with multiple fractures. That same night, the couple disappeared, leaving their home and car behind. Dixie never knew whether they disappeared on their own or with a strong suggestion from a big, scary black guy. "I'll bet the president of Kimberly-Clark would be proud to learn their missing truckload of Huggies is so hugely appreciated," she told Hooch. "I hope you sent a thank-you note."

"Don't we always?"

Dixie felt someone slip up catlike beside her.

"Hooch," Ski said, "you make that pickup?"

"Like clockwork. Being unloaded as we speak."

"Good. I need the truck for a delivery."

"The truck be all yours, Ski. Need any help?"

She seemed to think about that for a moment, eyeing Dixie all the while. Although the trio acted like brothers and sister, Hooch was the only one Dixie had ever seen with a date, and Ski was fiercely possessive of both men.

"Yeah, I do need your help," she said.

"Then let's be doing it." He ruffled Dixie's hair as he turned to go. "You, girlfriend. Don't be so scarce."

"Good to see you, too, guy." Dixie looked back at Brew, who was still on the phone. He waved her over.

"—forget it," he said into the phone. "We're even now. Thanks for the help." He wheeled around to face her and tapped a pencil on the desktop.

"I'm not sure this is what you want to hear," he said. "Nobody was working that part of Spring Branch the night the girl was hit. Nobody professional, that is. We can't rule out amateurs or someone passing through town."

"If it was somebody passing through town, we're sunk."

"Yeah, well an amateur would either freak out and skip town with the car or dump it far from the accident. He wouldn't calmly drive back and park it where he stole it, then trip away into the moonlight."

"That's how I see it, too."

"Does your man have enemies?"

"I don't think he stays in one place long enough to make anybody hate him. No family in town, no close friends." But Dixie knew that a person could make enemies without being aware.

Before leaving, she promised to attend the New Year's Eve party and forked over fifty dollars to send some teens to a big-screen pay-per-view bowl game. Yawning, she looked at her watch. As a skip tracer, she attracted strange friends who kept strange hours.

Arriving home at three A.M., she found a single light burning in the kitchen and a note propped against a plate of brownies on the table:

Your cupboard's bare. I found four eggs, shortening, some flour and sugar in the canisters & a partial can of cocoa, hard as brick until I beat hell out of it with a tenderizing mallet. I threw out the fuzzy green stuff in the fridge. God knows what it was before it started growing hair. 2 of the eggs I scrambled and ate. I used the other 2 in the brownies. Eat these, they taste fine. You owe me breakfast.

— Dann

Dixie studied the brownies, lifted one from the pile, and took a hesitant bite. It was good. In fact, it was excellent. Her can't-fail box type invariably came out tasting like cardboard.

She eased open the guest-room door to find Dann snoring and Mud curled up on the floor beside the bed. The dog raised his ugly head, yawning.

"Good boy," Dixie whispered. Mud lowered his chin across freshly manicured paws and winked out. The vet would no doubt send a whopping bill for the extra days of kennel service.

Dixie considered what to do about breakfast. Taking Dann to the local cafe and supermarket in Richmond should be safe enough with Mud along. If Dann liked to play chef, she'd buy whatever he needed. Home-cooked meals had been damn scarce since Kathleen died.

Cooking meals might also keep Dann too busy to cook up trouble. She could count on Mud to take Dann's leg off if he tried to leave the yard, but a desperate criminal with too much idle time might eventually outwit even the World's Best Watchdog.

Chapter Twenty-six

Sunday morning came and went in a blur. After pounding the pillow until well past ten, Dixie took Dann to breakfast and then to the grocery. They bought a carload of food, things like ginger root, which she couldn't imagine eating, and parsley, which she thought was used only as plate clutter.

By afternoon, the smells from the kitchen convinced her Dann knew what he was doing—pasta with shrimp, coffee made from freshly ground beans, and homemade pecan pie. He'd found her pecan stash in the pantry, the fifty-pound bag she saved out of each year's crop, and had spent the morning shelling pecans while she slept. She didn't have the heart to tell him about the automatic sheller in the barn.

"So," he said over coffee. "We get started first thing tomorrow?"

He had shaved, and she was still getting used to his new face. He looked younger, friendlier, less sinister.

Mud lay with his muzzle on Dixie's foot, faking sleep. She could feel his gentle pulse thrumming up her leg. Comforting.

Dann sat across from her in the breakfast nook, a diner-style booth Barney had built after Dixie and Amy went off to college.

"Forget that 'we,' " Dixie told him. Legally, she was treading a fine and hazardous line between illegal restraint and harboring a criminal, proving she could get in plenty of trouble without Dann's help. "Your part is to stay put and fix whatever's broken."

He rose abruptly and carried their coffee cups to the counter, his face turned determinedly away from her.

"Show me something that's broke. I'll fix it," he said curtly. He took a long time refilling their cups. Then his broad shoulders relaxed, and he turned, set the cups on the table, and settled back into the booth. "Meanwhile, I cook and keep the place picked up, right? So you can concentrate on finding evidence to clear me. That's our deal." His voice had lost its edge. He gazed at her with wide-eyed innocence.

The high-backed benches were padded in imitation leather, cadet blue, exactly the color of Dann's eyes. She hadn't realized until now that his eyes were the same shade of blue as Barney's.

True blue. The color of loyalty, royalty, and robin's eggs. Trustworthy blue.

Barney had been trustworthy, but Dann was still a suspect in at least one killing. Dixie couldn't afford to forget that. She looked at his mustache instead of his eyes. Definitely the mustache of a scoundrel.

"There's no guarantee I'll find anything," she said. "Or if I do, that it will help your case."

"Can't blame me for hoping, can you?" He wiggled his eyebrows.

Dixie hated that. When he wiggled his eyebrows, she couldn't help grinning.

"Hope is okay. But writing down everything you can remember about that night would be even better."

He groaned. "We've already been over it—"

"And the tenth time around you remembered something important."

"The salesman with the butterfly? Think he might be important?"

"You never said he was a salesman."

"I didn't?" Dann frowned, thinking about it. "He asked questions about selling, but like he didn't have much experience. Said he was working on a big deal."

"You said the Hornet was full of computer techies that night. Was he one of them?"

"No, he was talking land . . . or development . . . or something. Is that where you went last night, to talk to Augie?"

"Your friend wasn't working last night."

"Where the hell was he? Augie always works on Saturday. Big tip night."

"Sick with the flu, according to his replacement."

"That'd be the day man. Luke. So that's all? You were gone half the night—"

Dixie slammed her cup down. "Cripple that horse, Dann, and walk it by me real slow."

"What?"

"You're here because I have a soft spot for justice. And because I think *maybe* justice is being thwarted in your case. It's my call. This is my house. I'm not in the habit of reporting my every move."

For an instant his blue eyes flashed anger, then he blinked it away and looked embarrassed. "Sorry. Your personal life is none of my business."

Personal? He thought she was out with a lover? She felt a flush of color rise in her own cheeks. This situation was getting damned complicated.

Mud had jumped to attention and stood watching them beside the table. Dixie patted the dog's side to reassure him.

"Okay, here's what I found out. There were no local car theft rings working Spring Branch the night before the accident—which doesn't rule out a solo—"

"Someone just picking up wheels? That's possible, isn't it?"

"Possible," Dixie said, not believing it.

"Gets in a hurry. Tears around a corner and boom! Hits the kid. Then he's scared. Maybe drives around, realizing how much trouble he's in. Sneaks back. No cops yet, so he parks the car in my driveway and beats it on foot."

"Possible."

Dann studied her face, and she could see some of the hope go out of him.

"We have other angles to work," she said. "We have the guy with the butterfly tattoo, and we have all those techies to check out."

The blue eyes brightened a bit. "We do, don't we?"

Yeah. And only six days to find a lead that Belle Richards hadn't found in seven months.

After dinner, Dixie marshaled her resolve for a duty she could no longer put off. Christmas gift in hand and embittered feelings firmly set aside, she visited her mother. The Flannigans had always encouraged Dixie to forgive and forget.

Your mum's no saint, child, Kathleen had told her. *She's your blood mother, all the same, and you'll do right by her. We can't let wrong beget wrong, can we? Remember the good times. Remember she had a hard life.* Kathleen had combed Dixie's hair with her strong fingers. *To whelp a child sweet as you, a mother can't be too bad, now, can she?*

The first few years after her adoption, Dixie had lost track of Carla Jean completely. Then the year she graduated high school, a card came, "To my darling daughter on Graduation Day," postmarked Dallas. After that, Dixie received a postcard once a year, usually from somewhere in Texas, but once as far away as Phoenix. The cards stopped abruptly about the time Dixie joined the DA's staff.

The next communication was from a hospital. Carla Jean had been found wandering along Interstate 10, bruised, bleeding, and confused. She'd been riding with a friend, she told the paramedics who picked her up. The friend was angry, and Carla Jean told him to stop the car and let her out. He opened the door and shoved her; her head hit the pavement. By the time the ambulance reached the hospital, she'd slipped into a coma. She never told anyone who the "friend" was. On an ID card in her mother's handbag, Dixie was named as next of kin. Two weeks later, Carla Jean awoke from the coma remembering nothing about the accident and only bits and pieces of the past. Her motor skills were drastically impaired, but after a while she recovered enough to manage a walker. The doctors were encouraged. Then little by little, she lost all the ground she'd gained, along with her speech.

Now she lay in an oversize baby bed with chrome rails to keep her from falling out. The nurse had dressed her in a pink gown and brushed her thinning hair, gathering it back with a pearl-encrusted comb.

Carla Jean's green eyes sparkled as they had when she was young, but there was no depth to them. The doctors said she wasn't blind or deaf, but she no longer responded to people in the room. She could eat when someone fed her, soft foods, which required no chewing. She could hold her hand up if someone raised it, and she wouldn't know to put it down again until someone lowered it.

"You want some juice, Mama? It's apple, your favorite."

Dixie held a straw to the withered mouth, watched the liquid slowly climb to the top, watched the neck muscles work to swallow. She hated seeing her mother like this. In the old days, nobody could cheer up a room like Carla Jean. And during the brief weeks following the coma, when she had seemed most like her old self, she'd brought joy to the entire hospital, turning the simplest gathering into a party.

Carla Jean had spent her whole life dancing from one party to another, waiting for her dream lover to show up. She needed people, hated being alone. Dixie wondered now if her mother was alone in her mind. Or had her imagination created a dream world filled with love and laughter and handsome men?

"Your hands look dry, Mama. Let's put on some lotion to soften them." Dixie opened the Christmas package she'd brought and poured creamy perfume-scented liquid into her own hand to warm it, then rubbed it gently into the papery skin. "You always had such pretty hands."

She hated believing that Carla Jean knew some of her men friends had visited Dixie's room.

"Mama doesn't notice things," Dixie had told one of the older girls at Founders. "She's kind of dreamy, always imagining these wonderful things are about to happen. Then when they don't, she gets onto another idea, forgetting the first one, as if it wasn't important, anyway."

"Sure, hon, you go on believing that," the older girl replied. "But I've seen women who flutter their eyelashes and wiggle their butts at anything in pants, then play dumb like they're oh, so innocent. Won't take honest pay for sex, like that makes it dirty or something, but it's all right if a man drops a gift on the dresser afterward, a token of *affection*. Some men give especially nice gifts for kiddie poontang."

Dixie wasn't sure Carla Jean ever really understood she had a daughter. She treated Dixie more like a sister, was barely seventeen when Dixie was born. Only fifty-six now, but looking eighty-five. Had she ever come close to finding her white knight? Or could no man measure up?

"You want to eat now, Mama? The nurse brought some nice vegetables." When Dixie touched the spoon to Carla Jean's mouth, the thin lips remained closed. Dixie coaxed with a slight pressure of the spoon but got no response.

She buzzed for the nurse, then gathered up her coat and gloves. As she was about to turn from the bed, Carla Jean blinked. A tear slid from the corner of her eye.

Dixie grabbed a tissue and blotted the moisture away. Then she snatched a couple more tissues for herself and hurried from the room.

Chapter Twenty-seven

Homicide Division had moved some years ago from the maze of offices in downtown Houston to the Southeast Service Center on Mykawa Road. The idea was to spread out, thereby easing the tension that surfaces under crowded working conditions. Dixie had known Benjamin Rashly as an overworked homicide sergeant sharing a desk and chewing Tums as if he owned stock in the company. Now, as a lieutenant of Accident Division, he didn't belong in his old office, but he hadn't broken the habit of dropping by.

When she popped in at eight o'clock Monday morning, he sat scowling down at an arrest report in a thick folder.

"Hey, Rash. Got time to talk?"

He held up a hand for silence.

Now that she was no longer with the DA's office, getting Rashly to part with information on a police case was like trying to sweet-talk water from a well. On the drive over, she'd racked her brain for something she could trade for a look at the Keyes file. Official reports were public record. What she wanted were the bits and pieces that never made it to the official reports.

Rashly's white hair was thinning on top, revealing a pink spot about the size of a silver dollar. He'd gained a few lines in his square face over the years and some extra padding around his middle. Not bad at all, though, for his age, which she guessed at mid to late fifties, same as Carla Jean's. What a world of difference between this vital, active man and her wasted mother.

Knowing it did no good to rush him, Dixie poured a cup of coffee from a pot on a table outside the door, then settled into a gray plastic side chair. His office walls had been recently painted, sky blue, a nice change from dingy beige. The smell of solvent evaporating from the uncured paint made her coffee taste worse than usual. When he finished reading, he leaned on a fist and peered at her over his gold-rimmed glasses.

"What do you make of this?" He turned the file so she could see a yellow arrest sheet on a Hermie Valdez. "Three priors. One for accessory to felony theft, for which Valdez served six months, and two for harboring a known felon—her boyfriend, Alton Sikes. Both times, the cases were acquitted."

Dixie felt uncomfortable discussing anyone harboring a criminal when Parker Dann was probably showering at that very moment in her guest bathroom.

Rashly pushed the arrest sheet aside to show her a memorandum from the DA's office.

"Twice Sikes is arrested and breaks loose. Twice Valdez hides him out—"

"Your men have a little trouble holding on to this guy?"

"Give me a break, Flannigan. We're talking three years apart here, and Sikes is damn good with that jujitsu crap. Anyway, he serves nine months on the first burglary theft, gets out, goes back to his old ways, only he's moved up to robbery, knocks off three Kroger grocery stores. This time he serves eighteen months, and learns how easy it is to pick up fifty, sixty bucks at an automatic teller. Must've robbed thirty people first week out. Waits till a customer gets cash from the ATM, then waltzes up with a .38 Special and takes the money. Half the time, the victims don't file a report because the fifty they lost isn't worth the hassle.

"This last time, though, Sikes picks a guy who just took

three hundred dollars from the machine so he and his wife could drive to Austin. Their daughter's working on a doctorate at UT, and she'd taken sick. Sikes steps out with his .38. Eichorn, that's the victim's name, knows he can't get any more money from the machine because three hundred's the limit for twenty-fours. He refuses to hand the money over. Sikes must've been hopped up on something, because he doesn't hesitate, pumps four shots into the man's belly, nearly cuts him in half. Mrs. Eichorn, who's been sitting in the car out of sight, hears the shots and comes screaming around the corner, Sikes shoots her, too."

"Both dead?"

"Both hanging on. He won't make it. She will. Her testimony will convict Sikes—hell, it'll bury the bastard—but first we have to find him. We know Valdez is hiding Sikes. It's what she always does. I say, convince her she's going down with him this time and she might talk." Rashly stabbed the memorandum with a short, blunt finger, the nail surprisingly well manicured. As a homicide sergeant, he had chewed his nails, Dixie recalled. "How do we convince Valdez to roll over when the DA won't use her priors in court?"

"Not *won't*, Rash, *can't*. Valdez's lawyer apparently got the judge to disallow any reference to previous convictions. Not as easy as it sounds, actually. Nevertheless, the DA has to prove guilt in *this* case, regardless of past behavior."

"Same kind of chickenshit you used to pull on me, Flannigan."

She knew better than to take that bait. Rashly had never believed they were on the same side. Dixie refused to prosecute until she was personally convinced a suspect was guilty—then she wanted every piece of ammunition she could find to get a maximum sentence. While she never violated the disclosure rules, she danced plenty close at times, holding key bits of evidence to present at the last moment, when the defense felt confident and had dropped their guard. She hated plea bargaining. The guilty belonged behind bars, so the rest of the world could sleep easier.

"What are you doing here, Rash? This isn't your case anymore."

Rashly had worked himself to a wrath telling his story. He was flushed and short of breath, his head thrust forward in a familiar belligerent cant.

"I opened this case. I'll see it closed."

"You really want this guy," Dixie said.

"I hate creeps who prey on weakness. This couple, they're knocking on sixty-five. Woman's barely able to talk but still worried about her daughter—"

"What do you think would happen if you let Valdez go?"

"*Let her go?*"

"Who is it you really want, her or Sikes?"

"Sikes, of course, the shooter. I don't give a damn about Valdez." He narrowed his eyes thoughtfully. "We let her go, she'll be bustin' a gut to contact Sikes and tell him what a fine ruse she pulled on the HPD. But she's not stupid enough to lead us right to him."

"You can't use the kind of surveillance devices that're needed."

"Meaning you can."

"I'm a private citizen. What I hear and pass along is fair game."

"Not if it's obtained illegally."

"When have I ever done anything illegal?" They both knew they were dancing dangerously close to violating Valdez's right to privacy. In Texas, evidence gained illegally, even by a private citizen, was inadmissible. But Dixie wouldn't be gathering evidence. "Remember the Balsam case?"

As a young ADA with limited surveillance funds, Dixie had frequently used local talent. Take a kid fresh from his first juvenile arrest, get him to help out on a case. He wouldn't turn on his friends, naturally, but adults and outsiders were fair game, and he could usually round up a few buddies to help out—cheap. Balsam, a reluctant key witness, had disappeared. Patrol units were cruising his usual haunts, but he hadn't surfaced; yet Dixie felt certain he hadn't left town.

Then she remembered Balsam's obsession with fitness. She obtained some passes to local health clubs and gave them to a recently paroled kid she'd pegged as salvageable. He and his buddies were beginning to develop some impressive pecs when they spotted Balsam on the bench press. A few years later the kid asked Dixie to write a letter of recommendation when he applied to the Police Academy.

"Valdez won't make a move to contact Sikes," Dixie told Rashly, "unless she's convinced you aren't sitting on her doorstep."

"Hell, we don't have the manpower to sit on her doorstep."

"I've got real keen ears, Rash." As well as some new electronic bugs she'd been dying to try out.

"Let me get this straight. We release Valdez, after much moaning and complaining so she won't glom it's a trap. Then we back off until we get an *anonymous* tip to Sikes' whereabouts." Rashly stroked his smooth-shaven chin in contemplation. "He's not out on bail, so there's no bounty. Why would you do it?"

"Would you believe I think bad guys should be locked up?" When he rolled his eyes, she amended, "Would you believe I'd trade it for something *I* want?"

"Sounds more like it. What's the trade?"

"Information. A hit-and-run case last May, just after you moved over to Accident Division. Victim was a child, Elizabeth Keyes. I want to know what's in the file that wasn't put out for public awareness."

He scowled. "You thinking to get a private dick's license now?"

"Just something I'm looking into for a friend."

"Must be a damn good friend."

She shrugged.

"It's a closed case," he said. "I'd have to get the file from Records. Might take a while."

"Did you work on it?"

"Not personally, you know how it is around here, once you get promoted to a desk job. But I was cognizant."

Dixie smiled at his unlikely jargon. "Then let me pick your brain. You can get the file for me later."

"*Pick my brain?* Jeez, Flannigan, I *hate* that expression. Sounds ghoulish." He scooped up their empty coffee cups and headed out the door.

While she waited, Dixie flipped through her recollection of Belle's case file on Dann. Betsy had walked to school alone that morning because her two sisters were ill. The investigating officer sketched a map of the route the girls walked every day, which took them within a block of Dann's house and three blocks of the Green Hornet. Spring Branch was an old neighborhood. Fast-food chains, small office buildings, and retail stores lined the main streets, with residential areas tucked in behind. The girl's parents, Rebecca and Travis Payne, owned the Payne Cafe and Payne Hardware. Rebecca had been employed as head chef at one of the city's elite restaurants before she married Payne and opened her own place next door to her husband's business.

Rashly returned with two cups of steaming coffee. An aroma of Middleton's Cherry Blend pipe tobacco followed him into the room. Went out for a smoke, Dixie figured, to think over her offer.

"What do you want to know?" He handed her the coffee, then stood over her, one elbow resting on a tall gray file cabinet. Dixie eyed the drawers. The Keyes report wouldn't be here at Homicide, but downtown, in a cabinet just like this one.

"There's one angle your guys briefly touched on, but didn't follow up," Dixie said. "The possibility of Dann's car being stolen—"

"Yeah, we thought about that, especially it being a Cadillac. There's a bunch we've been trying to catch nearly a year now, steals high-profile cars—your Mercedes, your BMW, your Cadillac—sells them in South America, transported in cargo containers booked as carpet shipments. Roll the stolen vehicle to the back of the boxcar, fill the front with carpet. Inspector looks in, everything's copacetic."

"Sounds like a good lead. Why didn't your men take it any

further?" From the beginning, the cops had focused their investigation on Parker Dann. His prior arrest for driving while intoxicated hadn't helped him any.

"What lead? Dann didn't report his Cadillac stolen. Nobody reported seeing anyone messing around near his car. Nobody's fingerprints in it besides his own and the boy who cleans and waxes it. And no other vehicles in the neighborhood were stolen that night."

"Maybe it was an amateur. Stole the car, hit the girl, panicked, and put the car back where it came from." Might as well see if the idea sounded as weak to Rashly as it did to her.

"You're reaching, Flannigan. How many amateurs would remember to wear gloves? This was May, not December. Dann's prints were all over the steering wheel. Anyone wiping their own prints off would've wiped his off, too."

Dixie sighed. The case against Dann was looking tighter and tighter. "I noticed the girl and her parents have different surnames."

"Mother's been in and out of divorce court a couple times. Married again last year. Before that she was married to an architect. The youngest kid is his, but he adopted two from the woman's earlier marriage, then fought her in court for custody of all three kids. Lost, of course. Single male, what the hell did he expect?"

That would be Jonathan Keyes. "You check him out?"

"What's to check? Respectable businessman, partner in a big architectural firm downtown. Like most divorced fathers, he gets the kids every other weekend and alternating holidays. His weekend happened to be the one before Elizabeth Keyes was killed. The girls stayed a few days extra to attend some blowout his firm was having. He dropped them off at home the night before the *accident*. Get the inflection on that last word, Flannigan? This was *not* a homicide."

"Did you know one of Betsy's sisters was killed in a swimming mishap in August?"

"Not in *my* jurisdiction."

"Camp Cade, near Conroe. You didn't hear about it?"

"No reason I should. An accident, not even in this country. Our case was closed by then. You see a connection?"

Dixie shook her head. "Must be hard on the family, though, losing two children like that."

"Flannigan, why are you digging into this case? It's a done deal."

"Like I said, just—"

"I know, a favor for a friend. Well, tell your *friend*, Belle Richards, that you're on a short leash fooling around in police business." He picked up the Valdez file and quickly copied something on a notepad. "On this other thing, we never discussed it. I might've mentioned we'd like to know where Sikes is holed up, but I have no knowledge of any actions you might take on your own." He ripped off the sheet he'd been scribbling on, folded it, and handed it to Dixie.

"A posted reward would help that story hold up." Rashly was blowing smoke about not having access to Betsy's file. He could call up the computer version with a few keystrokes. The HPD had issued computers to every patrol unit and required officers to log their reports daily. But then his name would be logged in. He might have to answer questions about why he was looking into the case at this late date. "You know, Rash, a skip tracer isn't likely to finger a suspect without something in return."

"What the hell happened to our deal?" His jaw thrust forward.

Dixie got up to go. "Hey, the deal hasn't changed. You let me know the minute Valdez is released and I'll be on her like dirt on a doormat. Your old homicide buddies can make the Sikes collar and get some good press. Only, I may have to work the surveillance in between paying jobs. A reward could hurry the results."

Rashly heaved an agitated sigh. "I'll see what I can do. But listen, Flannigan, don't drop your guard. Valdez is tight with Sikes. It never ceases to amaze me what some women will do for the love of a man."

"Rash, you're getting downright romantic."

Outside his door, Dixie unfolded the scrap of paper with

Valdez's address and telephone number. She stuffed the note in her pocket. In exchange for the time she'd have to spend putting a tracer on Valdez, she hadn't gained much. But a deal's a deal. Maybe there'd be more in the case folder.

And Rashly had mentioned something about Jonathan Keyes that set a red flag waving in Dixie's mind. The evening before Betsy's death, Keyes had taken all three girls to a party. The next morning, the younger girls stayed home, conveniently sick, leaving Betsy to walk to school alone.

Chapter Twenty-eight

Dixie was glad to see the word *Garden* separating *Payne* from *Cafe*. Regardless of the spelling, she couldn't get past the image of hot soup in the lap or ground glass in the burgers—a restaurant dispensing pain as the house specialty. Payne *Garden* Cafe was a little easier to take.

Parked across the street in the Mustang, she studied the Garden Cafe and Payne Hardware, pondering what she might accomplish by going inside. She wanted to know Betsy Keyes, wanted to know her family, their routines and how those routines might have differed on the day the girl died. She wanted to know Courtney, as well. Dixie wasn't sure how it would help her determine whether the deaths were accidental, but she needed to fill in the picture.

That Rebecca Payne was creative, she deduced from viewing the cafe's exterior. Nestled among service stations, dry cleaners, and convenience stores, the Garden Cafe contributed a dash of vibrancy to an otherwise commonplace neighborhood street.

A glassed-in sun porch spread across the front. A terraced bed of herbs and flowers flanked the weathered boardwalk leading to the entry. Among chives, dill, and other green edibles, which Dixie recognized by their hand-painted pixie signs, potted poinsettias raised red topknots to the midday sun. In one corner, a stack of flat clay pots and a box of daffodil bulbs bearing a fluorescent PLANT NOW sticker hinted of the yellow blossoms that would spring up in coming months. Dixie liked it.

She entered through a golden oak door embellished with etched glass, a large brass knob, and a tinkling bell. The dining-room space, surprisingly narrow, boasted eight tables, four booths, a six-stool counter, and a specialty section defined by a few well-stocked shelves.

Right away Dixie noted an array of tiny clay pots planted with the same herbs she'd seen outside. An assortment of Mason jars filled with sauces and dressings bore the "Payne Garden Cafe" label. Two shelves of commercially packaged containers held items Dixie had seen in health-food stores— roots, extracts, bulgur wheat, millet, granola, salt substitute, fructose, spice blends, and exotic teas. A framed magazine article beside the specialty section touted the Garden Cafe as one of Houston's best kept secrets, "a down-home place serving delicious, healthful food at reasonable prices." Sounded like the best thing since apple butter.

Dixie selected a jar of spaghetti sauce with mushrooms and a packet of Italian spices to supplement Parker Dann's culinary skills and carried them into the dining area.

Taking a seat at the far end of the counter, she looked the place over. Only one table was occupied—a couple who had eyes only for each other—but the lunch crowd wasn't officially due for another ten minutes.

Then Dixie noticed the nearest booth was also occupied, and a stillness came over her. The youngest Keyes child, Ellie, lay asleep on the padded seat, a gaily crocheted afghan covering her small body. Seeing her, Dixie realized how worried she'd been that yet another accident might have occurred in the Keyes family. Except for a chapped nose, the girl seemed fine. Brown hair tangled around her chubby cheeks. A bright Raggedy Ann doll clutched in her arms, and one bare foot thrust outside the afghan, she looked angelic and vulnerable. On the table beside her sat a Kleenex box and a prescription bottle. According to Belle's notes, Ellie was barely six, Dixie's age the first time Tom Scully visited her bedroom. What made a person want to defile such innocence?

Dixie realized as she watched the sleeping girl's shallow breathing that she'd been revisiting the past much too often lately. She resolved to stop. If she continued to muddle her own childhood problems with the Keyes accidents, she'd never find the truth. As a rule, she rarely thought about the bad years. Too much good had happened in her life to dwell on misfortunes. But the world was filled with casualties of life's dark side, and if she could save just one child from harm, perhaps the past would redeem itself.

Her breathing fell into rhythm with the rise and fall of Ellie's chest. Then a mucus bubble formed at one tiny nostril, and Dixie smiled. A head cold was reassuringly ordinary. She plucked a tissue from the box and gently wiped Ellie's nose, as footsteps sounded behind the counter.

Dixie turned to find a pert twenty-year-old with springy black curls and lashes like paintbrushes. Her name tag said GILLIS.

"Sorry to take so long." She laid a menu on the counter. "I didn't hear the bell."

Dixie had hoped to meet Rebecca Payne, but the mouthwatering aromas issuing from the kitchen suggested the chef was preparing lunch.

"Gillis, I saw your magazine write-up as I walked in. It said to ask for the house specialty." Dixie hoped it wouldn't be yogurt or tofu. In her limited experience with "healthful" food, those ingredients seemed overrated and overly abundant.

"Today's special is Chicken Piccata. Mrs. Payne does wonders with herbs. The Brandied Beef on Sprouted Wheat is good, too." Gillis placed a white napkin and utensils on the counter. "Oops, there's the buzzer. The produce truck is finally here. Be right back."

Dixie studied the menu. After a moment, she heard a rustle behind her and turned to find a pair of solemn brown eyes staring over the top of the afghan. Ellie had pulled it high to cover her nose.

"Hello," Dixie said.

The brown eyes blinked.

"Bet you've got the sniffles. I hate having the sniffles, my nose all runny and sore. Can I get you anything? A glass of water, maybe? Orange juice?"

Blink.

"Hot lemonade? That always tastes good when I feel puny, hot lemonade and raisin toast."

This time the eyes bounced up and down as the child nodded.

"Good. I hate to eat alone." Gillis reappeared, as if on cue. Dixie ordered the Chicken Piccata and coffee for herself, hot lemonade and toast for the girl.

"That's a nice big booth," Dixie said, when the waitress left to turn in the order. "Think I could join you?"

The brown eyes moved side to side. "I'm kuh-*tay*-just."

"Contagious?"

"Got the flu." She coughed, a deep, phlegmy sound.

"Oh, well. I'm not one bit scared of the flu. Why, I've had the flu so many times I've lost count. If that's all you're worried about, you can stop worrying."

The child was sitting up now, letting the afghan slip down to her waist. Her round brown eyes looked unconvinced.

"Your mommy tell you not to talk to strangers?"

The nod again.

"Suppose I clear it with your mommy. Then will you consider letting me share your table?"

A bright smile accompanied the nod. When Gillis returned with salad, Dixie handed her a business card with D.A. "DIXIE" FLANNIGAN printed above her telephone number and a post office box. In this case, the D.A. was for Desiree Alexandra—but few people asked. She had a thousand cards printed each year in exchange for a few pounds of pecans.

"Gillis, would you introduce me to this very cautious and slightly contagious young lady, and then ask her mother if it's all right for us to have lunch together?"

Gillis looked uncertain, but read the name on the card exactly as it was written, introduced the little girl as Ellie, then disappeared into the kitchen.

"Happy to meet you, Ellie. Please don't call me Ms. Flannigan. I'm Dixie, plain and simple."

"Hi, Dixie-plain-and-simple!" Ellie piped, breaking into a fit of giggles.

"Whoa! I walked right into that one, didn't I? Where'd you learn such a good joke?"

"From Courtney." The light winked out of Ellie's eyes.

Dixie didn't want to put a damper on what promised to be a pleasant lunch. She filled the silence quickly.

"I don't know any jokes as good as yours, but I know the best *knock-knock* joke in the whole world. You know what a knock-knock joke is?"

Ellie nodded, eyes wide and solemn.

"Want to hear the best knock-knock joke in the world?"

Another nod, a tiny smile.

"Okay, but I think we should warm up to the best. Let's try this one: Knock, knock."

"Who's there?"

"Oswald."

"Os-wald who?"

"Oswald my gum."

The child's giggle was high and frothy, like champagne bubbles bursting. "My turn?" she said.

"Go for it."

"Knock, knock."

"Who's there?"

"Awch." She giggled again, anticipating her own punch line.

"Awch who?"

Giggle, giggle. "God bless you!" Giggle, giggle, giggle.

Dixie whooped, genuinely amused, but also hamming it up.

"Okay, are you ready now for the world's greatest knock-knock joke?"

"Yes!"

"Okay, you start," Dixie said.

"Knock, knock."

"Who's there?"

Ellie looked blank for a moment before she realized she'd been had. Then she grinned. "You fooled me!"

"Yep. That's me, an old fooler."

Gillis appeared with a tray. She set the hot lemonade in front of Ellie and Dixie's meal across from her.

"Mommy said I can join Ellie for lunch?" Dixie asked.

"That's right, but she did say to warn you that Ellie has a bronchial flu and might be contagious."

"I already told her that," Ellie said. "Come on, Dixie, sit down."

Ellie nibbled at the toast and sipped the lemonade. Dixie put away the Chicken Piccata, which was excellent despite the green specks that Gillis assured her were fresh herbs from the garden outside the door.

Even more than the meal, Dixie enjoyed the company. But she couldn't help envisioning Ellie's two sisters alongside her, as they appeared in the Christmas snapshot. According to Rashly, the older girls had a different father from Ellie, yet they looked very much alike and had identical coloring.

Ellie coughed. Dixie wanted to scoop her up, take her home, rub her chest with Vicks VapoRub, feed her chicken soup, and keep her safe. Rebecca Payne probably felt the same protectiveness, bringing Ellie to the cafe instead of hiring a sitter, terrified of letting her remaining child out of sight.

"You don't like your toast?"

"My tummy hurts."

"Oh." Dixie touched the back of her hand to the child's forehead, not sure exactly what she should feel. Warm. Maybe the girl needed aspirin or one of the the little white prescription pills—AMOXIL, the label said. Lord, she didn't know a thing about kids.

She called Gillis, who said Rebecca had gone next door to the hardware store to take Mr. Payne some lunch. Minutes later, Rebecca Payne appeared with Tylenol and water. Unlike her brown-haired daughters, Rebecca had radiant blond hair pulled back in a ribbon that matched her print dress. She wore a white cook's apron over a trim figure and stood about five-foot-seven. Not quite pretty, yet attractive, she had a bobbed nose and striking bottle-green eyes a bit too close together.

"The chicken was wonderful," Dixie told her. "Every bit as good as the restaurant critic proclaimed."

Rebecca's smile brought her closer to beautiful. "The newspapers have been kind, but I'm not one for false modesty. I serve some of the best food in town."

She settled Ellie for a nap. As she tucked the afghan around the child's neck, Dixie noticed Rebecca's left hand was missing the first two fingers.

Next door, at Payne Hardware, Dixie tried to think of an item she needed at home—garden hose, faucet washers—did people browse in a hardware store? Certainly, that would give her more time to check out Travis Payne.

The cowbell over the door rang more insistently than the baby tinkler at the Payne Garden Cafe. The air smelled of sawdust and machine oil. From somewhere near the back, a power saw buzzed shrilly.

Dixie scanned the room for the angry face in the news clip of Dann's arraignment. The only man in sight was a stout-nosed shopper wheeling an overburdened cart to the register.

"Get out here, Travis," he shouted over the power-saw whine. "I'm ready to go."

The whine ceased, and after a moment a sturdy, white-haired man in orange overalls appeared from behind a partition. Travis Payne didn't look nearly as fierce as his photograph. The two men chatted at the register like old friends.

Sidling in that direction, Dixie feigned an interest in a shelf of cleaning agents. She picked up a bottle of Tarnex.

"Travis, I can't see any advantage in that new department you're adding," Stout Nose stated.

"The computer center? Got to keep abreast of the times, Tate. You know that."

Dixie heard excitement in his voice, the same excitement her hacker friends exhibited when discussing their latest passion. Travis Payne had been bitten by the computer bug.

"Pah! A money pit, that's what it'll turn into. Who's going to buy a computer from a hardware store?"

"Lay you odds that department will *double* what the rest of the store brings in. *Double* it, just you watch. Soon as it's completely stocked and I get the word out."

"That's what you said when you added kitchen gadgets. Now you've got a truckload of pots and pans gathering dust."

Dixie noticed a neat yellow sign that marked the kitchenware section. Others advertised plumbing, electrical, and building supplies. A bright blue sign marked the computer area.

"Everybody these days needs a personal computer," Payne said. "Everybody. Including you, Tate. You can be my first customer." He had finished ringing up the sale. Now he stacked the merchandise on a cart.

"If I recollect rightly, my wife was your first customer when you put in that fancy decorator section. Rugs, curtain rods, lamps—now I ask you, what kind of hardware store carries such nonsense?"

"It's called forward thinking, Tate. Look at what's to come, not what's past. You'll see—"

"I know. 'Soon as you get the word out.' Well, I won't hold my breath. Be glad I'm not your business partner." Payne opened the door, and the customer wheeled his cart through, muttering, "Computers in a hardware store. That takes the cake."

The cowbell clanged wildly as Payne shut the door.

"May I help you, ma'am?" He smiled at her, pale blue eyes twinkling, white mustache defining his bow-shaped mouth, orange overalls tight over his roundish belly. Dixie wondered if he ever moonlighted as Saint Nick.

"I'm trying to decide between these cleaners," Dixie said.

"Take your time, ma'am. Take your time. I'll be in the

back working on some shelves when you're ready to check out." He scurried away, and a moment later she heard the power saw.

Travis Payne had to be ten or twelve years older than Rebecca, Dixie thought as she wandered idly down the rows of hardware, kitchen, and decorator items. A man happy in his work, business apparently expanding, his wife's business written up favorably in the press. The only dark cloud in their lives seemed to be the deaths of two children.

She found a bin full of key holders, including the kind Dann had used to hide a spare key under the chassis of his Cadillac. Payne had sold it to him. He would've known exactly where to look if he wanted to steal—or borrow—Dann's car. For that matter, anyone shopping in the store that day might have observed the sale.

In the new computer area, unfinished shelves covered half of one wall. Sealed boxes of merchandise sat in the middle of the floor draped with a plastic drop cloth. Expansion in progress.

Dixie focused on the Tarnex bottle in her hand. *What the hell was this stuff for, anyway?* According to the label, it instantly cleaned copper, brass, and other metals. Dixie wondered if it would make Kathleen's copper teapot shine like the one pictured.

She didn't like admitting it, but her sleuthing skills were producing less than brilliant results. At the moment, her best suspect in Betsy's death was the salesman who had stayed late talking with Dann at the Green Hornet, the man with a butterfly tattoo. The bar wouldn't open until late in the afternoon. She could ask Rashly to put out a bulletin with the man's description, but she was already indebted to the homicide chief for more hours than she wanted to spend. She'd take her chances later with the bartender. Meanwhile, she might as well have a talk with Ellie's real father, Jonathan Keyes.

Deciding the word "instant," when applied to cleaning, had unbeatable sales appeal, she carried the Tarnex to the register. Outside, she used the cellular phone in the Mustang

to call the architectural firm of Keyes & Logan. Like Ellie,
the receptionist had a stuffy nose. She kept saying "excuse
me," then sniffing.

"Mr. Keyes is oud of towd today," she said. "I can't give
oud his home dnumber, but he'll be back in the office
domorrow."

Keyes' home telephone was unlisted. Dixie could get it,
but she didn't like using resources unnecessarily. Tomorrow
would be soon enough to meet Jonathan Keyes.

She felt more compelled, at the moment, to check on
Dann. He'd been home alone with Mud for several hours.
Who knew what mischief he could be cooking up?

Before leaving Spring Branch, though, she might as well
visit the scene where Betsy was killed. Finding the corner, she
parked, then got out and approached the intersection from
the sidewalk where Betsy had walked. A willow tree grew near
the curb, bare limbs stretching over the narrow street. Shrubs
with low-hanging limbs encircled the tree in a bed trimmed
with bricks. In full leaf, as the limbs would've been in May,
they could easily conceal an approaching vehicle.

Parker Dann's house, Dixie recalled, was around the block
and two streets away. The most likely route from Dann's
house to the Payne Garden Cafe, Payne Hardware, the Green
Hornet, or the nearest freeway would pass through this intersection.

She drove to the Paynes' home address and discovered that
it, too, was on the route to Dann's house. In addition to seeing
the girls at the cafe and hardware store, Dann would naturally
have met them on occasion walking along the street or playing in their front yard.

At eleven years old, Betsy was probably mature enough to
baby-sit her younger sisters, and with their parents working
only a few blocks away, Dixie imagined the three girls spent a
lot of time playing at home alone. Dann, a commissioned
salesman, would have plenty of free time during the day to get
to know the Keyes children, if he chose to.

Dixie didn't know where her thoughts were leading, but
the proximity between Dann's house and the Paynes' house

troubled her. The fact that Dann was friendly and attractive, with trust-me blue eyes, bothered her even more.

The red Frisbee sailed across the yard.

Mud dashed after it, sprang into the air like a corkscrew, and snapped it out of the sky. Parker couldn't help admiring the dog's grace. Ugly as a mongrel from hell, and strong enough to tear a man's arm off, he was actually not much more than a lovable pup. Loved running. Loved attention. Loved chasing after the Frisbee.

Mud lumbered across the yard to where Parker stood waiting.

"Good boy!" He gave the dog a liver treat, his favorite. "What a fine fellow. Yes, sir!"

The treat disappeared in a gulp, Mud all eager to play again. Parker rubbed the dog's head and patted his side.

"Okay, boy! Let's go!" He sailed the Frisbee. As Mud ran after it, Parker closed the gap between them. They'd started playing near the porch. Now they were almost to the fence.

Earlier, Parker'd made the mistake of running too close to the front gate. Mud nipped the seat of his jeans with enough snap from those evil teeth that Parker knew the next bite would take a chunk out of his butt. He backed off fast. Now he was taking it slow and easy, and they were almost to the same spot near the gate.

So far, Mud hadn't noticed.

"The bluebird carries the sky on his back," Thoreau had written. Perhaps a red Frisbee carried freedom. With enough patience, Parker figured, it might carry him right through that gate, with Mud prancing happily ahead of him.

Parker had slipped the Frisbee into Flannigan's grocery cart when they went shopping, after the cart was full enough that she wouldn't notice. At the checkout counter, he distracted her by pointing out the latest Elvis sighting headlined on a scandal rag. If she saw the toy now and asked where it came from, he'd say, "Hell, I thought it was Mud's. Found it right there in the yard. Think somebody's kid threw it over the fence?"

"You're a good fellow, Mud!" Parker gave the dog another liver treat, more pats, more praise, then sailed the Frisbee right up to the gate. "Go get it, Mud! That's it! Good boy!" All the while running toward the gate himself. He closed the distance that Mud would have to run back, and the dog nearly stumbled when Parker wasn't where he expected him to be. But then he lumbered happily to Parker's feet, dropped the disk, and panted, pleased as hell with himself.

This time, Parker sailed the disk toward the porch. When Mud dashed after it, Parker stepped a few feet closer to the gate.

"Good boy, Mud! Bring it here!"

The dog raced back and dropped the Frisbee. Then he looked at the gate and back at the porch as if realizing something wasn't quite right.

"It's okay, boy. Yeah, you're a good boy, good dog." Parker spent a bit more time on the patting and praising. Then he sailed the Frisbee toward the porch.

Mud's hesitation was so slight, the disk had barely started its downward arc when he caught it. Then the dog stood looking back and forth—at Parker, at the porch, at the gate— holding the Frisbee in his mouth.

He sat down on his haunches and stared at Parker.

"Come on, Mud! Bring it here." Taking one of the liver treats in hand, Parker offered it invitingly. "It's okay, boy. Come on."

Mud looked at the treat in Parker's hand. He looked at the gate, then dropped the Frisbee, covered it with his big paws, and whined softly.

"Hey, boy, it's okay. It's me, your old buddy Parker." Kneeling, he offered the treat again. "Come on, fellow. That's a *good* dog. Smart dog." *Smart as hell.* "Bring it here."

Mud looked at Parker's outstretched hand, Parker sitting low to the ground now, no threat, no indication that the man might cut and run toward the forbidden gate. After a moment, the dog picked up the Frisbee, plodded to Parker's feet, dropped the disk, and accepted his liver treat, chewing it more slowly this time, as he watched Parker with a wary eye.

They were becoming great friends, all right. Fun was fun, but the dog knew his job.

"You're a damn good dog," Parker said, meaning it. He picked up the red Frisbee and decided he'd pushed his luck enough for now.

Chapter Twenty-nine

Cruising toward home on U.S. 59, Dixie turned on the windshield defroster and counted the days until court would reconvene next Monday, January fourth. Today was Tuesday, her second full day back in town, and she hadn't picked up a crumb of information linking the accidents that killed Betsy and Courtney Keyes. A squeamish part of her mind hoped she was barking up the wrong tree this time. No matter how coincidental, two accidents were preferable to two murders. She was determined to keep an open mind, in any case.

The Paynes had not seemed particularly distraught over the loss of their daughters. But then, Betsy's death had taken place in May, Courtney's swimming accident in August. This was December. Even after such tragedies, life goes on.

Dixie turned down the defroster's blast of hot air and tuned the radio to a news station. "Colder," the weatherman predicted cheerily, "with possible freezing rain."

What if she tried her damnedest, yet on January fourth had gathered no new evidence in Betsy's case? What made her think, anyway, that she could accomplish what Belle's trained investigators had failed to do? A skip tracer's job was pig simple—bring the bad guy in for due process. Period.

But she'd been truthful when she told Dann the justice

system would work better if its caretakers were more conscientious. She'd seen her share of bad guys over the years; Dann somehow didn't fit the mold. On the drive to Houston, she'd questioned him ruthlessly, and she believed he was telling the truth—which didn't rule out the possibility that he was so drunk out of his mind he didn't *know* the truth. Yet, in the five days they'd spent together, she hadn't noticed any usual signs of alcoholism.

If Belle Richards said the jury was ready to convict, Dixie would lay money on it. Assuming Dann's innocence, Betsy's killer was still on the streets. And if Dixie turned Dann in, without being convinced of his guilt, her conscience would needle her to the grave. As Barney would say, "The most painful wound of all is a hard stab of conscience."

Belle had left three messages. So far, Dixie had successfully ignored them, since talking to the attorney now would mean skirting the truth. Sooner or later, though, she'd have to return those phone calls; sooner or later, Dann would have to face the jury. The clock was ticking. Certainly, no one heard it louder than Dann himself.

He'd been a model prisoner these two days, but Dixie wasn't fooled. While biding his time, hoping she'd turn up new evidence, he was probably also plotting alternatives. And as the clock ticked on, he'd get panicky. Desperate men couldn't be trusted.

The pecan grove came into view: rows of trees, stripped now of their foliage, cast long bony shadows in the afternoon light. Closer to the house, the Flannigans had planted live oaks for year-round shade and wind protection. Kathleen's sporadic interest in gardening had produced seasonal vegetables and occasional flowers, but the beds had long since weeded over. Maybe Dann could clean them out. Maybe he could also stain the rail fence.

She was turning in the driveway when she remembered the Valdez job. Now, before Rashly released Hermie Valdez from jail, was the time to wire the house for sound. It would take only an hour or two. If Dixie hurried, she could pick up the equipment from home, install a few choice pieces at Hermie's, and still make it to Amy's on time for supper.

She parked the Mustang in the four-car garage, an old barn that had formerly housed the shelling and packaging machines of the pecan business. Barney had sold the equipment, except for one sheller, when he started sending the pecans to a commercial packager, and now the barn housed a variety of vehicles Dixie found handy at times—a tow truck, a taxicab, a gray van. She'd purchased all three cheap, from owners who wouldn't be driving anytime soon.

Jogging to escape the cold, she entered the house through the utility room, caught a whiff of cooking aromas, and heard Mud's toenails tick across the kitchen floor. When she opened the door, he was eagerly waiting. She rubbed his ears.

"What a fine guard dog Mud is."

Mud licked her hand. Then he pranced to the stove and sat down beside Dann, who stood over a burner stirring a pan that emitted the delicious aroma. The man looked totally engrossed.

The homey scene stirred a slew of emotions in Dixie. This kitchen needed someone who enjoyed filling it with the bubble and sizzle of food preparation. It was designed for that. After Kathleen's death, Barney had lost heart for anything more complicated than scrambled eggs, and Dixie's efforts had been dismal. She fell into the habit of stopping for carryout every evening. There was something comforting about coming home now to the aroma of good food cooking.

On the other hand, she'd never enjoyed a domestic moment with any man her own age. Not that she was a stranger to long weekends, sleepovers, breakfast in bed—but such occasions had a defined purpose in the dating-mating-copulating game. This situation was emphatically different. Did any of her books on law enforcement define appropriate behaviors for jailors and prisoners?

"You're early. Dinner won't be ready for an hour." Dann toasted her with the spoon. "My specialty, Chicken Piccata."

"Hmmm. Interesting choice." How could he know she'd had it for lunch? "But I'm expected at my sister's for dinner."

"Oh."

The spoon sagged in his hand. He looked so disconcerted she wondered if he hoped to win her allegiance with food. Not a bad gambit. She wasn't hungry, yet her taste buds were harkening.

A pasta pot bubbled on the back burner; a plate with three cooked chicken breasts sat on the counter. Dann looked at the stirring spoon, tasted it, and shrugged.

"Great sauce." He laid down the spoon, dipped a clean one, and held it out to her.

Mud bolted upright and bared his teeth. A growl rumbled deep in his throat. Dann jerked his hand back, spilling sauce on the stove top.

"It's okay, boy." As Mud relaxed, Dixie peered into the pan simmering on the stove. "What are those green specks?"

"Green specks? You mean the herbs? Here, try it." He scooped a fresh spoonful.

"I don't remember buying any herbs." She tasted the sauce, tentatively at first, then licked the spoon.

"We bought the parsley," Dann said. "But I found tarragon and chives in your garden."

Dixie stopped licking. "Those weeds out there? How do you know they're edible?"

"Relax, I'm not going to poison you. See?" He took another sip. "Actually, you'd have a nice selection of herbs and vegetables if they hadn't been neglected."

"You mean I could've been throwing those weeds on my chicken all this time and it would taste like this?"

"Sure. Of course, you also have a castor bean plant. Eat that and you're dead. The narcissus, too. Easy to mistake the bulbs for green onions." He picked up a knife and began slicing a chicken breast, his fingers quick and precise. "I noticed the bulbs need dividing."

Dixie tasted the sauce again. "How do you know what to put in?" Did everybody in the world besides her know how to cook?

"A recipe helps, but mostly I experiment with flavors I

like—celery seed with green beans, marjoram with carrots, dill or rosemary with chicken."

"Maybe if I pour some herbs on my steak it won't taste like boiled chip board."

Dann made a funny sound in his throat. Dixie wasn't sure whether he was laughing or choking.

"A *touch* of herbs," he said, "adds flavor. Toughness usually comes from overcooking. How long do you broil it?"

"Broil? I fry it till it's good and dead, then throw in some flour and milk to make gravy."

Dann winced. "Keep the pantry filled while I'm here, and I'll make sure you eat well. Gives me something to do. Otherwise, the only difference between here and jail is the company's better."

Dixie finished the bite of chicken and took another small piece. "Mud, I think that compliment was meant for you."

Mud's ears pricked up. He gave a soft bark. Dann chose the largest chicken slice and held it for the dog to eat.

"Hey, don't feed him that—"

But Mud already had his teeth in it.

"Piccata makes lousy leftovers," Dann explained lamely.

"Just what I need, a mutt with a gourmet appetite."

"That whole chicken breast probably didn't cost any more than his dog food. Look how he's enjoying it."

"Of course he's *enjoying* it. It's damn good." In fact, her untrained palate found it better than what she'd eaten earlier at the famed Garden Cafe.

"So," Dann said. "Going to fill me in on your day?"

Dixie licked her fingers and headed for the hall closet where she kept supplies.

"Not much to tell."

He followed her, Mud padding alongside. After a moment of silence, while Dixie unlocked the supplies closet, Dann cleared his throat.

"I know you're not obligated," he said. "Only I'm sitting here with my stomach in knots wondering when the firing squad's going to show up."

Dixie opened the closet door. She could think of no reason

to keep Dann uninformed. He'd be less antsy if he thought they were gaining ground.

"I talked to Homicide about getting a look at the police report." Quickly assessing the closet's contents, she selected a UHF transmitter, about the size of a cigarette pack, and a receiver. Between the two, she could listen to sounds and conversations in Valdez's home from as far away as a mile. "The investigating officers didn't find any evidence your car was stolen, but that doesn't rule it out. They did note your claim of a spare key hidden under the frame and the fact that no key was found."

She painted in the details of her day, making it sound more fruitful than it really was, relating her meetings with the Paynes and her phone call to Ellie's real father, Jonathan Keyes.

"Tomorrow I'll stop by Keyes' office."

"If he's a reputable businessman, an architect, what makes you think he's involved in car theft?"

"I don't." Dixie invariably found it easier to do a thing than talk about it. Explaining her abstract method of reasoning out a problem had never come easy, even as an ADA working with an investigative team. But Dann's question deserved answering. While she considered it, Dixie selected a telephone tap and digitizer, for transmitting phone conversations to a recorder outside the Valdez house. She packed the equipment into a battered metal toolbox with shock-resistant foam padding.

On a shelf beside the toolbox sat her camera.

"Ever take any travel photos?" One of her law professors had told her that every complicated idea could be explained with a simple analogy.

"Snapshots," Dann said, shrugging it off. "Can't say I've ever done anything as good as that Yucatán shot in your album."

Dixie stiffened. "You looked through my scrapbooks?"

He blinked, his mouth tightening. "I didn't see a KEEP OUT sign."

"And I didn't realize I'd have to mark 'hands off' on all my personal belongings."

"Okay, so I had an acute case of indiscretion." His voice was low and measured. "There's not a hell of a lot to do around this place."

"Tomorrow I'll buy some fence stain. You'll have plenty to do."

"Fine."

Mud, sensing the discord, nosed between them.

Dixie glanced past Dann to the kitchen, which he'd obviously cleaned and polished before cooking the dinner she refused to eat. She knew he was cozying up, hoping she'd start trusting him and let down her guard. But, hell, there was nothing secret in the house: nothing dangerous, except ammunition, which she kept in a locked cabinet, and guns, which she carried with her. And her badass-bitch routine didn't play comfortably in her own home. A long breath seeped out between her teeth.

"Sorry," she said. "Being a recluse breeds suspicion. I'm not used to having visitors." She turned back to the shelves, added a VHF beeper for Valdez's car and a canister of CS tear gas to the other equipment in the toolbox. She could feel Dann watching her.

"What're you going to do with all that?"

"A side job, in payment for looking at the Keyes file." Most of the stuff she wouldn't need. Like the shiv in her boot, it was merely insurance. She started to shut the closet, then saw the Pentax and realized she'd never finished answering Dann's question about why she wanted to talk to Jonathan Keyes. She picked up the camera.

"When I travel, I like to capture the sense of a place in six or eight shots . . . buildings, boats, cars, parks and beaches where people gather, close-ups of local people *doing* things, items that represent the culture—food, jewelry, clothing, whatever makes the area unique. When I'm finished, I know the place I'm visiting as well as my own yard. The photographs paint the entire experience." Dixie set the camera back on the shelf. "I approach an investigation the same way, which is what I was doing this morning. Trying to capture a true picture of Betsy Keyes and what happened the day she died. Jonathan Keyes is part of the picture. I need to know where he fits in." Dixie locked the closet and moved into the den.

"Makes sense, I guess."

She triggered a hidden electronic lock and opened a spring-mounted bookcase to reveal a row of narrow shelves. One shelf held stacks of gun shells. She removed a box of .45s for the semiautomatic and a box of double-aught buckshot for the combat shotgun.

She felt Dann's interest perk right up at the sight of the ammunition. Not much use to him without guns, even if he managed to break the electronic code—unless he was as handy at making bombs as he was at making Chicken Piccata. With a mental shrug, Dixie relocked the cabinet. Trust was a useful measuring tool at times, but she'd remember to check later for tampering.

In the kitchen, she took a photographer's vest from the coat closet. The vest's custom lining would stop a 270-grain shell from a .357 Magnum. Several of the vest's fourteen pockets contained items she occasionally found useful—sandwich bags, tape, putty, wire, a glass cutter, a Lock-Aid tool for instantly opening any lock except high security, a pair of binoculars.

Dann held a pocket flap open while she inserted the cartridges.

"This side job looks serious," he commented quietly. "Should I be worried about you?"

"Worried?" She looked up.

The top of her hair brushed his chin, and she found him studying her, eyes hooded and dark. A weighted silence hung between them. Dixie wasn't used to having anyone worry about her. Except Amy.

Dann swallowed, as if his mouth had gone suddenly dry. She noticed a web of laugh lines that framed his eyes and thought he must laugh a lot during less stressful times. She knew she should look away, but the concern that filled his gaze was very real. It was also strangely gratifying.

Kidnap victims often developed an emotional attachment to their captors, she'd read. Complete dependency on a person for food, shelter, human companionship, and approval created false endearment. Was that happening here? And if so, why was she feeling it, too?

An invisible cord seemed to draw them closer.

"What if something happens to you?" Dann said softly.

His voice had the rich sensuousness of dark velvet. She'd noticed it before; now it enveloped her like a plush, warm cloak. She liked the sound.

She also liked the strong line of his chin. And the way his brown hair waved over his ears.

Her chest felt suddenly tight, her breathing shallow. She zipped and unzipped a pocket flap. A strand of hair fell across her cheek.

He reached for it—

Mud's jaws snapped over Dann's wrist with the speed of a viper.

Chapter Thirty

Be just his luck, Parker thought, Flannigan getting herself killed. Mud holding him prisoner out here in the boonies till they both starved to death. Parker's arm still twitched when he thought about the damage Mud's teeth could've done.

He ran hot water over pans and liquid soap in the bottom of the sink.

The dog was dedicated to Flannigan, no argument there. Maybe it was just plain dumb, thinking he could win the dog over and waltz out the gate. Likely get himself chewed to a bloody pulp. Mud, all grins and wags till you made a move toward his master. Must play hell with Flannigan's love life.

Flannigan's love life—now why did that thought give him a start? Everybody had lovers. Woman her age, her looks. He tried to picture the kind of man she'd fall for. Lawyer type, probably. Or cop. Maybe that homicide cop who'd given her information on Parker's case. Traded information, Flannigan said. She does a side job, cop gives her a peek at the file. What kind of boyfriend would put a woman in danger? What the hell kind of a job, anyway, required a whole box of bullets and those electronic gadgets? Were they even legal?

Bounty hunters were known to straddle legalities when it suited them. Be worth a chuckle, discovering Flannigan fenced stolen art or ran a smuggling ring on the side. See her get busted. Some eager young cop locking Flannigan in handcuffs, throwing her in the slammer.

Jail was a bleak damn place. Wouldn't wish that on anybody.

He loaded the dishwasher, then picked up the piccata pan from the floor, where Mud had licked it clean.

"And you!" Mud sat up, his ears twitched straight ahead. "Some friend you turned out to be. Could've broken my arm, grabbing it like that. I wasn't going to hurt her. I was just thinking—"

Hell, what *had* he been thinking? Turn on the charm, get her feeling all mushy, maybe talk her into letting him go? He'd bet Flannigan'd never been mushy about a guy in her whole damn life, even as a scrawny teenager.

He appreciated her poking around for some evidence to clear him. Parker didn't read her as a do-gooder, either, just a helluva strong woman with a passion to see justice win out. "The first thing we do," Shakespeare wrote, "let's kill all the lawyers." Good idea, but maybe he'd have made an exception with Flannigan.

Halfway through his trial, Parker had lost faith in justice. Which was why he'd skipped, why he was even now working on a backup plan.

What happened earlier, though, with Flannigan, wasn't part of any plan. Her standing there, all soft curves and perfect face, not much more than a handful but with her tough-bitch veneer. Parker wondered what she'd have done if he kissed her. He looked down at Mud.

"Some friend."

The dog yawned and gave Parker his "Who, me?" look.

Scrubbing a spot of burned crust on the broiler pan, Parker recalled watching Flannigan drive away in the gray van. The guns worried him. Useless, though, worrying about something you couldn't fix.

Pans. He could fix pans. And food. Cooking took his mind off the shit he could do nothing about. Like an artist with a painting, get your mind wrapped around creating a meal, then sit down and eat it—double the pleasure. Better yet, share the meal with somebody. Couldn't eat a painting.

He'd had a chuckle looking at Flannigan's scrapbooks. Pictures of her growing up, her older sister, Amy, and the old folks. Nice life. Sometimes he wondered why he'd never settled down. Pretty wife, big shady yard, maybe a kid or two. A dog like Mud.

Crazy name for a dog, but there it was, right on his tag: MEAN UGLY DOG. MUD in parentheses. Flannigan had a sense of humor. Parker hadn't seen much of it, but it was there. Her mother must've had one, too, naming a daughter Desiree Alexandra. Found that in one of the albums, a spelling bee award from school. No damn wonder she called herself Dixie, with such a girly name to live down. Desiree Alexandra. Sounded like something from *Gone With the Wind*.

Parker stacked the clean pots and emptied the sink. Be dark soon. He hoped Flannigan wasn't getting herself into something dangerous.

He opened the pantry and took out the red Frisbee.

"Come on, Mud. Let's see how close I can get to the barn, and the cars inside the barn, before you turn mean."

Chapter Thirty-one

The Valdez house, faded yellow with black shutters, sat close to the street, flower beds overgrown with weeds, yellowed newspapers piled on the porch, oil stains spotting the cracked concrete driveway. Hermie Valdez's twelve-year-old Toyota was parked in the open garage. There was no other car in sight.

Dixie cruised past, looking for obvious signs of occupancy. Before leaving home she'd called Rashly. Hermie hadn't yet been released, so the house should be empty.

In its heyday, the early seventies, the southwest neighborhood had rocked with disco parties every night, swinging singles riding the fast track to corporate management. Now it was being ethnicized by Hispanics, Asian-Americans, African-Americans, and East Indians, with and without green cards, with and without drug and alcohol habits. On early mornings, men lined the street, waiting for the day labor truck to drive by, wondering if they'd be selected for work.

In place of the Mustang—a former police car that would likely attract attention in this neighborhood—Dixie was driving the gray van. It now sported a magnetic sign that said DOVER PLUMBING. She backed into the driveway behind the Toyota, parking nose out, then climbed down lazily from the cab. As she opened the truck's side panel to get her "plumber's" tools, she scanned the neighboring yards.

The van blocked the view from the street. Hermie's house stood between Dixie and the neighbors on the west. The house on the east side appeared dead empty. But Dixie felt someone's eyes on her. She hoped her blue overall with the Dover name patch looked convincing. Beneath it she wore the bulletproof vest and her sister-visiting clothes; she looked thirty pounds heavier. Fortunately, it was a cold night.

From the battered toolbox, she slid the Lock-Aid tool into her pocket and palmed the directional beeper, slapping the back of it with putty. She picked up the toolbox, closed the truck, and strode purposefully to the back door of the house. With luck she could be in and out in less time than a plumber could replace a faucet washer. Passing the Toyota, she slipped the beeper into the curved lip of the tire well.

She knocked on the door. After a moment, she opened the screen door and knocked again, louder. When still no answer came, for which Dixie was entirely grateful, she pressed the Lock-Aid against the dead bolt, pulled the trigger, and listened until the bolt magically clicked back.

"Plumber, ma'am," she called, as if someone had asked. She eased the door open. "Here to fix the leak."

Inside, with the door closed behind her, she flipped the light switch and scanned the kitchen. A cockroach scurried across the table, apparently startled from feasting on a partially eaten TV dinner. Next to the leftover meal was a bakery pumpkin pie and a new one-pound can of Folgers coffee. Despite the room's coolness, the pie was moldy.

Dixie strode through the house with her penlight to make sure no one was sleeping in a back room. It occurred to her that Sikes might be staying right here. Stupid, but possible. The .45 nestled in a holster under the overall, not particularly accessible; but a hell of a big plumber's wrench was tucked in her hip pocket. Her search revealed four empty rooms, with nothing more menacing than another Texas cockroach. Yet the feeling persisted that someone was watching.

Finding a wall phone in the kitchen and a Princess model

in the bedroom, she made sure they rang on the same line, then proceeded to install the tap.

The front doorbell buzzed.

Dixie froze, telephone wires dangling from her hand. A minute later, another buzz, followed by an impatient knock.

"Hermie! You in there, girl?" A woman's voice.

Dixie pocketed the phone tap. Hefting the plumber's wrench, she turned on the porch light, then opened the front door.

The woman outside stood about five feet tall, shorter even than Dixie, and wore an animal-print jumpsuit. She was plump, pretty, thirtyish, and curious as hell.

"Who're you? Where's Hermie?"

"Plumber, ma'am. Nobody's here but me."

"Well. How'd you get in if ain't nobody here?"

"Landlord sent me over to fix a leak. One leaky faucet can make a whopping difference in a water bill." Dixie drawled each word like pouring molasses.

"Ain't it just like that tight bastard to worry about a water bill when Hermie's been needing a new heater ever since winter broke? Anyway, I was hoping Hermie was home." The woman tried to look past Dixie, into the living room. "Listen, maybe I should come on in while you work. You know, a witness in case anything goes missing from the house?"

"I'm bonded, ma'am. Afraid I can't let you in, though. Shouldn't have opened the door, but you looked like an observant neighbor who might be worried about Ms. Valdez's property. Wanted to set your mind at ease, so to speak."

"Oh, well . . . thank you. Guess I do try to look out for my neighbors when they're not at home."

"Don't suppose you saw anyone else prowling around this house, did you? Landlord's concerned about burglars. Word gets around when a house sits empty."

"Hermie's coming home soon, ain't she?"

"Don't know anything about that, ma'am. You see anyone lurking around the property here?"

"Nobody but Hermie's no-good boyfriend, Alton Sikes.

Saw him slinking across the backyard last night. Don't know what she sees in that good-for-nothing."

"What was he doing in the backyard, do you think?"

"Lord knows. Looking for Hermie, I guess."

"You see where he went?"

"Why you so interested in Alton Sikes?"

"Sikes is not a resident here. The landlord would be upset to find him living on the premises while Ms. Valdez is away."

"Well, no, I don't think Alton's staying here. I'd've seen him coming and going, my house being right next door."

"You have any idea where Mr. Sikes lives?"

"On the street, you ask me. Hasn't got a pot to piss in."

"You'd think Ms. Valdez'd worry, him living on the street."

"Listen, Hermie'd do anything for that man, but she ain't stupid. Alton's a junkie. If he had a key to this house, he'd hock everything Hermie owned, and be as gone as a bee-stung cat. Wouldn't be no good to her then, if you catch my drift. She only lets him stay over when she's here to watch her things." The woman paused, and a secretive smile tugged at her lips. "Anyhow, I hear the cops want Alton again. Maybe he's back in jail, where he belongs."

Dixie gently coaxed the woman into leaving, then finished the phone tap. She found a place in the hall where a UHF transmitter would pick up sounds from any of the four rooms. Later, after the transmitter did its job, she'd have to come back and retrieve it. Otherwise, she was out eight hundred bucks.

Before driving to Amy's, Dixie stepped into the back of the van to shed her overall and vest. She unstrapped the .45, placed it in a compartment marked "sump pump," and straightened her tan sweatshirt. Climbing back into the driver's seat, she fluffed her hair, applied lipstick, grimaced, and wiped it off again. She felt as ready as she'd ever be for a visit with her sister's family.

Fog drifted across the road, diffusing Dixie's headlights. She exited the freeway, turned toward the inner-loop community of West University, and parked on the street in front of Amy and Carl's spacious home. Their gaslight boasted a hand-painted sign that said THE ROYALS. She refluffed her hair in the rearview mirror, thought again about applying lipstick, decided the hell with it, and hurried up the walk.

Amy was all smiles, warm cushiony hugs, and White Diamonds perfume. Dixie was surprised not to see Ryan bounding ahead of her.

"Ryan has the flu," Amy explained, tucking the tag on Dixie's sweatshirt out of sight as she steered her toward the dining room. "Started coughing this afternoon, and now he's in bed with a fever."

"Have you called the doctor? Does he need anything, some aspirin or something?"

"The doctor sent a prescription, and Ryan's comfortable. That's about all we can do."

"Well, darn." Dixie thought of Ellie Keyes, her chapped nose and queasy tummy. Kids seemed so pitiful when they were ill. Dixie felt helpless around them. The flu wasn't an enemy you could drag away in handcuffs. "How long will he be sick?"

"Until it runs its course. The doctor said it's rather virulent, especially with the bronchitis. The medicine will help a lot, and of course the usual, plenty of rest, plenty of fluids."

"Then it's not really serious." She knew Ryan would hate being bedridden.

Amy hesitated, a frown puckering her brow.

"It *is* a serious flu strain. There've been three deaths reported, from dehydration and pneumonia, but, Dixie, two of those were street people without anyone to care for them, and the third was an elderly woman."

"People don't *die* from the *flu*."

"Now, don't worry about Ryan. We caught it early. He has the best of care. He'll be fine."

Dixie insisted on peeking in on her nephew. Sleeping, he looked thin and vulnerable, his blond hair tousled, his cheeks pink with fever. Dixie shook the prescription bottle; Amoxil, same as Ellie's. Enough fat pink tablets to make him well, she hoped. Plenty of tissues. A full water pitcher. She had to grin when she saw the Cessna controls beside his water glass. The plane sat in the middle of the floor, where he'd apparently been taxiing it back and forth. As soon as he was well enough to go outside, she'd take him flying.

At dinner, Dixie put everything but family out of her mind, soaked up every warm, fuzzy feeling they threw at her, and even managed to avoid arguing with Carl. The food was not as good as Dann's Piccata, but far better than carryout. They opened gifts—ballet tickets for Amy, Rockets tickets for Carl. Her gift from Ryan was a stuffed talking bear, and from Carl and Amy a yellow silk pants suit.

"Since you quit working downtown, you never dress up," Amy explained. "Yellow is great on you."

When Dixie finally made going-home noises, Amy tried to talk her into staying over.

"Ryan will be awake in the morning, probably feeling well enough to stay up awhile. Dixie, we see so little of you these days."

"You mean since I'm not on TV every other week explaining to the press why we let another burglar/killer/rapist go free."

"You could do so well in your own practice," Amy said, bringing up a recurring argument. "I don't understand why you won't consider it."

"If you're tired of criminal law," Carl put in, "you could specialize in business law or civil litigation. What I'm saying, I know people who'd put up money to get you started."

Dixie didn't want to explain once again why business law bored the hell out of her and most civil suits were a blight on the system.

"Maybe someday." Waving that glimmer of hope usually placated them both.

"You will stay over, won't you?" Amy coaxed, when Carl picked up the TV remote.

Dixie thought she'd skirted that suggestion. She didn't want to mention having to work. Amy would want details, which she couldn't provide, and would worry all night, details or not.

"Amy, you know how much I wanted to see Ryan, but I didn't leave any food or water out for Mud, and I've been gone most of the day." No lies in that statement, and Amy liked Mud.

"Well, give Ryan a call in the morning. He'll be disappointed he missed you."

When Dixie looked in on her nephew one last time before leaving, the high color had faded from his cheeks. The boy looked pale and sweaty, but he was sleeping soundly, despite the stuffy nose and occasional cough. She kissed him, smoothed his silky, tangled hair, and left feeling totally useless.

The Valdez house stood dark and silent when Dixie cruised past, no sounds transmitting from inside, Toyota parked in the same spot. She checked the phone tap: nothing. Either Rashly hadn't released Valdez yet or the woman hadn't gone straight home. Dixie had hoped to finish the job tonight, finger Sikes and be done with it. Instead, she'd have to stay on hold until she heard from Rash.

Her stop at the Green Hornet Saloon fared no better. Augie was still out sick. Dixie didn't see anyone with a butterfly tattoo. She left the bar without finishing her beer.

At home, she parked the van in the barn alongside the Mustang. The outdoor floodlights brightened the porch and yard under the old oaks. Parker Dann sat in the antique rocking chair that had belonged to Barney, throwing a red Frisbee so Mud could lumber happily after it and bring it back.

Dixie's steps slowed as she approached the porch, listening to the familiar creak of the rocker, watching the red disk sail through the night sky and Mud's joyful leap to catch it. A curl of smoke rising from the chimney carried the smell of roasted pecan shells. Another homey scene, which gave Dixie another peculiar feeling.

Recalling the awkward moment in the kitchen earlier, she

felt a surge of expectation, and paused to collect herself. She was no stranger to physical attraction. Her longest, most comfortable relationship had been with a saxophone player, a real "stud muffin," according to both Belle and Amy. When his big break came, Dixie and the sax player had said good-bye with the same ease they'd felt dating each other. She was happy in her independence, and she certainly didn't need the complication of falling for a man who might be headed for prison. Nor could she afford to lose her objectivity. Dann was still a suspect in Betsy's death.

By the time she walked into the light, he stood lounging against the porch support. He had shaved and changed clothes. Instead of a jacket, he wore two shirts, blue plaid flannel over a blue chambray work shirt. His hair spilled rakishly forward, as if he'd been running a hand through it.

She couldn't deny a flash of tenderness when she drew close enough to see the worry in his eyes, nor a ripple of lust that made her mouth go suddenly dry. Her gaze fell to the sensual curve of his lips, the broad chest, the hard line of his freshly laundered jeans. She wiped her damp palms across the seat of her own jeans. She couldn't deny the feelings, maybe, but she could damn well resist them.

Mud trotted down the walk to nuzzle her hand, then padded quickly back to Dann's side. Where he belonged, she reminded herself. Where she'd told him he better by-god stay.

He kept glancing up, as if taking a cue from Dann on how to act. The cussed dog was forgetting who rescued him from mongrel heaven and raised him from a stumble-footed pup nobody would look at twice. She wanted to smack him on the nose. On the other hand, anybody Mud liked couldn't be all bad.

"You're home, then," Dann said as she climbed the steps. "Is it over?"

An electric drill and bit case lay on the porch.

"Where did that come from?" Dixie said.

"Found the tools going to rust in the utility room. Thought I'd fix that wobbly porch rail, but . . ." He shrugged.

Dixie saw the toolbox and an oily rag he'd used to clean the bits. The stripped-out hole had been filled with wood putty, and a new screw gleamed in the porch light. But the rail felt just as wobbly when she pushed against it.

"Tomorrow, I'll replace the strut and look around for some touch-up paint." He scooped the drill and bits into the tool-box.

Dixie didn't think replacing the strut would help, but at least it'd keep him busy and out of trouble. When she opened the door, the smell of apples and cinnamon drifted on warm air.

"You baked, too?"

"Just a pie." He carried the tools to the utility room and took her overalls and vest to hang in the kitchen closet. She saw him glance in the pocket where they'd tucked the ammunition.

"No, I didn't have to shoot anybody tonight," Dixie said.

He looked at her. "Sorry. Where I'm from, taking a gun out means you expect to use it. Hunting deer, elk, moose. Never people." He hung up the vest and shut the closet door. "Ever shot anybody?"

"No. That coffee looks good."

The dripolator gurgled and sputtered. Dann must have started it brewing the instant her headlights hit the gate.

He filled two mugs, then splashed a few ounces in the bottom of a cereal bowl, cut it with water, and put it down for Mud.

"You're giving him coffee?" Dixie said.

"A little won't hurt him. Who else am I supposed to drink with when you're not here?" He set two slabs of pie on the table. "Hope you didn't have dessert."

Actually, she had. Fruitcake off the grocery-store shelf, which she'd nibbled to be polite.

"You made this from those apples we bought?"

"I only know one recipe for apple pie that's *not* made from apples, and it tastes like soggy crackers."

"A frozen pie would've been easier."

"You haven't even tasted it yet."

She took a bite. "It's great." She had never grasped how anyone could start with a sack of flour and a few apples and end up with something edible. "Tastes like you've had more practice cooking than fixing porch rails."

He grinned, cut another pie sliver, and placed it in Mud's bowl.

"When I was about eight, I got a notion to drive my dad's tractor." He unbuttoned the cuffs of the flannel shirt, releasing the strain across his broad shoulders. "Mason, my older brother, had been driving it three years already. Pop says, 'Okay, Mase, take Parker out in the field and teach him.' We hadn't been in the field ten minutes before we started fighting over that tractor seat. Mason wanted to lord it over me. I was bratty enough to figure I knew everything. In the heat of battle, I ended up under the tractor."

That must be how he got the limp. Dixie had noticed it only on a few occasions, most significantly after the long drive to Houston.

"I was housebound for six months. Soon as I could hobble, Ma put me to work in the kitchen." He shrugged it off. "Guess you don't forget the basics."

Dixie carefully mashed the last few crumbs onto her fork and licked them off. Tasted a hell of a lot better than basic.

"So," Dann said, carrying their plates to the sink. "Tomorrow you see Jonathan Keyes. Then what?" He peeled off the flannel overshirt, tossed it on a chair back, and rolled up his sleeves to rinse the dishes.

Dixie liked the way the dark hair on his arms curled against the light blue chambray. She flashed on that first morning in North Dakota, that same dark hair curling across his bare chest. She looked down at her coffee.

"First I'll try to get a look at the police file. Then maybe I'll talk to the camp counselor who was on duty when Courtney drowned."

There was a moment of heavy silence.

"Think the deaths are connected?"

The flannel shirt slid to the floor. Dixie picked it up.

"Possibly. I try to avoid making assumptions, until the whole picture shapes up."

The soft flannel felt warm from his body heat and smelled faintly of bay rum. She liked bay rum. She draped the shirt over the chair back, smoothed the sleeves, smoothed the collar, her fingers lingering over the warmly scented fabric.

Chapter Thirty-two

Jonathan Keyes' office occupied one small corner in a black trapezoidal building in the Greenway Plaza business complex. Framed architectural sketches of skyscrapers and sprawling retail centers adorned the reception area. Dixie recognized several Houston buildings.

She also recognized the red bows and gold balls that nestled in a pine bough on the desk. Some designer in town was making a killing this year on decorations imprinted with computer chips. The elaborate spray almost obscured a tiny woman who sat at the privacy desk reading a romance novel. Dixie read the nameplate, SHERI MCLAUGHTER, and squashed a bow to peek at her.

"Cheers, Sheri!"

Snapping the book shut, the woman smiled brightly.

"Id's dso quiet here during the holidays," she said, her voice nasal from the head cold. "Even the delephones stop ringing. If I couldn't read, I'd go dnuts."

Dixie smiled to put her at ease. Anyone chained to a desk all day needed all the distractions she could muster.

"Sheri, I'm here to see Mr. Keyes—without an appointment, I'm afraid." She handed the receptionist her card.

"You're lucky." The woman blew her nose, clearing her

head as well as her speech. "He's one of the few people in the office this week. Nearly everyone took vacation days." She punched a number on the telephone console and listened a moment. "There's a D.A. Dixie Flannigan to see you, Jon. No appointment, but would you have time?" A pause, then to Dixie, "His office is third on the left." Waving Dixie toward a door, she went back to her novel.

Photographs of completed buildings dotted the hallway. The shots had been taken from a helicopter, Dixie figured, or some other high vantage point.

In Keyes' office, however, the paintings were abstract swashes of color, vivid purples and blues. Dixie looked for a building hidden among the brush strokes, but if one was there, she wasn't astute enough to find it. A teakwood desk faced the door. Behind it, broad windows offered an expansive view of downtown.

Keyes was working at a drafting table, jacket off, tie loosened, shirt cuffs turned up exactly twice. He was thin, about thirty-five, with short brown hair and big ears.

"Sit down, Ms. Flannigan," he said, without looking up. He made angular lines on a large drawing, using a ruling device attached to a free-swinging mechanical arm at one corner of the table, moving it along in precise increments. "I'll be a minute finishing up here . . . I assume you've come about the job."

Dixie sat in a guest chair upholstered in blue tweed.

"Actually, I have a few questions, Mr. Keyes. About your stepdaughters."

He looked up, pencil poised above the drawing. "Betsy and Courtney? What about them?"

"I can wait for you to finish. I'm doing some work for Belle Richards, tying up loose ends."

"Richards . . . *Richards?!* That's the woman who's defending the drunk that killed Betsy." He snapped the pencil down in a tray at the front of the table and moved the ruling device off the drawing.

"The man who *allegedly* killed Betsy. The charge hasn't been proven."

"And you're trying to dig up some nonsense to get the bastard off."

This was what she'd saved herself by not questioning the Paynes, Dixie thought.

"Mr. Keyes, if Parker Dann killed your stepdaughter, he'll go to jail. But if someone else was driving his car, then Dann's innocent and deserves to have the guilty person brought to justice, wouldn't you agree?"

Glaring silently, Keyes rose to stand across from her at the desk. The silence stretched.

He folded his arms.

"What do you want to know?" His shirtsleeves had inched higher, exposing a tattoo on his left forearm.

"On April thirtieth, the night before Betsy's accident . . ." Dixie took a moment making out the tattoo design—a butterfly with a human head. Keyes' name was Jonathan—Jon? A string of mental dominoes chinked into place. The description Dann had given her, six-foot-two, lanky, fit Jonathan Keyes like frost on a beer mug. She changed the gist of her question. ". . . you were in the Green Hornet. Is that true?"

Keyes pulled the desk chair out, sat down, and studied her with another long silence.

"The Green Hornet," she continued, "is a bar about four blocks from the scene of the accid—"

"I know where it is. Why are you asking?"

"Someone described you, said you were drinking late that Thursday night."

"What does that prove?"

"It doesn't prove anything, Mr. Keyes, but it's information we didn't have before. Why didn't you mention it?"

"Nobody asked."

"That bar isn't exactly in your neighborhood, is it?"

"You *know* exactly where it is. What you *want* to know is, why was I there."

"Why were you there, Mr. Keyes?"

He straightened the blotter pad, lining it up with the edge of the desk.

"I'd dropped the girls off at Rebecca's, and I was anxious about a meeting the next day. I stopped for a beer."

"That was a Thursday night. Was it usual for you to have the girls on a school night?"

"No . . . but it wasn't *un*usual. I get them the first and third weekends, plus alternate holidays. Easter weekend threw us off, then Rebecca had something planned for the following Wednesday, so I picked them up on the twenty-fifth, agreed to keep them all week, nine days, actually, since the following weekend was mine. Then we'd be back on schedule."

Dixie opened her wallet to a dog-eared calendar sent by her insurance agent every year. Time for a new one.

"You planned to take the girls back on May third, the following Sunday?"

"That's right, Sunday." He picked up a ballpoint pen from the desk and stared down at it. "But one of the Austin accounts we'd been pitching wanted to meet on Friday, May first. I had to fly up there with some rough layouts."

Dixie wondered why he wouldn't meet her eyes.

"Do you stop by the Green Hornet every time you take the girls home?"

"*Every* time? Of course not. What are you trying to do, turn this around so that *I'm* the drunk who ran Betsy down? Ms. Flannigan, I was on a plane at nine o'clock that morning."

But Betsy was killed at seven-fifteen. Not impossible, Mr. Keyes. Not impossible at all, if you had a reason to kill your stepdaughter.

"How late were you at the Hornet that night?"

"Till closing." He clicked the ballpoint to the writing position.

"Where did you go afterward?"

"Home. To bed." *Click, click.*

"With an early flight, it's surprising you stayed so late."

"Usually, I wouldn't, but I got to talking to someone—a salesman. He gave me some tips on how to pitch my account the next day—talked about selling fishing trips in the Caribbean, but I could see where the same techniques would work for me. Sales is not my strong suit, not what I usually . . . *godammit!*" He slammed the pen down on the desk. "That was Dann, wasn't it?"

"You didn't recognize him when you saw him in court?"

"I never went to court."

"The newspapers, then."

"I didn't recognize the bastard, okay? Probably saw his picture, if it was in the paper, but I'd had a lot on my mind . . . that new account to worry about, Betsy's death . . . maybe it wouldn't have happened if I hadn't taken the girls home three days early." *Click, click. Click, click.* "The cops did a good job catching the bastard as fast as they did. I don't care what he looks like, only that he's behind bars for the rest of his life."

The pen still clicking, he glanced at a Sierra Club calendar with days marked off in orange.

"Mr. Keyes, your other stepdaughter, Courtney, also suffered a fatal accident earlier this year."

Keyes turned to look at her slowly. A quizzical frown wrinkled his brow. "What's Courtney got to do with this?"

"Doesn't it seem a bit . . . *strange* . . . two fatal accidents only three months apart?"

He hesitated, then, "I don't see where you're going."

Dixie's pulse hammered wildly. This was the break she'd been searching for, if she could figure out what to do with it. Keyes was nervous about something . . . but why would he risk setting Dann up for hit-and-run after spending so much time talking with him in public? On the other hand, real killers were rarely as smart as the ones in mystery novels.

"Where were you the day of Courtney's swimming accident?"

"On my way to Austin again. Driving, since I planned to stay there several days. What the hell are you implying?"

"I'm not implying anything. Just trying to see how it all ties together."

"It doesn't *tie together.* Betsy was killed by a drunk driver. Courtney . . ." He looked away again. *Click, click. Click, click.* "I taught those girls to swim, and they were good. Too good for some freak accident like that to happen. Those camp counselors were negligent."

"What exactly did happen?"

He shook his head, as if baffled. "All anybody could determine was that she must have tangled herself in the vegetation growing near the bank, maybe cramped up and couldn't pull free."

"When did you hear about the accident?"

A muscle in his jaw jumped.

"When I returned from Austin. Rebecca had left a message on my answering machine. She knew where I was, godammit? She had both numbers. If her child-support payment hadn't shown up on time, she would have tracked me to the North Pole, but to tell me my daughter was—" He glared at Dixie, his eyes moist. "I returned in time for the funeral. Just."

Dixie wasn't sure what to make of him. He was either extremely distraught or a hell of a good actor.

"You said daughter, not stepdaughter."

He brushed a thumb under his nose, then snatched a tissue from a box beside his drafting table.

"I adopted the girls when I married Rebecca. Courtney was a year old, Betsy three. We were married five years, and I raised them as my own, loved them every bit as much as I love Ellie. In fact, Rebecca and I would've divorced long before we did if it weren't for the kids."

"Did you pay child support for all three girls?"

"Of course. Until the accidents."

Would a man resent paying child support for children not his own by birth? Maybe. Especially after his ex-wife remarried.

"Did their new stepfather ever suggest he would like to adopt Betsy and Courtney?"

"I'd have fought Travis on it if he tried."

"You sued Rebecca for custody of all three girls during the divorce, is that right?"

His eyes sparked. "Maybe Betsy and Courtney would still be alive if the judge had ruled in my favor."

"What do you mean by that?"

"I mean Rebecca—Oh, hell, I don't know what I mean. Nothing, I guess. It's just that Rebecca only fought me on it for spite. I don't believe she ever really wanted kids. She, well, when she got pregnant with Ellie, we'd been having problems. I was ready to file for divorce, but how could I when she was carrying my child? After Ellie was born, we actually got along better . . . for a while."

Something was going on here, something dark that Dixie couldn't quite get hold of. This man might be every bit as sensitive as he appeared. But maybe not.

"Did Rebecca ever mistreat the children?"

"Mistreat? You mean, like abuse them?" He shook his head. "No, she took good care of them. She never hit them or screamed at them or anything like that. At least, if she did, I didn't know about it. You can bet I'd have used it in court. Rebecca's just . . . indifferent, I guess."

"Indifferent." That was mild compared to what most divorced men said about their ex-wives. Mild for a man who'd fought his ex-wife fiercely for custody of her children by a former marriage.

"Did you think Rebecca was an unfit mother?"

"Listen, what I sued for was joint custody. I wanted a role in their lives, wanted to help them grow up, become young women. Rebecca doesn't have a lot of patience with kids. Don't get me wrong on this, she fulfills her motherly duties, feeds and cares for them, but she was never *pals* with the girls. I enjoyed taking them places, doing things together as a family. One reason for our divorce was Rebecca's jealousy when I paid what she considered too much attention to Betsy and Courtney. She'd send them to her mother or off to camp at every opportunity."

Pals? Dixie knew her own background was once again causing her hackles to rear up, and she had to resist letting her personal feelings distract her, but damnit all, even in her professional experience she'd seen too many men unnaturally attracted to children. Keyes would not be the first man to adopt his own private sex toy. And when abused children matured, they often became confident enough to speak out against their abusers. Maybe Keyes created "accidents" to keep his stepdaughters from talking.

Nothing in Belle's notes had mentioned sexual abuse, though, and Dixie hadn't seen the police file yet. She needed to keep an open mind concerning motive.

"With Betsy and Courtney dead, your child-support payments are considerably reduced."

Keyes' head snapped around. His face flushed.

"You meddling bitch! You really are trying to pin something on me. Get out. I wouldn't have told you a goddamn thing if I'd known what you were up to."

"Why did you talk to me, Mr. Keyes? You certainly weren't obligated to."

He stood up, stared at her silently for a moment, then calmly picked up the ballpoint pen and dropped it in his pocket.

"Why shouldn't I talk to you?" His voice was controlled now, deliberate. "There's not a chance in hell Parker Dann is going to walk. And Courtney's death? That was an accident. Case closed."

The *Houston Chronicle* Building was twenty minutes from Keyes' office. On the way, Dixie phoned Rashly from her car phone. She wanted his personal take on Jonathan Keyes, but Rash was out. A friend of Dixie's who worked in the newspaper's file room quickly found the article about the drowning death at Camp Cade. The two-inch blurb carried no new information.

Dixie's friend telephoned the *Conroe Courier,* Conroe being a substantial community only five miles from Camp Cade, and cajoled a file clerk into pulling the early August issue and reading the related article over the phone. After giving the camp location and describing the swim event that led to the drowning, the writer cited counselor Edith Frey as the person who found Courtney.

Courtney Keyes was known to be a good swimmer. Therefore, when the ten-year-old girl failed to appear at breakfast, and it was learned she had gone for an early swim, no
one was immediately alarmed. A bunk mate was dis-
patched to find the girl, however, and when she couldn't
be found, it became evident something was wrong. A
search party covered the area in and around the lake.
Counselor Edith Frey dove repeatedly for almost an hour.
Finally, she located the child's body entangled in vegetation growing near the bank.

The piece went on to mention the excellent rating the
camp maintained, stating that this was the first serious accident in nineteen years. Dixie took down the counselor's name
and called Conroe directory assistance for her telephone
number. A mellow woman's voice said, "Frey."

The one-word greeting was difficult to read. Dixie decided
to play it straight, more or less, as she had with Keyes.

"Ms. Frey, my name's Flannigan, and I'm doing some
background work for the law firm of Richards, Blackmon and
Drake. You were present at Camp Cade last August at the
time of the drowning death of Courtney Keyes. Were you
aware that Courtney's older sister was killed in a hit-and-run
accident only three months earlier?"

"Good Lord, no! I thought she had only the one sister, the
little five-year-old." Ellie was six now—must've had a birth-
day. The woman's gentle drawl brought visions of frosty mint
juleps, magnolia trees, and women with big skirts and frilly
white parasols.

"The newspaper account of Courtney's drowning," Dixie
said, "mentioned she was a good swimmer. Was she familiar
with the lake?"

"Heavens, yes. Courtney had been swimming in it every
day for two weeks."

"Would you tell me in your own words exactly what happened?"

Frey recounted the story much as the newspaper had, adding that Courtney had been hell-bent on showing her mother

she could beat the previous year's champion swimmer, and she'd had a good chance of doing it.

"As it turned out, though, her poor mother had to be called with a grim message that morning," Frey recalled.

"You told her over the *phone*?"

"Actually, no, but we tried," she admitted. "You see, parents are invited to spend the last day with us at Camp Cade. To watch the sporting events and have lunch. It's a big family day. We didn't want Courtney's mother walking in unaware of what had happened."

"When did she arrive?"

"We'd barely finished cleaning up after breakfast—though I suppose that took longer than usual. Apparently, the lady had gone to her restaurant before her staff arrived that morning to prepare enough food so she could take the day off. By the time we connected with someone at the restaurant, Mrs. Payne was already on her way to camp."

"How did she take it?"

"Oh, lordy. I was the one who had to tell her. At first, that poor lady insisted we were wrong, that Courtney was too good a swimmer, it had to be some other child. Finally, she let me drive her to the hospital."

"Ms. Frey, were you satisfied with the explanation of how the girl died?"

"What do you mean?"

Dixie hesitated. Sometimes her questions didn't make a lot of sense, even to her; they just seemed to need asking.

"If Courtney was familiar with the lake, and a good swimmer—?"

"Even the best swimmers can get a leg cramp. We caution the girls not to swim alone, but . . ." Frey sighed, the weight of a thousand "should've's" behind it.

"Ms. Frey, I appreciate your being frank with me. I know it can't be easy, going over all this again. I won't take any more of your time—"

"Wait, there's one other thing that's been bothering me. I didn't tell the police because I didn't find out until later, and it might have been nothing important. . . . Courtney told her bunk mate she'd seen someone prowling around camp that morning. The girl said Courtney left the cabin before sunup, following this . . . person."

"Did she describe the prowler?"

"No. The bunk mate thought Courtney was imagining the whole thing, but . . . I have to tell you, Courtney wasn't a child who spooked easily. She was a tough little girl."

An image came to Dixie of another tough little girl, spunky, even when sick with the flu. If the accidents that killed Courtney and Betsy were not truly accidents, if the girls were murdered, could spunky Ellie Keyes also be in danger?

Chapter Thirty-three

Ellie squirmed, trying to find a cool spot under the covers of the roller bed in Daddy Travis' storeroom. She didn't want the covers off, because then she felt shivery. The air squeezed under her jammies and made her teeth chatter.

Her foot tangled in the sheet. She kicked, trying to get it off. For a while she had slept, dreaming she was a princess, dressed in a white nightie and standing on the edge of a volcano, like in *Rings of Fire*, the museum movie she saw with Daddy Jon. There weren't any princesses in the movie, but there were volcanoes spitting fire and spewing hot oozy stuff. Somebody wanted Princess Ellie to jump in the fire, but she ran away instead and hid behind a rock.

The sheet was tangled more than ever, and now her other foot had slipped outside the covers.

If Daddy Jon were here, she would sit on his lap to hear a story. He'd make the voices funny and squiggle his fingers up her back in the scary parts. If it got really scary, like in "Jack and the Beanstalk" when the giant went, *"Fee fi foe fum! I'll grind his bones,"* Daddy Jon would tickle her till she wet her panties.

Ellie wriggled the foot that was outside the covers so her toes could breathe. When the cool air touched her foot, she didn't feel so hot. Only now she had to cough. Coughing made her throat hurt. Maybe a drink of water would keep her from coughing.

But her water glass was empty. She must have drunk all the water Mama brought.

She wondered what had happened to the box of candy Daddy Jon tucked in her Christmas stocking. She knew it was from him and not Santa, 'cause she'd seen the same wrapping paper in Daddy Jon's closet. Had she eaten it all before she got sick?

Daddy Travis had brought some cough drops, the cherry kind that didn't taste icky. Opening her eyes a sliver, Ellie pulled the cover back and felt around on the table until she found one of the cough drops. She didn't like to open her eyes wide, 'cause they burned. Anyway, her lashes were stuck together with something oogy. Fingers shaking, she unwrapped the cherry drop and sucked on it. Maybe now she wouldn't cough.

Oooo-ooh. But now she was cold, her teeth chattery, from having her arms outside the covers. It made her bones hurt.

She kicked at the tangled sheet and wished Courtney were here. Courtney would make things better.

Ellie scrunched into a ball, pulling her foot free of the sheet finally and pulling the other foot back under the covers to get warm. Scrunching a corner of her pillowcase, she wiped away the tears that oozed through her lashes.

Chapter Thirty-four

Dixie left the *Houston Chronicle* Building, and picked up the van parked in a truck zone, with her mind darting about like a runaway balloon on a windy day. She'd learned more in two hours than she had in two days. Jonathan Keyes. Counselor Frey.

She wanted to know more about Keyes.

Frey's story about the prowler Courtney saw the morning she drowned had more than half convinced Dixie that both Keyes girls were murdered. And Jon Keyes, on his way to Austin that morning by car, would've passed within twenty minutes or so of Camp Cade. After talking to Counselor Frey, Dixie had sat with her finger on the DISCONNECT button, a gnawing uneasiness in the back of her mind, wondering if she should call Rashly and tell him what she'd learned. She couldn't help worrying that Ellie might also be scheduled for an "accident."

But Ellie was Jon Keyes' blood daughter, which could mean she was safe—at least for a while. Even if Keyes had been molesting his adopted daughters, he might never be attracted to Ellie in the same way. Yet, Dixie's uneasiness persisted. Pedophiles were unpredictable. Sometimes one child in a family would be singled out, while siblings went untouched and were totally unaware of what was happening. Other times, children became desirable when they reached a certain age, and were discarded after they passed that age. Some molesters preferred boys, some liked *both* sexes as long as they were tender and unspoiled. It was a sick, sick, sick mind that found children sexually appealing. Dixie had studied the subject, but didn't begin to understand it.

Pointing the gray van toward North Houston, toward Keyes' home address, according to the file, she dialed Southwest Airlines on her cell phone. He'd been nervous when Dixie asked where he was the morning Betsy was killed. His alibi may not be as tight as he hoped it was.

A flight for Austin, the ticketing agent told her, left Hobby Airport every morning at 8:35, another at 9:05. Betsy had died around 7:30. With precise timing, Keyes could have taken Dann's car, waited at the intersection he knew Betsy would cross on her way to school, killed her, returned the car to Dann's driveway, and still made the 9:05 flight to Austin.

Jon Keyes also had the perfect opportunity to arrange for the younger girls to get sick at the party the night before—a mild food poisoning, perhaps—assuring Betsy would walk to school alone. And since Dann often ate at the Garden Cafe, Keyes might have seen him there, heard Dann talking to Betsy, maybe even learned that he lived nearby. Keyes' flexible work hours provided the opportunity to follow Dann and discover his habit of stopping at the Green Hornet on Thursday nights. Meeting up with him at the bar could've been planned. Encourage Dann to drink—maybe even slip a few sleeping pills into his glass.

Dixie drummed the steering wheel, waiting for a light to turn green. Her pulse refused to slow down. For the first time since she'd heard about Courtney's death, she felt close to learning the truth.

The tough question was motive. If Keyes was the sick sonofabitch Dixie suspected, he killed Betsy to keep his dirty secret from being discovered. Maybe he turned his attentions to Courtney only to discover she wasn't as reluctant as Betsy about speaking out.

Horns blared, and Dixie looked up to see the signal light had changed. She stepped on the gas.

Suspicion wasn't enough to reopen an accident investigation and call it murder. If she went to Rashly with her half-baked story about Jonathan Keyes, he'd laugh her out of his office. Somehow she'd have to dig up solid evidence first. Keyes' neighbors, his partner, his clients . . . none would know the man's sick sexual preferences . . . that's what made such cases almost impossible to prove in court. Pedophiles didn't brag to their friends.

Worrying about Ellie made Dixie think of Ryan. She put in a call to Amy.

"He's feeling much better already," Amy told her. "Well enough to complain about missing your visit."

When Ryan came on, his voice sounded muffled and conspiratorial, as if he'd put his mouth close to the phone.

"You have about a hundred pieces of E-mail on my computer."

"From that ad you put on the Internet?" Dixie sighed. "Ryan, I wish you'd—"

"Some of them sound pretty good. And a couple are *really* interested. We need to E-mail some answers before the best ones get away. If you don't have time, maybe I could—"

"That's all right! I'll make time." She promised to drop by that night to empty the E-mail box.

A Metro bus stopped to pick up passengers, and Dixie was trapped behind it, cars speeding past in the next lane. The smell of diesel exhaust invaded the van's cockpit.

Ryan was certainly determined to find a boyfriend for her. Apparently, dating was no longer a private matter. Personal columns in newspapers. Video dating services. Now the Internet.

She wondered if Jon Keyes had a normal dating life. Girlfriends . . . who would know about his girlfriends? She picked up the cell phone and punched in his office number.

"Keyes and Logan." The receptionist's cold sounded less nasal. Maybe she'd taken some decongestant.

"Hi, Sheri. This is Dixie Flannigan. I was in earlier today, to see Mr. Keyes. How's the book?"

"The hero's in jail! They think he killed a man, beat him to death with his bare hands. Can you believe that? Somebody's framing him. I just know it! And I think it's Joanna's father, that old miser!"

"Must be some hunk of a man, to even be suspected of beating someone to death."

"Strong . . . but gentle when he's with Joanna." The woman's voice held a dreamy quality that reminded Dixie of Carla Jean.

"Speaking of hunks, I noticed Jon Keyes wasn't wearing a wedding ring."

"Nooooooo." The girl lowered her voice. "He's been divorced since before I came here."

"Anybody in the wings?"

Sheri hesitated. "You know, I've never seen him with anybody steady. We have company dinners once or twice a year, and Jon always brings somebody different. Once he even brought his daughters, and no date at all."

"Daughters? They don't live with him, do they?"

"Well, I wouldn't bring it up, if I were you. It's really sad." The woman told Dixie about the accidents, pretty much the same version she already knew, with one addition. "Jon had been working really hard all summer on the Zimmerman account in Austin—you know, that big new mall going in downtown—and when that poor little girl drowned, Jon just about lost it."

They chatted for a few more minutes. Dixie managed to learn that Morey Zimmerman was the contact at Zimmerman-Fogarty Enterprises. She disconnected, then immediately dialed information for the number and spent the extra buck to have an operator make the connection.

"Mr. Zimmerman's secretary, please. This is Sheri, from Keyes and Logan." Dixie squinched her nostrils to sound congested. When a mature female voice came on, Dixie improvised: "We're backtracking on some airfare overages, and I'm hoping you can verify a couple of dates for me. Would your records show if Mr. Keyes arrived in your office as scheduled at eleven o'clock on the morning of August first? That was a Saturday."

When Dixie disconnected a few minutes later, she had learned that Keyes arrived on time for a noon luncheon appointment with Zimmerman. Austin was about three hours from Houston by car. He'd have lost maybe forty-five minutes by detouring east to Camp Cade that morning. And on May first, he had arrived a few minutes late for the meeting scheduled at ten o'clock. Perhaps taking the 9:05 flight had been cutting it close.

She turned the van into a quiet suburban neighborhood. Live oak trees lined both sides of the street, and trimmed boxwood or Ligustrum hedges framed deep yards. Jon Keyes' house sat in the middle of a block, architecturally distinctive. A pair of four-foot-high nutcrackers flanked the entrance, and a snow-flocked Christmas tree was visible in the living-room window.

Dixie parked at the curb and strolled to the front door as if expecting someone to be home. She rang the bell, glancing around as she waited. In this sort of neighborhood, at least one or two homeowners would be retired. She saw a white Ford Taurus parked in a driveway down the street.

After ringing the doorbell again, she rounded the house to check out the fenced backyard. The DOVER PLUMBING sign on the van would keep the neighbors from getting too anxious, as long as she didn't set off the alarm system. Keyes had the real thing, not just a decal. In back, a swimming pool had been installed, with a child's slide, and possibly a heating system, since the pool wasn't covered for winter disuse. Some live oak leaves floated on the chlorine-blue water. The houses in this subdivision were twenty to thirty years old, and swimming pools were not part of the original packages. Keyes had given his house a pool along with the face-lift.

Leaving the van parked in front of Jon Keyes' house, she walked three doors down to the house with the white Taurus. A wreath of dried pinecones and holly springs brightened the entrance. When Dixie rang the bell, it played "Frosty the

Snowman," and a tall, willowy woman of about sixty-five frowned through a sidelight before opening the door.

"Yes?"

"Mrs. Beringer?" Dixie had read the name on a magazine sticking out of the wall-hung mailbox. "I'm doing some follow-up work on an accident that occurred last spring. Did you know Betsy Keyes?"

The woman sucked in a sharp breath. "Yes, of course."

"Do you recall if Betsy had any close friends here in the neighborhood? Other children her age? Or perhaps a baby-sitter who might have known Betsy?"

"Well, yes. The Gilbert child, Rona, sits for all the little ones in the neighborhood. I'm sure she sits for Mr. Keyes on occasion."

"Rona's what, about fourteen, fifteen?" At sixteen, kids usually went to work at McDonald's or Wendy's or KFC, Dixie had noticed.

"Fifteen, I believe."

"And the Gilberts live where?"

"The two-story blue house on the corner."

"Thank you." Dixie turned to leave.

"I certainly hope the drunk who murdered that child is going to be put away long enough to teach him a lesson."

"Yes, ma'am."

The Gilbert house had toys in the yard and a bicycle parked beside the front door. A basketball hoop was mounted over the garage door. Dixie rang the bell and wasn't surprised when a teenage girl answered. Nobody's quicker to the phone or the doorbell than a teenager.

"Rona Gilbert?"

"Yeah." Her brown eyes widened.

"Dixie Flannigan. I'm following up on the Betsy Keyes accident. I understand you knew Betsy."

"Yeah, sorta."

"Do you often sit with Ellie when Mr. Keyes goes out?"

"Yeah, not often, I guess. He doesn't go out much."

"I suppose Betsy was old enough to sit with the younger kids . . . before the accident."

The girl looked away. After a moment, she said, "Yeah, when he wasn't going to be gone a long time."

"What's a long time? Did he ever stay away overnight?"

"Once, you know, when he had a meeting out of town."

"And he left *all* the girls here?"

"Yeah." Rona grinned. "Betsy and I stayed up all night watching videos."

"Did Mr. Keyes ever take Betsy or one of the other girls somewhere and leave the other two with you?"

"No, well yeah. The doctor. When one was sick, I'd stay with the others."

"Do you remember Betsy being upset about anything shortly before the accident?"

Rona's eyes widened again. "Yeah, she was always clicking that toy thing."

"Toy thing?"

"This thing, you know, you get at Halloween. Metal thing, and you press it and it goes *click-click*. Betsy carried it everywhere."

"She started carrying it last Halloween?"

"Yeah. No! I don't think I saw her with it until a long time after Halloween, after Christmas, maybe even after Easter, or some time around spring break. Yeah. I think, maybe, around spring break. Is it important?"

"Do you have any idea what Betsy was upset about?"

"Yeah, well, no. I guess she might've been getting hassled at school. That's what always gets me moping around."

"She didn't mention any problems at home?"

"You mean with her dad? I guess he might've been on her case. Yeah, my dad gets on my case, I get zoned out."

"Did Betsy's dad get on her case often?"

"Yeah, well no. I guess, you know, like most dads—oh! There's the phone, sorry!" The teenager glanced over her shoulder as the telephone rang again. "Mr. Keyes comes home sometimes for lunch. Maybe you can ask him."

Dixie barely caught the last few words before the door slammed. She arrived back at the van to find Jon Keyes turning into his driveway. He jumped out of his car and shouted.

"What the hell—?"

Dixie didn't think he'd be willing to talk about what was upsetting Betsy during the weeks before she died. Just to get his reaction, she considered asking him anyway. She was itching to confront the sonofabitch.

But his undisguised anger as he stalked toward the van suggested provoking him further would be a bad idea. And Barney had taught her to never throw a rope until it was properly looped. She didn't want Keyes wriggling out of her lasso. Starting the engine, Dixie sketched a cheerful wave and drove away.

An hour later, after drive-thru barbecue for lunch, she found herself parked across the street from Payne Hardware. Jon Keyes hadn't picked Dann's name out of a hat. They must have bumped into each other somewhere before meeting that night at the Hornet, casually enough that Dann didn't remember. After considering the acoustics in the cafe, she couldn't imagine anyone overhearing ordinary conversation there, unless they were seated side by side at the counter. But in the hardware store, she'd had no trouble at all overhearing the banter between Travis Payne and his friend Tate.

She entered Payne Hardware to the metallic ring of a hammer hitting big-headed nails. Sawdust bit at her nostrils. Payne, jangled away from his work by the cowbell, came bouncing around the corner in his orange overalls, a big welcoming smile spread across his face.

"The copper polish lady! Hope that Tarnex worked for you."

"Actually, I haven't used it, yet." She scooped up one of the magnetic key holders from the basket near the register. "If I put a spare car key in one of these, where's the best place to hide it?"

Payne didn't even pause to consider. He must have been asked often enough to have an answer ready.

"Not on the driver's side—first place a thief looks. Very first place. Not in a tire well, either. Too easy to feel under there without even stooping down, if you see what I mean.

Not under the hood, unless you have an external hood latch, and then not too close to the engine heat."

"Under the front bumper, maybe?" Actually, professional car thieves never bothered searching for spare keys. They could pop a door open and have a car started in sixty seconds flat.

"Me, I'd put it on the passenger side, rear, right up on the frame."

Dixie smiled. "Is that where yours is?"

He twinkled. "Now that'd be telling, wouldn't it?"

She picked up a key chain with a penlight smaller than her pinkie. Cute.

"Will that be all today?" Payne asked.

"A friend said you could help me choose some fence stain."

"Certainly! Fence stain, you say. Cedar fence? Pine? Redwood?"

"Cedar." She had hoped he'd ask who the friend was so she could casually mention Keyes' name. Apparently fence stain didn't stimulate Payne's interest as much as key holders and computers. A gallon of Barnwood Brown practically jumped in her cart without much discussion. "When I was here yesterday, I noticed you have a good selection of . . . baking pans."

"One of the best cookware departments in town—Chantal, Le Creuset, Chef's Pride. Have a brand in mind?"

"Which would you buy?" Dixie couldn't pretend to know about cookware.

"For baking, I'd have to go with Chef's Pride, I suppose, mostly because of the variety. Let me show you . . ."

Leading the way to the kitchen section, he explained the difference between reflective and nonreflective baking surfaces, nonstick coatings, and the various utensil shapes. Dixie examined a bright red enamel pot with a price tag she thought had to be a typo.

"Two hundred dollars for one pot?"

Payne chuckled. "Top of the line. Some cooks won't use

anything else. We have good brands for half the price, though."

Dixie noticed the shelves were heavy with expensive stock. Selecting a medium-priced loaf pan, she put it in the cart. She browsed from one area to another while they talked.

"Have you been at this location long?" she asked Payne.

"Three years next week. Three good years. Bought the place after taking early retirement."

"My neighborhood hardware store doesn't carry nearly the variety of items you offer. What made you decide to handle housewares and decorating supplies?"

"I listen to people. Things they haven't been able to locate, hard-to-find items, if they can get those here, they'll shop for other items as well. Started with kitchenware. Then I built the garden center, the decorating corner, and now I've added the real attraction, computers."

None of the areas he mentioned looked completed, Dixie noticed. "Must be an inventory nightmare, though."

"No, no, no. First you set up your space. Then you add your products, then your support products. That's where I am now, adding software and accessories."

But he was still finishing shelves?

"Were you in the hardware business before you retired?"

"Geologist, one of those professions that suddenly got overstocked and outdated." He laughed, his belly shaking like Saint Nick's.

The cowbell jangled, and Rebecca Payne stormed through the door.

"I thought I recognized you. You've been stirring up trouble with my ex-husband."

"Rebecca," Travis said, "this is a customer. She's not—"

"She's a spy. She was at the cafe yesterday talking to Ellie. Now Jon calls asking about someone named Flannigan, the same name that's on this card, and says he's going to start another custody suit." She shoved Dixie's business card in Travis' face.

"Custody?" Travis frowned. "Well, Ellie's his daughter."

"She's *my* daughter, and he's not taking her." She turned

on Dixie, green eyes snapping, forefinger jabbing at Dixie's chest. "YOU get out of here!"

"Mrs. Payne—"

"Out!"

"I'm not working for Jonathan Keyes. In fact, I wanted to ask you some questions about him—"

"Out!"

"Did Jon Keyes ever show more than a fatherly interest in your daughters?"

Rebecca sucked in a sharp breath. "OUT!"

"I only want to help—"

"Travis! We don't need her money. Throw her out of here."

Payne hesitated, then very quietly he said, "It's our right to refuse service to anyone." Anyone. His Saint Nick twinkle was gone, replaced by a hooded wariness.

Chapter Thirty-five

Now that she'd alienated the Paynes as well as Jonathan Keyes, Dixie knew she'd have to tread carefully. Everybody filed harassment suits these days. With only six days before Dann's trial resumed, she couldn't waste it arguing with a judge.

Wrestling mentally with what would be her next step, she cruised past the Valdez house. It sat dark and quiet as ever. Dixie wasn't surprised. The longer Hermie Valdcz sat in a cell with a few incorrigibles, and the more prostitutes she watched sail in and out, scarcely warming a bench, the itchier she'd be to roll over on Sikes to save herself. But if Rashly was planning to withhold the Keyes case folder until Dixie located Sikes, she wished he'd get on with his part.

She spent a couple of hours at the courthouse, looking up construction jobs Keyes had worked on and reading transcripts of the custody hearing. Even with her contacts, the files took time to acquire, time to read, and in the end proved to be about as useful as a sewed-up pocket.

Keyes' building designs held no surprises. They were fairly basic, mostly steel and glass boxes. A few of the newer ones boasted interesting stone facades. No unusual lawsuits or worker's comp reports. The custody hearing provided more fascinating reading.

KEYES: *I like to take my girls out of town on occasion. To the beach. Do things with them. Why should their mother get to veto everything we want to do together?*

JUDGE: *Such as what, Mr. Keyes?*

KEYES: *Overnight camping, hiking in the mountains, weekends at Galveston—you name it, Rebecca's against it.*

In the end, the judge denied joint custody, but granted Jonathan Keyes generous visitation rights, in return for substantial child-support payments, considering Rebecca was making a pretty fair wage as a chef.

Leaving the courthouse, Dixie remembered her promise to visit Ryan. She found him sniffling and still somewhat pale, but no longer feverish.

"Check out this letter, Aunt Dix. I deleted all the obvious geeks—you know, too old, too young, too wimpy. This one's got a son, fourteen, and a daughter, thirteen."

DWM, 41, with Curb Appeal. My clan heads for the South Dakota cycle rally this summer. If you're "born to be wild," let's fit your seat to the leather on my spare Harley before road fever is upon us.

A color photograph that accompanied the letter showed a brawny, ponytailed man in a black leather jacket and black boots on a huge black motorcycle. Two equally brawny teenagers posed beside him on smaller bikes. They looked like a trio Dixie might see eventually in a police lineup.

"Ryan, I'm not sure this is a good idea." It was a *terrible* idea. "Suppose one of these men showed up on my doorstep one night—uninvited."

"Can't happen, Aunt Dix. All they know is your E-mail

address, actually *my* E-mail address, which exists in cyberspace."

"Cyberspace?" To curtail his enthusiasm, maybe she should ask Amy to arrange another dinner with Old Delbert Snelling. "Are you positive there is absolutely no way anyone can trace your E-mail address to this computer? To this house?"

"None. Aunt Dixie, you need to join the technology age. You're riding a bicycle in a space shuttle zone. Look at what you can do—"

He pushed the mouse around its pad, and the monitor lit up like *Star Wars*. This wasn't the first time Ryan had endeavored to impress Dixie with his keyboard wizardry, but this time she paid attention. Close attention. Because this time she realized she'd overlooked the most obvious way to learn more about Jon Keyes.

Valdez's house was still dark, Augie was still on sick leave from the Green Hornet, and the Gypsy Filchers wouldn't arrive at their headquarters until midnight. Sometimes Dixie wished her life had a fast-forward button. The Filchers had given her a private number to call if she needed to reach them in a hurry. She dialed the number from her car phone and punched in a code. The callback came from Hooch. He had some friends, he assured her, who could take a peek at Jon Keyes' financial records without anyone knowing.

"You're sure they're discreet? And they know computers *as well as* business?"

"What they doan know, girlfriend, you doan need or doan want." He directed her to a corner in the Heights. "No way you ever find their place alone. I'll take you."

Having lived most of her life in Houston, Dixie found it hard to imagine a place she couldn't locate with good directions, especially in the Heights, a formerly prestigious neighborhood near downtown. Hooch was standing on a dark corner when she drove up in the van. He swung up into the passenger seat, his ruined face grinning on one side. She wondered how many people he'd given heart attacks, lurking around in the dark like a grotesque phantom.

He directed her down a dead-end street, through a gate posted with HIGH VOLTAGE signs, into an alley behind a shipping company, and then down a set of stairs that opened into a narrow, musty-smelling hallway. The hallway turned twice before Hooch knocked on a plain wooden door, identical to other plain wooden doors. For several moments, Dixie heard voices raised in argument behind the door.

"Who are these people?" she muttered. "Do they *live* here?" Who would live in such a secluded, uninhabited place?

"Pearly White and Smokin'."

"Those are names?"

The door finally opened two inches, and a man of about seventy peered out at her, bald, with a trim white beard, half-size reading glasses, cherry-red suspenders, and cloudy brown eyes full of suspicion. He stood about as high as Dixie, but looked as if he might have been taller in his youth, as if someone had washed him too often in hot water.

"Smokin'!" Hooch greeted the little man with a high-five. "Pearly White told you we was coming, didn't she?"

"Yep, yep. She didn't say when."

"I said directly," came a crisp voice behind the door. "Said they'd be here directly, and here they are, right on time." A white-haired woman even shorter than the man pulled the door wide and smiled at Dixie. "Why, Hooch, you didn't say she'd be so pretty. Did you? I don't recall you saying she'd be pretty."

"Must've slipped my mind, Pearly White. You take care of what she needs, though, and I'll be owin' you."

"It's me that's got what she needs." The little man grinned, all suspicion gone. He took Dixie's arm and tugged her into the room. "Yep, yep. Come right on in here."

Hooch faded into the shadows and was gone.

The room held a big-screen TV, VCR, and two recliners at one end. The TV/VCR straddled a black line that had been applied to the carpet with electrical tape. The line divided the room precisely in half, with one chair on either side. At the other end of the room sat two pairs of sawhorses. A wooden door had been laid across each pair to make two desks, one on either side of the black line. Each desk was covered with computer equipment and software manuals. Dixie recognized some slight differences in the two sets of equipment. One monitor glowed with a screen saver that looked like July Fourth fireworks, the other with tropical fish swimming serenely across a sea-green background. On one desk, beside a cigarette dispenser, an ashtray was filled to overflowing.

Smokin sat down at the chair with the ashtray and fireworks.

"Let's have it. Who do you want to know about and what do you want to know?" He selected a lengthy butt that was still burning and puffed on it.

"Can you look into someone's bank account?" Dixie asked. As the girls' legal father, Jon Keyes could carry life insurance on them. His bank records would show whether he was hurting for money. Unusual fluctuation in the account could mean heavy gambling debts or an expensive drug habit.

Smokin grinned and smashed out the cigarette butt. "My specialty."

"*Your* specialty? Since when is a bank job your specialty?" Pearly White sat at the other computer and touched a key that dispensed with the fish. A cursor blinked expectantly. "What about credit cards, sweetie? Credit card purchases can tell so much about a person."

"She said 'bank.' Not credit cards, *bank*. Got wax in your ears, old woman?" He touched a few keys. "How about police records? This fellow got a sheet? Drug trafficking? Burglary? Disturbing the peace?"

"The child wants to know about his money, not his work habits. Now what was that name, dear?"

Dixie gave them the meager information she had on Jonathan Keyes. They both typed it in, and minutes later the monitors were filled with information.

"We're in, sweetie. Now what do you want to know?"

Good question. "Can we look at general cash flow? Say, over the past two years?"

"No problem."

"Yep, yep. I knew he'd have a sheet," Smokin said. "Eight traffic tickets last year. Speeding, illegal turns, failure to stop. Yep. Let's see what else we can find."

He typed a string of characters and the words on the monitor changed. Dixie tried to read over both sets of shoulders.

Regular deposits showed that Keyes earned a substantial salary from his architectural firm. He wrote most of his checks during the first half of the month, spending approximately the same each month on household expenses, travel, entertainment, and insurance premiums. His car insurance was high, perhaps due to the traffic violations. His mortgage payment was modest in relation to his earnings.

When Betsy and Courtney died, Keyes received $10,000, most of which he paid out again on what looked like funeral expenses. Child-support payments dropped after each death, but the amount, though generous, was insignificant compared to his income. Nothing Dixie saw pointed to unreasonable spending.

"Look at this transaction, sweetie." Pearly White pointed to a withdrawal. "That money was transferred to another account in the same bank. Would you like me to check that out?"

"Go for it."

"*Go for it,*" Smokin mimicked. "While you two are pussy-footing around over there, I've got the fellow cold for assault and battery. Yep, yep."

"Really? Who was the complainant?" Dixie looked at Smokin's monitor and saw for herself: Travis Payne. According to the notation, Rebecca had wanted Keyes to pay his child support quarterly instead of monthly. Keyes got into a shouting match with her. When Payne stepped between them, Keyes punched him out.

"Yep. He's a rounder, that one. Bet the FBI has a sheet on this perp."

"Isn't it illegal to tap into FBI files?" Dixie hadn't counted on digging that deep.

"Depends." Smokin lit another butt from the ashtray. "Anyhow, what do you think *she's* doing over there? Think that's legal? Tell her, old woman, is that legal?"

"Here's his savings account." Pearly White whistled softly. "You should have stayed in architectural school, old man." Keyes' savings account held $75,000. "See this highlighted symbol? That means there's yet another account." She toggled a key and found a certificate of deposit in Keyes' name for $500,000. This time Dixie whistled.

"Mr. Keyes' money would earn a much higher return invested in mutual funds," Pearly White said. "He needs a financial planner, sweetie."

"*I* should have such problems," Dixie said.

"Is this man a partner in the firm, dear? We could check out his company accounts."

"Do it."

They found three accounts, one for taxes, another for everyday business, and a third for escrow on jobs in progress.

"Nothing here looks out of order, dear. The business seems to be prospering nicely."

Dixie had to agree. Financially, Jon Keyes was squeaky clean.

"Dadburn it! FBI has *nothing* on this bozo. Was he in the army? Navy? Marines?" When Dixie shrugged, Smokin said, "A rounder, this guy? Angry, feisty, ready to fight? Probably marines." His fingers flew over the keys.

Dixie summoned an image of Jon Keyes: agitated, angry. Reasonably well built. Not bad-looking. She wondered why he'd never remarried. The obvious reason sickened her.

"Mr. Keyes travels a bit," Pearly White said.

She had pulled up a list of credit card purchases, several for airline tickets. The trips to Austin were numerous, as expected. Dixie asked Pearly White to scroll backward to the months before Betsy's death. They found a purchase for a tour package to Disney World in June. The package was canceled two weeks later—three days *before* Betsy's accident. Because of his big job in Austin? Or because he knew Betsy wouldn't be available for a trip to Disney World?

"Who else you want to check out?" Smokin jabbed keys with one hand while he stubbed out a cigarette with the other.

Dixie already had what she'd come for, and she was tempted to call it a night. But that would be poor investigative technique.

"Rebecca and Travis Payne," she said.

"Bonnie and Clyde team?" Smokin's left hand danced over the keys, his right hand jabbing the mouse.

Pearly White tossed him a look, as her own fingers picked up speed. Moments later Payne's banking records were on-screen. Dixie asked her to scroll backward two years to about the time Travis and Rebecca married. He had added Rebecca's name to his account and she apparently transferred her savings, because the joint account showed a sudden increase of $132,000.

"That's a sizable dowry, sweetie," Pearly White commented. "I didn't realize women handed over their money so easily these days. This Mr. Payne doesn't have much of a head for business, does he?"

"Not much of a head for crime, either." Smokin was fingering keys wildly and without much success. "Not a blamed thing on record locally. What is this fella, a monk? Not even a dadburned traffic ticket."

Previously, the Payne account had operated close to the margin. As Pearly White scrolled forward in the file, small amounts moved in and out of the account, then four months after the $132,000 was deposited, it disappeared.

"Now you see it, now you don't," Dixie said. That was the month Rebecca opened the Garden Cafe. "See if she opened a business account in the same bank."

She had. The money was used as the initial deposit.

"If you don't mind," Dixie said, "go back to Travis' records."

"No problem." Pearly White touched a key. The joint account reappeared, with a window containing the cafe business account. The lady beamed.

"You get a kick out of this, don't you?" Dixie said.

"It's like eavesdropping, sweetie. Everybody likes to do it, but few would admit it."

"Ever get the urge to change some of those numbers?"

"You mean, transfer a few digits into my own pocket? Don't I ever! Especially when you know the money was probably acquired illegally. But, sweetie, that's a quick way to become a guest of the federal government."

"What about just looking? Is it dangerous?"

"Yep, yep," Smokin piped. "But only if someone's doing a security scan—"

"Wait! Back up." The Paynes' joint account had rocked along for several months barely above zero balance. Then a $20,000 deposit popped up. "Where did that come from?"

"Maybe they sold something." Pearly White scrolled slowly through the numbers.

A few days later, the $20,000 disappeared without reappearing in the cafe account. Pearly White made another window and brought up the business account for Payne Hardware. The $20,000 transfer had hit barely in time to avoid a bounced check.

"Whatever they sold must have belonged to Travis Payne," Dixie said. "And he needed the money."

"Dear, I'm surprised Mr. Payne stays in business. Look at this."

The cafe account, shortly after it was opened, showed a transfer of $30,000 to the hardware account. Both deposits to Payne Hardware occurred in the first year after Travis and Rebecca married, and were followed by a frenzy of spending.

Twice the following year—in June, the month after Betsy's death, and August, after Courtney was killed—a $50,000 deposit was made to the joint personal account, then transferred almost immediately to Payne Hardware. Insurance settlements?

Fifty thousand dollars seemed like a heck of a big policy to carry on a child, especially when Jon Keyes seemed to have paid the burial expense. Of course, some policies paid double for accidental deaths.

One thing was clear, Travis Payne profited by marrying Rebecca, and profited after the death of each child.

"That twenty-thousand-dollar deposit," Dixie said. "Is there any way to find out where the money came from?"

"Is it important?"

"I don't know." But all the other big deposit amounts were accounted for by Rebecca's initial cash injection or by insurance on the two girls. "Guess I'm just curious."

They spent another half hour looking for additional bank accounts for either Rebecca or Travis, while Smokin pecked away at records Dixie didn't even want to know about. Nothing turned up. Once again, Dixie was ready to call it a good search and go home when she realized there was one person she had ignored completely: Parker Dann. Belle Richards would not be happy if Dixie uncovered additional evidence *against* Dann, but for her own peace of mind Dixie needed to know.

"Hope this perp's got more going than the last one." Smokin hunched over his keyboard as if World War III were at hand. Fascinated, Dixie watched him dip into files she would've spent hours, possibly days, acquiring at the courthouse. The arrest last May was there, of course, and the previous DWI charges, as well as a speeding ticket from January.

"Sweetie, this man is a much better catch than your Mr. Keyes," Pearly White commented. "He has bank accounts in three states. And some nice investments."

Dixie's mouth dropped open. Dann appeared to be worth several million dollars, if he chose to cash it all in. Having been inside his house, she'd expected his big commissions to be offset by heavy spending—expensive dining and drinking tabs, maybe some gambling. According to his accounts, though, he lived sparely and invested most of what he earned. Although he drove a luxury car, currently impounded as evidence, his home and furnishings were modest if not downright paltry.

Quarterly, a check was paid to a Monica Dann in Montana. An ex-wife, Dixie would've guessed, if Belle hadn't already told her that Dann was never married. Probably his mother, then. In addition to normal expenses, a monthly check was also sent to someone in Wisconsin named Heather Burke. The debits went back four years, and were paid out of an account in Baton Rouge, Louisiana.

"I wonder if Ms. Heather Burke sold him some property," Pearly White said, calling up deed registration files.

"Burke?" Smokin said. "Yep, yep. That's the name right here on this paternity suit."

Paternity suit? Dixie leaned over Smokin's shoulder. Heather Burke, twenty-one, had filed a paternity suit against Parker Dann four years earlier, claiming him the father of her two-year-old son. Dann was forty-two now, so he'd have been thirty-five to Heather's eighteen when the child was conceived. Seventeen years older than Heather. According to the records, she had lost the suit. So why was he sending her checks every month?

Chapter Thirty-six

Dixie wrapped up the computer search and arrived home an hour earlier than she'd told Dann to expect her. She found the red Frisbee on the back step and the house dark except for one light in the den. Mud met her at the door. The house seemed incredibly quiet.

"Hey, boy." She scratched Mud's ears. "What's going on?"

The kitchen sparkled. She couldn't detect any cooking aromas. But then, even though she was home early, it was long past supper.

When she flipped on the kitchen light, a loud *thump* sounded in the den. Following Mud, she swung past the refrigerator, where a note was anchored by Ryan's picture magnet: *Your plate's ready to go in the microwave.*

In the den, Dann sat at the desk, reading. He looked up, all blue-eyed innocence, when she entered. Dixie's hunch alarm clanged like crazy. He'd been up to something. Mud settled at Dann's feet, his ugly mug across one shoe.

"Guess I lost track of the time," Dann said, looking at the desk clock. "Got some great books in here."

"I didn't realize you were a reader." Actually, she'd seen a bookcase at Dann's house filled with an interesting variety of reading material. But he didn't know that.

"Passes the time." Using one of her business cards to mark his place, he closed the book. Dixie read the title: *Whip Hand* by Dick Francis, one of her personal favorites. In fact, she seemed to recall leaving it face out on the shelf the last time she read it. Handy.

"Did you eat? I made Stroganoff." Dann stood and pushed his chair under the desk.

Tense, Dixie thought. *He didn't expect me and didn't hear the car drive in.*

"How about popping my plate in the microwave," she said, "while I wash up?"

He glanced at the book on the desk. "Sure. Give me about six minutes."

She waited until he was out of the room, then slipped behind the desk and opened the drawers. Nothing screamed out as having been disturbed, but then she wasn't the world's neatest when it came to filing and paperwork.

She scanned the room, thinking maybe the *thump* she heard was Dann dropping something rather than shutting a drawer. She had no doubt Dann was clever enough to escape if he took a mind to; she hoped he was also smart enough not to try. Perhaps he was merely nosing around in her scrapbooks again. No harm there. She studied the bottom bookshelf where the five volumes stood, all in order, their dates marked on the spine.

In the shelf above, a volume of *How Things Work* was misaligned. She pulled the book from the shelf, and looked behind it. Nothing prevented it from sliding all the way in. She laid the book on the desk. It fell open to a section on locks—safe locks, automobile locks, mechanical, electric, electronic, even magnetic strip locks. It appeared that Dann was either trying to get into something, or trying to get out.

When she entered the kitchen, after quickly washing her hands in the bathroom, he was pouring coffee.

"How'd it go today?"

"Better than yesterday. That Stroganoff smells good."

Dixie had come home debating whether to relate what she'd found on Jon Keyes. Now she was more intent on learning what Dann was plotting. If he tried something stupid, like breaking open the ammunition cabinet, it would, at the least, cost her an expensive lock. Worse, he might actually blow himself up trying to make an explosive device. Another volume in her bookcase carried the instructions for homemade bombs.

She sat down at the table where he'd placed a plate of steaming beef and noodles, a dinner salad, a basket of hot pumpernickel bread, and a glass of water with a lime slice floating in it. Whatever else Dann was, he knew how to eat well. And since he knew how to follow recipes, he'd have no problem figuring out how to do just about anything, digging through her library.

Tasting the Stroganoff, she realized just how much she was going to miss the gourmet fare when this business was over. Mud, watching her eat, doing his best to look starved and pitiful, was likely to miss it, too. Dixie had noticed the bag of dog food in the pantry wasn't disappearing at its usual rate.

Dann brought two cups of coffee and joined her at the table.

"Food okay?"

"Absolutely."

"Cheesecake and blueberries for dessert. The boxed kind, but it tastes pretty good."

"Think I'll skip dessert. It's late." She continued eating, without looking at him. Mud, watching every forkful, obviously expected her to share. *Dream on.*

"Guess you had a long day," Dann said. "Not very talkative."

Dixie buttered a piece of bread.

"Dann, you ever hear the old story about a Shogun who saw one of his Samurai coming up the road, bloodied and battered? 'What happened to you?' the Shogun says. 'I have been robbing and killing your enemies to the East, my Lord,' the Samurai tells him. 'But I don't have any enemies to the East,' says the Shogun. The Samurai pauses for a moment, then says, 'You do now.' "

Dann smiled tentatively. When she didn't smile back, he

sighed. "Guess there's a message for me in that story. Unless you're planning a new career on the comedy circuit."

Dixie put the bread down and pushed her plate away.

"Dann, I'm not your enemy."

"No." He frowned at his hands, clasped around his coffee cup. "Not unless my court date arrives and you haven't turned up a miracle."

"Do we need a miracle? I thought I was just looking for evidence."

"And not finding any."

"We still have time."

He carried his cup to the sink and dumped the coffee down the drain. He stood with his back to her, neck and shoulder muscles rippling with tension.

"I looked every one of those jurors in the eye that last day. The prosecution showed photographs of Betsy lying beside the road like a pile of discarded clothes. I thought about how I'd feel if I were one of the jury listening to the prosecutor's case. I'd throw my sorry ass so far in Huntsville Prison the world wouldn't even be driving cars when I got out."

Dixie was tempted to tell him what she'd learned about Keyes. But first she needed to talk to Belle Richards and find out if the lawyer thought the information would make enough difference to alter Dann's case.

"If there's evidence out there to find, I'll find it."

"I wish I knew." His eyes held a solemn resolve she'd never seen there before. "I wish I *knew* if there was any evidence out there to find. I wish I could promise you absolutely that I wasn't behind the wheel when my car hit Betsy. *I just don't friggin know.* But two things I *can* promise. One. I'd never intentionally hurt you, or hurt Mud, or cause you any unnecessary anguish. Two." He sighed again, his gaze never wavering from hers. "I won't go gently to prison."

After transferring the contents of the ammunition cabinet to the Mustang's trunk—just in case that was sparking Dann's sudden interest in locks—Dixie spent the few remaining hours of the night wrestling with sleep. Rows of numbers and letters bounced around against a glowing computer screen in her brain. She'd hoped to avoid returning Belle Richards' phone calls until she had something concrete to present in Dann's favor. But the attorney would need time to reorganize her case presentation for court on Monday. Only five days remained, most of them weekend or holidays.

When the alarm finally rattled Dixie out of bed, she pulled on some clothes and headed straight for the phone, knowing Belle's habit of keeping early office hours. The lawyer picked up on the first ring.

"You weren't joking when you said you'd let me worry right up to the last minute, were you, Flannigan?"

"Did I get your attention?"

"Trust me, you better have good news after keeping me waiting. What's going on?"

"First, let's set your mind at ease. Parker Dann is here."

"Where?"

Dixie glanced through the hall at the guest-room door. Mud would be dutifully on guard beside Dann's bed.

"A friend of mine is keeping an eye on him. But I have some other news."

She told Belle what she'd learned about Courtney's swimming "accident," about Jonathan Keyes talking to Dann at the Green Hornet, and finally about her suspicion of Keyes. Belle was silent for a long beat.

"I see where you're pointing," she said finally. "But you of all people, *Ms. Former Prosecutor*, must be aware of how nasty it would look to present unsubstantiated allegations against Keyes which, if they're wrong, could ruin his reputation." She hesitated. "I don't suppose you unearthed any actual proof?"

"Child molestation is hard enough to prove when the victims are still alive. I seem to recall that you won a couple of my cases by merely planting a 'seed' of reasonable doubt in the jury's ear."

"Never a seed so insidious. If a jury didn't buy it one hundred percent, they might convict Dann in a backlash of sympathy for Keyes."

"I was afraid you'd say that. So here's a seed with the sort of hard numbers juries like." She told Belle about Travis Payne's $50,000 deposits and erratic spending sprees after the deaths of both stepdaughters. This time she could almost hear the lawyer's mental wheels grinding. Juries could imagine a man murdering his stepchildren for money. Travis Payne's "motive" was so obvious Dixie wondered why Belle's investigator hadn't picked up on it. Everybody considered Betsy's death an accident. No one had noticed that Payne pocketed a substantial amount of insurance money. According to Belle's notes, he claimed he was at the hardware store repricing inventory when Betsy was killed. No one was there to substantiate his whereabouts. Dixie would bet a similar situation existed during the time Courtney was killed. Small business owners often worked odd hours.

She hated providing evidence that implicated an honest man, but suspicion was not conviction. If the jury believed the "evidence" against Travis Payne cast reasonable doubt on Dann's guilt, they'd acquit. The DA would investigate Payne, but they'd never arrest him without substantial evidence. Meanwhile, Dixie would turn over to the prosecuting attorney all her information against Jon Keyes, and the right man would go to jail. Maybe.

"After the swimming accident," Belle argued, "my investigator questioned the counselors at Camp Cade and didn't see any connection."

"No reason they should. For your people, as well as the police investigators, the two deaths were separated by months and miles, and were totally dissimilar. I got news of both accidents within forty-eight hours."

"Still, I should've picked up on the coincidence." She paused. "Why did you go to all this trouble?"

"Let's say I don't trust packages that are too neatly tied."

"If you're right, Keyes put together a tidy frame against Dann, all right, a package that twelve people in the box were ready to buy." Belle fell silent again, and Dixie knew she was still processing the information. "Frankly, it sounds like Payne is more likely to have the calculating sort of mind to follow through on such a diabolical plan. Maybe he really is the killer."

It didn't surprise Dixie that Belle would favor Travis Payne as the prime suspect over Jonathan Keyes. Even the best lawyers were squeamish about looking into the cesspool labeled "Sex Crimes Against Children." As soon as Dann was cleared, Dixie would have to go after Keyes on her own.

"You'll need to send another operative to follow up on Travis Payne," she said, describing her run-in with Rebecca. "I don't think either of the Paynes will talk to me again. Also, you'll need to verify the fifty-thousand-dollar deposits were indeed insurance claims. If so, when were the policies written, who was the actual beneficiary, and how much insurance does Payne carry on Rebecca and Ellie?"

"Gee, Flannigan, it's been a long time since anyone told me how to do my job. Are you bucking for a consultant's fee, too?"

"Justice is its own reward, Ric. Haven't you heard?"

"That's a nasty rumor. Don't let my clients hear it."

"On one condition. Let me know what you find out on this."

"You're worried about Ellie Keyes?"

"Naturally, I'm worried." And she'd been digging around in this case too long to drop it now. She wanted to know everything Belle found out.

"Hang loose, right where you are," Belle told her. "Checking the insurance records won't take long."

Two minutes after Dixie hung up, the phone rang. She scooped up the receiver.

"Once again, Ric, you exceed my expectations."

"And once again you baffle the hell out of me." Benjamin Rashly's tobacco-gruff voice rumbled in Dixie's ear.

He would be calling for only one reason.

"Valdez is out?"

"Released ten minutes ago. On her way home right now."

"Shit."

"I've been talking to my doctor about that. Gets harder

every year." Rashly chuckled over his obscene joke. "Get on it, Flannigan. A deal's a deal."

"I'm on it, Rash." Even as Dixie clicked off, she shrugged into her overalls and vest. She hooked a jacket out of the closet—the weatherman had predicted another temperature drop—and stuffed the cellular phone into a pocket. She didn't want to miss Belle's call while she staked out Hermie Valdez.

The plumbing van had worked before, and although Dixie usually preferred to change tactics, time was short. Her "plumbing" tools were already loaded. She pulled the van into the driveway of a vacant house she'd spotted half a block down from Valdez. Before jumping out, she tossed a shovel and plumber's snake to the ground.

A police car stopped at the Valdez house. Departmental escort was rare, probably a direct order from Rashly, including instructions to take their time, allowing Dixie a few extra minutes to get positioned. A large, angular woman in rumpled clothes emerged from the cruiser, slamming the door rudely.

Turning on the portable receiver clipped under her coat, Dixie heard Valdez enter the house. Footsteps on the wooden floor came through loud and clear.

Dixie chose a likely spot and started digging, not putting much muscle in it. Should anyone ask, she was searching for a clogged sewer line. Until Hermie contacted her fugitive boyfriend, the only thing to do was wait. And dig.

For the first hour, Dixie listened to footsteps from room to room, drawers opening and closing, a shower running, a hair dryer wailing. Then Valdez must have decided to take a nap, because the house grew quiet.

By that time, Dixie had dug a trench about a foot deep and six feet long, with no idea whether a sewer line was anywhere within fifty yards. Her legs were growing numb and she shivered so hard the UHF receiver shook loose from her belt. She barely caught it before it hit the ground. For once the weatherman had been right about the temperature.

When the phone in her pocket bleeped, she was glad for the chance to sit down in the van's cab, out of the cold.

"The policy on Rebecca and the girls," Belle said, "was written two days after the wedding. And get this, the insurance agent is Dennis Payne, a younger brother of you know who."

Which explained why the policies were so large, Travis throwing business at his younger brother. "Closed that sale fast, didn't he?"

"Twenty-five thousand on each child, a million each on Travis and Rebecca, double for accidental death, with the surviving spouse as beneficiary."

"Those two fifty-thousand-dollar boosts to Payne's cash flow disappeared like ice on a griddle. I bet he could spend the hell out of two million."

"Are you swinging toward Payne now as the killer? You think he really murdered those girls?"

Dixie didn't, but she knew that's what Belle wanted to believe, so she could sell it easier at Dann's trial. If Belle thought she and Dixie were thinking along the same lines, the information flow would continue.

"He sure looks good for it," Dixie hedged.

"Payne's the one who got the goodies. By the way, did you know this is not Rebecca's third marriage, but her fourth?"

"Woman has a hell of a hard time hanging on to men." Dixie's breath was fogging the van window. She rolled it down to keep Hermie's house in sight.

"Trust me, she does all right. The first husband lasted nineteen months. Rebecca got a nice settlement, ninety thousand dollars and a cabin on Lake Livingston. Apparently he moved out of state. Now what were the other phantom deposits you asked me to check out?"

"Payne's account showed a thirty-thousand-dollar deposit, which came from Rebecca. Then in June of last year, twenty thousand dollars was deposited to the joint account. It might've been a personal sale—furniture or jewelry, but it might also be a small insurance claim. Maybe something was stolen."

"Actually, I think there was something here . . ." A sound of paper rustling. "Something about—yes, here it is. Same policy, dismemberment clause. Rebecca lost two fingers in an accident."

Dixie recalled seeing the disfigured hand. Running a restaurant must be more dangerous than she realized.

"Does it say how the accident occurred?"

"A power saw. Travis was builing a shelf unit for the hardware store. Rebecca was helping. That's all it says."

Dixie felt the hair rise between the goose bumps on her arms.

"I just flashed a gruesome old joke, Ric. Remember the one about the down-on-his-luck farmer with the three-legged singing pig? Farmer shows the pig to a friend. Pig sings a moving rendition of 'Old Rugged Cross,' bringing tears to the friend's eyes. He wants to know how the pig lost his leg, and the farmer says, 'If you had such a wonderful singing pig, would you eat him all at once?' "

"Jesus Christ, Dixie! That's gross. You think Travis cut his wife's fingers off on purpose?"

"Maybe the fingers were an accident. But maybe that twenty-thousand-dollar check spurred a gruesome plot to keep the money flowing."

Dixie shuddered at the thought. It was no more gruesome than her own theory that Keyes murdered his stepdaughters to keep the world from discovering his sexual perversions. Her money was still on Keyes, but . . . an image of Travis Payne slipped into her head . . . Santa Claus in orange overalls, friendly, cheerful, optimistic.

Belle said, "You mean, he couldn't cut off more of his wife's fingers when he ran short of money, but he could create a traffic accident and bump off one of the kids."

"After all, they're not his k— Oh, fuck!" Dixie had glanced toward the Valdez house. "The car's gone."

"What?"

"I'll get back to you."

She jabbed the OFF button and turned on the VHF receiver. After a moment she heard a faint blip. Valdez's Toyota was almost out of range.

Chapter Thirty-seven

Dixie maneuvered the van around a detour for construction. The transmitter's signal was stronger now, but not strong enough. One missed traffic light and Valdez could zip out of range.

Abruptly the signal faded. Hermie must have turned down a side street. Dixie drove three blocks, then flipped a mental coin and turned right.

Blip. Stepping on the gas, she closed the distance. Valdez was headed into an Asian-American district near downtown, east of the George R. Brown Convention Center.

The cellular phone rang.

"Dixie?" It was Amy. "I called the house first, but that nice Mr. Dann said you'd gone out, said he was a friend of yours, doing some work for you there at the house, so I took a chance on catching you in your car. That's right, isn't it? He *is* a friend?"

"Yes, he's a . . . friend." *Jesus, Amy, I don't have time for this now.* Valdez turned again. This time Dixie was close enough to keep up.

"It's Ryan. Now that he's almost over the flu, he's being a real pill. I told him you'd see him tonight—"

"Tonight?"

"Dinner! Remember? Carl's barbecuing a turkey. You promised to be here."

"All right, I will, but right now—"

"Great. Now here's Ryan."

"Wait, Amy, let me call—"

"Aunt Dix." Ryan was using his spy voice, close to the phone, muffled. "You won't believe this latest E-mail. A pilot, a real air force pilot. That oughta blow Snelling out of the race."

"Ryan, there's no race." The Asian-American neighborhood ended at a warren of semi-abandoned buildings where ethnic boundaries tangled like frayed threads. Valdez parked in front of a row of four shotgun shanties, a slumlord's version of town homes.

"I think I should reply, Aunt Dix. Tell him to meet us when we fly our models on Sunday."

"No, please, wait till tonight. I want to be there." She cruised past Valdez's Toyota just as the big woman, wearing a shiny purple coat, climbed out of her car and stomped toward the back of the houses. Dixie couldn't tell which door she entered.

"Well, okay. I just hope he doesn't find another girlfriend. Here's Mom."

"No, Ryan, I need to hang—" But he'd already handed off the phone.

"Dixie, Carl bought a huge turkey," Amy said. "Why not invite your friend? There's always room for an extra plate."

Jeez, Amy. "Okay, I'll ask him. I really have to go now."

Turning at the next block, Dixie pulled to the broken curb and parked. She would have to walk back to the shanties, locate Valdez and make sure Sikes was with her, then phone Rashly to make the collar. Her plumber's garb was no good here as cover. People in this neighborhood didn't call white-bread to fix their pipes.

Fortunately, it was cold, the neighbors all indoors. She pulled on a knit cap to cover her hair and turned up her collar to hide as much of her face as possible. After silencing the ringer, she shoved the cellular phone in her pocket, locked the van, and headed toward the row of shacks. Not too fast, not too slow. Confident, as if she belonged here. Trying to ignore the shiver sliding down her spine.

Touching the .45 holstered under the overall, and flexing her ankle against the shiv in her boot, she felt safer. After all, she had no intention of trying to take Sikes in herself. Like a good hunting dog, all she had to do was find and point.

The sky had clouded over, blocking the late morning sun, turning the day even colder than it started out. The shabby clapboard buildings that crowded the narrow street appeared empty, until an eye peeked through a broken window covered over with cardboard or voices seeped through the dry rot that riddled the walls. She stepped off the sidewalk to avoid a pile of ruptured trash bags where a boarded-up grocery store had been built in front of an old house, pushing outward almost into the street. A few boards had been pried loose and the smell of burned cooking grease hung in the air.

Compared to the buildings she'd just passed, the row of shanties might be touted as upscale housing. Finding a torn window shade proved easy: most of them were either torn or threadbare and nearly transparent. Unfortunately, the shanties almost touched one another, leaving no room for side panes. The front windows looked into living rooms, the back windows into bedrooms.

At the first house, two kids sat watching cartoons on a portable television. A scrawny Christmas tree behind them was hung sparsely with tinsel. The second house appeared vacant. If someone was farther back, in the kitchen, Dixie couldn't tell. In the third living room, empty beer cans littered a coffee table, a magazine lay facedown on a raity sofa. At the fourth house, two women argued over a red polka-dot dress.

Circling to the back, Dixie entered a narrow alley separating the four houses from an identical row that faced the next street over. Valdez might have gone into one of those, after parking on the wrong block to throw off anyone following. But the woman didn't strike Dixie as especially cunning. Other than a few extra turns, Hermie had taken no precautions against being tailed, and Dixie was certain she hadn't been spotted.

Stepping to the back of the third house, the one with beer cans and a magazine in the living room, she peeked through a tear in a bedsheet covering the window. Except for the light that shone through an open bathroom door, the bedroom was dark. She heard voices. Then bedsprings creaked, as if someone had sat down.

Dixie ducked under the window, crossed to the other side, and found another peephole. A man wearing a T-shirt and jeans had stepped up to the bed. He unbuttoned his pants. His face caught enough of the light from the bathroom for Dixie to recognize Alton Sikes.

Stepping away from the house, she dialed Rashly's number and gave him the address. Then she slipped into the shadows to watch and wait. It didn't take long.

How Sikes got wind of what was coming down was a mystery. Maybe guys like him were born with genetic fuzz busters. He was ready when they kicked in the door. Dixie couldn't see the fracas, but it sounded like the homicide cops were chasing Sikes up one wall and down the other. Five minutes later, when they brought him out front in handcuffs, Hermie Valdez had disappeared.

"She'll turn up." Rashly looked British in a navy-blue Burberry coat with a plaid muffler. "What's important is Sikes is going down. This time he'll stay down." He knocked his pipe against a shoe heel to free the burned tobacco, then took a pipe cleaner from his pocket.

"Thought you stopped smoking," Dixie said.

"Yep." He forced the pipe cleaner through the stem. "Maybe next month I'll stop again."

Dixie had hung around not so much to watch the bust as to talk to Rashly about Jon Keyes and Travis Payne. The detective, watching his men go about the business of securing the scene, took a leather tobacco pouch out of a coat pocket.

"Rash, while you were investigating the Keyes hit-and-run case, how much did you learn about the custody suit Jon Keyes filed during his divorce from Rebecca?"

"Divorce? That was old business long before the girl was killed. Why are you digging into that?"

"Didn't it strike you as strange that a single male would file for joint custody of two girls that weren't even his?"

"When it comes to divorce, nothing two people do to each other would surprise me. Besides, he adopted them. Legally, they're his kids."

"Keyes is nervous about something."

Rashly dipped his pipe into the pouch. Flakes of cherry-blend tobacco fell to the sidewalk.

"When nervous gets to be a crime, Flannigan, we'll have criminals lined up clear to Oklahoma waiting for a bunk at the prison." He packed tobacco into the pipe bowl with his thumb and began searching his pockets for a lighter. Finding it, he cupped his hand over the pipe, drawing deep to get the tobacco going, then started across the narrow street, leaving her in a cloud of smoke. "Go take a load off your feet, Flannigan. Sit in my car. Maybe you'll find some light reading material in the backseat."

The Keyes case folder. Dixie had almost forgotten why she'd agreed to help Rashly round up Sikes.

She found the same traffic tickets for Keyes that Smokin had turned up, and the assault charge Payne filed when Keyes punched him out in their argument over the child support. Otherwise, neither had a prior arrest. According to one investigator's notes, Keyes had been a model father since the divorce. Picked up the three kids on his weekends, returned them on time. Showed no hostility toward his ex-wife. As divorced father of the year, he would get a ten.

Then Dixie found a report from Social Services. In late April, a doctor had called a social worker to the hospital emergency room after Jon Keyes brought Betsy in with acute abdominal cramps and vaginal bleeding. It turned out that she was having her first menstrual cycle. Keyes didn't realize that's all it was. According to the doctor, Betsy's cramps were more severe than she expected, based on the film she'd seen in health class.

Dixie felt her skin go clammy as she recalled her own first

menstrual period. She'd hoped it would keep Scully from bothering her. "Damned if you aren't getting to be the little woman," Scully'd said. "Budding out up top. Bleeding like a woman, even smell like a woman. Too bad you don't have a little sister." Every month, Dixie exaggerated her stomach cramps to Carla Jean, who promptly sent her to bed and clucked over her. Scully's visits hadn't stopped, but at least he didn't come around during that one week of the month.

Jon Keyes had not believed Betsy's cramps were normal, even for a girl's first cycle. When he discovered the doctor had phoned Rebecca, Keyes drove his fist into the doctor's face so hard it loosened a tooth. That's when Social Services had been summoned.

Rashly opened the driver's side door and, leaving it open, sat down heavily behind the steering wheel. He took a long draw on his pipe, coughed as he exhaled, then looked over his shoulder at the report Dixie was reading.

"Still hot on Keyes? What is it about the guy that ruffles your tail feathers?"

Dixie's take on Keyes wasn't something Rashly would understand.

"When something looks too good to be true," she said, "maybe it needs a closer look." On paper, Jon Keyes was merely a concerned father. On paper, Travis Payne stacked up more marks as a killer. But his friendly smile and twinkling eyes had seemed sincere.

Rashly blew a fresh trail of gray smoke into the winter air.

"Good guys happen, Flannigan. We don't see many in our line of work, but they're out there, going quietly about their law-abiding lives. Maybe Jonathan Keyes is one of them."

"Maybe." She stepped out and away from the car.

Rashly started the engine and drove off. The other police cars had already moved on.

As Dixie passed in front of the shanties, heading back to the van, quizzical faces peered through tattered window shades. The kids had abandoned their cartoon show to watch the real action outside their window. Dixie winked as she passed, and they ducked below the sill, giggling. She had the feeling hundreds of pairs of eyes followed her progress down the deserted street. In the distance, traffic sounds attested that the city had not stopped going about its business, but here in this gray gutter town the quiet engulfed her. She flexed her shoulders and lengthened her stride.

Nearing the corner of the boarded-up grocery, she stepped off the sidewalk. A flash of purple lunged from the shadows, shrieking in high C and wielding a rusted iron pipe. The blow caught Dixie across the temple, knocking her to the ground. She rolled a moment too late, blocking the next blow with her forearm, and felt something crack.

Hermie Valdez, huge in her purple coat, swung the pipe again, missing this time and screeching with fury. Dixie reached for the .45.

Hermie kicked it out of her hand. A three-inch heel stomped down on Dixie's shoulder—pain shot through her chest.

Dixie caught Hermie at the knee and yanked. The woman crashed into the dry rot-riddled grocery front, but stayed on her feet. With her good hand, Dixie reached for the boot knife.

Hermie swung the pipe again, but this time Dixie rolled to her knees, bringing the knife around and arcing upward, into Hermie's arm. Hermie screamed, eyes riveted on the blade slicing through her coat and flesh, but she held tight to the pipe as she backed away.

Dixie stumbled to her feet. Blood ran into the corner of one eye from the blow to her temple. She blinked, keeping Hermie in sight, and edged forward with the knife.

The .45 had slid into the pile of trash bags. Doubtful she could reach it before Hermie swung the pipe down on her head.

"You the white bitch come snooping round, telling Sheila you a plumber. I tole her they ain't no leaky faucets in that house. Why'd you call the cops on my Alton?"

"Alton killed a man." Dixie eyed a streak of blood sliding down Hermie's coat.

Hermie clutched the pipe in both hands, waving it side to

side in front of her. Nervous. She didn't like the knife, but she didn't look scared of it, either.

"We's going away together, me and Alton. Today. Leave everything. Walk away and start over. Why'd you have to come here and mess us up?"

"Start over stealing and killing?"

"I never stole nothing in my life. And that man Alton killed? Was a accident. Alton, he's weak sometimes, but he's a good man when he's off the candy. Needs a new start is all."

"When has Alton ever been off the candy, Hermie?"

"Promised me. We leave together, he leave the habit behind."

"If it was that easy, why didn't he do it long ago? Before he killed a man?"

"I *told* you, that was a accident. I got some money saved. Alton been hiding out, waiting till my last paycheck come today. Could've made it. But *you*—"

She lunged, swinging the pipe at Dixie's head.

Dropping low, Dixie came in under Hermie's arm, leading with her injured shoulder and bringing the knife butt down hard on Hermie's wrist. The pipe fell. Dixie kicked it aside and shoved Hermie against the wall, the blade nicking the skin at the woman's throat, forcing her head back.

Hermie's mouth hardened. Her eyes burned down into Dixie's.

Dixie could feel Hermie's body tighten to strike out again. She was bigger than Dixie and a mean scrapper. Dixie didn't want to use the knife, but she had to do something quick. She slid the point lightly along Hermie's neck to her cheek, leaving a trail of ruby beads. The furious eyes narrowed.

"You're not afraid of losing your life, are you, Hermie? But what about your looks? One jab . . ."

The mouth trembled ever so slightly. Dixie slid the point up Hermie's cheek, not cutting but nicking the skin as it crossed the cheekbone.

A thin, barely audible whimper escaped the woman's lips.

"You could take me, Hermie. But I don't think you can move fast enough to avoid losing an eye."

Hermie held the stare another moment. Then she sagged against the wall.

"Take that blade outta my face. I won't fight no more."

"At least, not until my back is turned." Holding the knife steady, Dixie fished a small roll of duct tape from a vest pocket under the overall. Finding the folded end with her teeth, she pulled it out a few inches.

"Put your hands out. Hold them together in front of you."

Taping was awkward left-handed, but Dixie got enough duct tape on Hermie's wrists that she felt safe in lowering the knife. She found the cellular phone and dialed.

"You owe me one," she told Rashly.

Chapter Thirty-eight

"Ow!" Dixie flinched as Dann tried to help her out of her coat.

"What happened? You look awful—hey, that's blood. You cut your head."

"Just a scratch." She had stopped at a service station to wash the blood off her face, but she couldn't get it all out of her hair, and her jacket would have to go to the cleaners.

"That's no scratch. You need stitches."

"It'll be okay, Dann. Really. I just—I need a hot shower and half a dozen aspirin."

He got two aspirin and a glass of water while she shrugged out of her vest. She tried to hang the vest up, but her arm wouldn't move that high. She dropped the vest on the floor.

"What's wrong with your arm?"

She swallowed the aspirin and drank half the water.

"It'll be fine. Maybe I'll put an ice pack on it after I shower."

In the bathroom, she turned on the water and started to peel off her clothing, but again, her left arm wouldn't cooperate. The wide-leg overall presented the least problem. One long zip and she kicked out of them. She managed to pull the sweatshirt off one-handed by reaching behind her, bending over at the waist, and skinning the shirt down over her head. Getting the arms off was another problem, the boots even harder. By the time she had stripped to her underclothes, she was drenched in sweat. A sliver of pain shot through her arm and shoulder.

She sat down on the toilet seat, nauseated, dizzy. She leaned over, head down, and stayed that way for a while. After her head cleared, she saw a key chain lying on the tiles beside her foot, the key chain she'd picked up at Payne Hardware. Shoplifted, apparently. Scooping it up, she flicked the tiny flashlight on and off, then laid it on the sink and stepped into the shower. Warm water sluicing over her head took some of the pounding away.

Stepping out, she felt the need to sit down again, but stayed on her feet. Toweled off. Toweled her hair. Then wiped the fog off the mirror and got a surprise at the sight of her injuries. Her shoulder was bruised from collarbone to armpit. One area the size of her palm had turned a deep, ugly yellow. Her forearm was purple and swollen, and the cut on her head gaped.

Dann tapped on the door.

"Hey. Everything okay in there?"

"Yeah, thanks. I'm okay."

"I made some ginseng tea. To take some of the soreness out. Want it in there or in the kitchen?"

"I'll come out."

Her terry-cloth robe slipped on easily, without much pain, but she hated to think about dressing for dinner at Amy's.

Dann's ginseng tea smelled funny and tasted bitter.

"Drink it anyway. Tough broad like you doesn't get squeamish over a cup of tea." He had packed a deep tray with ice cubes, covered with a folded towel. Dixie sat down in the breakfast nook and laid her arm on the ice. Dann placed another ice pack on top. "You need this x-rayed. Might be broken."

"It's not broken."

"Oh. Now Superbroad has X-ray vision."

"Don't we have some of that aspirin cream in the first-aid kit? Rub some of that on it."

"Aspirin cream won't heal a broken bone." He brushed her hair away from the cut on her head.

"Ow!"

Mud, dozing under the table, sat up abruptly, then laid his heavy muzzle on her foot.

"I'll have to trim away some of your hair," Dann said.

"So trim it already. It's hair. It'll grow back." She'd have to think of some way to hide the bandage from Amy. Maybe a scarf. Did she have any scarves. "Ow!"

"I didn't touch it yet! I bumped your sho—you got something wrong with this shoulder, too?"

"A bruise."

"Bruise?" Ignoring her protests, he peeled back her robe to look at the shoulder. "Hellfire, woman! You need a doctor."

"It'll be okay. Rub some of that aspirin cream on it."

"Later. First an ice pack."

"Then take this one. My blood's turning to slush."

"Blood?" He dabbed alcohol on the cut and opened a box of bandages. "Superbroad ought to be fueled by high-test, at least."

"Hey! Why are you on my case?"

"Somebody needs to be. You take off without telling anyone, out there getting yourself banged up, nobody knows where you are. Your sister calls here—what am I supposed to tell her?"

"You improvised fine. Got yourself invited to dinner—OW!"

"Dammit, Dixie, this cut needs stitches."

"There's a sewing basket in the closet."

He sighed, long and heavy. "Maybe I can get a butterfly bandage to work."

Silence filled the minutes while he trimmed her hair around the cut, his touch gentler than she knew she deserved. She hated being fussed over, and had never been a cheerful patient. And she still wasn't used to having anybody besides family worry about her. Maybe she could at least lessen the worry about his own immediate future.

Reaching into her robe pocket, she took out the key chain with the mini-flashlight.

"You know that tunnel you woke up in last May first?" Catching his hand, she dropped the key chain into it. "I brought you a delayed Christmas present." His skin was warm and smooth against her palm.

"Present? What is it?"

Dixie wished suddenly that it was more than a two-dollar key chain. "It's just . . . sort of symbolic."

His gaze held hers, and a slow warmth filled her. She hadn't allowed herself to consciously acknowledge how devil-ishly attractive he was—the strong brow, the slightly irregular features, the compelling mouth.

He wiggled his eyebrows. "When do I get to open the present?"

"Oh." Her fingers still covered the key chain in his hand. She released it.

As he looked at the key chain, a puzzled expression came over his face for a moment. He grinned, finally, and flicked the switch.

"Miniature flashlight." Then a muscle jumped in his jaw, and a slow energy seemed to fill him, lifting his shoulders, quickening his breath. "A light in the tunnel."

"I gave Belle Richards enough clout today to swing your case hard in the right direction."

She watched him taking it in, trying to be cool but unable to deny the relief. He sat down abruptly.

"I didn't do it, then," he said softly, staring down at the key chain, flicking the light on and off. "Somebody else . . . in my car." He looked up. "Who?"

Dixie hesitated. "There's no absolute proof *against* any-body." That was the truth, although Belle would make the evidence sound as absolute as possible in court. She told him briefly about Travis Payne, since that was the scenario he'd hear from Belle. "The important thing is presenting the jury with an alternative possibility so strong they'll have no choice but to acquit."

She laid her good hand over his and squeezed gently.

"No guarantee. But I'd hate to be in the ADA's shoes come Monday." Seeing Dann's reaction, she realized how much she had wanted him to be innocent, and how worried she was that he might not be.

As the realization continued to sink in, his facial muscles relaxed, the jaw softening. The crease between his eyebrows all but disappeared. He looked down at their hands on the table. When Dixie started to withdraw hers, he captured it, rubbed his thumb lightly over her knuckles.

"Dixie, my own attorney didn't work as hard for me as you did."

"It was your attorney who sent me to find you. If not for her—"

"I know. But Richards was paid to believe in me. You just . . . did."

Dixie wished she could say that was true. Her passion for truth had driven her long before she met Parker Dann.

"There ought to be . . . something . . ." Dann's voice had gone hoarse. He cleared his throat. ". . . I can say . . . do . . . more than . . ." He sighed, then raised his eyes to meet hers. "Thanks."

Held by the intensity of his gaze, she realized that some part of her had believed in him. There was a decency about him that transcended even the mocking insolence he'd displayed at first.

"You're welcome." She liked the way his hand felt on hers. She wished the rest of her didn't feel like hamburger.

He must have noticed the pain in her face. He stood.

"We, uh, need to do something with that shoulder. You'll have to take the, uh, sleeve off, give me some room to work on it. I'll make some more tea."

When he turned to put the kettle on, Dixie slid the robe off and wrapped it tight across her chest, feeling incredibly bare beneath it.

He took the cup, rinsed the grounds out of the bottom, and

scooped a spoonful of something out of a plastic bag. Dixie watched him, noticing the way he moved. Any other man his size would look clumsy handling china cups. But he had a powerful grace, as comfortable in the kitchen as he was battling a South Dakota blizzard, as comfortable as she imagined he'd been on that tractor seat all those years ago.

He put the smelly tea in front of her and moved the ice pack to her shoulder.

"No, keep your arm on the cubes in the tray," he ordered when she started to move it. "How's the soreness?"

"Better. Almost gone." Actually, her arm really didn't hurt as much now. Probably frozen.

He dabbed peroxide on the cut at her temple, then drew the cut together with a Band-Aid, rubbing it lightly in place. When he was satisfied the bandage would hold, he took her arm from the tray and applied the analgesic lotion. His fingers gliding over her skin aroused every nerve. She guessed the arm wasn't frozen, after all.

"Drink your tea," he said gruffly. "It's getting cold."

She sipped and grimaced.

"Now the shoulder," he said, squeezing more lotion into his hand, warming it.

She turned sideways in the booth, her back to him. He rubbed the warm lotion on her back, his touch unbelievably tender.

"I was worried something was wrong when you took off in such a hurry this morning," he said. "After last night, I thought you might give up and turn me in." His fingers traveled around the front of her neck, stroking the hollow beneath her collarbone, down to just above her breast.

"Last night, I was almost ready to turn you in." Dixie held very still, allowing the delicious sensations to soothe her. His hand moved gently up, over her shoulder, and down her arm.

"Hey, you've got a bruise back here as big as a dinner plate. What the hell happened out there?"

Dixie recalled the flash of purple as Hermie Valdez raged out of the shadows, swinging her lead pipe.

"I made the mistake of coming between a woman and her man."

His thumb brushed the line of her jaw as he finished the stroke, back around her neck and over her collarbone, maddeningly sensual. Dixie knew she was making a mistake, but her hand seemed to rise of its own volition. She caught his fingers in hers and brought the back of his hand to her lips.

The moment seemed to stretch forever. Then she felt his breath feather her hair, and he buried his face in it. He kissed the top of her head, his arms encircling her gingerly from behind.

"You'll never know how lousy I felt," he whispered, "when you came in hurt. All bruised and bloody. I knew it had something to do with your helping me."

Dixie closed her eyes and enjoyed the awakening of senses she'd been suppressing. She was very, very glad Parker was innocent of involuntary manslaughter. She only wished she knew what he had going with Heather Burke.

Chapter Thirty-nine

"Mom, Dad! They're here!" A wreath of bells and holly jingled brightly as Ryan bounded out the door of the Royals' contemporary split-level home.

Dixie tugged at a yellow scarf covering her head wound, which matched the yellow silk pants suit Amy had given her. She'd found the scarf at the bottom of a dresser drawer, probably another gift, and she hoped the combination didn't make her look as much like a big Easter chicken as she felt. Dann kept looking at her like she'd beamed down from another planet.

"Relax," he said, when she fidgeted with a gold chain necklace she'd added at the last minute. "You should be going to a doctor, not to dinner, but you look fantastic."

Easy for him to say. She wished now she'd worn her jeans and hoped Amy and Carl wouldn't make a big deal out of her wearing girl clothes. One thing she had to admit, though: the silk felt terrific against her skin. Even when she'd worked in the DA's office, wearing a suit every day, she rarely attended events that required dressing up. And the minute she got home, she slipped into jeans.

Dann had driven, since her left shoulder wouldn't move two inches without jolting her with pain. Before she could open the Mustang's door, he was around the car and offering her a hand. Dixie felt a twinge of nostalgia. Barney had always insisted his "girls" wait patiently until he opened doors for them. In those final months, with all the trips to doctors, Dixie often had to steel herself against jumping out to help Barney from the car. Instead, she sat ticking off long, tedious moments as he extracted himself from the passenger seat and shuffled around to open her car door. He'd been a gentleman all his life. She wasn't about to deny him the few dignities he clung to as that life withered away.

Dixie accepted Dann's hand and stepped to the sidewalk. "Is this collar high enough?"

"Looks fine."

She tugged it higher. "I don't want Amy to see any bruises. She's always on my case, worried I'll get hurt. She thinks I should be a tax lawyer."

"Maybe she's right." He squeezed her left shoulder, sending a mild jolt along her collarbone.

"Hey, ow!" Dixie looked up to find his face etched with a teasing mockery she'd come to recognize as a challenge. On the drive over, he'd continued to insist that she see a doctor.

"Wow!" Ryan said, bounding up to meet them at the curb, staring. "You look different."

"Different how?" She had put on eye shadow and lipstick. Maybe it was too much. "I look okay, don't I?"

"Yeah, you're okay. Kinda *yellow*."

He studied Dann. Dixie introduced them, ruffling Ryan's hair and grabbing a quick kiss before he could escape. He folded something into her hand.

"The E-mail printout," he said.

"Okay." Dixie nodded, hoping to show her appreciation without too much encouragement. One big reason for being here tonight was to stop the Find-a-Fellow-for-Dixie game that had somehow gotten started.

"Read it," Ryan urged, "so I can get your reply on-line before Mom makes me shut the computer off for supper." He slid a sideways glance at Dann, frowned, and then looked back at Dixie, taking in the makeup, the yellow suit, and the cinnamon midheel pumps she'd found in the back of her closet.

"Where's your boots?" he demanded.

"Thought I'd give them a rest tonight. You don't like these?"

"They're okay."

He sniffed the air, scowling. Maybe she'd overdone the perfume.

As they approached the house, with Ryan bounding ahead of them, Dann whispered, "You smell like a sea breeze."

Was that good? Or did it mean she smelled like dead fish?

The house, however, smelled great, like pine boughs and smoked turkey. Amy, in rose-pink hostess pajamas, tiny gold bells tinkling at her ears, and Carl, in his "Texas Chili Peppers" barbecue apron, came in from the kitchen. Dixie introduced them to Parker Dann. Carl eyed her clothes, glanced at Dann, and grinned wickedly. Dixie's face flushed. The men shook hands, sizing each other up.

"Dann . . . Dann, Parker Dann," Carl said. "Unusual name. I've heard it somewhere."

"There's a pro golfer named Palmer Dann," Dixie said, blurting the first lie that came to mind. Dann's trial hadn't been featured in the newspaper lately, only a few lines near the back. But she'd forgotten Carl's habit of reading the news cover to cover every day.

"Pro golfer?" Carl said. "No, that's not it . . ."

Amy drew Dixie aside.

"Where have you been keeping him? He looks just like that actor, that . . . what's his name? The one with the other two men and a baby?"

"Amy, don't you ever watch *recent* movies?" Dann did look a bit like Tom Selleck, though. A *young* Tom Selleck. Or maybe Sean Connery. Dann had a face that would age well.

"Dixie, any man that can fill out a shirt like he can is worth having around just to look at." Amy tucked the yellow scarf behind Dixie's ear, patted a stray hair in place. "And look at you! Positively glowing. How long have you two been dating?"

"Whoa! Slow down. Who says we're dating?" Dixie watched miserably as Carl guided Dann toward the dining room. She hoped Carl's name-remembering had been diverted. Amy would have a nerve attack if she discovered Dann's true claim to fame.

"Now, Dixie, when was the last time you brought a man to our house for dinner?" Amy gushed. "What does he do? Sort of a handyman, you said? He was doing some work at your house?"

"That wobbly porch rail. But he actually sells heavy equipment. You know, cranes, backhoes."

A high-pitched buzz sounded from the hallway. Everyone looked up as Ryan taxied the Cessna model across the rug, between their feet and into the dining room, where Carl was opening a bottle of Piesporter. The airplane crashed into Dann's shoe.

"What's this?" He picked the plane up and examined it.

"Ryan," Amy said, "apologize to Mr. Dann for bumping into him with that thing."

"Sorry."

"No harm done." Dann smiled graciously at Amy, then turned back to Ryan. "Model 185. Classic."

"You know about airplanes?" Ryan rushed to take it, the remote in his other hand.

"Sold Cessnas for a while," Dann said. "Long time ago. The 185 was top of the line in single engines."

"Wow! Did you ever ride in one?"

"Had to get over being airsick first. Can't sell an airplane sitting on the ground. Later, I got my pilot's license and flew one occasionally."

"Cool!"

Carl handed around glasses of wine. "About that waterfront property," he told Dann. "What I'm saying, you'll find some good investments along the Texas coast."

"Seabrook, Galveston?"

"Rockport. Nice little town farther south," Carl said. "You should check it out."

"You're thinking about moving?" Dixie asked.

Dann shrugged, his face inscrutable. "My neighbors aren't as friendly as they used to be."

Dixie wondered if he was about to drift on, now that his future didn't include prison. The thought of it bothered her. Maybe he'd drift back to Louisiana, back to Heather Burke.

"Waterfront lots can be risky," Carl said. "What I'm saying—"

"Dinner's ready!" Amy announced. "Let's sit down before it freezes over. Parker, take this chair beside Dixie's."

Dann pulled out Dixie's chair at the round table and waited for her to be seated. Amy beamed at the conspicuous courtesy, while Ryan claimed the seat on the other side of his new airplane buddy. It seemed Dann knew how to win hearts of all ages.

"Do you have a real airplane?" Ryan asked.

"We could rent one for a couple hours. Want to go up some time?" Dann looked at Carl for approval.

"For real?" Ryan's eager gaze grabbed Dixie's as if seeking assurance that Dann wasn't pulling his leg.

Dixie shrugged. "Better pray he flies airplanes better than he fixes porch rails."

Amy passed a heavy platter, which Dixie almost accepted with her lame arm. When she hesitated, Dann took it for her.

"Look at this—baked yams!" He forked one onto Dixie's plate. "I love these things. How about you, Ryan?" He helped Ryan's plate, then his own, before setting the dish down. "Your mom sets a heckuva fine table."

Amy's proud smile was enough to make Dixie glad Dann had come to dinner, despite a growing uneasiness. Her family had warmed quickly to his easy charm and directness. But behind his charming demeanor lay a past with more twists than a pretzel factory.

"How did you two meet?" Amy asked, passing the cranberry sauce.

"A friend of Parker's," Dixie blurted. "Heather Burke."

Dann's wineglass clinked as he knocked it over, catching it just before it hit the table.

"Sorry." He dabbed at the spilled droplets.

Amy's eyes had widened, heart undoubtedly skipping a beat. The cut crystal was a family heirloom.

"The glass was . . . nearly empty," she stammered. "Carl, open another bottle, would you? I'll refill Parker's glass with what's left in this one."

While they bustled around with the wine, Dixie looked up to find Dann staring at her, a twinkle of malice in his blue eyes.

"How'd you happen on the name of Heather Burke?" he murmured.

She riveted her attention on cutting a bite of turkey. "Open a can with no label and you never know what will pour out."

"Mr. Dann," Ryan piped, "can we go flying before school starts? That's Monday."

"Don't pester him, Ryan," Amy said. "Parker, you don't sound as if you were born around here. Where did you grow up?"

"Montana. Until I graduated college. Then I traveled to northern Florida to sell time-share condos. Sold cruise packages in Maine. Indian art in Arizona, ski equipment in Colorado." He dropped a casual hand on Dixie's bad shoulder. "Texas is my favorite, though. Met some friendly, interesting people here. Stubborn as crabgrass, but friendly."

Under the table, Dixie gouged her salad fork into Dann's leg. She turned to smile at him sourly. Flinching, he lifted his heavy hand from her shoulder and slid a glance at her. His blue eyes were as teasing as a small boy's.

"Where'd you sell airplanes?" Ryan piped.

"Montana, Canada." Dann's smirk disappeared before he turned to Ryan. "Crop dusters, mostly. Ranchers up that way use a plane to get around. Especially the Hollywood ranchers."

"That's right!" Anything to do with movies always sparked Amy's interest. "*People* magazine said a number of actors have bought ranches in Montana."

"Wouldn't mind going up myself," Carl said. "I've flown in your commercial puddle jumpers, sixteen-passenger jobs, and a charter jet once, but never a private plane like Ryan's there—what I'm saying, a real one."

"Haven't taken one up in a while," Dann said. "But my license is still good. We could make a day of it."

"Sounds like fun," Amy said. "Carl, are you going to pour that wine or just hold it?"

Dixie watched her family grow more and more enthralled as Dann described the difference between high-wing Cessnas and low-wing Beechcraft. They liked him, had opened their big hearts and scooped him right in. There was something warm, vital, and electric about Parker Dann. Watching how easily he talked to Carl about investments, complimented Amy on her cooking, patiently answered Ryan's unending questions about flying, Dixie could see how he'd made all the money in those various bank accounts. Damn him, her family could no more resist his piratical charm than a fly could resist flypaper. He was one hell of a salesman.

Today he cut a particularly dashing figure, in blue flannel slacks and a crisply pressed white shirt. His hair waved over his ears, slightly longer, she imagined, than was normal for him. He looked like everybody's favorite hero. Dixie found herself wishing that Smokin had never uncovered the disturbing trail to Dann's past.

"Those little planes aren't dangerous, are they?" Amy asked. "Oh, I suppose they *have* to be, but . . . so *many* people fly them these days. I feel so adventurous!"

"You'll go up in the plane, won't you, Aunt Dixie?"

"Well . . ." Her earliest heroine had been Amelia Earhart. But that was before Dixie's first air travel, a flight to Disneyland with the Flannigans.

"Your aunt spits in the eye of danger," Dann said, lightly brushing Dixie's bruised shoulder. "Isn't that right?"

Dixie bit down on a curse. "Maybe we should wait till spring, when the weather's better." She *hated* flying, even in first-class splendor on a supersafe 747, with earphones, relaxation music, and movies to take her mind off the fact that she was hovering miles above the earth in a sardine can with wings. She *wanted* to love it. But she truly *hated* flying. "Anyway, since Parker hasn't flown in a while, maybe he should go up alone first."

Ryan looked like someone had stolen the goodies out of his Christmas stocking. Carl, seeing Dann finish his dinner roll, handed him the bread basket.

"Not something you'd forget, I imagine," Carl said. "Like riding a bicycle. You get on, and it all comes back."

"Except when you fall off a bicycle, the buzzards don't circle." Dixie snatched a roll for herself.

"Now, Dixie," Amy said. "Stop being a wet blanket and pass Mr. Dann another piece of turkey."

Dixie took the plate and shoved it at Parker. He grinned at her with bland, mocking impudence.

New Year's Eve morning, four days before Dann's trial date, Dixie awoke late with a gripping ache at the back of her head and a talking bear clutched in her arms, two good indications she'd enjoyed more than a fair share of wine at Amy's dinner party the night before. The stuffed bear, a gift from Ryan, said things like "Hug me, I hug back."

"Take me with you," it pleaded now as Dixie stumbled to the bathroom.

Parker Dann had made such an impression that Amy and Carl had invited him to dinner on New Year's Day. Dann insisted on bringing dessert. Everyone assumed Dixie would be pleased with the arrangement. She wasn't sure how she felt about that.

Pain shot through her shoulder as she opened the medicine chest to look for aspirin. Her whole body couldn't feel worse if it'd been used for a hockey puck.

The rich smell of bacon wafted from the kitchen. She pictured Dann at the stove, Mud standing guard, and wondered how long it would take to resume her normal routines—burnt toast for breakfast, junk food for lunch, salad greens for dinner. Mud would never forgive her when his bowl offered only dry dog food. Maybe she could find an exotic brand for special occasions.

She swallowed the aspirin with water from her tooth cup, then decided to brush her teeth. Rinsing her toothbrush, she eyed the dental floss, reasoned that wounded people deserved some exemptions, and picked up the hairbrush.

Belle had left a message saying she couldn't talk to the ADA until Monday about withdrawing the charges against Dann. The ADA wouldn't be happy about reopening the investigation—especially against two such upstanding citizens as Jon Keyes and Travis Payne. After coming so close to a conviction, pure cussedness might keep him from dropping the case. But Belle Richards wasn't dubbed "Texas' hottest defense lawyer" for nothing.

In any case, except for delivering Dann to court and collecting her fee, Dixie's job for Richards, Blackmon & Drake was finished. Yet, truthfully, it didn't feel finished at all. Possibly because Dann was still living in her house.

There was something distinctly disquieting about that. She remembered falling asleep last night with a tingling realization that he lay just across the hall, as alone in his bed as she was in hers. For a swift, wine-induced moment, a sweet madness had swept over her. She'd thrown the covers back and put her feet on the cold floor before regaining her senses— how would she feel if she cuddled in his bed and he rejected her?

Worse, what if he responded to her sexual overtures, then later drifted on his way? Except for the brief moments of tenderness when she came home wounded, Parker had never expressed any emotional interest—she didn't count his obvious moves on the drive to Houston, when he was trying to romance her into dropping her guard.

Not that she was totally opposed to relationships based strictly on physical needs. Hadn't she always been the one to keep men at an emotional distance? Now she wasn't sure how to get close.

Perhaps they'd both feel different after he was no longer her prisoner. If Belle was successful in her talk with the ADA, Dann would be a free man in four days. Surely he wasn't crazy enough to skip town now that his case stood a good chance of being dismissed. Dixie could reasonably send him home, let him spend the weekend in his own digs.

On the other hand, this was New Year's Eve. The bars would beckon. After a few drinks, Dann might feel panicky and, even with his acquittal practically in the bag, might convince himself he'd never walk out of the courtroom a free man.

Dixie flipped a strand of hair forward to cover her bandage. It wasn't Parker Dann that made the job feel unfinished. It was six-year-old Ellie Keyes. Freeing Dann wasn't enough if Ellie was still in danger, or was right now being molested by her father.

Fortunately according to the visitation schedule, Ellie would be spending New Year's weekend safely at home. Dixie planned to resume her investigation of Jon Keyes first thing Monday, but maybe she should just drop by the Garden Cafe today and see how Ellie was weathering the flu. Exchange a few knock-knock jokes. If she went early enough, Rebecca would be busy in the kitchen.

"You're an old softie," the bear said when Dixie elbowed it off the commode lid.

"And you're a blabbermouth." Dixie gingerly pulled on clothes and scooped up the bear, parking it in the breakfast nook when she entered the kitchen.

"Only two eggs," Dan reported, standing over the stove. "So I made French toast and bacon. How's that?"

"Smells great. I'll pick up more eggs when I go out."

"Out? Did you see the weather?" He turned off the burner under the toast. "Is this another dangerous assignment?"

"No. Just wrapping up a few loose ends." She plucked a slice of bacon off the platter and halved it with one bite. "How do you get this to cook so evenly? Mine's always burned on one end, raw on the other."

"Vigilance," he said. "Vigilance and patience."

She could hear frustration in his words, along with something she didn't recognize until she looked up to see the worry in his eyes. The chattering voice in Dixie's mind abruptly went quiet.

"Nothing dangerous today," she said. "Honest." He could go with her, she supposed, except then she couldn't visit Ellie. Dixie took the pot from him and poured the coffee. "Maybe I'd better get used to waiting on myself now."

They sat down to breakfast with a huge silence between them. Dinner at Amy's had muddied their relationship. No longer were they merely jailor and jailee.

"Guess you didn't believe in me as much as I thought," Dann said. "Since you know about Heather."

"I know you won the paternity suit. I know she was eighteen and you were thirty-five."

Another silence.

"Dann . . ." *Parker*. Since he was no longer a prisoner, she didn't need to distance herself further by using his last name. "Parker, my instincts about people are good but not infallible. I had to check you out."

He moved his toast around the plate, soaking up honey. He hadn't eaten much, she noticed.

"Heather was a very *mature* eighteen."

Dixie didn't know what to say to that. Eighteen was eighteen.

Parker pushed his plate aside. "Guess men don't look at age the same way women do. A few drinks, a warm, willing female."

"Whoa! You don't have to explain anything." Dixie had no desire to hear the intimate details. She carried her dishes to the dishwasher.

"Heather was a secretary to one of my clients," Dann persisted. "One day the client dissolved the company. No warning, bam! Big CLOSED sign on the door. Heather's out of a job, I lost a big contract. Guess misery loves company. We went out a couple times. Nearly three years later I get these papers in the mail. She knew the baby wasn't mine. Her relationship with her boss had been more than she let on, but he disappeared and I looked like an easy mark. Guess she figured I wouldn't do the tests." Parker paused. "Tell you the truth, I kind of wished the kid *was* mine."

"You send her money every month."

He took his plate to the sink and scraped his uneaten breakfast into the garbage disposal.

"He's a great kid. Working, raising him alone, be easy for a woman to feel desperate, jump the first guy who shows an interest. Maybe the few bucks I send give Heather a chance to make choices."

A sudden image invaded Dixie's thoughts—a tawdry princess, too young to be a mother, with too many men knocking at her door but no handsome prince to help her turn them away. Life sure got complicated at times.

Dixie grabbed her jacket from the closet. She felt a huge need to be alone for a while, and the overcast sky outside suggested she finish her errands fast. On her way out the door, she tossed Parker the talking bear.

"Hug me," it said. "I hug back."

Parker plunked the bear on top of the refrigerator and opened the door. Dixie had left before he could find out if she was okay about last night. He'd enjoyed visiting her family, hamming it up. And he'd seen another side of her, a softer side—tough bitch turned mild-mannered, insecure little sister. But Dixie had gone real quiet after he accepted Carl's invitation to dinner tomorrow. Parker hoped she didn't feel he was mooching in where he didn't belong.

Now why the friggin hell was he standing here looking in the refrigerator? Oh, yeah, *tonight's* dinner. He took out a ham and the orange juice, then a package of frozen black-eyed peas from the freezer. After splashing some juice in Mud's dish, he filled a glass and drank half of it.

He'd miss Mud when he left. Wasn't right leaving a dog alone all the time. He'd miss Flannigan, too. Last night, lying there in the dark, he couldn't get her face out of his mind, the way she'd looked after a couple glasses of wine. Relaxed. Happy. Enticingly female. And there she was, maybe twenty steps beyond his own bed. He'd been halfway to the door before realizing only a total jerk would show up in her room uninvited. If she was interested in sharing some time between the sheets, she'd have put out signals.

" 'Love is an irresistible desire to be irresistibly desired,' " he told Mud, who'd lapped up his juice and sat watching Parker juggle the ham. "Robert Frost wrote a lot of shit about love. Maybe he even got some of it right."

Parker put the ham in the oven and the black-eyed peas on a rear burner to cook. Until he came to Texas, he'd never thought about eating black-eyed peas on New Year's Day for good luck. Now he wouldn't dare miss them. Who knew what bad luck he'd suffered in years past simply from not eating black-eyed peas?

Mud watched him adjust the flame under the pot, then padded to the ultility room and came back with his Frisbee.

"Aw, I don't think so. Looks cold out there. Cloudy. Like it might rain."

Mud looked at the door. Looked back at Parker. Padded to the door and waited, the red toy clamped in his mouth.

"Okay. Half an hour, that's all."

Parker opened the coat closet and shrugged into his parka. Before pulling on his gloves, he went to the den and took out the volume of *How Things Work* that described automobile ignitions.

Mud had been all teeth and determination every time Parker threw the Frisbee toward the gate. But when he tossed it into the garage, no problem. And when he jimmied the lock on Dixie's taxicab, and the Frisbee landed inside, the dog had lumbered in to retrieve it. Later, Parker whistled Mud up onto the seat to ride shotgun. Providing he learned how to hot-wire the ignition, Parker figured he'd have no trouble at all *driving* out the gate, so long as the dog went with him.

Finishing the juice, Parker set the glass in the sink and scooped up the book. When he shut the refrigerator door, the bear fell off and bounced.

"I love you," it said. "Do you love me?"

He thumped the bear down on the table and went outside with Mud.

Chapter Forty

The rain turned mushy as Dixie drove the twenty miles from Richmond to Houston and parked across the street from Payne Hardware and the Garden Cafe. When she stepped from the car, sleet stung her face, reminding her of the trip with Parker through South Dakota. Had it been only a week ago?

Ice-slickened sidewalks triggered her phobia about falling, but she planted her boot heels and ignored the queasiness. If she could weather a South Dakota blizzard, she could handle Houston ice. Surprisingly, the anxiety lifted.

A note on the door said Payne Hardware was closed until Monday, but the cafe was open until two o'clock, according to the sign. She was determined to check on Ellie, even if it meant another argument with Rebecca. Gillis greeted her at the counter.

"Cheers!" Dixie said, sliding her last handful of Hershey's Hugs toward the waitress. "Why's the hardware store closed? Did the Paynes go somewhere for the holiday?"

"Mr. Payne went to visit his folks in Denton, but Ellie's still down with the flu, so Rebecca stayed in town. We fixed up a little bed in the storeroom near the kitchen. Ellie's sleeping."

"My nephew caught it, too," Dixie said. "But he's feeling better already."

Gillis poured Dixie a cup of coffee, her fourth that morning. "Some kids are strong like that. Poor Ellie seems to feel worse every day. Can't kick the fever."

"She's been to the doctor, hasn't she?"

"Oh, sure. He gave her these little white pills, and I guess they're helping. Mrs. Payne says Ellie just needs plenty of rest and liquids. Mr. Payne was really angry, though, that they couldn't all drive up together to see his folks. I've never seen him so upset."

The bell over the door tinkled delicately. As Gillis left to wait on the new customers, Travis Payne's bank records filled Dixie's mental computer screen. White numbers popped in and out of a blue spreadsheet as money moved from one account to another. Fifty thousand dollars after each death. When Payne installed the new computer section at the hardware store, his balance plummeted to an all-time low. Yet, he had mentioned adding software and accessories. Where did he plan to get the money?

First rule of detection, Flannigan: look at who profits. A mom-and-daughter "accident" would mean two million and change to Payne's bottom line.

Today was only New Year's Eve, not the actual holiday, and it was also a Thursday. Smart retailers didn't close in the middle of the week—unless, of course, there was reason to believe one might be coming into some money . . . maybe taking advantage of the bad weather? Slick streets, low visibility, car suddenly out of control, Payne conveniently thrown free while his wife and stepdaughter smash into a concrete embankment. Quick cash.

Dixie swallowed the last of her coffee. Gillis had told her that Rebecca and Ellie stayed at home. So maybe Travis-Santa Claus-Payne was just a lamebrained businessman with strong feelings about keeping families together at Christmas and no sinister motives.

Outside, the weather had turned miserable—freezing, sleeting, with a wind nearly as cruel as the one in South

Dakota. A braking motorist slid through the intersection, missing the Mustang by a hair. Not the ideal time to be running errands, Dixie realized, but things needed to be done.

At the supermarket, she picked up everything on Parker's list, then stood pondering a display of champagne. Usually, she wasn't much of a party person on holidays. Last year she'd fallen asleep watching a movie on her VCR, missing the big Twelve-O-O entirely. But tonight she'd have company. Parker would likely cook something special. She picked up a bottle of champagne to ring in the New Year, hesitated, then added five more bottles to her cart.

Traffic on the freeway was all but stopped. Houstonians were uncomfortable driving under icy conditions. As a veteran now, she zipped ahead, taking the Mykawa exit to Homicide Division. At Rashly's office, she dropped off the first bottle of champagne. He held it at arm's length to read the label.

"You get five thousand dollars for an hour's work, and this is the best you can afford?"

"Surely you don't expect me to buy you the good stuff. Your palate's so deadened from smoking that pipe, you couldn't taste the difference between Chateau du Pape and turpentine."

"I get satisfaction from reading the label."

"You're saying a hundred-dollar bottle reads better than the twenty-dollar variety?"

"How the hell do I know? The good stuff's always in French."

Dixie tipped him a wave. "Cheers, Ben."

"Hey." He tossed her a gold foil bag, embossed with holly leaves and sealed at the top with a gold medallion. "You did damn good on that Sikes thing."

She peeled the medallion off carefully, already certain what was inside. Every year Rashly ordered dark sweet chocolates with liqueur centers, straight from Switzerland. So good they should be illegal. Better than drugs or sex, Dixie had once told him. On her way out the door, she aped a swoon.

The second bottle of champagne she took to Amy and

Carl, with a split of nonalcoholic bubbly for Ryan and a large container of orange juice. Carl liked to make mimosas on New Year's morning.

"Why don't you join us tonight?" Amy said. "Bring Parker. Carl picked up a stack of videos. We can make popcorn."

Dixie managed to beg off by reminding Amy they'd be over for dinner the next day.

The last three bottles of champagne were intended for the Gypsy Filchers. They wouldn't be in, of course, but they had methods for keeping track of visitors to their headquarters, even in the daytime. She tapped in the code on the nine-digit keypad. When the elevator doors opened, she placed the three bottles of champagne precisely in the center of the car, and tucked an envelope down between them. Inside the envelope she had placed five one-hundred-dollar bills, five percent of the fee she'd collect later from Belle Richards, wrapped in notepaper with the single word THANKS. They'd never miss her at the party.

When the twenty-minute drive home looked like turning into an hour, the roads getting slicker every minute, Dixie picked up the cell phone to call Parker. A coating of ice glistened on rooftops. Long icicles hung from eaves. Power lines drooped under the extra weight. Trees lacy with frozen droplets sparkled red and green in the streetlights, turning the city to a winter wonderland that quickened Dixie's holiday spirit. The phone fuzzed out a couple of times before she finally got a connection.

"I hate to tell you this," Parker said, "because it probably means you'll be late for dinner again, but Jon Keyes has been calling every ten minutes for the past hour."

Keyes? "Did he say what he wanted?"

"Only that it's urgent."

Dixie wasn't eager to have her good mood spoiled, but if Keyes was still pissed about her checking up on him, maybe he'd let slip something she could use. She rang the number he'd left with Parker. The area code sounded like Austin. "Mr. Keyes?"

"Oh, Jesus, thanks for calling. After yesterday, I wasn't sure you would, but I didn't know who else to ask. The cops won't help, and I've got this awful feeling—"

"Slow down." He was talking so fast she could barely understand him. "Tell me what's wrong."

"It's Ellie." She heard him take a breath. "I phoned to check the messages on my machine. I taught the girls to call anytime, for any reason, or just to talk, only this time Ellie sounds . . . strange, like she's hurt or lost . . . I've never heard anything like it. The cafe closed early and Rebecca won't answer the goddamn phone—"

"Where are you?"

"In Austin. Flew in for a meeting—"

"Maybe Ellie's medication—"

"Medication? Has she been sick? Why the hell didn't Rebecca tell me?"

"It's only the flu. You didn't know?"

"I haven't talked to Ellie since Sunday. This goddamn job is running me ragged—"

"I was at the cafe this morning. Gillis said Ellie's still pretty sick. Maybe Rebecca took her to the doctor." *Ellie seems to feel worse every day*, Gillis had said. Ryan was almost fully recovered.

"I think I have the pediatrician's number here." Keyes' voice grew muffled, as if he had tucked the receiver under his chin. "Here it is. I'll call him, but . . . you're a private investigator, right?"

"Well . . ." Not exactly a *licensed* investigator.

"If Ellie isn't at the doctor's office, if they haven't seen her, I want you to find out what's going on."

"Mr. Keyes—"

"I don't care what it costs, whatever your rate, I'll pay."

"That's not the—"

"You can't imagine how awful Ellie sounded, like she was . . . I don't know . . . scared."

Perhaps Rebecca changed her mind and decided to join Travis in Denton. But Gillis had said Ellie was still ill.

"Jon, does Rebecca have family or close friends she might have left Ellie with?"

"You obviously don't know my ex-wife. She's—well, Rebecca doesn't make friends, and except for a card or gift at holidays, and to arrange visits for the girls, she's scarcely spoken to either of her parents in years—"

"Her parents are divorced?"

"Since Rebecca was a kid. Christ, maybe that's why Rebecca's so desperate for attention, why her world revolves around the man in her life. I don't know how Travis takes it. It nearly drove me crazy—"

"Some men would find that flattering."

"I suppose it was, at first. But the woman clings like briar nettles. She won't let you breathe. She was even jealous of the time I spent with the girls—"

"Your adopted daughters."

"Ellie, too, after she was born. I've spent more time with those kids since the divorce than I did in all the years we were married."

Jealous of her own kids? Dixie recalled Keyes' similar comments in the custody hearing transcripts. She wasn't entirely sure she trusted his motives.

"Mr. Keyes, go ahead and call that doctor, then get back to me. I'll have someone telephone the hospitals." She gave him her cell phone number.

"What's going on?" Parker said when Dixie rang him back.

"Ellie left a cryptic message on her father's answering machine. Now Ellie's disappeared, and he's worried. Frankly, so am I. Something feels wrong." Dann agreed to call the hospitals, starting with those closest to Spring Branch. Dixie had scarely disconnected, when Jon Keyes called back.

"The doc says Rebecca brought Ellie in on Monday. She had the flu that's going around, and he prescribed some antibiotics for the bronchial symptoms. Told Rebecca to call him if Ellie wasn't better in a couple of days. He hasn't heard from her since, so he assumed Ellie was recovering."

It's a nasty strain, three people have died.

"I also called Rebecca's mother in Plano," Keyes said. "She told me Rebecca was planning to drop Ellie off with her, then drive on up to Denton where Payne's family lives.

About an hour ago, Rebecca called back, said the roads were icing over. She owns a house on Lake Livingston, and she was going to stop there overnight, start out again when the weather clears."

The people who died were street people without anyone to care for them, Amy had said. Kids were more resilent than street people. But maybe Rebecca didn't realize this flu strain was more dangerous than most.

"Jon, do you know where the cabin is located?"

"Somewhere east of Huntsville, about an hour from Houston. I was only there once, right after we married."

"Let me see what I can find out. I'll call you back."

"Are you thinking of driving all the way up there tonight?"

"Unless there's a phone . . ."

"I asked Rebecca's mother. There's no phone at the cabin, no answer on Rebecca's car phone. You think something's wrong up there, don't you?" When Dixie didn't answer immediately, he started rambling. "Rebecca wouldn't ignore Ellie's health. She never actually neglected any of the girls. Maybe she doesn't pay them a lot of attention, but . . . Oh, Jesus, that's what you think, isn't it? That Rebecca's so wrapped up in her business and her new husband that Ellie isn't getting the care she needs."

"Mr. Keyes, all I'm thinking is maybe Rebecca needs some help, up there in the woods alone, with Ellie sick. If we can find out where the cabin's located, maybe someone from the local sheriff's department would drive out and check on them."

"Okay. Okay . . . let me think. Maybe Rebecca's mother—"

"Call her back. Meanwhile, I'll see what I can dig up."

She punched in a number for Belle Richards. "Did you bring Dann's file home with you?"

"With all the work I have to finish before Monday? Of course. What do you need?"

"That lake property Rebecca Payne received in the settlement from her first husband, do you have an address on it?"

"It's in the boondocks, Flannigan. Trust me, there won't

be a street address. But maybe there's something . . . here it is." She read off the state road and general location. "Hey, I talked to the insurance investigator. Remember that gross story you told me about the three-legged pig?"

"What about it?"

"What would you say if the pig cut off its own leg so the farmer wouldn't starve?"

It took Dixie a moment to shift her thoughts and let the question sink in. She suppressed a shudder.

"You're suggesting Rebecca cut off her own fingers? *On purpose?*"

"The investigator is convinced, although he couldn't prove it. Travis left the room to wait on a customer, heard the saw start up and run for a few seconds. When he got back, there's Rebecca holding a shop rag around her bleeding hand, calmly dialing 911. Travis sees the fingers lying on the floor, wants to wrap them in ice, but can't bring himself to pick the things up. Yuck."

"Betsy was in the room when this happened?"

"She was in the room, but claimed she was sweeping up sawdust and didn't see the accident. The investigator thinks she did see it, or at least saw enough to suspect what really happened. When he asked where she was when her mother screamed, Betsy said Rebecca *didn't* scream."

"Damn, what's she made of? Stone?"

"Rebecca claimed she was too shocked to scream when it happened, and the pain didn't start until afterward."

"That fits with reports I've heard of gunshot wounds."

"But get this. The investigator said Rebecca called to ask about her dismemberment clause and how soon she could expect a check while she was still in the ER waiting for the doc to look at her hand."

A chill seeped through Dixie's bones. Had Rebecca maimed herself for $20,000? The money had lasted no more than a month in her husband's bank account.

"Ric, what would seeing something like that do to a kid? She'd be scared to death her mother was crazy."

"I can't see a sane woman calmly hacking off her own fingers."

What was it Rashly had said? *It amazes me what some women will do for a man.*

Dixie felt sick. "If a couple fingers are worth twenty thousand dollars, is fifty thousand a fair price for a child? Are we saying Travis got a taste of easy money and talked Rebecca into murdering her own children to finance his business expansion?"

"You're the one who pointed out that Rebecca has a hard time hanging on to husbands."

"It sounds so crazy. No crazier, I suppose, than the man who killed Halloween." Houstonians would be a long time forgetting that one. The man poisoned his own kids' candy before sending them out trick-or-treating.

"It's always easier to believe such atrocities of men. Trust me, Flanni, women account for fifty-five percent of domestic violence."

But *mothers* were supposed to love their kids. They could be thoughtless, sure, careless, forgetful, self-centered. But underneath all that, mothers loved their kids. *A mother does not look the other way while her husband kills her children.*

Does a mother pretend her "boyfriends" are not visiting her daughter's bedroom? Dixie swallowed hard, recalling the nights she had prayed Scully wouldn't come, or that her mother would stay sober and not pass out. Now she remembered something else. Mama always bought her something special after one of Scully's visits, usually a box of cherry cordials. Dixie had loved cherry cordials. The thought of them now made her want to throw up.

"I'm not ready to rule out Jon Keyes," Dixie said, realizing that she *had* softened toward him. The fear in Keyes' voice had been too real . . . of course, Ellie was his blood daughter, while Betsy and Courtney were not . . . did that make the two older girls expendable?

"Maybe Rebecca's accident was really exactly that, just an accident," she told Belle. "But maybe getting that first insurance check incited Travis' greed." Now her own voice sounded shaky and filled with fear. She cleared her throat. "You realize, of course, if both kids had been killed in one accident, we might never have caught on. I'm surprised the killer—whichever of them it was—didn't consider that."

"Perhaps the first fifty thousand was supposed to put Travis' business forever in the black."

"Like a gambler's lament? The next race, the next game, will be the one that scores big, paying off the old debts?"

"Dear God, Dixie, we're talking about *children*! You make it sound so . . . dispassionate, like buying a lottery ticket. It's giving me the shivers."

"What gives me shivers, Ric, is knowing that Travis Payne is out of money and Ellie is missing."

Chapter Forty-one

Ellie kicked the covers off. She was hot, hot, hot. Dreaming of peanut butter-and-chocolate ice cream, her favorite of all thirty-one flavors. Mommy had bought her a cone and told her not to drip on the rug, but the ice cream kept melting, running down her fingers faster than she could lick it off.

She started to run, *hurry, get off the rug*, but the rug wouldn't go away! She ran fast. The rug stretched to meet her feet, curling up at the end like a big tongue, lapping at her teasing her.

Screaming, Ellie turned and ran the other way, melted ice cream sticky on her face and hands. The rug curled faster and faster and faster, licking at her legs, covering her like a scratchy blanket.

Ellie stomped and kicked, trying to get the scratchy rug away from her legs. Then she fell and tried to crawl, but the rug wrapped itself round and round and round, sealing her up like a bug in a cocoon.

She punched at it, tearing away big chunks of sticky fuzz with her fingers, but it was no use. Every time she tore away one chunk, another grew in its place.

She was hot . . . so hot . . .

Chapter Forty-two

New Year's Eve, Interstate 45, Texas

Dixie rummaged through the glove box until she found a map of Walker County and the area surrounding Lake Livingston, where the cabin was located. Hail peppered the Mustang's roof like buckshot as she joined a stream of holiday traffic on the interstate. The hour was early enough that holiday revelers were still reasonably sober. Later, the bar fights would start. Maybe bad weather would curtail the usual fireworks disasters.

Tuning the radio to an all-news station, Dixie adjusted the volume over the noise of the hail. Severe thunderstorms were expected in a nine-county area, temperatures in the teens. She wondered if Rebecca's cabin had sufficient heat, imagined Ellie shivering in a dark room, brown eyes bright with fever, face chapped, lips parched. . . .

Noticing her death grip on the wheel, her heavy boot on the gas pedal, Dixie forced the image from her mind. What help would she be to Ellie if she plowed into another car?

The cabin was still more than an hour away. What if Rebecca told Travis she was stopping at the cabin, and he decided to join her? His "traffic accident" squelched, what better place to effect Ellie's death than a lonely cabin in the woods—the child already ill?

However, Jon Keyes was on the edge of hysterics, which wouldn't help anyone. Dixie dialed home; got a busy signal. Who the hell was Parker talking to? *If Travis is determined Ellie won't survive the flu,* she thought, *if he's doing something right now to escalate Ellie's symptoms, I don't have a snowman's chance in hell of getting to the cabin on time.*

She needed to round up some help. She dialed the Walker County Sheriff's Department.

"We're overloaded with traffic accidents," the desk officer said curtly: "I'll send somebody out as soon as possible—"

The connection went dead. Even cellular networks depended on phone lines, which were probably being brought down steadily by ice. She dialed Homicide, was disconnected twice before getting through, and got an earful of static, but she also got a live voice, hallelujah, and asked for Ben Rashly. He was out, could anyone else help her? She couldn't think of anyone who would respond without a lengthy explanation, which she'd never accomplish with the phone fading in and out. She thumped the steering wheel in frustration. Why did communication devices always fail when you needed them most?

A weather report bleated from the radio. Dixie turned up the volume. Nothing had changed. But she was outside the city now, away from the worst traffic. Maybe she could make some time. Moving into the fast lane, she passed a bus that kicked up a blinding barrage of hailstones.

Travis Payne claimed he was handling inventory during the hit-and-run, leaving Rebecca at home with two sick kids until a sitter arrived. The Paynes live a block and a half from Parker, who was a regular customer at Payne Hardware as well as the Garden Cafe. Travis and Rebecca both could know Parker's habit of drinking at the Green Hornet every Thursday . . . and about the spare key carrier. With the younger girls in bed asleep, either of them could have jogged to Parker's house, taken the car, and waited at the intersection Betsy would have to cross. What if Betsy had walked to school with a friend that day? Would both children have been killed?

In the dark, Dixie couldn't see the snapshot on her visor,

but she could envision the three sets of brown eyes. Trusting eyes. A mother's love ought to be unquestionable, a child's absolute certainty.

Remember your mother had a hard life, Kathleen Flannigan had said about Carla Jean. *Remember the good times.* Had there been good times? Dixie recalled Carla Jean's high spirits and endless fairy tales featuring handsome young knights. Perhaps there *had* been good times—before Tom Scully.

Dixie pictured Betsy's protective arms embracing her sisters. Had she known even then they needed protection from their stepfather . . . and their own mother?

On the radio, a local furniture store owner shouted, "*We save you money!*" Dixie changed to a traffic report. "*Accident outbound on Interstate 45 at Spur 336, traffic backed up on both sides . . .*"

She was less than a mile from the snarl. Brake lights dotted the road ahead like a ruby necklace, as cars slowed down. Zipping across two lanes, Dixie took an exit a bit too fast, then searched the map until she found a detour that would take her all the way to the cabin. She'd have to risk driving on rough roads, but she doubted they'd slow her down as much as the traffic jam.

There had to be somebody who could get there faster.

McGrue!

She dialed the Texas Highway Department and left an urgent, detailed message.

Dialing home again, she heard Dann pick up but couldn't hear anything he said—and he evidently couldn't hear her. As a last hope, she dialed the Gypsy Filchers' private line, got the machine, as always, and punched in her pager number, not really expecting anyone to call back. Brew, Ski, and Hooch would be heavy into their New Year's Eve party by now.

Brew's call came less than five minutes later. He sounded as if he already had a snootful.

"Hey, Dix, thanks for the bubbly. You coming—"

"Brew, I need your help. I've a hunch a six-year-old is in trouble." Nothing would sober him up faster. She rushed through an explanation, expecting her voice at any moment to be garbled in static. "If you know anyone in the Lake Livingston area, send them to the cabin."

He promised to call around, but Dixie could hear music and laughter in the background and wondered how much help she could count on. At the moment she couldn't be choosy.

The road dipped into a densely wooded section of Sam Houston National Forest. Trees crowded the roadside, limbs whipping the icy air. The unpaved road, flanked by deep drainage ditches, snaked sharply in curves that defied her headlights. Dixie slowed her speed.

On the day of Courtney's swim meet, Travis claimed he was at a computer conference near the airport—conveniently near Camp Cade. But with Ellie also at camp, that meant Rebecca was at home alone and already planning to attend the last day activities. What had Jon Keyes said? We all enjoy swimming, snorkeling . . . The prowler Courtney mentioned to her bunk mate that morning may have been Rebecca or Travis . . . checking out the lake. Rebecca would know her daughter's risky habit of swimming alone.

Did the child see her killer's face as she was drowning?

The Mustang hit a pothole, invisible under the wash of rain and ice that covered the road. The tires bounced and skidded. Dixie knew she was driving too fast, but she had to keep moving.

Tracking her route by the dim map light on her dash, Dixie saw that she was nearing the turnoff to the cabin. She slowed for the turn—*Shit! That's not a road, nothing but a muddy path*—whipped the Mustang to the right, wrenching her injured shoulder, and felt the tires slide before miraculously gaining traction.

Pines danced crazily overhead. Deciduous skeletons bent icy limbs across the road, scraping the Mustang as it barreled along. The darkness was absolute; her headlights bounced off sheets of rain and ice. Dixie slowed again, fighting the car's constant slide toward the ditch.

A feeble light shone through the trees—it had to be the cabin. Only one car in the driveway. No sign of Travis, then.

No sign of help, either. Rebecca had certainly picked a remote spot. If Ellie's condition worsened, who could blame
Rebecca for not getting her child to a hospital in such miserable weather? For choosing instead to keep her daughter warm
and snug until the roads cleared? And what could be easier
than withholding proper care and medicine from a sick child?

*But what kind of mother could sit calmly watching her child
die?*

The same mother who calmly waited at a curb until her
daughter stepped into the intersection . . . or in a murky
lake, ready to strike like a snake in the water.

Shaking off a feeling of doom, Dixie turned into the
double ruts that served as a driveway, killed the engine behind
a Chrysler LeBaron, and tried once more to reach the sheriff.
McGrue. Anybody! When only static crackled in her ear, she
wanted to hurl the cussed phone into the mud and stomp it.

Instead, she checked the stun gun on her belt—fresh batteries—too bad the .45 was still in the van with her
"plumber's tools"—and climbed out of the car.

Sleet peppered her face. She shivered and zipped her
jacket. Light flickering on the window shades suggested a fireplace inside the cabin. Apparently, her image of Ellie shivering in a cold, dark room had been nothing more than Dixie's
own macabre imagination.

A lithe shadow moved from one window shade to another.
Must be Rebecca.

Hunching against the driving rain, Dixie opened the
screen and knocked on the door. After a minute, she knocked
again, harder. When the door swung open, Rebecca's green
eyes widened in surprise, then narrowed in suspicion. Her
blond hair was tied back in a pink gingham ribbon that
matched her full skirt. Her white blouse had a lace collar
pinned with a gold heart. Little girl clothes.

"What are *you* doing here?" Rebecca demanded. "Did you
follow me?"

Dixie slipped a booted foot across the threshold.

"Ellie's father is worried about her. After talking to your
mother, he asked me to drive up and make sure you're both

all right." She angled her body into the room, so that if Rebecca tried to close the door, Dixie's foot and shoulder would wedge it open. Unfortunately, it was her lame shoulder. Icy rain blew through the doorway, spattering the wooden floor.

"Of course Ellie's all right! She's fine."

"Then you won't mind if I come in and talk to her."

"Yes, I do mind. You tell Jon Keyes he's wasted his money. It isn't even his weekend to have her. Now get out." She swung the door, but Dixie put up a hand to hold it.

"Mr. Keyes received a call from Ellie that led him to believe she might be in danger."

"*Danger?* She's sick, that's all. Oh, all right, come in before you flood the kitchen."

The room was warm and bright. In the glare of a bare overhead bulb, ladder-back chairs cast long shadows on the wall. A chopping board, a colander of vegetables, and the bony remnants of a chicken on the counter suggested Rebecca had been cooking. The aroma rising from a pot on the stove suggested chicken soup.

"Ellie's in here."

Rebecca led the way to a small bedroom with two sets of bunk beds. Ellie lay in a lower bunk under a patchwork quilt. Raggedy Ann shared her pillow. The child's hair lay in damp ribbons around her sleeping face. Nearby, a serving cart held a water glass, with a swallow of water left in the bottom, and a medicine bottle. Dixie recognized the prescription she'd seen at the cafe. Alongside the medicine sat a steaming bowl of soup, a spoon, and a napkin.

False alarm? Rebecca was apparently doing her best to help Ellie get well.

Ellie's eyes opened slowly. They looked sleepy and feverish, but recognition brightened within when she saw Dixie.

"Hi, Dixie-plain-and-simple." Her voice sounded tired yet reasonably alert. "Why are you here?"

Dixie was asking herself that same question. She sat down in a chair beside the bunk. "Came to see how my favorite jokester's doing with that nasty flu."

"I was sick, but now I feel better."

Dixie took the girl's hand. It felt warm, the pulse steady, maybe a little fast. She didn't have a hell of a lot of experience taking pulses.

"Your daddy says you phoned him this morning. Can you tell me what you were calling about, what you wanted to tell him?"

Ellie looked blank for a moment. She glanced at her mother standing in the doorway.

"I *dreamed* I called Daddy Jon," she murmured.

"Do you remember why you called? In the dream, that is." A pause while she thought about it. "No."

"Well, is there anything you want me to tell him when I get back?" Dixie was striking out here, and she should be glad, relieved—hell, she *was* relieved. But after all the tension, the long ride, the certainty that Rebecca was the worst kind of monster, finding Ellie on the mend was something of a letdown. A welcome letdown, but hard on the nervous system all the same.

"Tell Daddy I want to see *The Nutcracker* again."

"I think it's over until next year."

Ellie licked her dry lips. Her eyelids drooped. "Then I want to go again next year."

"I'll tell him that, if you'll promise to concentrate on getting well."

"How?"

"Well, take all the medicine your doctor gave you." *The doctor said he hadn't heard from Rebecca . . .* Dixie picked up the prescription bottle, shook it, watched the white tablets bounce around inside. "Drink plenty of water and juice and eat the nice soup your mother made."

"If you'll leave," Rebecca said tightly, "maybe it will still be warm when she eats it."

"Your mommy's right, I have to be going, but your daddy wanted me to give you this." She kissed Ellie on the cheek, the skin warm against her lips. The girl smelled slightly sour from being sick and not bathing for a while, but felt soft and tender, just as Ryan had at that age. Dixie was glad she'd made the trip. It was worth all the trouble to know Ellie was okay. "You have a good time tomorrow at your grand-mother's."

Ellie looked at her mother. "Are we going to Gramma's?"

"Well, of course we are," Rebecca said. "You just forgot." Looking daggers at Dixie, she picked up the soup bowl and stood beside the chair.

Dixie tweaked Ellie's ear and stepped back.

Rebecca scooted the chair closer and started feeding Ellie the soup. It must taste as good as it smelled, judging by Ellie's speed in putting it away. Dixie's stomach growled; she hoped Dann had saved her some dinner.

What now? she wondered, walking back through the kitchen. She couldn't exactly scoop Ellie up and take her home, which is what she wanted to do. She'd get some of her friends in the Highway Patrol to watch for Travis Payne. Maybe she'd even take a trip to Denton herself, make certain Travis didn't engineer an accident for his wife and stepdaughter on their way back to Houston.

Dixie's nerves refused to settle down. Her active imagination had pictured Ellie shivering and starving, Rebecca throwing buckets of freezing water on the tiny feverish body to accelerate the bronchitis. What she'd found instead was a mother taking care of her child, opting to spend the night in a cozy cabin rather than risk several hours on a dangerous highway, even making homemade soup under less than ideal cooking conditions.

Stalling, trying to make sense of her own emotional turmoil, Dixie stopped at the kitchen tap. She wasn't thirsty, but she drew a glass of water anyway while she assessed the array of herbs and soup vegetables beside the chef's knife and chopping board. Had Rebecca brought all this food from home, expecting to cook it at her mother's house? Or had she stopped somewhere after deciding to take the detour to the cabin?

Carrots, celery, onions, garlic, mushrooms, parsley, something else green and leafy, salt and pepper, some kind of sprouts. A bottle of herbal diuretic? Dixie picked up the bottle and read the ingredients—uva ursi, juniper berries, and a

long list of other herbs. The fat pink tablets reminded Dixie of
something, but she couldn't quite—

Daffodil bulbs? The open box was pushed against the
counter's backsplash.

Why would Rebecca bring the box of daffodil bulbs from
the cafe garden? Dixie recognized the fluorescent PLANT NOW
sticker on the front and a diagonal tear close to the top. The
box was partially empty. She tipped it, held her hand to catch
the bulb, which looked a little like garlic—in fact, it looked
exactly like the garlic among the soup vegetables, or what
Dixie had *thought* was garlic. This must be one of the exotic
edible flowers Dann had mentioned.

Turning the box to read the back, she saw a line drawing of
daffodils in bloom, along with drawings of other flowers from
the same family, according to the blurb, jonquils and narcissus. Dann had said something about narcissus . . . had
found some in her garden and said they were like the castor
bean plants—*eat them and you're dead.*

Shit!

And now she realized what was familiar about the pink
diuretic tablets: They looked exactly like Ryan's prescription
tablets. The pills in Ellie's prescription bottle were small and
white. Yet, according to the label, the medicine was the same,
Amoxil.

Three people have died . . . Amy had said . . . *mostly
dehydration and pneumonia.* Rebecca had switched the pills.
Not only was Ellie not getting the medicine she needed, the
diuretic would accelerate dehydration.

Dixie raced back to the bedroom, slipping the Kubaton
from her pocket with her good hand. . . . *Don't frighten the
kid, do it but don't frighten Ellie, no time to deal with her fears
when she could right now, oh, God, be dying from the poison in
that goddamn soup* . . . Rebecca was touching the spoon to
Ellie's lips . . .

Dixie slipped the Kubaton under Rebecca's arm, into the
soft tissue deep in her armpit. Rebecca flinched and sucked
in a sharp breath. Dixie kept the pressure steady.

"Mrs. Payne, would you set the bowl down and come to

the kitchen for a minute, please? I want to show you something. *You don't mind if I steal your mommy for a minute, do you, Ellie?" Talk slowly, soothingly. Keep the Kubaton right up there where it hurts. Hold her arm down with the injured — ow! — hand. Watch it, now, she's tall, she can break your leverage.*

Rebecca leaned toward the cart, but with Dixie holding her arm, she couldn't reach it. Dixie relaxed her grip a tad so Rebecca could set the bowl down —

The soup bowl slammed into her face. The soup stung her eyes. Blindly she grabbed for Rebecca's arm, felt it slip away, heard Rebecca run out the door.

"Mommy?"

"Ellie, it's okay." Dixie wiped her face on her sleeve. "Stay right there, please."

Dixie ran after Rebecca.

Something in the soup burning her eyes. Pepper? Okay if it's pepper, no problem just pain, but what if it's daffodil-god-damn-bulbs and the poison enters the system through the eye-ball?

Dixie heard the kitchen door open, felt a blast of wet, icy wind, saw a blur that had to be Rebecca.

No time! Grab her. Dixie dove at the open doorway, trying to keep her burning eyes open, hoping Rebecca was in her path.

Nothing. Rebecca was outside.

Outside in the dark with her good eyesight, and Dixie still couldn't see, even in the light. *Let her go. The important think now is getting Ellie to a hospital.*

She stumbled to the sink, splashed water into her cupped hands, held it to her eyes, blinked rapidly into the water, *which was plenty cussed cold.* Scooped more water, rinsed her eyes again. And again. Fumbled for paper towels.

She could see now, blurry but she could see —

The knife was gone. The big chef's knife beside the cutting board had disappeared. *To hell with it — and to hell with Rebecca — she had to get Ellie out of here.*

•   •   •

Parker scowled at the string of taillights ahead of him on the exit ramp.

"Don't have time to wade through a mile of stalled cars," he told Mud. "Dixie could be in trouble."

The dog made a high, thin sound and moved closer on the truck seat, the red Frisbee captured beneath his front paws. Picking up on his own agitation, Parker figured.

Suddenly he remembered the kind of vehicle he was driving.

"Hellfire! Why didn't I think of that sooner?"

Flipping a switch that set the tow truck's yellow light bar to blinking, he turned the wheels hard right, jumped onto the grassy embankment, and headed downhill—sliding as the truck hit an icy patch—then rumbled along the shouler. When a pickup nosed into his path, Parker leaned on the horn and kept driving.

Lucky thing he and Mud had taken their first Frisbee drive that morning. When Parker couldn't get through on Dixie's damn cellular phone, no way could he sit worrying whether she was in trouble. Between Jon Keyes' vague recollections and a guy at the Walker County Sheriff's office, he'd gotten enough information to scribble a rough map, which was now taped to the dashboard, ignition wires dangling beneath it.

He blasted the horn at a fellow trying to flag him down. Lowering the window, he shouted "Emergency ahead!" and rumbled past heavy traffic without slowing. The map showed a cutoff coming up soon. He saw it a second too late, made the turn too wide, and slid toward the ditch.

Then the tow truck's big wheels dug in, and he was headed into the thicket. Branches whipped the windshield. Darkness closed overhead as the fickle moon disappeared behind a cloud.

"Ellie," Dixie whispered.

The child's eyes were closed, her breathing ragged.

The poison working? Or the flu?

Seeing the broken soup bowl, Dixie picked up a piece that was smeared generously with soup and shoved it into a Ziploc bag from her vest pocket. Wrapping the quilt around Ellie, she lifted her with the bad arm. She needed the other arm free to open doors and ward off plunging knives.

Rebecca wouldn't stab the child. It would defeat her plan. If Dixie hadn't come, Rebecca might've pulled it off, even in the wake of the other "accidents." She'd laid the groundwork and had taken advantage of the weather. Ellie's doctor knew she had the flu, had treated her and prescribed medication. Everyone at the cafe knew Ellie was still sick, but Rebecca's plan to visit her mother and go on to Travis' parents' house for the holiday would seem plausible, since Ellie had started feeling better. The weather turning worse was good enough reason to change plans, and how could she know Ellie would take such a sudden downturn? No close neighbors, no telephone to call for help.

A ribbon of pain pulsed in Dixie's shoulder. Hoisting Ellie higher, she took most of the weight on her collarbone, less pull on the arm. She turned off the kitchen light and waited by the door for her eyes to adjust.

Rebecca's plan could still work, if she killed Dixie and lost the Mustang deep in the national forest. It might not be found for years. Then all she had to do was stall around until Ellie was beyond saving and "rush" her to the nearest county hospital. If asked, Rebecca would claim Dixie never showed up.

Who'd suspect poison? Jon Keyes and Parker Dann would scream loud enough to get attention, but even an autopsy wouldn't reveal certain poisons unless they were specifically included in the testing. Salt certainly wouldn't be noticed. If daffodil poison *was* somehow detected, Rebecca could claim it was an accident, that the bulbs must have gotten mixed in with the garlic.

Dixie didn't believe Rebecca would stab Ellie and ruin her chances of collecting the insurance money—but she couldn't be absolutely certain. She couldn't be certain Rebecca was even sane.

Ellie's breathing was deeper and steadier now. Dixie hoped the sound sleep was natural, her small body fighting the illness. But maybe daffodils were narcotic. She had to get Ellie to a hospital right away.

Dixie peered through the screen door and saw only blackness under the trees. She didn't like going outside where darkness would hide Rebecca's movements, where every tree trunk posed a potential ambush.

Groping along the wall beside the back door, she found a second light switch, hoped it was porch light or, better yet, a floodlight, and flicked it on. A grim yellow glow brightened a patch near the porch. But the darkness beyond looked blacker than ever, the Mustang invisible beyond the yellow circle. Too much risk stepping from brightness to dark.

No light then. She flicked it off and waited until she could see the trees as blacker shapes in the night sky, and the vague hump that was the Mustang. Easing the screen door open, she heard a distant truck engine and wished for the tenth time this place wasn't so remote. Maybe McGrue or the Walker County Sheriff was headed her way. But the truck sounded too distant to be any help.

She would have to do it fast . . . car keys ready . . . open the rear passenger door . . . drop Ellie on the seat. Her most vulnerable moment would be bending over, back exposed, Ellie in her arms.

Do it now!

The mushy ground plucked at her boots as she ran, Kubaton clutched to strike—the stun gun would be too dangerous with the child in her arms. Eyes wide and darting, she searched the shadows for movement. Freezing rain stung her skin. Ellie was dead weight, Dixie's grip clumsy at best.

The child moaned, stirred. *Be still, honey, or that arm won't hold you.*

Keys in the lock, door open, Ellie down on the seat—

The car door slammed into Dixie's backside, striking her

calves. Staggering, she dropped Ellie and tried to turn. The car door slammed again, striking her bad shoulder—

"Mommy?"

"Shhh, it's all right, Ellie." Dixie shoved the car door hard, but Rebecca had already stepped around it, knife striking out. Swinging the Kubaton with its heavy ball of keys, Dixie felt it strike flesh and bone, then Rebecca's knife ripped through Dixie's injured shoulder.

She jabbed the Kubaton butt-first, striking instinctively at the soft tissue beneath Rebecca's chin, connecting, knocking the woman back. Then she felt the knife slash her forearm.

"Mommy?" Ellie sitting up, wanting out of the car.

Fumble for the stun gun, fingers clumsy with blood.

The glint of the blade coming fast. Dixie dodged, heard the scrape of metal on metal, brought both arms down hard on Rebecca's spine—

A spotlight, from the road. Bright. Blinding.

"Flannigan, you all right?" Dann's voice? And Mud, barking as a truck rumbled closer.

Rebecca's face terrible in rage, the knife high, arcing—

Dixie's heart pounding furiously. *Oh, dear Jesus, she's not crazy. She's a killer, all right, but those eyes are stone-cold sane.*

"Mommy!" Ellie at the window, holding her stomach, tears streaming. "Mommy!"

Rebecca reaching for the car door.

Don't let her get the child, don't let her get the child, don't let her get the child—

Butt against the door, HARD! Slamming it shut. Rebecca's two fingers caught, mashed. Screaming.

Stun gun hard and long at Rebecca's solar plexus.

Knife slashing blindly—

Searing pain across Dixie's throat . . . blood . . . blood . . . then slowly . . . finally . . . no more slashing.

A siren approaching.

Red and blue light disks dancing in the rain-whipped sky.

Blackness.

Chapter Forty-three

Saturday, January 2, Houston Police Department

Q. Mrs. Payne, what time did Betsy leave your house on the morning she was killed?
A. A little after seven. She liked going to school early.

Ben Rashly himself was conducting the interview with Rebecca. Dixie and Belle Richards stood watching them through one-way glass.

"She should have counsel present," Belle said.

"Offered and refused." Dixie tugged at the bandage on her throat. Her stiches from the knife wound itched like poison ivy. "Think she's ready to confess?"

"Shifted from cop to cop, county to county—I'd say she wants to just get it over and done with. Which is why she needs counsel."

Seconds after Parker arrived at Rebecca's cabin that night, McGrue had pulled up in his patrol car. Rapidly sizing up the situation, he'd unfolded his spindly frame across the frozen ground like a lightning flash and secured Rebecca before she could recover from Dixie's stun gun. Dixie was still dazed, blood pouring from her neck. She was grateful to see Mc-Grue instead of a stranger—no lengthy explanations.

He placed Rebecca in the backseat of his patrol car and blazed a trail into town, with Parker, Dixie, and Ellie following in the tow truck as far as Walker County Hospital. An intern stitched up Dixie's neck while Dixie tried to explain that it was Ellie who needed immediate attention.

"In the girl's weakened condition from the flu, complicated by severe dehydration," the doctor explained later, "the small amount of poison in that soup would have killed her." Another day or two on the diuretic pills Rebecca had substituted for Ellie's prescription would have killed her, too. Apparently, Rebecca had grown impatient.

Despite the orange jail-issue jumpsuit she wore now, and an absence of makeup, Rebecca looked prim and attractive. Her blond hair had been gathered into a loose braid. She sat straight and alert, staring at Rashly.

Q. The two younger children? Where were they?

A. In bed. I'd mixed Ipecac in their breakfast juice, so they wouldn't feel like going to school, and some Tylenol PM, so they would sleep through my morning run.

As Dixie suspected, Rebecca had jogged to Parker's house and found his spare key hidden under the Cadillac's frame. Then she drove his car to the intersection she knew Betsy would cross.

Before asking his next question, Ben Rashly stared at Rebecca for a long moment. Dixie could see a bead of sweat form on his forehead.

Q. Mrs. Payne, what did you do when you saw your daughter starting across the street?

A. I pulled away from the curb and stomped the gas pedal.

Q. And . . . after the car hit Betsy, what did you do?

A. I felt the bump and looked in my rearview mirror at the body lying beside the road. . . . I honestly thought the killing would end there.

Rashly glanced at the video camera, checking the red recording indicator, Dixie figured. Then he relaxed in his chair and pulled out his pipe. He wouldn't light it, but Dixie knew the process of filling it was calming for him, especially now that he had what he needed on tape.

Q. Mrs. Payne, your daughter Courtney attended Camp

Cade, where she drowned on August first of this year, is that correct?

A. Yes.

Q. And you visited the camp that morning?

A. Yes.

Q. What time did you arrive?

A. I don't know. Early. Long before sunup.

Q. Was Courtney expecting you?

A. Yes, but later. For the swim meet. I knew she'd go out for an early practice, no matter how many times we'd warned her not to swim alone. She hated losing.

Q. You waited for her there at the lake?

A. She didn't see me under the water. . . . It was like drowning a kitten, like drowning a gray tabby whelp on a summer afternoon.

Rashly looked at her for a moment.

Q. What was that you said? A whelp?

A. Kittens. Six of them, their mama got hit by a car, and my friend Gary Stahling brought them over in a box. He was two years older, a sixth-grader, always showing off.

Rashly sat up and laid his pipe in an ashtray. Evidently, the interview was taking a direction he hadn't counted on.

Q. You were in fourth grade, then. That would make you what, eight? Nine?

A. Nine, I think. A heavy rain had filled Aunt Alice's red plastic swimming pool to the rim. She soaked in it every afternoon during that dry summer, to cool off.

Q. You lived with Aunt Alice?

A. She lived with us. After Daddy left, she came to take care of me while Mama worked—though I told Mama I didn't need taking care of.

Q. What happened—with the kittens?

A. Their eyes weren't open yet . . . the box smelled sour where the kittens had wet it . . . mewling, crawling atop one another . . . *My pop says I should get rid of 'em,* Gary told me. He picked a kitten up by its neck and plunged it into the pool. Its tiny paws batted the water . . . then the body jerked and was still. *Now you do one,*

Gary said. I hesitated, though not long enough for Gary to notice, then I scooped up the squirmy body. I remember it curled its paws around my finger. I felt its heartbeat . . . strong, racing furiously in the cool water . . . then weaker until it sagged like a lump of clay.

"Look at Rebecca's face," Dixie whispered to Belle. "She could as easily be talking about cooking a soufflé or doing the laundry."

"My grandfather used to gather his cat's litters in an old pillowcase and drown them in the bathtub," Belle said.

"Lucky for you he stopped with kittens." In her own ears, Dixie's new gruff voice sounded like gravel. Rebecca's knife had nicked a vocal cord. "Nothing serious," the doctor had said, "but don't talk for forty-eight hours, and then only sparingly." Dixie was trying it out.

Q. Mrs. Payne, what happened that morning at Camp Cade? When you saw Courtney swimming in the lake?

A. A stubborn child, Courtney was. Willful. As stubborn as those kittens. After the fourth kitten lay heaped beside the pool, our back door slammed open, and Aunt Alice screamed at us: *You kids! What are you doing there?* She grabbed a handful of my hair and batted me across the ears. *Gary Stahling, you get on home,* she said, *or I'll give you some of what this one's getting.* Gary reached for the dead kittens, to put them back in the cardboard box. *Leave 'em,* she yelled. Gary stumbled past the swimming pool and lit out around the house.

Rebecca's hands, which until now had lain relaxed on the table in front of her, were knotted into tight fists. She seemed almost in a trance, reliving a moment she must have visited a thousand times in her mind to make it so vivid.

A. *Look at those poor little dead things,* Aunt Alice said. *Kid, you got a mean streak like your daddy.* My daddy was a gray photograph in my bureau drawer . . . a blue button Mama ripped from his coat the day he walked out—Mama screaming at him not to go. *Don't say anything bad about my daddy,* I told Aunt Alice. *He's coming back.* She laughed, her bathing suit all pink and shining like a fresh-cut watermelon. *Think your mama'd take him back?* she said. *Him walking out, leaving her with no money and a snot-nose brat to raise?* I tried to squirm out of her grasp. *Daddy's coming to take me with him,* I told her.

Rebecca abruptly stopped talking. She looked away from Rashly.

Q. He didn't come back, did he?

A. Mama cried . . . the day Daddy left. *You're the reason he's gone,* she yelled at me. *We did fine till you were due to be born. Then I lost my figure and your daddy started slipping around with that Cindy Lou from the dime store.* Cindy Lou looked like the women in the magazines at the bottom of Daddy's closet. Mama looked like Aunt Alice.

Q. Mrs. Payne, your youngest daughter, Ellie—

A. I'll tell this my way, or I won't tell it.

   Rashly nodded, reassuringly.

Q. You go right ahead, ma'am. You were saying . . . ?

A. Aunt Alice made me carry the kittens to the garden. The ground was hard-packed. Digging in it, even with the sharp-edged shovel, blistered my hands. The blisters burst and stung. *Make them holes deeper,* Aunt Alice said. *Don't want no mongrel sniffing around, raking 'em back up.* I scooped out another layer of dirt. Then Aunt Alice laid a kitten in the hole . . . its mouth sagging . . . the pink tip of its tongue hanging out. *What good were they?* I asked, hating her for what she'd said about Daddy. *They couldn't eat or play or anything.* Her fingers struck, like a snapping turtle, pinching. *You heartless little snipe. Someone ought to drown you like you drowned those helpless little kittens.* I hated Aunt Alice for being there, for taking Mama's side about everything and taking Daddy's chair at the table. I jammed the pointed shovel into her fat leg, gouging blood. *Jesus Christ! You little shit!* The blood bubbled up and oozed over her knee.

Dixie felt a chill roll down her back. Rebecca's face had flushed with rage. The veins in her neck bulged out in the harsh overhead light.

When she didn't speak for a moment, Rashly prompted her gently.

Q. And then . . . ?

A. I threw down the shovel and ran. Aunt Alice pushed herself to her feet. She looked like a big pink slug, fat rippling on her arms and neck . . . blood running down her leg. I stumbled over the kitten box and fell, striking the hard plastic pool with my nose and splashing facedown in the shallow water. Tried to get up, but Aunt Alice held my shoulders. I coughed and choked and looked up through water that was turning red with the blood from my nose. Aunt Alice's face was there above the pool . . . all flushed and grinning like an evil jack-o'-lantern. *You want to make things dead, brat? Kill helpless creatures? I'll show you how it feels to be helpless.* She pushed me down . . . fighting back was useless. Then the pressure let up. I shot out of the water, gulping air. *You gonna kill any more kittens, brat?* Her eyes bulged . . . then suddenly she tumbled into the pool, on top of me. At first I didn't know what had happened, thought she was still trying to hold me down. My lungs were on fire, my head ringing. I managed to crawl from under her weight and got my head above the water. Once I could breathe, I realized she wasn't moving. The blood had stopped pouring from her leg. Her wheezing had stopped. I climbed out of the pool, scooted into the shadows near the back porch, and sat watching her for a long time . . . afraid she was dead. And afraid she wasn't.

Ben Rashly rubbed a hand over his face as if to wipe away the grisly image. He glanced toward the one-way glass.

"Jesus," Belle said. "Can you imagine how alone and frightened that child must have felt?"

"Not half as alone and frightened as her own daughter when she was pulled to the bottom of that lake." Dixie frowned at Belle. "You're *not* saying you'd represent her?"

"You know I can't, after hearing this confession. What I'm saying is if I were her attorney, I'd never let her answer these questions."

Q. Mrs. Payne, can I get you anything? Some water?

Rebecca shook her head, but Rashly nodded at the one-way glass, and someone behind Dixie left the room.

A. Old Mr. Belsen from next door called an ambulance. He took me in his house and wiped the dried blood off my nose. The men in the ambulance said Aunt Alice must have suffered a heart attack while digging in the hot sun. Injured herself with the shovel and passed out in the pool. Nobody noticed the blisters on my hands. After a while . . . when the police didn't come to take me away . . . I realized they might not know I killed Aunt Alice . . . that I plunged the shovel into her leg and caused a heart attack. I was glad she was dead.

"Textbook classic," Dixie told Belle. "Early abuse, cruelty to animals."

"Dixie, at nine years old, she believed she was a murderer."

"She *was* a murderer. She murdered the kittens."

Q. Who took care of you after . . . your aunt died?

A. Mama paid the old couple next door, the Belsens, to let me stay with them after school. Mr. Belsen knew my father. A *fine man, good with his hands*, Mr. Belsen told me, while he sawed pieces of wood to build birdhouses and window planters he sold in town. *Your father used to come over, bring a big jug of iced tea, and we'd talk into the night. A dreamer, your daddy. Always scheming to make a dollar.* I sanded the pieces when Mr. Belsen finished cutting them. . . . Sometimes I imagined my daddy and I were building things together. But *Mrs.* Belsen didn't like me. White hair, broomstick legs . . . she spent a lot of time in bed—because of her bad hip. Said her walker was too slow. She'd just push a buzzer and yell. *What are you doing out there?* Her bedroom window opened right beside the workshop . . . and she had this loud, whiny voice. *Doesn't that child have homework or something? Bring me a Coke.*

She could think of a thousand reasons to ring that buzzer. The detective who had left the room came back in carrying a tray with a pitcher of water and two glasses. He opened the door to the interrogation room carefully and set the tray on the table. Instead of leaving, he checked the camera, then leaned against a wall, just out of Rebecca's line of sight. She seemed not to notice.

Rashly poured two glasses of water.

Q. You and Mr. Belsen, though, you got along okay?

Rebecca nodded.

A. Three days a week, he took his birdhouses and planters to a store in town. He said I should answer the buzzer—for a skinny lady, Mrs. Belsen could put away a lot of Coke and snacks—but while Mr. Belsen went to town she always took a nap. She didn't like Mr. Belsen spending time with me. . . . He could do a lot more woodworking, I thought, without her pushing that buzzer. One night, I got an idea from a movie on TV. An old lady was in the hospital. She had a buzzer like Mrs. Belsen's, and the nurses hated her. While she was sleeping, someone put a pillow over her head until she stopped moving. A few days after I saw the movie . . . I was screwing mailboxes together for a big order. Mr. Belsen couldn't finish even one birdhouse for having to run inside to his wife. As I fitted a shiny brass screw into a hole and tightened it down, I thought about that movie. When Mr. Belsen left for town, I stood outside his wife's doorway. She'd fallen asleep with her reading glasses on . . . a line of drool down to her chin, and a soft whistling coming from her nose. . . . I crept in carrying a pillow from the spare bedroom . . . took off her glasses—she didn't even flinch—and straddled her, quickly pinning her arms so she couldn't move . . . the pillow over her face. She twitched and tried to throw me off . . . but she wasn't very strong. I held the pillow for a long time after she quit moving.

Rebecca paused, after the long rush of words.

"She was just a child," Belle whispered. "With all that anger inside her."

Dixie shook her head. She couldn't share Belle's sympathy.

"Lots of kids have parents walk out on them. They don't all start killing."

Rashly tossed another glance at the camera. At any moment, Rebecca could decide to ask for a lawyer, and the interview would be over.

Q. Did you continue to stay with Mr. Belsen after his wife died?

Rebecca frowned and glanced away.

A. For a while. He had a lot more time, without her around. He didn't talk as much, though . . . and sometimes he'd build too many birdhouses when the store wanted more planters. He'd forget to eat. Then he got sick, and his daughter took him to live with her. Mama never noticed the Belsens were gone until a real estate sign appeared in the yard.

Rebecca stared into the distance.

Q. Mrs. Payne, your youngest daughter, Ellie—

A. I'll get to that! In good time.

She sat another few moments without speaking. This time Rashly didn't coax her, and after a moment the words started flowing again, like a roll of toilet paper unwinding across a slick floor.

A. I tracked down my father the year I graduated high school. He'd moved to the city and, as Mr. Belsen predicted, was a successful businessman. I met his new wife, before she disappeared into the kitchen . . . slim, pretty . . . younger than my father. He sat in a wide blue recliner, a plump cat curled up beside him. *I thought you'd come back for me,* I told him. *Well, now,* he said, *looks like you did fine. All grown-up, going off to college.* Two children ran in, yelling, *Daddy! Daddy!* . . . the oldest, a blond replica of her mother. The boy, about four years old, crawled up on my father's lap. . . . Before I left for college, I took an ax and chopped up the wooden frame I'd made for that gray photograph of my daddy.

Rebecca paused long enough to drink a glass of water in one long swallow. Rashly refilled the glass, and she held it, staring down at the liquid as if at a crystal ball. Several moments passed before Rashly ventured a question.

Q. You married while still in college, is that correct?

She smiled, glancing up at him, almost flirting.

A. I met Charles my second year . . . he was pre-med, tall, striking. We spent a weekend in Dallas . . . scarcely leaving the hotel room. A week later I moved into his apartment complex . . . after six months we were married. Charles was interning by then, and never seemed to have any time at home—even though I kept myself pretty for him. . . . One night he didn't come home at all—sent a letter saying he could no longer live with my "smothering." Since when is it *bad* to *care deeply* for someone?

For the first time since the interview started, Rebecca looked ready to cry.

Q. But you married again?

She slid another coy smile at Rashly.

A. When I met Randy, I knew what had gone wrong with Charles and how to keep it from happening again—I got *pregnant* before the end of our first year. . . . Randy was so sweet . . . bringing me flowers, like when we were dating. After Betsy was born, I tried to explain it's bad to spend too much time with a child—parents need time alone. I sent her to stay with Mama for a month, so we could have some time together. Randy flew into a rage. . . . I took a job, put Betsy in day school. At night, she'd be tired from playing all day and fall asleep early, so Randy and I got some time alone. . . . Then he started going out at night with his friends. . . . I could see him drifting away, just like Charles, so I got pregnant again. He did stay home more at night . . . sweet, attentive . . . but there was always Betsy.

"Jesus Christ," Belle whispered. "She did it for attention."

"Ric," Dixie said. "I think we've finally met the Queen Bitch of the Universe."

Rashly's face mirrored their own horror. When he urged Rebecca to continue, his voice sounded weary.

Q. Then Courtney was born . . .
   Rebecca's eyes brightened.
A. And we bought a new house! I stayed home to make it
   perfect for us. We had a perfect life, perfect! . . .
   Rebecca paused, and her features hardened.
A. Until the day Randy never came home. This time I didn't
   even get a letter, just a divorce notice. . . . But it was
   because of the girls that I met Jon Keyes. He was running
   in the park and stopped to say what a beautiful family I
   had . . . pushed the girls on the swings . . . treated us
   to ice cream cones. We married three months later. To
   keep the girls busy, I enrolled them in music, ballet, summer camp. And planned romantic vacations for Jon and
   me. . . . But he wanted every moment to be family time.
   He brought the girls gifts from his frequent business
   trips. . . . Brought me candy—which I threw out, knowing how easily I could begin to look like Mama. One day I
   looked in Jon's eyes and knew he was going to leave. I told
   him I was pregnant—I wasn't, but I soon got that way with
   all the extra attention he gave me. After Ellie came, Jon
   spent every spare minute with them—with his *girls*—Ellie, Courtney, and Betsy. We couldn't do anything, go
   anywhere, without three stones dragging us down. . . .
   When Jon left me, he tried to take them—and they'd have
   Daddy all to themselves, wouldn't they? I put a stop to
   that! . . . Then I met Travis. He gets upset when his
   business doesn't go well, but . . . someday everything
   will be perfect. . . . I can always have more children, if
   he wants them. The important thing is that Travis loves
   me. He won't leave. I know he won't.

Chapter Forty-four

Dixie pushed through the mahogany doors of Richards, Blackmon & Drake tugging at the yellow scarf covering her neck bandage. She was wearing the blouse from her yellow silk pants suit, with a brown tweed jacket she'd found in the depths of her closet, a skirt the color of dark chocolate, plain brown pumps, and her camel's hair overcoat.

Receptionist Grimm lifted an appreciative eyebrow.

"Got your fighting clothes on, I see."

Dixie grinned. "Knockout in the first round!" After reading Rebecca's deposition, the ADA had conceded to dropping the charges against Parker. Dixie tipped a casual salute and reached for the brass doorknob to head for Belle's office.

"Ms. Richards has someone with her," Grimm said.

"I know." Dixie's grin widened.

"Ah, like that is it?" A lascivious smile spread across the woman's stern face. "Here. This worked for me." She flipped a Hershey's Hug to Dixie from a bowl on her desk.

As she caught the candy and turned down the hall to Belle's office, a flush of unexpected heat filled Dixie's face. She had nothing to blush about, though. Not yet. Now that Parker was no longer a fugitive, she hoped to change all that.

In court that morning, Dixie had hung around long

enough to hear the DA's announcement that he was dropping the charges against Parker, then she'd left to visit the nursing home, having missed her usual Sunday visitation. She entered her mother's room feeling that something tightly constricted was unfolding inside her. Carla Jean lay as distant as ever, skin translucent, bright green eyes unfocused. Dixie had taken her mother's hand, papery and almost weightless. "We both deserved a better life, Mama. I'm finally ready to get on with mine. Wherever you are in your mind, I hope there's a shining white knight alongside you." She pressed the frail hand to her lips, and left with the first deep sense of peace she could remember feeling around her mother since the days before Scully.

When Dixie swung into Belle's office, the tension inside the room was thick enough to cut. The lawyer, classy in a slate-gray suit, sat at her desk, watching her client.

"Confession might be good for Rebecca's black soul," Belle was saying, "but it sure ruined the DA's morning."

Parker stood at the window, his back to the door, staring out at the Houston skyline.

"Reading it didn't do much for my morning, either. The woman stole eight months of my life—yet, I feel guilty for being angry."

"Two kids were murdered," Dixie croaked in her new voice. "No amount of confessing can undo that. The fact sits like gunpowder in your belly. Makes you feel like exploding all over somebody."

After a few more moments of silence, she heard Parker's weighted sigh. "Guess you do know the feeling." He turned to face her.

Despite the disquieting knowledge that he might drift out of her life at any moment, Dixie couldn't suppress a certain hopeful anticipation. He was like no man she'd ever known, earthy, honest, caring, and when he turned on that devilish charm, a rogue as well as a gentleman.

"Think about Ellie," Dixie said. "Without our involvement, without you telling me about the poison narcissus in my garden, she'd be dead, too. Now she'll grow up healthy and well loved." Dixie had been at the hospital when they released Ellie to Jon Keyes. Still sniffling but well on the mend, the child had not even asked about her mother.

Belle opened her desk drawer and jingled a set of car keys.

"They released my Cadillac?" Parker said. "What about evidence?"

"Rebecca was smart enough to wear gloves. Unless she foolishly kept your spare car key, there's no evidence that she ever drove the car."

"You're not *still* thinking of representing her?" Dixie said suspiciously.

"She hasn't asked, but with a plea of diminished capacity—"

"You saw her in that deposition room, Belle. She's not crazy. She knew exactly what she was doing when she killed those girls."

"Trust me, any woman who would sacrifice her own children to buy a man's love is emotionally and mentally unstable."

"You're a soft touch, Ric. Rebecca Payne doesn't deserve you."

Belle's gray eyes leveled at Dixie. "Innocent until *proven* guilty, remember? Rebecca suffered her mother's jealousy and wrath all those years—"

"I was there. I heard it all, too. Remember?"

"Can you blame her for frantically clutching at her own husbands? In the end, they did exactly what she'd always feared. They walked out."

"Even Travis?"

Belle shrugged. "He'll have his own load of guilt to shoulder. After all, she did it for him."

Parker scooped up the car keys, the evidence release form, and his overcoat. He looked at Dixie as he headed for the door.

"Mind giving me a ride to pick up my car?" He'd taken his clothes home that morning when she drove him there to change into his suit for the trial.

"Sure," she croaked. She tipped Belle a wave and caught up with him.

"Don't talk," he said.

"I can now. It's been more than forty-eight hours." He was walking faster than she'd ever seen him move.

"You sound funny. I don't think you should push it."

All New Year's weekend, he'd played Doctor Mom. She supposed it wasn't easy to stop. The weather had stayed cold and wet. Parker picked up a dozen old movies from the video store and made three kinds of soup. She loved the attention, but she'd soaked up all the warm fuzzies she could stand for a while.

"Where to, after the auto depot?" Her throat did feel as if a pin were stabbing right through it every time she spoke.

"I don't know."

He jabbed the elevator button. The doors opened instantly. Dixie tried to recall whether she'd ever summoned the elevator from the forty-seventh floor and had it appear instantly.

"Still planning to sell your house?" she said.

"I don't know."

They rode down through all forty-seven floors in silence. His anger was still palpable. Dixie could understand how he felt. Despite the DA's dismissing all charges, Parker's life—his home, his job, his reputation—would never be the same. Much of his frustration came from realizing that monsters can walk among normal people without horns and fangs to identify them.

"Think you might know anytime soon?" she asked. She had parked across the street at the Galleria Mall garage. He took her arm when the WALK sign blinked on.

"Know what?" he said.

"Whether you'll be leaving town."

He looked down at her as they crossed the street, and she was glad to see his blue eyes had regained their cynical amusement.

"Would you care?" he said.

"You've spoiled Mud rotten. He'll be heartbroken if he doesn't occasionally find chicken piccata in his dish."

"And you?" They had reached the car in the underground garage. Parker stood so close she could feel his body heat, even through her coat. One corner of his mouth went up in a bland, impudent smile as his knuckles gently grazed her jawline. He lowered his voice so that it carried to her ears only. "Would you be heartbroken?"

She loved the way he smelled—bay rum, warm male skin, the pleasant aroma of coffee on his breath.

"What makes you think a badass bitch like me has a heart?"

"Anybody Mud likes can't be all bad."

His lips felt exactly as she'd expected, strong but soft.

"What do you say we pick up the beast," he said softly. "Drive down to the beach. Look at some of those waterfront properties Carl told me about?"

"It's January."

"Then we'll have the beach all to ourselves."

"We'll freeze."

"I'll see what I can do to keep you warm."

If you enjoyed Chris Rogers's debut mystery,
BITCH FACTOR,
you won't want to miss the second
sizzling Dixie Flannigan novel:

RAGE
FACTOR

Look for Chris Rogers's
RAGE FACTOR
at your favorite bookstore,
coming in hardcover
from Bantam Books in February 1999!

About the Author

Chris Rogers lives in Houston, Texas, where she is at work on her second Dixie Flannigan novel, *Rage Factor*.

SUE GRAFTON

"Once again, the finest practitioner of the 'female sleuth' genre is in great form...."
—Cosmopolitan

"Ms. Grafton writes a smart story and wraps it up with a wry twist."
—The New York Times Book Review

___27991-2	**"A"** IS FOR ALIBI	$6.99/$8.99 in Canada
___28034-1	**"B"** IS FOR BURGLAR	$6.99/$8.99
___28036-8	**"C"** IS FOR CORPSE	$6.99/$8.99
___27163-6	**"D"** IS FOR DEADBEAT	$6.99/$8.99
___27955-6	**"E"** IS FOR EVIDENCE	$6.99/$8.99
___28478-9	**"F"** IS FOR FUGITIVE	$6.99/$8.99

"The best first-person-singular storytelling in detective novels."
—Entertainment Weekly